JOURNEY

to an
UNTAMED LAND

A Novel

JONITA MULLINS

ISBN 13: 978-0-9789740-2-2 (previously published by WinePress Publishing as 978-1-4141-2695-1)

ISBN 10: 0-9789740-2-6 (previously published by WinePress Publishing as 1-4141-2695-6)

Library of Congress Catalog Card Number: 2013908543

DEDICATION

To Bette Gabehart, my Haskell High School English teacher,
who insisted I enter my writing in competitions; to my freshman
composition teacher at Oklahoma State University, who
convinced me to major in English and pursue a writing career;
and to Betty Howard, editor of Daily Blessing magazine, who
gave me my first writing job and helped me hone my craft.
Thank you.

Jonita Mullins

CHAPTER ONE

Pittsburgh, Pennsylvania
April 16, 1820

Clarissa Johnson stood quietly on the long, wooden dock of the Pittsburgh port. A cool morning breeze pulled strands of chestnut brown hair from the green silk bonnet she wore. The young woman could scarcely take in the bustle of activity at one of the busiest river ports in the country.

A square jaw, strong chin and wide mouth gave Clarissa a look of confidence that she did not feel. In fact, she felt as if the earth were moving beneath her feet. She gave a little shake of her head to try to clear the swirling sensation. *It's just the water and all this rushing about,* she told herself to try to calm her nerves. *It has nothing to do with the fact that I'm changing my life forever.* But she knew that wasn't true. The bustling of the waterfront matched the turmoil in her heart.

Clarissa gripped the handle of her carpetbag a little tighter and closed her eyes to shut out the sight of the water lapping at the piers and causing the boats to gently rock up and down.

"Quite an impressive operation here isn't it?" a voice suddenly beside her caused Clarissa to jump. She opened her eyes to see one of the other members of the mission family standing at her elbow.

The young man at her side was not much older or much taller than Clarissa but had a pleasant open face and nice smile. He wore his light brown hair pulled back in a club held with a simple cord of leather. His gray wool coat was serviceable, but clearly not of an expensive cut.

Clarissa remembered that he had been introduced as a mechanic, but she could not remember his name. She had been introduced to so many new people since they had all assembled at the United Foreign Mission Society's headquarters in New York last week.

"Yes, it's quite impressive," she said, hoping the name would come to her as they talked. "I had read that the Pittsburgh port was busy but I never realized there would be so much bustling about."

"'Gateway to the West' is what they call it," the young man returned, his clear brown eyes scanning the wharf. "Everyone traveling west by the rivers leaves from here."

"Do you know when we will board?" Clarissa asked, wishing that they could finally begin the journey.

Though she had left her home in Colchester, Connecticut two weeks ago, the journey would not begin in Clarissa's mind until they left Pittsburgh. For it was from here that she truly would be "jumping off" into the vast wilderness of the American frontier and leaving behind the comfortable familiarity of her small New England hometown.

Until the keelboat pulled away from the dock, she could still change her mind, as her mother had twice reminded her when she boarded the stage in Colchester. And Clarissa was afraid that if they didn't board the keelboat soon, she might change her mind. Her stomach was developing knots from the waiting.

"Shouldn't be much longer, I'd think," the young man replied. "I've seen our trunks put aboard so surely they'll be calling for passengers soon."

He turned an appraising eye upon Clarissa, appearing to study her carefully.

"Have you been aboard a boat before, Miss . . . Cleaver, isn't it?" he asked, coloring a little as if embarrassed that he was at a loss about her name.

Clarissa smiled and felt herself relax a bit. "It's Johnson," she responded. "Miss Cleaver is over there with the Spaulding family."

"I'm sorry," he stuttered his apology. "Afraid I'm bad with names."

"No need to apologize," Clarissa assured him. "I've been

trying to remember yours and can only remember that you said it was French."

"It's Requa," he supplied. "George Requa, from Mt. Pleasant, New York."

"Mr. Requa," Clarissa repeated, offering him a gloved hand. "Clarissa Johnson of Colchester, Connecticut. And to answer your question, yes, I have been aboard a boat. My family would take a summer holiday at New Haven most years. I love being out on the water."

"I'm afraid I don't have much experience with boating myself," George confessed. "I hope I don't embarrass myself by taking ill." He stuffed his hands into the pockets of his coat, as if suddenly self-conscious about his lack of travel experience.

Clarissa eyed the squat keelboat that they would soon board as she tucked a strand of hair back into her bonnet. The wind was getting up again, increasing the chill in the air.

"I doubt that one of those keelboats gets any speed at all," she offered. "You'll probably not notice the motion much, unless the winds make the river a bit choppy. I find it helps to keep your eye on the shoreline if you feel unsettled in your stomach."

"Thank you, I'll remember that," George said. Then he added, "It's good we have a doctor in our group . . . should someone take ill, I mean."

"Yes," Clarissa agreed. The fact that a medical doctor would be part of the mission was one of the reasons that Clarissa's parents had finally agreed to allow her to join it. While they approved of her desire to do some good with her life, they had been quite reluctant at first to consider their oldest daughter's wish to travel out to the Indian country to teach at a mission school.

Clarissa could remember the conversation clearly from several months earlier. She had sat with her family at the Sunday dinner table discussing the morning's sermon presented by a visiting minister. The Rev. William Vaille had told about the organization of a mission society in New York that had just secured permission to establish a school among the Osages in the new Arkansas Territory.

The society was seeking workers to assist with this mission

effort. They were most in need of teachers, having secured Rev. Vaille as the pastor and secretary for the mission, as well as a medical doctor and certain craftsmen such as a blacksmith, stone mason and carpenter.

While her younger sisters had amused themselves during the sermon by watching a snowfall out the church windows, Clarissa's attention had been riveted to Rev. Vaille's description of the beautiful prairie where the mission would be located. *Perhaps this is my answer,* she thought. *I can play the courageous and benevolent teacher and no one will ever know I'm just running away.*

As her family sat around the dinner table following the morning church service, the discussion had immediately turned to Rev. Vaille's plea for teachers for the mission.

"Dr. Dwight says every Yale graduate should give one year of service on a mission field," Clarissa's younger brother George said as he carved into the boiled beef and potatoes Betsy had served. "I plan to go . . . someday," he added quickly, seeing his mother's look of alarm. "I fully intend to graduate first."

George was in his first year at Yale College, a fact that everyone in the family was proud of. Dr. Timothy Dwight, president of the college, had long been a leader in encouraging the development of mission organizations. The United Foreign Mission Society Rev. Vaille had helped form was a combined effort of the Presbyterian and Congregational Churches of New England.

"Mission work is a laudable effort," Clarissa's father said. "But I hope you'll give it some serious thought before you head off to the wilderness, son. I'll need you at the mill as soon as you graduate."

"Yes, father," George said agreeably enough, but Clarissa knew her brother longed for some grand adventure before settling into the dull work of running a textile mill.

"Well, these missionaries are to be admired," Emily Johnson stated. "To head off to an untamed land, where the privations must be terrible, would certainly take a true dedication to the Lord's work." She sipped at her water goblet thoughtfully. "We should be careful to keep them in our prayers."

Clarissa took a deep breath, drawing up her courage. "I'd like to go," she said, her voice coming out in a timorous squeak.

Everyone at the table stopped what they were doing to turn and look at her. Even her two sisters who until now had shown more interest in buttering their rolls than in the conversation about missions work were looking at Clarissa as if she suddenly had grown a second head.

Her mother set her goblet down so quickly a bit of water sloshed out onto the rose damask tablecloth. "But, Clarissa," she said, clearly struggling to gather her thoughts. "It's so far. Who knows how long you might be away before you could get back. And to go alone? It's well enough, I suppose, for someone who is married. You should wait until you're ma. . ." She stopped abruptly. "That is to say, until . . ."

"I'd like to go," Clarissa repeated, this time more forcefully to stop her mother from embarrassing them both. "I have teaching experience. They need someone to teach the young girls. I could do some good, I think."

Clarissa saw her parents exchange a look. And she knew at that moment that she would be going to the Indian country. Though it took several more discussions to secure their permission, they had finally relented and agreed to allow this journey into the unknown.

"I believe the captain is calling for boarding," Mr. Requa said, interrupting Clarissa's reverie. "Shall we join the others?"

With a hand at her elbow, the young man walked with Clarissa across the wooden wharf, their footsteps echoing on the planking suspended above the river. At the gangplank, a queue of fellow travelers waited their turn to board the keelboat piloted by Captain Josiah Douglas.

Joining their fellow missionaries, George and Clarissa fell in line behind the Chapman family. Rachel Chapman turned and gave Clarissa a smile. "Well, at last we are on our way," she said. "I was beginning to despair of ever making our departure."

On the journey from New York to Pittsburgh, Clarissa had shared a coach with the Chapmans and had gotten to know them better than the other members of the group. Rachel was an attractive woman with pale blond hair and gray eyes.

Though only a few years older than Clarissa, she was the

mother of four active young children. Clarissa had been astonished that Mrs. Chapman would not hesitate to take her children out beyond the reaches of civilization, especially after she had told Clarissa her family name. Mrs. Chapman was from one of the wealthiest and most politically connected families in all of Connecticut.

Her husband, Rev. Epaphras Chapman, would serve as the superintendent in charge of the mission. He had traveled with an advance party of five men from the mission society to St. Louis where they would purchase the bulk of the supplies and tools they would need for building the mission complex.

"Come, come, children," Rachel turned to her young charges. "Careful here on the gangplank. It might be a bit wet and slippery." Somehow she managed to get her arms across the shoulders of them all as she gently urged them forward to the boat.

George Requa smiled as he and Clarissa followed behind the Chapmans. "Motherhood seems to be her calling," he spoke in a low voice to Clarissa.

She nodded in agreement, but said nothing as the captain, resplendent in his navy uniform with gold buttons, offered her a hand to step aboard. Carefully lifting her woolen skirt, Clarissa set her booted foot onto the deck of the keelboat and followed the Chapman clan in getting their first look at their traveling accommodations.

The boat was bigger than it appeared from the wharf, some sixty feet long and fifteen wide. The pilothouse was whitewashed with a jaunty blue trim around the top. An American flag rose above it with its 20 stars and 13 stripes snapping crisply in the breeze.

Around the deck, boatmen went about the business of preparing the boat for launch. When the passengers had all boarded, Captain Douglas stepped to the helm and cleared his throat to gain everyone's attention. "Ladies and gentlemen," he said in a booming voice used to calling out sailing orders, 'welcome aboard the finest boat upon the Ohio River today." The captain was a heavy-set man with full mutton chop whiskers. He was an imposing figure, his bearing as authoritative as his booming voice.

As Captain Douglas continued his welcome, Clarissa found her attention turning more closely to her traveling companions. While there were a few passengers who were not a part of the mission group, the bulk of her fellow travelers standing around the deck would be making the journey with her all the way to the Indian country. Altogether there were twenty-three in the mission family, eight of them children. Five more men had traveled ahead and would meet them at St. Louis.

Mr. Requa had joined Dr. Palmer and they were standing near the captain. Dr. Marcus Palmer was a much taller man, a bit thin and angular with dark hair that curled around his ears. Not more than a year or two out of medical school, he was also from Connecticut.

Near them was the Spaulding family. John Spaulding would be the other teacher for the mission. His wife Alice, young son Billy and sister-in-law, Eliza Cleaver, huddled close to him.

Four other single women made up the mission party. Two, Phoebe Beach and Susan Comstock, had been hired to be housemothers for the boarding school. They were a study in contrast – Phoebe was dark-haired and rather stocky while Susan had honey blonde hair and was quite tall and thin. Amanda Ingles, a plump redhead would work as the cook for the mission. And Sally Edwards, a dark-haired girl who looked not more than eighteen had been hired as a seamstress.

Two married women whose husbands were with the advance party already in St. Louis made up the remaining women traveling alone. Lydia Fuller was the wife of the farm director for the mission. She had ginger colored hair that reminded Clarissa of her sister's tabby cat. She seemed rather pale as if she was recovering from an illness and she always held a handkerchief close to her mouth to cover a rather persistent cough. Martha Woodruff, the oldest of the women traveling west, was married to the mission's blacksmith.

Near them stood Asenath Vaille, wife of Rev. William Vaille with their three children. Mrs. Vaille was a pale, willowy young woman with a complexion like a china doll. Clarissa thought she seemed too fragile to be making such an arduous journey west.

But then she remembered the penetrating look Mrs. Vaille had given her when they were introduced, as if she too were questioning Clarissa's decision in going to the wilderness. Did she suspect that it was not some great devotion to the worthy cause of missionary work that had brought Clarissa to this journey? Clarissa looked away as Mrs. Vaille glanced in her direction and turned her attention back to Captain Douglas.

"My steward, Mr. Pennywit, will direct you to your cabins and see to your needs," the captain concluded his speech. "Don't hesitate to ask for assistance. We'll be casting off within the half hour."

Mr. Philip Pennywit was in his mid-thirties and had the look of a man who had long worked on the river. He spoke with a Virginia drawl and was fair-haired with a full beard and friendly gray eyes. He was immediately assailed with questions from the passengers.

Clarissa felt Rachel Chapman crook her arm around her own. "Now, dear," the motherly woman said, "I think it best that you stick close with us Chapmans for the journey." Looking around the boat's deck at the men who were lifting the gangplank and stowing the last of the cargo below, she added, "We'll give them the benefit of the doubt for now, but some of these men look a bit rough around the edges. It will not do for all of you unmarried women to go about the boat unescorted."

"Yes, ma'am," Clarissa agreed politely, though she doubted that any of these rough looking roustabouts would give her a second look. Clarissa considered herself rather plain and had never been a woman to have men buzzing about her. More likely they would be drawn to another of the unmarried women on board – Miss Eliza Cleaver.

Pretty and petite, the young woman wore her abundant blonde hair in long, curling ringlets in the fashion of the day. Clarissa watched as Eliza played with her nephew around the oarsmen's benches on the keelboat deck. The hood of her blue wool cape had fallen back and her curls bounced in the breeze. Clarissa could tell that Eliza had already caught the eye of several of the men on board.

Miss Cleaver, age sixteen, was traveling to Arkansas Territory with her sister Alice and brother-in-law John and their son. Billy Spaulding at age three was one of the youngest members of the mission party. John Spaulding would teach the male students while Clarissa was to teach the girls.

"Shall we go down and look over our cabins?" Rachel asked, pulling Clarissa's attention back to the Chapmans. At Clarissa's nod, she motioned her children to gather around her.

"Thomas, you lead the way," she said to her oldest son, a fair-haired boy of nine who looked to be growing out of his gray wool pants. "I'll be all summer sewing new clothes for that boy." Rachel smiled proudly, causing Thomas' ears to redden and seven-year-old Abigail Chapman to lapse into giggles. Clarissa winked at her and her younger sister Leah. James, a precocious six-year-old, trailed behind them, reluctant to miss any of the activity above deck.

The group joined other passengers looking over their living space for the journey that would take several weeks to complete. Mrs. Chapman declared the cabins to be neat and tidy though to Clarissa's eye they looked terribly small and cramped. Clarissa would share a cabin with Mrs. Martha Woodruff and with two of the other single women, Sally Edwards and Phoebe Beach.

Each cabin had two sets of stacked bunks and all would be full for the journey. With their trunks set beside the beds, there was barely floor space to walk around the cabin. A small wooden cabinet held a white, unadorned water pitcher and basin on top, with a chamber pot tucked discreetly inside its one drawer. A high wooden shelf along the back wall with hooks beneath were all that was available for storing items.

Hearing the order to cast off, passengers made their way to the top deck again, wanting to watch the procedure for pulling the heavy keelboat away from the dock. Captain Douglas stood at the wheel of the boat with Mr. Pennywit nearby to relay orders. The muscled oarsmen had taken position at the benches fore and aft of the pilothouse.

Other boatmen, using long poles, strained to push the keelboat away from its mooring at the wharf. Once clear of other boats tied at the port, the rowers would lower their oars and with powerful strokes pull the boat into the current of the wide Ohio River.

Clarissa stood with the Chapmans around her, but her eyes

were not on the activity aboard the boat. She kept her eyes on the bustling port, watching it grow smaller as the boat moved downstream.

She felt the jerk of the boat as the rowers bent into their oars for the first mighty stroke. She saw the expanse of muddy water widen between the boat's stern and the wharf.

Now there was no changing her mind and no going back. She could not know what would lie ahead for her as she journeyed into the vast American frontier. But she knew it could be no worse than what she was leaving behind.

CHAPTER TWO

Ohio River
April 16, 1820

Time on the river seemed suspended. The keelboat had
been underway for over an hour, yet it seemed only a few
moments since the oarsmen had pulled away from the dock.
Clarissa found it interesting to pass through the outskirts of
Pittsburgh, noting how the buildings became smaller and further
apart as they moved away from the port.

A river road on the shore was busy with traffic. Freighters
with large, loaded wagons pushed their teams of four, six and
even eight mules toward the port. Farmers moved at a slower
pace in their wagons hauling seed or other supplies back to their
homesteads. There were plenty of riders on horseback and other
folks walking along the road. Many waved at the passing boat.

The children on board had spent the first hour of travel
rushing from one rail to another, as if fearful of missing any of
the interesting sights along the way. Clarissa exchanged smiles
with Mrs. Chapman as they watched the children.

"They don't seem to realize we're going to be on this boat
for weeks and weeks," Rachel said. She and Clarissa stood at
the starboard rail where it was warmer in the lee of the
pilothouse. "If I know my brood, they'll soon tire of this running
about and will be begging for something to eat. They were all
too excited to even touch their porridge this morning."

Clarissa would not admit that she too had eaten little of the
early breakfast served at the hostelry though it was more

nervousness than excitement that had quelled her appetite. She marveled at the equanimity that Mrs. Chapman showed at the prospect of this long journey. It seemed fraught with possible dangers and difficulties to Clarissa, who had been born, grew up and lived her entire life in only one house on a quiet street in Colchester.

Though she had seen some of Connecticut, had visited the seaside of New Haven often and had even traveled to New York on a few occasions, this months-long journey was a first for her. To venture beyond the protection of her family and hometown had taken a courage that had surprised even her. If staying at home had not seemed such a dismal prospect, she would never have struck out on this mission undertaking.

"Thomas . . . Leah, come away from there," Rachel called to two of her offspring when they began to lean too far over the rail as if hoping to catch one of the fish that occasionally broke the surface of the mud brown water.

Thomas and his younger sister Leah turned from the rail and hurried to their mother.

"Mother, may we go fishing?" Thomas asked breathlessly when they reached Rachel's side.

"Fishing!" she exclaimed with a knowing smile. "Whatever for?"

"For something to eat!" Leah answered promptly, as she hopped from one foot to another, her long strawberry blond curls bouncing. "We're hungry!"

"Hungry!" their mother echoed. "After eating such big bowls of porridge as you were served for breakfast this morning?"

Leah's gaze fell to her high-button shoes now no longer dancing in excitement. "Well," she answered slowly, "it has been such a very long time since breakfast."

Even Thomas had to laugh at the crestfallen face of his sister. They both had been caught at not having eaten their breakfast.

Mrs. Chapman surveyed her children as James and Abigail joined the group. "Perhaps the cook might have something prepared," she said. "If we ask politely we may entreat him to share a bit with us. What do you think?"

"Yes," Leah quickly agreed. "We will ask him very politely."

"Will you join us, Miss Johnson?" Rachel asked, turning to Clarissa.

"Thank you, but no," Clarissa responded. "I may join you after a while."

Seeing Rev. and Mrs. Vaille close by, Rachel conceded to leaving Clarissa alone on deck.

Clarissa watched the Chapman family as they made their way below. Rachel had her arms clasped through Thomas' and Abigail's as if they were all great friends. It was clear that their mother's sense of adventure was shared by the children. Perhaps that was why this journey seemed to be taken in stride by all of them. It was simply an exciting adventure, not a flight from which there was no return.

Clarissa turned and leaned against the rail, glad for a moment of solitude. She knew there would be few such moments aboard this crowded boat. She watched the slow passing of the distant shoreline. Birds dipped up and down above the water, their keen eyes searching for the ripples of insects on the surface.

Having left the city behind, the shore was heavily lined with trees and underbrush, not quite ready to put on their spring growth. The smell of the river was a unique mixture of mud and fish and heavy vegetation, not entirely pleasant to the senses.

The rhythmic slap of the oars created an almost hypnotic sound. How serene the river seemed, unlike the churning within the young woman's spirit. Every dip of the oars carried her farther from her home, her family, her work, in some ways even her identity. She was no longer Clarissa Johnson of Colchester, Connecticut. But who was she? A missionary? A teacher?

She remembered her sister Millie's quizzical look as she had helped Clarissa pack her trunk for the journey.

"But why do you want to go all the way to that Arkas place?" she had asked, as they sorted through Clarissa's dresses. Millie was the youngest of the family and still a bit childish even at age thirteen. Having paid little attention to all the talk about the Osage Mission, she seemed genuinely puzzled that her sister would decide to go there.

"It's Arkansas Territory," Clarissa corrected. "And you know why I'm going. I'm going to teach at the mission for the Indians."

"But you already are a teacher," Millie argued, "at the Colchester School for Young Ladies. You don't have to go to a mission to be a teacher."

It's because I'll never be anything but a teacher, Clarissa thought bitterly, but she did not give voice to that thought. Instead, she tossed aside another silk dinner dress and tried to explain to her sister without revealing the ache in her heart.

"The young ladies of Colchester have plenty of teachers," she said. "But the girls of the Osage tribe don't have any. I can make a difference there."

Millie was silent for a while as she folded the simple brown wool dress Clarissa handed her. "Are you going to marry an Indian?" she asked, cutting far closer to the heart of the matter than she realized.

"Millie!" Clarissa exclaimed, as if the idea had never occurred to her and never would. "Of course not!"

"Well, that's what George says," the girl explained in her defense for making such a shocking statement. She often parroted her older brother whom she idolized. "He told mother she shouldn't let you go to Arkans Territory because you'll end up marrying an Indian and bring shame to the family."

"George doesn't know what he's talking about," Clarissa replied curtly, "and he ought to keep his ignorant opinions to himself." She rolled up a couple of cotton petticoats and stuffed them down into a corner of her trunk with more force than necessary.

"George isn't ignorant," Millie defended him. "He goes to Yale."

"That's no proof of intelligence," Clarissa huffed, really angry now. "Some of the most insipid men I know go to Yale." *Robert went to Yale,* the thought came unbidden to her mind as if to offer proof of what she said. But she wouldn't dwell on Robert or the tears would come again and she was through with crying.

"George shouldn't offer opinions where they are not wanted." Clarissa turned quickly away from her sister and began to sort through her gloves. *And he doesn't know anything about shame,* she finished in her head.

Even weeks later on the Ohio River, Clarissa felt the same heat of anger and embarrassment bring color to her cheeks. She turned away from the boat's rail and let the cool morning air blow against her face.

Her movement caught the attention of Rev. and Mrs. Vaille and the couple approached her. Clarissa fiddled with her gloves, hoping her emotions were no longer written across her face. She didn't want the solicitous pastor and his wife to inquire if something was wrong.

"Well, Miss Johnson," William Vaille addressed her with a slight bow. "I trust our journey has not been too strenuous on you thus far."

"Not at all, Rev. Vaille," Clarissa replied, looking up at him. "I'm not unaccustomed to travel, though this is my first trip by keelboat."

"You'll find it monotonous after awhile, I'm afraid," the pastor said, his shock of thick black hair blowing in the breeze that seemed to be picking up as the boat moved into more open farmland. "The scenery ceases to be quite so fascinating when you've seen miles and miles of the same thing."

"But you traveled this way before with a group of serious men," Mrs. Vaille countered softly, her blue eyes gazing up at her husband who was taller than her by at least half a foot. "I think the children we have aboard will make our journey quite lively." The Vailles' three children were ages nine, seven and three and had already proven to be as lively as the Chapman children.

Clarissa smiled as she thought of the Chapmans. "I'm sure you're right, Mrs. Vaille. The children will find ways to entertain us when the scenery fails to do so."

"Well, don't get me wrong, ladies," Rev. Vaille smiled down at his wife. "There is some very interesting scenery to be viewed on the journey. It's just that there's a great deal of general nothingness in between those highlights."

"I thought your description of the Indian country was quite beautiful," Clarissa said. "I can't imagine the great expanse of open prairie that you talked about."

"Yes, as New Englanders we're used to the woodlands that keep us closed in and always guessing what's just around the bend. Out on the prairie you can see for miles. It can actually be quite intimidating at first. But it is beautiful nonetheless."

"William tells me the grasses grow taller than he stands," Mrs. Vaille said again looking up at her husband's lanky frame. "Now that is something I cannot wait to see."

"It's a well-watered area where we'll be building the mission," Rev. Vaille explained as the young mechanic, George Requa, sauntered up to join their group. "Our location, in fact, is very near a river the Osages call the Neosho. It joins with two other rivers at a place called Three Forks. There's a little trading community developing there. The fur trade is important to the Osages and game is abundant in the region."

"What type of game?" Clarissa asked, feeling a little fearful at the thought of wild animals roaming near the mission. She unconsciously drew her wool cape a little closer about her.

"Yes, what animals are found in the region?" Mr. Requa asked, clearly eager to learn more about the country they would soon call their home.

"We saw several large herds of deer and elk," Vaille replied. "And at the Verdigris trading posts we saw pelts of beaver, fox, wolves, bear, mountain lions, panthers and, of course, the bison."

"I've seen a drawing of a bison," George said, leaning against the boat's railing. "Are they really as large as I've read?"

"We didn't chance to see any bison when we were there," Rev. Vaille said. He gestured widely with his arms to illustrate his point. "But from the looks of the hides we saw, yes, I'd say the bison is a very large animal indeed."

Just then the boat began to pitch slightly causing the small group of passengers to lose their footing. Mr. Requa quickly took Clarissa's elbow to steady her, but just as quickly, in a gentlemanly fashion, released her arm.

"Are you alright?" he asked.

"Yes, thank you," Clarissa replied. "What caused that?"

"McKee's Rocks," Rev. Vaille and George both answered as the boat continued to pitch up and down. Clarissa took hold of the rail to steady herself. Mrs. Vaille reached for her husband's arm. Clearly the boat was encountering rough waters.

"I see you've traveled this way before," William Vaille said to Mr. Requa.

"No," George replied, a bit sheepishly. "I've never been this far west before in my life." Then he pulled out a well-worn paperback book from his coat pocket. Holding it up he said, "I've been reading this."

Clarissa read the title. "*The Navigator*. What is it about?"

"It's a travel guide to the Ohio and Mississippi Rivers," George explained. "A man named Cramer wrote it. He gives a detailed description of what a traveler will encounter all the way to New Orleans."

"Then you've read about McKee's Rocks," Vaille said, as they were joined by the Chapman family who were coming up top to see what was going on. Dr. Palmer followed behind them and all began to move carefully toward the front of the boat.

Mr. Pennywit, the steward, met them at the bow. "Nothing to be alarmed at, folks," he assured them in his distinctly southern drawl. "The rocks in the river here make it a tad rough, but we've never had any difficulty in getting through them." He stood with his hands behind him and feet apart like a soldier at ease. "The river level is high enough that we need not worry about damage to the boat."

The bow of the keelboat continued to dip up and down as they made their way through the riffs of white water. Clarissa, like most of the other passengers, clung to the railing enthralled by the beauty of this river suddenly gone wild.

Though Leah Chapman, the youngest there at age four, clutched her mother's skirts, even she seemed to enjoy the ride. Soon enough though, it was over and the river returned to its placid demeanor, flattening out across the countryside with barely a ripple upon its surface.

"Mother, I don't feel so well," Abigail Chapman said, holding her stomach. Her face was white, making the few freckles across her nose stand out.

Mrs. Chapman lifted the girl's chin to check her closely. "Feeling it in your stomach, are you?" she asked.

Dr. Palmer stepped closer and laid a gentle hand on the

girl's shoulder. "Give her a bit of soda water," he advised.
"She'll be right in a few moments."

"Oh, Dr. Palmer," a voiced called from the stairs that led
below deck. Everyone turned to see Mrs. Martha Woodruff
making her way toward them. The older woman was out of
breath by the time she reached their group.

"What is it, Mrs. Woodruff?" the doctor asked.

"It's Miss Edwards," she explained, still trying to catch her
breath. Her hat was slightly askew and strands of grey hair
wisped around her face. "You need to check on her. She's taken
quite ill."

"I'll get my bag and meet you at her cabin," Dr. Palmer
said, already hurrying across the deck. Mr. Pennywit followed
after him.

Rev. and Mrs. Vaille joined Mrs. Woodruff and they made
their way back toward the cabins.

"Well, it seems the rough water doesn't agree with
everyone," Mrs. Chapman observed. "Come, Miss Abigail," she
said, taking her daughter's hand. "Let's get something for your
stomach."

Turning back to George and Clarissa, she addressed the
young man. "Mr. Requa, will you act as escort for our Miss
Johnson?"

George straightened suddenly from his relaxed position
against the rail. "Certainly, Mrs. Chapman," he said, seeming
uncomfortable at such a request.

Clarissa turned abruptly to the rail and looked out over the
water. She certainly didn't want to be a bother to the man.

He came and leaned on the rail close to her. "You were
right," he said simply.

Against her will she turned to look at him. "Right about
what?" she asked, her curiosity outweighing her annoyance.

"It does help to watch the shoreline," George said with a
grin, a lock of brown hair falling across his forehead. "If I
hadn't I would have been joining Miss Edwards and little
Abigail," he confessed in a conspiratorial tone. "Thank you."

Clarissa couldn't help but smile. "You're welcome," she
said.

CHAPTER THREE

Ohio River
Late April, 1820

As Rev. Vaille had predicted, the journey lost some of its luster for Clarissa as the days passed and life aboard the westward bound keelboat settled into a predictable pattern. The boat stopped frequently at the little river towns scattered along the Ohio, but their stays were usually too brief to give them time to go ashore. The oarsmen, a temporary crew, debarked and the boat now utilized only the powerful current and the wind in two large sails to move it downstream.

At each little town, Clarissa watched some passengers board and others debark if they had reached their destination. Freight was unloaded at some stops and more taken aboard to be delivered to a port of call further downstream.

Several cold rain showers had driven the passengers below deck for long hours at a time. With the skies overcast, little light came through the portholes and the crowded cabins seemed dreary. The children grew restless with their confinement and even the Chapmans who normally shared their mother's cheerfulness were out of sorts and complaining about everything.

"We need to find something to occupy the children," Mrs. Chapman sighed one morning as several of the women lingered in the dining hall of the keelboat after breakfast. Sipping the strong black coffee the cook had served, they listened to the steady drum of rain above them.

The soothing sound was interrupted, however, with a little girl's piercing scream. All the women started and turned toward the door from where the cry came. Mrs. Chapman set down her coffee cup and half stood as if she recognized the child's cry as her daughter's.

At that moment Abigail Chapman ran into the room, along with her new friend Elizabeth Vaille. They were followed by Thomas Chapman whose hands were filled with an enormous black and yellow bullfrog.

Around the tables they all three scampered then turned back into the passageway that ran the length of the cabin deck. The girls' screams echoed off the wooden beams above.

"Well, forevermore!" Mrs. Woodruff exclaimed in a brief moment of silence that followed.

Then more screams and running feet told them that the rest of the children had joined in the chase. Once more they entered the dining hall and all eight of them rounded the tables and dashed back into the passage. It was difficult to tell who was chasing whom. Little Billy Spaulding's chubby legs could barely keep up with the others.

Now the screams had become gales of laughter and Clarissa covered her mouth to keep from joining the merriment. The look of shock on Mrs. Chapman's face told her this was not the time to laugh.

"Children!" Rachel said in a stern voice. She moved from her frozen position, gathered her skirts from the wooden dining chair and strode purposefully to the hall. Mrs. Vaille and Alice Spaulding rose and dutifully followed.

Clarissa exchanged a smile with Sally Edwards and Amanda Ingles who sat across from her. Then all the ladies pretended a great interest in their coffee cups while listening to the three mothers separate their offspring and send them all to their respective cabins. Thomas was dispatched to the upper deck to release his captive bullfrog.

Rev. Vaille and John Spaulding entered the dining hall from the captain's cabin where all the men had been discussing the next few days of their journey. As the two fathers aboard the boat, they had recognized that there might be a need for their presence.

"What's all this?" Rev. Vaille asked as the three mothers returned from dealing with their wayward children.

"It's been handled, dear," Mrs. Vaille said in her quiet voice. "The children will be confined to their bunks for the next half hour to give them time to think about their behavior."

"What had they gotten into this time?" John Spaulding asked. Not as tall as Rev. Vaille, Mr. Spaulding had a slight build and with his boyish face and blond hair he seemed more like a student than the teacher he was. Round spectacles perched on his nose and always seemed in need of being pushed up.

"One of the rivermen had given Thomas a bullfrog to play with," Mrs. Chapman explained as she returned to her chair. "But he decided to torment his sisters with it instead." She picked up her coffee cup having returned to her usual cheerful demeanor. "As I was saying before," she smiled wryly, "we need to find something to occupy these children."

"I could work with the girls on their reading and penmanship," Clarissa volunteered, surprising herself a little at her boldness.

"An excellent idea," Rev. Vaille agreed as he took a seat beside his wife. "What about you, Mr. Spaulding? Would you be willing to take on a class of restless boys?"

"Certainly," John readily agreed. "We can cover geography, math and history for the boys. Perhaps the captain would allow us the use of the dining hall."

"I wouldn't mind to help the girls with some needlework," Sally offered. The young woman with dark curls had already demonstrated her skills as a seamstress with beautiful embroidery work. Poor Sally continued to struggle with a persistent sickness that left her hanging over the chamber pot most mornings. Even now she had dark circles under her eyes and a worn look about her face. "Perhaps we could do that in the afternoons." She flushed a little at saying this.

So it was agreed that school would be in session, much to the groans of the children when they heard the plan. The mornings would begin with devotions and prayer led by Rev. Vaille. Then following breakfast, Clarissa and John Spaulding settled their young charges at the dining tables for two hours of school before dinner.

The children were allowed an hour of play time following dinner and then George Requa and Sally joined the makeshift school to work with the children on crafts – needlework for the girls and wood carving for the boys.

Following supper, after the children were sent to bed, the adults gathered again in the dining room for Bible reading and some form of entertainment. Mrs. Chapman shared readings from a book of sonnets, Amanda Ingles had a lovely voice for singing some fine Irish folk songs, or sometimes they all joined together in singing hymns.

One evening after they had retired to their cabin for the night, Sally shyly asked Clarissa if she could beg a favor of her.

"Of course, Sally," Clarissa said as she began to unpin her hair. "What is it?"

"I'm not so good a reader myself," the young woman confessed. "Never had much chance for schooling. I was wondering if you might help me with my reading."

Before Clarissa could answer, Phoebe Beach, another cabin mate, offered her opinion. "What use will book learning be where we are going?" she asked, not unkindly while she prepared for bed. "There'll be few books to read out on the frontier, but I imagine there'll be plenty of work to keep us busy."

Phoebe had been hired to serve as a housemother for the Osage students who would board at the school yet to be built. A stocky young woman, she was plain of face and plain spoken as well. But she clearly loved children and had already become a favorite with the youngsters among the mission family.

"Learning is never a waste of time," Mrs. Woodruff interjected as she buttoned her cotton nightdress and then began to loosely braid her long dark hair, streaked generously with gray. "I applaud Sally for wanting to better herself."

The girl flushed and looked down at her hands folded in her lap. It seemed such kind words were unknown to her and Clarissa saw tears in her eyes.

"You're right, Mrs. Woodruff," Clarissa said. "Aren't we going to the wilderness to help the Indians learn? I'll be happy to help you, Sally," she reached out and patted the girl's hand. "We can work together during the children's play time."

"Oh, thank you, Miss Johnson," Sally sighed. "It's always been a dream of mine to be able to read."

"You'll be reading in no time," Clarissa said, and then added, "and please call me Clarissa. We're all becoming good friends . . . no need to be so formal."

"Oh, I couldn't," Sally countered. "Not to such a fine, well-to-do lady as yourself."

"Nonsense," Clarissa said, suddenly feeling uncomfortable. "Surely class and station will have little meaning for us on the frontier."

"Perhaps not for you," Phoebe again interjected as she climbed into the top bunk above Mrs. Woodruff. "But for those of us like Sally and me, we've always been put in our place by those above us. You learn right quick not to be too familiar with your betters. Ain't that right, Sally?"

Clarissa looked at Sally, but the girl would not meet her eye. Now that Clarissa thought about it, Sally always seemed to keep her eyes down as if she had perhaps been scolded by someone in her past for displaying anything but a servile attitude.

"It would just be better if we kept our place," Sally said quietly as she too climbed into the other upper bunk above Clarissa.

Clarissa exchanged a look with Mrs. Woodruff who simply shrugged and then slipped into her own bed. Clarissa pulled her nightdress over her head and then blew out the lamp. Climbing into her bunk, she quickly pulled the blanket up to her chin against the cool night air.

For a long time, Clarissa lay staring up at Sally's bunk, unable to sleep or to quiet the thoughts that tormented her brain.

Sally thought her well-to-do because she was educated and owned more than three dresses. But Clarissa knew her family was not wealthy by any means. Her father managed a small textile mill. Their home was not located in one of the finer neighborhoods of Colchester, but in a decent middle class section near the center of town.

No, if her family had money she would never be making this journey west.

Unbidden her father's voice came to her. "Is it the money?"

she had overhead him ask one afternoon as she walked by his study where he was meeting with Robert, her intended. Something in his tone, a note of distress, had caused her to stop outside the door.

"We could try to increase the dowry," her father continued. "I'll talk to her mother. See what we can do."

"By how much?" Robert had asked.

His words were like a knife to her heart.

Her father was being forced to pay a man to marry her, a man who had for the past year led everyone to believe he was happy to marry her. No protests of love came from Robert's lips now. He offered only a cold, calculating question. *How much?*

With her hand to her mouth to suppress a cry, Clarissa had hurried away from her father's door and ran to her bedroom upstairs. The worst few days of her life had followed as she had to pretend to have not overheard the conversation. But the words had never stopped echoing through her head. *How much? How much?*

As she lay in her bunk, they echoed still and she could not keep the hot tears from coursing across her face. Whatever her father had eventually offered him, Robert's answer had been . . . not enough.

CHAPTER FOUR

Cincinnati, Ohio
May 3, 1820

At last the rainy days passed and sunshine returned to the Ohio River valley. The passengers were so glad to be freed from the confines of the cabin deck that they were all at the boat's rails one morning in late April. The children were like birds set free from a cage. Back and forth they raced across the boat's deck, once again taking in all the sights along the river.

Clarissa and Mr. Spaulding decided to conduct their classes at the oarsmen's benches since they were no longer in use. The powerful current of the river was the only force moving the boat this day.

But Clarissa's three young students were not in a mood to copy simple sentences on their slates. Abigail Chapman and Elizabeth Vaille, both aged seven, were whispering secrets about their plans for their afternoon play time. Young Leah Chapman kept dropping her chalk and crawling under the bench to retrieve it.

A few benches further aft, John Spaulding was having even less success in keeping the attention of Thomas and James Chapman and Richard Vaille. None of the boys were interested in Columbus' exploration of the New World when they had a world of exploring to do aboard their own boat.

Finally Clarissa and John exchanged a look and in complete agreement declared class dismissed for the day. Their students were up and gone before the words were even out of Mr. Spaulding's mouth. Off they raced to where Phoebe and Eliza

Cleaver were sitting with Sarah Vaille and Billy Spaulding, the three-year-olds too young for school.

Clarissa watched the children for a while as Phoebe engaged them in one of the silly games she was always creating for them. What a contrast between the plain Phoebe whose only aspiration was to be a good mother and Eliza the pretty 16-year-old who would, with a little maturity, become a truly beautiful woman.

Phoebe was dressed in a serviceable dark wool skirt and blouse, with a misshapen black hat that had seen better days flattened against her head. Eliza wore a blue-sprigged muslin gown of the latest fashion and a pretty straw hat held in place with a bright blue bow tied at a jaunty angle under her jaw.

Good thing for her she is pretty, Clarissa thought with some bitterness as Dr. Palmer walked up and began to engage Eliza in conversation. Though Eliza was from a fine family, she was now orphaned and in the care of her sister Alice Spaulding. Dependent upon the sparse livelihood of her brother-in-law, a mission teacher, Eliza would certainly have no dowry. But then, such a beauty probably wouldn't need one.

"Oh, Miss Johnson," Sally's voice intruded upon Clarissa's pensive thoughts. "Isn't this sunshine lovely?"

Clarissa looked up to see Sally standing at the bench where she sat. The young woman had a book in her hands, not an unusual sight these days. Since beginning her studies with Clarissa, it was as if Sally could not get enough of books.

Clarissa only hoped her Osage students would be as eager to learn. Few things were as gratifying to a teacher as a willing student. Clarissa was glad she had thought to pack several books for the journey west.

"Yes, I could sit out here all day," Clarissa agreed. She patted the bench beside her. "Won't you join me in the sunshine?"

"Thank you, Miss Johnson," Sally said. She had never lost the deferential tone she always used with her teacher. She smoothed the skirt of her simple fawn-colored cotton gown as she sat down. Though it was completely unadorned with any ribbon or lace, the dress was well-made and fit her perfectly. It was a clear example of Sally's fine work as a seamstress.

"Where did you learn to sew, Sally?" Clarissa asked her young friend. "You certainly are adept with a needle."

"My mother taught me," Sally replied, her eyes downcast, her voice sad. "Her chatelaine is the only possession of hers I still have."

"Your mother is passed on then?" Clarissa said gently.

"She died when I was eleven. So did my father and brother. It was a cholera epidemic."

"Oh, Sally, I'm so sorry," Clarissa said. Perhaps this was the reason Sally always seemed so forlorn. Clarissa could not imagine what her life would have been like had she lost her parents at such a young age.

"Were you raised by family . . . your grandparents?"

Sally hesitated for a long moment before answering. She kept her eyes upon the distant shoreline, a look of pain visibly etched upon her face. "My only relative was a distant cousin, much older than I," she finally said. "He did not want me . . . so he sold me."

Her stark words shocked Clarissa. "Sold you?" she repeated in disbelief.

"He indentured me . . . for seven years," Sally explained. "I worked in a lace factory owned by my master. He . . ." Sally stopped herself. Tears welled in her eyes.

Clarissa sensed there was something awful in the unspoken words of her companion. But she had not the courage or will to press Sally to say more. She didn't want to know what Sally's life had been like.

Fortunately for both young women, the voice of George Requa interrupted their conversation.

"Miss Johnson," he called from across the deck where he and the children had been romping in a game of keep-away with Miss Beach and the other housemother, Susan Comstock. "Miss Edwards, come join us."

Sally stood quickly, as if glad for the interruption, though she barely raised her eyes above the book that she clutched in front of her like a shield. She and Clarissa joined the other young people of the mission family.

"Mr. Pennywit tells us that we'll be coming in sight of Cincinnati shortly," George explained when they reached him.

No one among the missionaries seemed more taken with the adventure of traveling down the Ohio River than George Requa. He had perused his book *The Navigator* until it was nearly ragged and he quizzed the boat's steward endlessly about what lay around each bend of the river. For someone who had never before ventured west of his home of Mt. Pleasant, New York, George was becoming an expert on travel down the Ohio.

The children raced toward the bow of the boat and threw themselves upon the rails as if expecting the city of Cincinnati to magically appear before them. Phoebe and Susan, the two housemothers, were right behind them, already taking their job of caring for the children quite seriously.

George, Sally, Clarissa, Eliza and the sweet-voiced Irish cook, Amanda Ingles, followed at a slower pace. All the passengers were eager to arrive at Cincinnati. Captain Douglas had informed then over dinner the evening before that their boat would be docked at the Ohio town for two days and everyone would have an opportunity to go ashore.

"I'll be so glad to reach Cincinnati," Eliza said as she adjusted the bow of her hat. "I've grown weary of this boat and want to go shopping. Oh, I do hope they have some decent shops out here."

"I'll be glad to have a meal that consists of something other than salted beef and biscuits," Miss Ingles said in her lilting Irish brogue. Amanda had often wished that she could get into the boat's kitchen and show the cook how a meal ought to be prepared.

"Now, Miss Ingles," George teased. "We've enjoyed salted pork and salted fish as well."

"And nothing but biscuits," Amanda rejoined, laughter bubbling around her words. "I'll have some wonderful yeast bread whilst we're here, if I have to prepare it meself."

It was some time before the boat rounded a bend in the river to come into sight of Cincinnati. Mr. Pennywit had told them that the Ohio town had a population of about 10,000 and would be one of the largest they would encounter on their journey. Like Pittsburgh, here the riverfront was also lined with wharves and boats docked at the piers.

By the time the boat was being maneuvered into its own slip

at the wharf, every passenger was on deck and standing at the rails. Long days of travel seemed to have left them all tired of the confining cabins and eager to go ashore.

Later that evening the missionary families occupied two long tables at a local inn and restaurant. The children had already been fed and Phoebe, Rachel Chapman and Asie Vaille had taken them off to bed. Besides a good meal, the travelers expressed that they were looking forward to hot baths, and a night's rest on the inn's real feather beds. The thin mattresses in their cabins were not the most restful of sleeping accommodations.

While enjoying their meal of fried catfish, fresh spring greens, warm yeast rolls slathered in butter, and raisin pie all washed down with plenty of coffee and tangy apple cider, the missionaries curiously assessed their surroundings. With the exception of Rev. Vaille, Clarissa and her fellow New Englanders had never been this far south or west before. As they discussed their surroundings, it seemed to them they had reached the very fringe of civilization and the speech, dress and customs of this frontier town fascinated them.

Their host, a Mr. McKinley, proudly told them he was a Revolutionary War veteran and like many other veterans from Kentucky and Virginia had been given land in Ohio for his service. His speech was a friendly mixture of his southern and Scottish heritage.

Along with his plump and cheerful wife, McKinley kept their New England guests amply supplied with rolls, cider, hot coffee and conversation. Their three older children also worked in the restaurant which bustled with the evening's supper crowd, most who seemed to be regular customers at McKinley's Inn.

"Tell us about the fort we saw when we docked," George Requa asked of Mr. McKinley as he replenished coffee cups all around. "It looked to be abandoned."

"That's old Fort Washington," McKinley replied, as he made his way around the table. "Earliest fort built out here in the Northwest Territory. It was named for the great General George Washington, ye know."

"But it's no longer in service?" George pressed.

"Nay, most of the Indian troubles are past us now," McKinley replied. He paused at the end of the long oak table. "The soldiers have all been moved to forts further west. Folks around here have started salvaging the lumber and re-using it. There won't be much left of the old place before long."

"Indian troubles," Amanda Ingles repeated. Her eyes were nearly as large as the yeast roll she held as she generously spread butter and homemade jam on it. "What kind of troubles?" The bliss she felt as she bit into the roll contradicted the worried tone of her words.

"Ye've heard of Tecumseh, the Shawnee chief, have ye not?" McKinley responded. The missionaries nodded. The great chieftain's name was known throughout the states.

"Well back in '91, he started getting the Indian nations in these parts all stirred up. Said they were going to form a confederation and drive out all the white men from their lands. The Miamis lived in these parts and they started attacking settlements up and down the river. Even the Osages came over the Mississippi to fight. The soldiers had a time putting down the uprising. It was a frightful thing for long months around here, I can tell ye."

"The Osages!" Alice and Eliza exclaimed together, the sisters' voices in perfect harmony of both pitch and fright.

Everyone at both tables was instantly alert. Even Rev. Vaille seemed surprised at this bit of information and he leaned forward in his chair. "How were the Osages involved?" he asked.

"Well, I don't know as I can give ye all the details," McKinley said thoughtfully, as he wiped his hands on the white apron he wore. Then casting his eyes around his establishment, he spied the gentleman he was looking for. "But Ben, there, was an officer under Governor St. Clair. He can tell ye all about his fight with the Osages."

The missionary family all turned to look at the man Mr. McKinley pointed out. Ben – Captain Benjamin Knowles, unaware of the sudden interest in him, was munching quietly on his supper of shepherd's pie and ale. He was dressed in the garb of a frontiersman: leather britches, rough wool shirt with sleeves rolled up to reveal a red undershirt. His full bushy beard seemed grown to compensate for his balding pate.

"Ben," McKinley called to his patron. "Come over here and tell these folks about St. Clair's Defeat. And about how that Osage lifted ye'r wig."

Captain Knowles took his time in chewing his last bite of food and then wiped his mouth on the linen napkin he'd tucked into his shirt front. "McKinley," he replied in a voice far more refined than his appearance would suggest him capable of, "you've heard that story a thousand times."

"I know it," McKinley responded. "But these folks ain't and they're heading out to the Osage country."

"Go on, Captain," another diner called out from across the room. "We haven't heard a good war story in a couple of months."

The captain stood slowly and picked up the straight-backed chair he had been sitting in. Carrying it to the tables where the missionaries waited, he placed it at the end between them. Then straddling it like a horse with his arms resting on the back, he said thoughtfully, with a bit of a twinkle in his eye, "Well, it's a good story. I guess I can tell it again."

Unconsciously, Clarissa leaned forward in anticipation of the story as did most everyone else in the room. George caught her eye from across the table and gave her a wink. Clarissa didn't know if they were about to hear the truth or a tall tale, but it would surely prove entertaining.

"We started out from Fort Washington in the fall of '91," Ben began his story. "We were heading northwest toward the Miami village of Kekionga. I was an officer, rank of captain, and we had close to 2,000 troops, most of them green as newborn pups."

Ben's voice was a low, rich baritone and it was clear he knew how to tell a good war story. Not a sound was heard in the room as everyone set down their dinnerware and listened in rapt attention.

The captain told how the troops under General Arthur St. Clair had marched in ragtag fashion toward Kekionga. The weather had turned cold early and the poorly equipped and poorly committed troops were wet, tired and demoralized long before reaching their objective. By the time they were within 50 miles of the Miami village, the troop size had been reduced by several hundred as the green recruits, and even some officers, deserted in droves.

They camped on a ridge near the Wabash River one evening, believing the Miami and Shawnee warriors were nowhere nearby. It proved to be a gross miscalculation on St. Clair's part.

Instead, the Indians had gathered a force of nearly a thousand warriors, and with good information as to the troops' whereabouts, they were preparing to attack at dawn. The Indians were led by Little Turtle of the Miamis and Blue Jacket of the Shawnees. A small group of Osages were also part of the war party.

"It was as if they knew exactly who the officers were among us," Ben said, his voice low. "They specifically targeted us in their attack. We realized later that we were the 'white hairs' to the Indians. We were all wearing our powdered wigs – the fashion of that day, you know." Ben rubbed his balding head and a smattering of laughter rippled around the room. "The British were paying the Indians for scalps and there was extra if the scalp was lifted from an American officer."

Poor gunpowder made whatever advantage the American troops might have had ineffectual. Soon they were engaged in hand-to-hand combat. The Indians were fierce fighters and, having more at stake in the battle, were more determined than the raw troops.

"I found myself in a struggle for my life," Ben said. Everyone was holding their breath by this time.

"An Osage warrior came at me, his screaming war cry making my blood run cold in my veins. He knocked my sword from my hand and then took hold of my white wig, intent upon lifting my scalp with his tomahawk." Captain Knowles grinned sheepishly. "But since there was no hair underneath the wig to grasp, the thing simply came off in his hand."

The men and women in the mission party all gasped in astonishment. Susan Comstock covered the big "O" of her mouth with both hands. Others in the room, familiar with the story, were grinning in appreciation.

"Well, he'd apparently never seen such a thing before, because he looked at it as if it were alive," Ben went on. "It gave me just enough time to roll out of his reach and take up my sword some few feet away. When I turned back to him, he was gone – and my wig was gone with him!"

Now the room erupted in laughter and Ben laughed right along with them.

"You'd think they'd get tired of hearing it," Ben said to the New England visitors. "But they never seem to."

"Did you face any more Osages?" Dr. Palmer asked in his quiet, thoughtful manner. The rest of the diners had now returned to their meals and their own conversations.

"No, I never did," Ben responded. "By the time I lost my wig, General St. Clair was ordering a retreat. I'd seen enough of the fighting after that and retired from the military. But I always wondered if that Osage had tried to claim his scalp money for my wig."

"Are there Osages in this area now?" John Spaulding asked.

"Not to my knowledge," the captain replied. "They've settled even further west, from what I hear, down near the Neosho River."

"That's where we intend to set up our mission," Rev. Vaille explained. "The Osages aren't still inclined to violence, are they?"

"From what I know," Ben said, "they've made their peace with the Americans. But the Cherokees, Choctaws and Pawnees are another matter. Like I said, the Osages are fierce fighters."

Captain Knowles' words were met with thoughtful silence among the missionaries. They looked at one another in an unspoken exchange of concern. They all had been advised about what they would possibly face when they signed on to this mission. They had been warned by the mission society more than once. But Ben's story made the dangers they were traveling toward seem all the more real.

Did I jump out of one trouble into another? Clarissa wondered, as she and the other missionaries later made their way to their rooms at the inn. *"What have I done, Father God,"* she prayed silently. *"What have I done?"*

CHAPTER FIVE

Ohio River
May 8, 1820

It was with a shared reluctance that the mission family re-boarded the keelboat after two days in Cincinnati. They all had taken the time in port to shop for necessary items, to walk about the bustling riverfront and enjoy the very comfortable accommodations at McKinley's Inn.

As they continued downriver, the weather turned warmer and none of the passengers wanted to spend any more time than necessary in the stuffy conditions on the cabin deck. Though the river was high from the recent rains, the drift of the current was as slow as molasses and swarms of mosquitoes buzzed along the marshes at the water's edge.

Clarissa kept her silk fan waving, to try to cool herself and also her young students who were bent over their slates perfecting their presentation of the letter E. The whining of a mosquito at her ear was becoming quite annoying and making it difficult to concentrate.

The girls sat on the deck in the shade of the pilothouse while Clarissa occupied one of the wooden chairs brought up from the dining hall. The young teacher smiled as her students worked on their penmanship, their brows furrowed in concentration. In the distance she could hear the chatter of the boys who were trying to make reed flutes from river cane Mr. Pennywit had gathered for them.

Clarissa had attempted an embroidery lesson with the girls on behalf of Sally Edwards who had taken to her bed with a fever. The heat made the girls quarrelsome and uncooperative, however, and as punishment, they were now writing E one hundred times.

Concern for Sally was another reason Clarissa found concentration difficult. She had grown fond of the young woman as they had worked on her reading lessons together. Though Sally continued to insist on a formality based on their different stations, Clarissa considered Sally a friend. She hated to see her suffering, not only from the heat, but with a fever as well.

When Dr. Palmer had examined Sally, he seemed very concerned. Sally was still having trouble keeping food down and was too weak to fight the fever. Dr. Palmer was considering bleeding her, but would only do so as a last resort.

Martha Woodruff and Mrs. Lydia Fuller were sharing the task of bathing Sally in cool water and feeding her small amounts of broth. Sally was so sick, she barely seemed conscious of the women's efforts.

Lydia was the wife of the mission's farm director, Stephen Fuller. They had sold their farm in New York to embark on this mission undertaking. Stephen was already in St. Louis.

"She'd rest better if we could change her gown," Mrs. Fuller said as she bent over the young woman. At Clarissa's insistence, the women had moved Sally to the lower bunk to make it easier for the women to care for her.

"I don't think she has another nightdress," Mrs. Woodruff said softly as she wiped the damp ringlets of dark hair away from Sally's face. "But we could put her in one of mine. It will be a little large on her but more comfortable than this one."

Together Martha and Lydia worked to pull the sweat-dampened gown over the girl's head. When they had completed the task, Mrs. Fuller gasped as she glimpsed a criss-cross of scars on Sally's back.

"Gracious Lord," Martha whispered.

"Who could have done such a thing?" Lydia asked as the two women exchanged a look of grave concern. Together they slipped Mrs. Woodruff's gown over Sally's shoulders and settled her once again upon the bed.

"Her master, no doubt," Martha responded, her mouth set in

a grim line. "Sally hinted that he had been a cruel man. But I never expected such as this."

She took Sally's gown and placed it in a pile of linens to be washed. "I noticed that she always dressed back in the corner behind her bunk," Martha went on. "I thought she was simply modest, but I suppose she was trying to hide those scars."

"Do you think we should tell Rev. Vaille . . . or the others?" Lydia asked.

Martha looked thoughtful for a moment. "Perhaps just Dr. Palmer," she finally said. "What's done is done and there's no changing it. Having everyone know about it won't help those scars and it might only cause her shame. But the doctor should know. It might have some bearing on why she's so weak and can't seem to fight this fever."

By the following morning, Sally's health was somewhat improved. When Clarissa and Phoebe returned to their cabin following breakfast, they found the young woman sitting up in bed and eating some tea and toast Mrs. Woodruff had brought her.

"Well, it's good to see you up," Phoebe told her cabin mate. "Amanda will be happy to know you're eating a bit. She thinks food is the cure for anything that ails you."

"Ah, but not just any food," Clarissa joined in the lighthearted banter, hoping to cheer Sally a bit. "Amanda assures us that with her cooking we'll tame the wilderness and bring civilization to the frontier. All in the power of her pot roast and dried apple pie."

Sally smiled wanly, but kept her eyes on the tray of food. Mrs. Woodruff chuckled, knowing the ginger-haired cook lacked no confidence in her culinary skills.

Clarissa gathered up the school books she would use for her lessons this morning. "Perhaps if you're feeling better this afternoon, we can read together," she offered.

Sally lifted her eyes briefly, "Thank you, Miss Johnson," she said, her voice thin and weak. "I would like that."

Phoebe touched Sally's shoulder and gave it a gentle squeeze. "We're all keeping you in our prayers," she assured the girl. Then the two young women left again.

They had not been gone long, when a knock sounded at the

door. Mrs. Woodruff went to open it and found Dr. Marcus Palmer in the passageway, his black doctor's bag in hand.

"How is our patient today?" he asked as he ducked his head to enter the cabin.

"Some improved," Martha answered. "She's managed to eat a little this morning."

"That's good," Dr. Palmer responded, crossing the small cabin and placing his hand on the young woman's forehead. "Fever seems down too."

The doctor placed his bag on the floor and settled himself on one of the trunks Mrs. Woodruff had drawn close to the bunk for seating. Taking Sally's wrist, he measured her pulse while studying her pale and drawn face. Sally refused to look at the young doctor. Mrs. Woodruff stood at the foot of the bunk, hoping the doctor would have a positive assessment of Sally's health.

Dr. Palmer was quiet for a time, as if pondering Sally's condition. Finally he spoke to the young woman. "Miss Edwards, is your stomach still troubling you?"

"No," she replied. "It's better now."

Again the doctor paused and then sighed. "Miss Edwards, I need to ask you some questions," he said. "Of a delicate nature," he added. "Whatever you tell me will be held in strictest confidence." He looked up at Martha. "Isn't that right, Mrs. Woodruff?"

"Yes," she agreed. She had spoken with the doctor the evening before about the scars upon the girl's back. She assumed he was going to question Sally about them.

"Miss Edwards," Dr. Palmer said quietly, "have you missed your monthly cycle?"

Sally nodded. The movement of her head was so slight that the doctor might have missed it if he had not been watching her closely.

Mrs. Woodruff saw too and she took in a sharp breath, showing she had recognized immediately what the doctor was implying.

"Are you with child?" the question came gently.

A sob escaped Sally's lips and she sagged against the pillow, the picture of despair. Tears coursed down her cheeks as she whispered, "It's not as you think. I tried to resist him . . . ." Her sobs overwhelmed her and she turned away from the doctor to face the wall.

"Who?" Dr. Palmer asked.

"Her master," Mrs. Woodruff supplied the answer, her voice edged with anger.

"Does he know you carry his child?" the doctor asked.

"No," Sally whispered.

"Might he not have done the honorable thing and . . ."

"He is married," Sally responded. "And I am not the only one he has violated. He turned another girl out when he learned of her condition. Left her to the streets."

Dr. Palmer clinched his jaw and his fist. Though a gentle man by nature, he felt his own anger rising. Such conduct was unconscionable and the doctor could barely comprehend the man's cruelty.

"Sally, I am sorry to have caused you pain," Marcus said. "But I felt I needed to know your condition in order to help you."

Sally turned to look at the doctor. "You have been nothing but kind to me," she said. "It is not you who has caused me pain."

Dr. Palmer looked up at Mrs. Woodruff to see that the older woman's eyes were also filled with tears.

Then turning back to Sally, he sought to give her some comfort though he felt his words would be inadequate. "Miss Edwards, be assured that neither Mrs. Woodruff nor I condemn you for this difficult circumstance you find yourself in. We will do all we can to help you."

"Yes, dearie," Martha agreed. "With the help of the Lord and your friends you will get through this."

Sally looked from one to the other, resignation clearly marked upon her face. "Thank you," she said simply.

"I'll leave you to get some rest now, Miss Edwards," Dr. Palmer said. "Try to sleep. It will help you regain your strength."

Obediently Sally nodded and closed her eyes.

Then Marcus stood, took up his kit and motioned to Mrs. Woodruff to follow him out of the room. Once they stood in the passageway, they exchanged a look of shared empathy for their young charge. Keeping their voices low, they discussed her condition.

"Will she be alright?" Mrs. Woodruff asked.

"I am concerned," Dr. Palmer responded honestly. "This journey will not get any easier and she is in a weakened state. I wonder if we perhaps should not send her back."

"To her master?" Mrs. Woodruff questioned sharply.

"No, never," Marcus assured her. "He should be horsewhipped. I fully intend to notify the law to have the man investigated."

"A lot of good that will do," Mrs. Woodruff said bitterly. "From what Sally has told me, he holds indenture papers on most of the girls in his factory. To the law, they are little more than property and it's unlikely he'll be punished in any way."

"Surely Sally has some family who would take her in," the doctor said.

"She has none," Martha contradicted. "That's why she ended up in the cruel clutches of such a man. And I suspect she did not complete the term of her indenture. If she is sent back to New York, she might be returned by the law to him."

Dr. Palmer sighed and ran a hand through his hair in frustration. "I fear for her if she continues this journey. And soon enough her condition will become obvious to everyone. Though we gave her our word of confidentiality, I believe we should, with her permission, tell Rev. Vaille of her circumstances. He may know better than I what should be done for her."

"Perhaps you are right," Martha agreed. "Better that everyone should know the truth than to speculate and gossip."

"Sally will need our support and prayers if she is to survive this journey," Dr. Palmer said with a somber tone in his voice. "I'll check in on her again this afternoon. For now I must look in on Mrs. Fuller. She has taken ill as well."

Martha watched the doctor make his way down the narrow hall to the other end of the passenger deck. Then she turned back into the cabin. Sally lay quietly upon her bunk, but Martha could see the tears coursing silently down her face.

CHAPTER SIX

Louisville, Kentucky
May 12, 1820

A few days later, Clarissa and her fellow missionaries were gathered in the boat's dining hall in the late afternoon before the cook was to serve supper. Sally was still bedfast as was Mrs. Lydia Fuller and all four of the Chapman children who had taken the fever as well. Miss Comstock was watching the children so that their mother Rachel could attend the meeting Captain Douglas had called.

He stood before the group at the front of the room as the passengers sat in rows behind the long dining tables. "On the morrow, we'll be docking at the village of Louisville, Kentucky," Captain Douglas said. "This is necessary because we have reached the only real obstacle to riverboat travel on this river."

George Requa leaned into the table where he sat with Clarissa, Phoebe and Amanda Ingles. "The Falls of the Ohio," he explained in a stage whisper.

Clarissa and Amanda exchanged smiles at Mr. Requa's eager knowledge of every aspect of Ohio River travel.

"Because of the difficulty these rapids present, we will be required to offload all cargo here so that it can be hauled by land around the falls," Captain Douglas explained. "Most passengers will want to disembark and travel by land as well . . . especially the women and children."

Clarissa's thoughts immediately turned to Sally. Traveling by boat was hard enough on her, how would the jostling of a wagon affect her. Mrs. Woodruff had, with Sally's permission, told Clarissa and Phoebe of the young woman's circumstances. Outspoken Phoebe had made a few choice – if not particularly Christian – remarks about the black-hearted factoryman who had forced himself upon poor Sally. Her suggestions of appropriate punishment, which included the removal of certain body parts, had made even Sally smile.

Clarissa had felt great empathy for Sally. In her she felt she had found a kindred spirit – a fellow desperate soul running from the prying eyes and wagging tongues of a small New England town. It made her wonder if others among their group had seen this mission they would create among the Osages as not a refuge for the Indians, but for themselves.

Clarissa pulled her attention back to the portly captain as he explained that Louisville had sprung up here at the falls to provide the services needed to get over and around them. Captain Douglas would hire an expert Louisville pilot to steer his boat through the river rapids.

"If all goes well for the boat," the captain said, "we will be docked on the other side of the falls awaiting your arrival by coach. I suggest you pack and carry with you any valuables you would not wish to be damaged. Passage through these rapids will toss about anything that is not nailed down."

The dining hall buzzed with conversation as the captain took questions. George declared that he was going to remain aboard and ride through the rapids.

"Now why doesn't that surprise me?" Amanda smiled.

Later that evening Rev. Vaille, Dr. Palmer and Mrs. Chapman privately gathered in the captain's office to discuss the task of getting their group around the falls. Transporting the sick was a concern for them all.

"Your children should be fine," Dr. Palmer assured Rachel Chapman where she sat in one of the black leather chairs. "In fact, I believe a change of scenery will see them greatly improved."

Mrs. Chapman gave him a wry smile. "Yes," she said, "confinement is the greatest discomfort my children face at the moment."

"And what of Mrs. Fuller and Miss Edwards?" Rev. Vaille asked. He leaned against the captain's massive mahogany desk, his long legs stretched out before him. As pastor of the mission family, he was responsible for everyone on board.

"Mrs. Fuller was somewhat improved today. With the assistance of Miss Comstock and Miss Ingles, I believe she will tolerate a wagon ride adequately." Dr. Palmer leaned forward in his chair, a look of worry on his face. "It is Miss Edwards I am most concerned about. She is not worse, but she cannot seem to get better. I am at a loss of what to do to help her."

"And what about her child?" Mrs. Chapman asked. She and Rev. Vaille had been advised of Sally's condition earlier.

Dr. Palmer sighed, staring down at his hands. "I fear most for the child," he confessed. "Moving Miss Edwards from her bed could not have come at a worse time. I truly wonder if we should not find a place for her to stay in Louisville."

"You mean leave her behind?" Mrs. Chapman asked. "I am not comfortable with doing that."

"I agree," Rev. Vaille said. "We have no idea if these small frontier villages even have a medical doctor. And to leave her alone, with strangers? I can't think that Miss Edwards would be agreeable to that."

"You are probably right," Dr. Palmer nodded slowly. "I suggested to her that she might be better off returning to my brother in Connecticut, but she begged me not to send her back." Dr. Palmer's brother, Edward, was also a physician with a practice in Greenwich.

The trio was silent for a time, each considering the best way to assist Sally. William Vaille paced in front of the captain's desk and Mrs. Chapman unconsciously pleated the garnet-colored fabric of her skirt in a worried gesture. Dr. Palmer stared at the floor, feeling he had failed his young patient. He silently ran through his mind all the possible remedies he might try to bring a cure of the fever that had gripped her. He could hear the voice of his brother in his head, berating him for his inability to help a patient recover.

"Could we afford to hire a coach just for Miss Edwards and perhaps two of the women to assist her?" Rev. Vaille addressed his question to Mrs. Chapman.

"Certainly," Rachel quickly agreed. "We'll do whatever we can to keep her comfortable. Perhaps several quilts packed around her would ease the jostling of the carriage."

"Yes," Dr. Palmer agreed. "We can at least do that for her. If the driver will maintain a slow pace, she shouldn't suffer too ill an effect from the journey."

"Will Captain Douglas be willing to hold up the boat for Sally?" Rev. Vaille wondered aloud.

"We'll insist that he does," Rachel responded.

Late the next morning, the missionaries boarded the large wagons that had been procured for their journey around the Louisville Falls. Each carried a small bag with the valuables they did not want to leave aboard the keelboat. The Chapmans, the Spauldings and Eliza Cleaver occupied one wagon, while the Vailles, Lydia, Susan and Amanda climbed into the second wagon. George Requa and Dr. Palmer were to remain aboard the boat.

Sally was settled into a carriage along with her three cabin mates. Wrapped in a quilt belonging to Mrs. Woodruff, the young woman leaned heavily on Clarissa as the coach made its way along the river road through Louisville.

"I'm sorry to be such trouble," Sally said quietly at one point in the journey. Most of the time she drifted in and out of sleep for Dr. Palmer had given her a small dose of laudanum.

"You are not a bit of trouble," Clarissa argued, gently pushing back Sally's thick black curls.

"You know we'll do anything we can for you," Phoebe added, reaching across the carriage to pat Sally's knee.

"I just wish you hadn't had to undertake this difficult journey," Mrs. Woodruff chimed in. "It's been so hard for you."

Sally smiled wanly at the other women "I'm not sorry I came," she said. "No one has ever treated me as kindly as all of you."

Tears sprang into Clarissa's eyes. Sally was gravely ill, possibly dying, yet she was grateful in her circumstances. How awful her life in New York must have been. It made Clarissa ashamed that she had indulged in such self-pity over a broken engagement. She had thought nothing could be worse at the time.

As the rhythm of the swaying carriage lulled all the women to sleepy reverie, Clarissa thought back to the day her mother had confirmed what she had feared. Robert had asked to be released from their engagement. "He's not ready for the serious commitment of marriage," her mother had said, but there was an edge to her voice that told Clarissa she was quite angry about the matter. Clarissa never let her parents know that she had overheard the conversation between Robert and her father.

For the next week, she stayed in bed, feigning a bad head cold to explain her puffy red eyes and swollen nose. Her sister Jerusha, at sixteen, was perceptive enough to understand. She brought Clarissa special treats that Betsy had baked along with hot chamomile tea, and tried to cheer her with the gossip and goings on from the School for Young Ladies. "What shall I do, Jerusha?" Clarissa asked her sister as they had talked together one afternoon.

"You will go on with your life," Jerusha had responded simply.

A jolt of the carriage wheel brought Clarissa back to the present. She glanced out the window at the passing scenery. So here she was . . . getting on with her life. But would fleeing her past cost her as much as it had cost Sally? She shuddered as she watched the afternoon shadows fall across the road they were traveling on.

CHAPTER SEVEN

Ohio River
May, 1820

The following day, Sally took a turn for the worse. Again her fever raged and she tossed and turned upon her bunk in near delirium. Dr. Palmer seemed almost frantic in trying to find a remedy for her situation. Someone among the mission family stayed at Sally's bedside at all times, keeping cool cloths on her forehead and trying to get her to take some nourishment.

Sally drifted in and out of sleep as the keelboat continued from Louisville toward the Mississippi River. As her condition deteriorated, a pall seemed to hang over the boat and its passengers. The children themselves were unusually subdued, sensing the concern shared by their elders.

Even as they approached the mighty river of the American West, the missionaries could not muster the excitement that would normally have greeted such a milestone. George Requa had looked forward to reaching the Mississippi since the boat had left Pittsburgh weeks earlier, yet even his enthusiasm was tempered by his concern for Miss Edwards.

The boatmen, too, kept their usual celebration of nearing the Mississippi in check. Normally reaching the great river without any major mishaps was a cause for opening a few casks of rum and drinking themselves to oblivion, according to Mr. Pennywit.

But Captain Douglas had locked the storage room where the rum was held and ordered all hands at their usual posts. He did so out of respect for his missionary passengers and for the poor young woman who lay seriously ill in her cabin below. He promised the crew an extra day of leave when they reached St. Louis and the men seemed satisfied with that.

On the morning that they would enter the Mississippi, Mr. Requa stood at the bow of the boat with Dr. Palmer and Philip Pennywit. They were passing a series of old Indian burial mounds and Mr. Pennywit was regaling the two men with stories of his journeys on the mighty Mississippi.

"We've been fortunate to make it here without hitting any snags," Pennywit said in his Virginia drawl. "But we'll likely not be so fortunate on the big river."

"Why is that?" George asked.

"The Mississippi is wide, but not always deep," the steward explained. "Debris in the river, sandbars, quicksand, all are constantly shifting in the current. Even though Douglas and I have plied these waters many times, we can never anticipate everything the river will throw at us. You always have to be on your guard and prepared for the worst."

"How many times have you traveled the Mississippi?" George wanted to know.

"This will be close to 20 trips to New Orleans for me," Pennywit said, "most of them with Josiah Douglas. But it will be my last time to travel with the captain."

Dr. Palmer turned to him in surprise. "You'll not be serving under Captain Douglas?"

"Nay," Pennywit said with a grin. "I'll be captain of my own boat next trip I make. She's being built even now in Cincinnati."

"Well, congratulations," George said, turning away from the rail to offer his hand to Philip. "Having your own boat is an accomplishment."

"Aye, I've worked for years for this," the steward nodded with satisfaction as he gripped Requa's hand. "Though a keelboat is not like a ship," he explained. "They aren't even named. Most keelboats are dismantled in New Orleans and the lumber sold. It's too cumbersome a craft to take all the way back upriver. It will be a frightful chore just getting this one to St. Louis."

"How long until we reach St. Louis?" Marcus asked before George could. He was anxious to arrive at the only true city they would visit from here on in their trip west. He hoped to be able to find some assistance for Miss Edwards there. It troubled him greatly that he had been unable to help Sally fight the fever that held her in its grip.

"With no obstacles, about a week," Pennywit responded. "It will take mules and men to pull us upstream. If St. Louis wasn't such an important market, we'd not take the trouble to fight the current. We'll take on the rest of your party and a load of furs for New Orleans."

"Will we be in port long?" George asked, having turned back to lean on the boat's rail. He kept his clear brown eyes on the western horizon as if willing the mighty Mississippi to finally come into view.

"The captain has promised the crew a day of shore leave," Pennywit drawled. "And we'll not arrive in St. Louis without receiving an invitation to dine with Governor Clark. So three days, possibly four."

"Governor William Clark?" George asked with excitement in his voice. He turned to look at the boat's steward. "Of the Corps of Discovery?"

"The same," Philip grinned, clearly enjoying Mr. Requa's interest in the great explorer. "Governor Clark loves to entertain guests with his many exploits in search of the fabled Northwest Passage. He has at his home a veritable museum of natural history. He didn't send all his specimens to President Jefferson, you know."

"And he would actually ask us to dine with him?" Requa asked. "I'd think he would be far too busy with the affairs of government and would have far more important guests among St. Louis' wealthy traders."

"Aye, he's a busy man," Philip agreed, "especially now with an election coming up. But any visitor to the city is of interest to him, for you bring news from back east. St. Louis is not so large a town that there won't be a crowd of folks gathered at the dock to greet us. Just to get the news."

"But surely St. Louis is large enough to have a hospital?" Marcus asked, "Or at least a physician?"

His question seemed to sober the two other men. While they may have momentarily forgotten poor Miss Edwards, Dr.

Palmer had not. Her plight haunted him and taunted him, calling him a failure, unworthy of the name Palmer. That is certainly what his brother would say.

"No hospital," Pennywit answered quietly. "Though the Sisters take in the sick at the abbey." He paused for a moment. "And I'm afraid the only physician hasn't a good reputation among the better class of citizens. Seems he drinks a bit."

Marcus sighed and ran his hands through his dark, curly hair. What had he been thinking, coming out here to this wilderness? Did he really expect that he could somehow make a difference? They had yet to arrive at the Osage Mission and already he had failed. He felt Sally's life sifting through his hands and there seemed nothing he could do to stop it.

Below, on the cabin deck, Rev. Vaille knocked on the door of Sally's cabin. Mrs. Woodruff opened the door to admit him and his wife. Their questioning look was met was a slight shake of her head. Sally was no better.

"We came to sit with her for a while," Asie Vaille whispered. "You need a chance to walk about. It's very pleasant on deck right now and we're nearing the Mississippi."

"Thank you," Martha responded, weariness evident in her voice. "If she wakens, try to get her to drink some water. Dr. Palmer says she needs liquids." She took her straw bonnet from the bedside table, placed it on her head and tied its black ribbons beneath her chin.

At the door, she paused and looking back at her young charge lying so still and pale upon her bed, she smiled sadly. "I fear she is not long for this world," she whispered.

Mrs. Vaille gave the older woman a gentle hug. "If that is so, then she goes to a better place than what she has known in this world," she said. "But we must keep faith. She may rally yet . . . for the sake of her child."

Martha nodded and dabbed away a tear from her eye. "Yes, we must have faith." Then she slipped out the door.

The young couple took their place at Sally's bedside. Rev. Vaille sat on a heavy brassbound trunk drawn up to the bed and Asie sat on the bunk's edge. Taking Sally's limp hand, she rubbed it gently. The girl's breathing rattled frighteningly in her chest.

William withdrew a Bible from his coat pocket and began to leaf through its pages. Sitting at the bedside of someone passing from this life was not something new to him for he had led a large church in Connecticut and had often been called to the bedside of a member of his congregation. He sighed deeply as he turned to John's Gospel and quietly read Jesus' words of assurance, "I am the resurrection and the life."

Sally stirred and slowly opened her eyes. Though glazed with fever, her dark brown eyes lit with pleasure at seeing her pastor. "I prayed you would come," she said, her voice just a hoarse whisper.

Asie's eyes immediately welled with tears. "Can we do something for you, dear?" she asked. "Would you like some water?"

Sally nodded, closing her eyes again.

William helped to lift the young woman and Asie held the tin cup from the table to her lips. Sally took a few sips, but then began to cough.

Mrs. Vaille held the cup still as the girl painfully fought through the coughing fit. Then Sally sank back upon her pillow, exhausted.

"Rest now, dear," Mrs. Vaille said, returning the cup to its place on the table. "We'll stay right here with you."

Sally nodded, struggling to regain her breath. For a time the only sound in the cabin was the dreadful wheezing in her chest. William sat with head bowed in prayer.

After a time, her breathing eased and she seemed to have drifted back to sleep. But then Sally opened her eyes and reached for Mrs. Vaille's hand.

"Does everyone who goes to church enter heaven?" she asked quietly, looking at Rev. Vaille.

"Sally, if you have professed your faith in the Lord and been baptized, then you have the assurance of heaven," Rev. Vaille said, offering words of comfort.

Sally shook her head slightly. "But going to church," she whispered somewhat fearfully. "Does going to church get a person to heaven . . . even if . . . even if they've done something terribly wrong?"

"Sally, the Bible says if we confess our sins, he will forgive us," William began, but Mrs. Vaille gently interrupted him. A light had dawned in her eyes. Clearly Sally was not concerned about her own salvation. She did not fear meeting her heavenly Master, but her earthly one.

"Dear, the Bible tells us that not everyone who says, 'Lord, lord,' is truly a follower of the Lord," Mrs. Vaille said. "Those who have lived a life displeasing to God will hear him say, 'Depart from me. I never knew you.'"

Rev. Vaille looked at his wife with confusion on his face, but he finally gave a nod of understanding at what Asie was saying.

He placed his hand over his wife's and Sally's. "God knows who are his true children," he assured the young woman. "Even among those who sit on church pews. No one will enter heaven by mistake."

Sally nodded, seeming satisfied. She placed her free hand on the slight swell of her abdomen. "Then we will truly be free of him," she said, caressing the child within her. She closed her eyes, a slight smile of contentment on her face.

Asie bowed her head, tears spilling from her eyes. Clearly Sally had reconciled herself to her own death and she did not fear it now.

William squeezed her hand, but neither said anything more. Sally soon drifted into sleep, her breathing shallow, but easier than before. When Clarissa came some time later to take her place at Sally's bedside, the pastor and his wife left with sorrow upon their faces.

An hour later as Clarissa sponged Sally's face and arms with a cool cloth, the girl's eyes fluttered open as if startled from a dream. She looked about for a moment as if trying to remember where she was. Seeing her teacher, she reached for her hand. Clarissa grasped it, suddenly scared to be alone with the dying girl.

"Oh, Miss Johnson," Sally breathed. "You've been so kind to me."

Clarissa shook her head. "Not at all," she said, unsure of what to say. "You have been my best student."

"I learned to read," Sally murmured, a bit of wonder in her voice.

"Yes and there are many more books still for you to read," Clarissa said, hoping to sound encouraging.

"More books to read," Sally repeated, but she sounded as if her mind had drifted to other matters. She gripped her teacher's hand more firmly.

"They won't put me in the water, will they," she asked, fear in her voice. "I'm afraid of water."

"No," Clarissa assured her, wishing she could run from this moment. She didn't want to talk about death.

"I have a little money saved," Sally went on. "Use it for a headstone." Clarissa wanted to stop her ears. Tears lumped in her throat and she could not swallow around them.

"Tell them to get a stone big enough for my baby's name," Sally began to cough. "Her name is Angel . . . for that is what . . . she will be."

Clarissa could no longer keep her tears in check. "Don't talk so, Sally," she begged.

A wracking cough tore at the dark-haired girl. Clarissa gripped her hand with both of her own as if trying to hold Sally in this life.

"Let me get Dr. Palmer," Clarissa whispered as the coughing fit subsided.

"No," Sally shook her head. "No, there is nothing he can do," she gasped for air, "and it grieves him so."

Sally lay quietly for a moment. "Tell Dr. Palmer it is not his fault," she said of her caring physician. "I asked God to let me be free and he has answered my prayer."

Clarissa could not hold back her sobs. "Don't go, Sally," she begged. "Please don't go." But she was already gone.

Above deck all hands and passengers were at the rail, watching the keelboat slip into the current of the Mississippi River. Even in the gathering dusk, the river held each of them spellbound, seasoned sailor and novice traveler alike. Mr. Pennywit told them the boat would tie up for the night on the western shore where barge crews for hire waited to pull the keelboat upriver.

Dr. Palmer stood a little apart from the others, staring into the muddy water. A long-legged egret gleamed white along the shoreline where it fished in the mud flats. Then with a shriek at the boat disturbing its waters, the bird rose up and took flight.

The doctor felt a shiver run up his spine and he knew. Another patient had died. He hung his head and let the pain of it seep into his soul.

Mrs. Woodruff must have sensed it too. She turned from the rail and made her way by lantern light down the stairs to the cabin deck. She opened her cabin door to find Clarissa kneeling by Sally's bed, her body shaking with sobs. Quickly she crossed the room and gathered the young teacher into her arms. Together they sat in the dark and cried.

CHAPTER EIGHT

Cape Girardeau, Missouri Territory
May 15, 1820

Mrs. Chapman had refused to allow Sally to be buried in the wilderness. They would stop at Cape Girardeau, the first village of any size they would come to on their way upstream to St. Louis. Captain Douglas knew of a small Catholic church there, led by a French priest. Sally would be laid to rest in the well-kept cemetery by the church.

The missionaries would have preferred a Protestant church, but were content to know that at least her grave would be cared for. Father Henri Mallett assured the mission family that he would secure a headstone as Sally had wished.

The group gathered at her grave in the morning. Phoebe Beach and Susan Comstock had kept the children on board, but all the remaining missionaries paid their last respects to the young woman whose life and death struggle had touched them all. Even Captain Douglas and Mr. Pennywit were present as Rev. Vaille read the Twenty-Third Psalm over the plain pine casket.

Clarissa kept her eyes to the ground, knowing that if she looked into the sorrowing faces of those around the grave, she would break into sobs again. She was frightened at the torrent of emotions she felt. Anger mixed with a profound sadness. It was so unfair. How could God have allowed sweet Sally to die so needlessly? All she had wanted was a chance to start a new life. Why had it been cut so short?

A gentle breeze stirred a field of wildflowers beyond the

little cemetery. A solitary bird sang its trilling melody in a gnarled old oak that stood like a sentinel beside the log church. The sweet smell of spring hung in the air. All seemed quiet and peaceful here, a sharp contrast to the dark sorrow that hovered over the group of mourners.

As Rev. Vaille said the final Amen the missionaries each dropped a handful of the rich loamy earth onto the casket. Nearby two Negro men waited at a respectful distance for the memorial to end so they could complete the burial.

Father Mallett walked with the travelers through the little village back to the waterfront. George Requa kept a hand at Clarissa's elbow, helping her across the uneven ground. She liked the feel of warmth from his touch.

Amanda Ingles walked arm in arm with Mrs. Fuller nearby, her heart heavy with grief. John and Alice Spaulding walked behind them and the soft murmur of their voices somehow seemed comforting to Clarissa.

They paused at the wooden wharf where their keelboat was docked. Father Mallett shook hands with Rev. Vaille and Mrs. Chapman. He assured them again that Sally's grave would be cared for.

"We appreciate your kindness," Rachel said. "It is good of you to care for Miss Edwards even though she was not Catholic."

The elderly priest smiled. "You will find out here on the frontier that such labels are not so important," he said with a slight French accent. "We all name Christ as Lord; we can fellowship together, no? Especially in the fellowship of sorrow?"

"Yes," Rev. Vaille agreed as Dr. Palmer stepped past him and made his way toward the boat. He watched the young doctor step up the gangplank to the boat's deck. "Our sorrow makes us all brothers."

The remaining mission family made their way back to the boat also. In a short time Captain Douglas was giving the order to ready the boat for another day's journey toward St. Louis.

In the following days, as the keelboat struggled up the Mississippi against its mighty current, the missionaries came to understand why travel upriver was not undertaken unless the value of trade made it worthwhile. The boat would only make a limited number of miles each day, pulled with long ropes by mules or men, usually by slaves.

The New Englanders had experienced only a few encounters with slavery in their travels down the Ohio and Rev. Vaille in particular seemed bothered by the fact that their journey now required the crack of a whip upon a man's back. He stayed below deck most of the time to avoid the sight that was so troubling to him.

The other missionaries tried to return to their routine of providing schooling for the children, though Clarissa found it hard to concentrate on teaching. She had never dealt with death so intimately before. It had always been a distant, abstract idea to her, certainly not something to claim a life so young.

Sally's passing was a sobering reminder of mortality to Clarissa and all the missionaries, most of whom were under 25 years of age. In preparing for their journey to the untamed land of Arkansas Territory, they had been warned of possible threats from the elements or perhaps hostile Indians or frontiersmen. Sally's death made it plain that their mission might be one of many more dangers, unseen and unstoppable.

Dr. Palmer continued to check on Lydia Fuller, whose own persistent cough was a concern and the children who intermittently developed a fever. Most of the time he kept quietly to himself, brooding over Sally's death. Eliza and the others tried to engage him in their evening gatherings, but he remained aloof.

They reached St. Louis a week after entering the Mississippi River, late in the afternoon. Most of the passengers had come to the upper deck to watch the boat dock. They had to shade their eyes to look into the western sun, while the boatmen used their long poles to carefully steer the keelboat into place at the wharf.

As Mr. Pennywit had predicted the riverfront was crowded with people, many who had come at the sound of the boat's whistle to see it arrive. Josiah Douglas carried newspapers from all the eastern cities and these would be posted at the custom house where St. Louis' residents could read them. Another set of papers would be delivered to Governor Clark.

The waterfront was teeming with activity, though it was not as large as that of Pittsburgh or Cincinnati. The town definitely had the flavor of the frontier. There were scarcely any women present; Clarissa counted only three as she scanned the crowd. Many of the men were dressed in the garb of the storied mountain man – fringed leather jacket and some type of animal skin for a hat. The sight of so many young women at the boat's rail had caught the attentions of these men and they stared at the boat with as much interest as the missionaries felt towards the citizens of St. Louis.

Standing in the shadow of one of the long, low warehouses was an Indian. James Chapman pointed and exclaimed, "Look!" before his mother could quiet him. The children all gaped in open curiosity, and the adults just barely hid their own curious glances. This was their first encounter with an Indian.

"He's Osage," Rev. Vaille said quietly and the word was whispered along the line of missionaries clustered at the boat's rail. The man was tall and muscular and wore a blanket draped across one shoulder while the other was bare. His head was shaved except for a long "scalp lock" down the middle. He stared impassively at the keelboat.

"That's Big Tracks," Mr. Pennywit said from where he stood behind the line of missionaries. "He's one of the Osage chiefs, probably in town to negotiate a fur trade."

"Big Tracks," George repeated with awe in his voice.

Clarissa felt a tingle go up her spine and wondered at her reaction . . . at everyone's reaction. Ministering to the Indians was why they had made this journey, but now seeing an Osage made it real for the first time.

"His village is at Three Forks," Rev. Vaille added. "I heard of him on our journey out last year, but we never met him."

"Do you think we'll meet him while we're in St. Louis?" John Spaulding asked.

"If you'd like to meet him, you'll only have to pay a visit to the Chouteau Fur Trading Company. That's their warehouse there," Pennywit said, indicating the log warehouse where the Osage stood. "The Osages trade fairly exclusively with the Chouteau brothers."

The missionaries as a group turned from the railing and

plied Pennywit with more questions about the Osages. Though he'd had only limited dealings with the Osages, Pennywit knew about them through the Chouteaus, a French family who owned one of the largest fur trading companies west of the Mississippi, rivaled only by that of John Jacob Astor. Captain Douglas would take on a load of Chouteau furs for the journey south.

"The Osages have three chiefs," explained the boat's steward as he tugged his hat a little lower to shade his eyes. "Big Tracks is the youngest. His group is called the Arkansas Band because they moved from Missouri down to the Arkansas River at Three Forks. The other two chiefs have villages on the Osage River and the Verdigris River."

The Osages had become professional hunters and made their livelihood following the great herds of deer, elk and buffalo out on the vast open plains. Having established a good trade relationship with the French settlers in Missouri, the Osages also acted as trade brokers between the French and the Plains tribes. Guns and horses were moved along the trade routes by the Osages.

"It would seem they have a good head for business then," John Spaulding commented as the keelboat bumped against the pier and the boatmen began securing it with heavy ropes.

"Yes," Pennywit agreed, "though they still prefer the barter system to paper money. But many of the tribes out here are astute traders from long practice. The area where you'll be settling is crossed with old trade and hunting trails, some of them having been used for hundreds of years."

So the Osages are relatively civilized then?" Rachel asked hopefully. "We were led to believe they were still quite savage."

"Well. . ." Pennywit drawled the word out thoughtfully, seeming to consider his response with care. His hesitation worried Clarissa. She glanced back toward the Chouteau warehouse, but the Osage chief – Big Tracks – was no longer standing there.

Pennywit finally stated, "Savage is a word I've never much cared for. It's a hard land out here and folks do what is necessary to survive, including the Indians."

Pennywit had no time to say more for Captain Douglas began calling orders to prepare the boat for de-boarding. The steward hurried off to do the captain's bidding, leaving the missionaries to ponder his words.

Within just a few minutes, however, their attention turned again to the St. Louis waterfront. Thomas Chapman had spied his father making his way toward the keelboat. "There's papa," he cried.

Instantly his siblings were jumping up and down and waving to their father, the Rev. Epaphras Chapman. "Papa, Papa," they called to him. Even Rachel waved a greeting to her husband with a lace-gloved hand.

Rev. Chapman smiled and lifted his hat to return the greeting. Behind him were four other men, all striding toward the boat. These were the advance party for the Union Mission. They had arrived in St. Louis four weeks earlier and had spent the time purchasing supplies for the remainder of the journey, and the tools and materials needed for building the mission in the wilderness.

Rev. Chapman was a man of average height, but possessing a boundless energy which he displayed now as he weaved among the crowd of onlookers toward the boat's gangplank being lowered to the wharf. He brushed back wavy brown hair and resettled his hat while bounding down the wharf to step onto the plank.

His children ran from the bow toward him and all of the mission family followed closely behind. All were eager to greet the men making their way aboard.

William Requa, George's older brother followed Rev. Chapman. He was a stockier version of George, wearing his shoulder-length hair pulled back with a leather cord. He filled out the light brown coat he wore with obviously well-formed muscles. He was a stone mason by trade.

Susan Comstock elbowed Eliza and whispered, "Now there's a fine looking man," as Requa boarded the keelboat.

Stephen Fuller's eyes scanned the group of missionaries, searching for his wife Lydia. Fuller was to serve as the farm director for the mission. A tall, thin man, he had reddish brown hair, a full beard and light hazel eyes. He sighed with relief when he saw his wife.

The other two men making their way up the gangplank were

quite a contrast. Alexander Woodruff at age 50 was the oldest member of the mission family. Gray was sprinkled liberally through his beard and dark hair. But Woodruff, though short of stature, was by no means frail or aged. As a blacksmith, his muscled arms rivaled those of William Requa's.

Coming last aboard was Abraham Redfield, age 21. He was tall and gangly and looked as if he had not yet reached his full height, for his long arms and raw-boned hands dangled out from his coat sleeves by a few inches. His sandy hair and light blue eyes made him look young and he seemed shy about greeting the other missionaries.

Rev. Chapman was quickly engulfed in an embrace by his family and Woodruff and Fuller sought out their wives for a personal reunion as well. Will Requa greeted George with a handshake and slap on the back. It was clear the brothers were happy to see one another.

For a time everyone seemed to be talking at once. Introductions were made all around by Rev. Vaille for Clarissa and several of the others had not met the men of the advance party before today. Frankly seeing these men, all who seemed strong and capable, helped to put Clarissa's mind at ease. Quickly forgotten was the Osage chief Big Tracks as everyone trooped to the boat's dining hall for a first meeting of the entire mission family.

"Mr. Requa and I traveled to the Osage village here in Missouri with Jean Pierre Chouteau," Rev. Chapmen shared with the missionaries over supper that evening at a St. Louis hostelry.

He had spent the entire meal with his youngest daughter Leah sitting on his lap. She now dozed with her head on his shoulder until Rachel gently reached over and eased the four-year-old onto her own lap.

Sipping a final cup of strong, black coffee from a tin mug, the mission superintendent related the details of their journey to the Osage River. "The main body of the tribe resides there," he said. "We talked with their chief, Pawhuska, about the mission. He listened politely but did not seem to feel much interest in our efforts."

"We had to smoke the pipe with him and the lesser chiefs,"

Will Requa added, a look of distaste on his face. "Noxious stuff, tobacco. I could barely manage to inhale it. The Osages found that very amusing."

"Mr. Chouteau assured us we would offend them if we didn't partake of the pipe," Chapman added. "It's an important ritual for them."

"Were you able to communicate with them?" John Spaulding asked. "They have a grasp of English, I hope."

"A few spoke English and a few more spoke French," Requa said. "They've intermarried with the French trading families so several are bilingual. Osage seems a peculiar language from what I could tell. It may be a challenge for us to learn it."

"That's where Chouteau's son Auguste will be helpful to us," Rev. Chapman added. "He has several trading posts in the Three Forks area and his father has offered us whatever assistance he can give. He has an Osage wife . . ." here he paused and exchanged a look with Will Requa that Clarissa found interesting. "He's fluent in the Osage language," he concluded.

The missionaries learned that Auguste Chouteau had traveled with Chief Big Tracks to St. Louis and they would have an opportunity to meet him while they were in port. Whether they would meet Big Tracks was uncertain. Clarissa didn't know if she was disappointed or relieved that they might not face their first encounter with the Osages while in St. Louis. Teaching Osage girls was one matter, facing the fierce-looking chief was another altogether.

CHAPTER NINE

St. Louis, Missouri Territory
May 24, 1820

As Mr. Pennywit had predicted, as soon as Governor Clark learned of Captain Douglas' arrival in St. Louis he issued an invitation requesting that the captain and his missionary passengers dine with him on the following evening. George was ecstatic at the thought of meeting the famed explorer.

"Lawsy," said Phoebe when she learned of the governor's invitation. The missionaries were gathered in the boat's dining hall, eating a hasty lunch on the day after their arrival in St. Louis. All planned to set out to explore St. Louis and do some trading at the mercantiles along Market Street. "I'll not be going to the governor's house. I'd rather eat with Mr. Big Tracks than with such an important man in his fine house." She shook her head vigorously and feigned a shudder.

"But Phoebe," Clarissa argued, though she couldn't help but smile at the young woman's emphatic expression, "everyone in the whole country would like to meet Governor Clark. How can you pass up such an opportunity?"

"Me and Susan have already decided," Phoebe said. "We'll stay aboard and watch the children like always. Won't we, Susan."

The sweet blonde sitting next to Phoebe nodded in agreement. "I'd be too nervous to dine with the governor," she said in her soft little-girl voice. Amanda Ingles also felt reluctant to visit the governor and gave a nod to Susan's sentiment.

In the end, only twelve of the mission family decided to

accept the governor's invitation. The party would include Thomas Chapman who had begged so hard for the opportunity to meet his hero that his parents had finally agreed to allow him to attend. The nine-year-old boy was made to solemnly promise to be on his best behavior.

The group of missionaries, along with Captain Douglas and Mr. Pennywit, set out from the docks to walk to Governor Clark's home on Main Street located only a few blocks from the waterfront. The afternoon was pleasant and the mood of the group was high for everyone knew of William Clark's famous exploration in 1804 and all were eager to meet the man who was legendary throughout the United States.

"Such a large group of us won't be an imposition, will it, Captain?" Asie Vaille asked. "We certainly don't want to strain the governor's hospitality."

"Not at all," Captain Douglas huffed as he strode up Market Street. "Governor Clark has one of the largest homes in St. Louis and one of the finest, too, I might add. He's entertained larger groups than ours on many an occasion."

"He'll certainly give you a tour of his museum," Mr. Pennywit added. "He has a most extensive collection of animal specimens and Indian craft works. Quite interesting to look over and the governor is glad to show it to his visitors."

Clarissa found herself growing nervous as the group turned onto Main Street and made their way to the imposing home on the corner. She and the other women had helped each other wash their hair so as to look their best for the evening.

Clarissa had donned the nicest dress she had packed – a scarlet faille with black lace at the throat and cuffs. The sisters, Alice and Eliza, were both wearing blue though of sharply contrasting colors. Eliza was in a pale cornflower blue while Alice wore a more mature shade of navy. Mrs. Chapman was quite stunning in pink silk with a matching hat.

Rachel had a firm hold on young Thomas' hand as they approached the governor's house. She constantly pulled at him to keep the boy out of the puddles formed in the ruts of the street. Having scrubbed him thoroughly despite his protests, she told him she wanted her son to arrive looking like a proper young gentleman.

The governor's guests mounted the steps to his home and were met at the door by a Negro servant who escorted them into a large parlor. "Please have a seat," the man said with a slight bow. "The governor will join you shortly."

All the ladies were seated, along with Thomas, but the men remained standing around the room that looked as if it were part of the famed museum. Dark paneled walls were lined with curios of the American west – antlers of various animals, native weaponry of different sorts, and paintings of landscapes wild and beautiful. Clarissa could scarcely take it all in and gave a start when her eyes fell on a large black bearskin rug, head and claws still intact, spread out in front of the massive fireplace.

George saw her widened eyes and gave her a wink. "Hope I never encounter one of those in the woods," he whispered from where he stood opposite her chair. Clarissa nodded her agreement, afraid to even speak. In this room one got a sense of the vastness and wildness of the American frontier and it felt rather intimidating.

In a few minutes the door to the room opened and in stepped Governor William Clark. Clarissa had seen a drawing of the explorer in a New Haven newspaper and recognized him instantly. The men all turned from their study of the room and Captain Douglas stepped forward to grasp the governor's extended hand.

"Good to see you again, Captain," Clark said. "Welcome to my home," he extended his greeting to all in the room with a sweep of his hand.

The captain then made introductions of the missionaries to the governor of Missouri Territory – soon to be the state of Missouri. The men all shook hands with the governor, including Thomas whose eyes were big with awe and excitement. The women all followed Mrs. Chapman's lead and merely nodded when they were introduced.

"An impressive display you have here, Governor," Rev. Chapman said.

"Oh this," Clark waved his hand almost dismissively. "This is nothing compared to the council chamber." He looked down at Thomas and smiled. "I suppose you'd like to see it?"

Thomas nodded and exclaimed, "Yes, sir!" then looked

quickly at his mother for her approval. She gave him a reassuring smile.

"Well come ahead then," Governor Clark said.

He led the group to a low brick building that sat beside the house. Inside a large room, nearly 100 by 30 feet, was filled with all manner of artifacts. In the center was a large table surrounded by chairs. "I meet with various Indian delegations here," Clark explained.

Around the room were brightly painted buffalo robes and woven blankets, numerous saddles and bridles, spears, powder horns and other weapons, and all manner of fancy handwork made with beads, porcupine quills and stones. Much of what was displayed had been gifts made to him by the Indian delegations. But there were also displays of the specimens Clark and his Corps of Discovery had collected on their journey across the continent to the Pacific Ocean.

Will and George Requa, with Thomas between them, eagerly wandered through the whole room examining everything carefully. They were like three boys given free rein in a candy store. Clarissa smiled at their eagerness, thinking George looked rather handsome in the lamplight.

John Spaulding and Rev. Vaille peppered the Governor with questions about the Osages which he seemed happy to answer. Dr. Palmer spent most of the time studying the skeletal specimens held in a case near the fireplace.

Alice and Eliza soon tired of the display and took seats at the council table. As they whispered between themselves, Clarissa thought they seemed rather rude, but Governor Clark appeared not to notice as he made his way around the room to point out something of particular interest to one of the missionaries or to answer their questions.

After a time, the houseman stepped into the hall and approached Governor Clark.

"Miz Matthews says dinner is ready, sir," he stated.

"Excellent," Clark said, rubbing his hands together as if greatly anticipating Mrs. Matthews' meal. "Shall we return to the house?" he said to his guests.

As they made their way back to the governor's home, Clark offered an apology for the absence of his wife. "I'm afraid Julia isn't feeling well," he explained, "and won't be joining us. But my son, Meriwether, will no doubt be waiting for us inside."

The missionaries as well as Captain Douglas and Mr. Pennywit found the meal as interesting as the tour of Clark's museum. On the menu were foods Clarissa had never tasted before. She had been slightly hesitant to try the buffalo steak set before her by a young Negro servant, but she found it to be quite lean and tender.

While the group enjoyed the meal, the governor shared several stories about his famous journey in search of the Northwest Passage. He told of the Indian guide, Bird Woman, who carried her newborn on her back as they traveled westward across mountain ranges that rivaled the Alps of Europe for beauty and treachery.

"And you'll meet my sergeant from the Corps when you arrive at Three Forks," the governor told them as dessert was served. "Though he holds the rank of captain now. Served under Andy Jackson at New Orleans. Nathaniel Pryor acts as a sub-agent to the Osages and has a fur outfit down at French Point."

"Your sergeant was very helpful in negotiating the land purchase for us with the Osages," Rev. Chapman said. "We met Captain Pryor at Three Forks and he took us out to look at the property on the Neosho."

"Pryor's a good man and he'll be helpful to you and your mission," Clark responded. "Though he does tend to favor the Osages over other tribes and that sometimes creates tensions when there are conflicts."

"Are conflicts common in the area?" John asked, pushing up his spectacles in a nervous gesture.

"Conflicts are common among human nature, don't you think?" Clark answered with a smile. Then he sobered, leaned back in his chair and added, "The Osages have their enemies in the region. The Pawnees and Comanches are particularly aggressive tribes and the Cherokees in Arkansas Territory have clashed with the Osages as well."

"Will that put the mission in a dangerous position, then?" Rachel asked as she carefully folded her napkin and placed it by her plate. Clarissa noticed that Thomas, who was sitting to his mother's left, studiously copied her napkin placement. Then she noticed George and his brother Will, who sat directly across from her, were doing exactly the same thing. The servants began to clear away the dishes.

"I daresay you'll not receive any threats directed against the mission," Clark said after a moment's thought. "But you'll want to take care not to get caught up in the tribal conflicts. Never let it appear that you are choosing sides. I have found that the Indians are extremely loyal to those they consider friends, but they have long memories against their enemies. You don't want to make enemies among the Osages, but especially not among the Cherokees."

As the missionaries returned to the keelboat after dinner that evening they were sober and quiet. Though the governor had shared several other incidents from his journeys with them – some quite humorous – his warning about taking care not to make enemies seemed uppermost in their minds.

Alice clung to John's arm as they walked together in the gathering darkness of the summer evening. "Are you sure this is what you want to do?" Clarissa heard her ask, despite the fact that Alice kept her voice low. Clarissa walked just behind the couple with Eliza and Dr. Palmer.

"I'll not find a teaching position anywhere in New England," John replied. "Not after what happened. You know that."

Alice sighed. "Yes, I know." Her voice held deep resignation.

Clarissa glanced toward Eliza out of the corner of her eye. The girl kept her eyes on her feet which kept her face hidden by the brim of her hat. But she heard Eliza give a heavy sigh as well.

It seems we're all running away from something, Clarissa thought. *Every one of us.*

CHAPTER TEN

St. Louis, Missouri Territory
May 26, 1820

Captain Douglas remained two more days at St. Louis restocking his boat with supplies and taking on a load of furs, pecans and honey for the New Orleans market. During this time, his missionary passengers spent their days exploring the western town on the Mississippi River.

On the day following their visit to Governor Clark, Mr. Pennywit had reminded them at breakfast that St. Louis would be the largest town they would encounter west of the Mississippi and any purchases of supplies or toiletries should be undertaken while they were in port here.

Clarissa, Phoebe, Amanda and Susan, who now shared a cabin together, had set out after breakfast to visit one of the emporiums on Market Street. All had received their first pay from the mission society before leaving New York and realized they had better make what purchases they needed today.

Clarissa's hope was to find some fine soap and buy it in a quantity to last for several months. A few evenings earlier, Amanda had shared the recipe for homemade soap – it seemed that Amanda was an expert at cooking soap as well as yeast rolls – but her soap recipe held little appeal to Clarissa.

Out on the edges of civilization, they would likely be required to make their own soap. Hearing Amanda describe the process of leaching wood ash to obtain lye and then boiling it with hog fat from animals they would have to butcher themselves had left Clarissa almost retching into her boiled beef and biscuits. She was a teacher not a soap maker and hoped she would not be called upon to participate in the process.

As the four young women walked along the board sidewalk, they quickly became aware that their presence was creating a bit of a stir around town. Though each was dressed in their workaday clothes of simple cotton or muslin, the attention they were receiving would suggest they were dressed in Sunday finery and strolling some posh avenue in New York. Men in the vicinity swept off their hats and made grand gestures of bowing and speaking to them. Most politely kept their distance, but a few actually began to follow them as if the sight of a woman had them mesmerized.

Clarissa found this attention rather threatening and Phoebe seemed annoyed and muttered under her breath about "backwoods barbarians." Amanda and Susan giggled together and seemed to enjoy the admiring looks from men clearly starved for female company.

It was a relief to Clarissa to step into Grady's Emporium and Fine Clothing where a few other women were also shopping.

The store greeted the young missionaries with the usual sights and smells of a general mercantile. The fragrance of leather boots and saddles mingled with the metallic scent of farm implements and casks of nails and the briny fragrance of salted meats and barrels of pickles. The emporium was stuffed to the rafters with merchandise and clearly enjoyed a brisk business.

Clarissa quickly located the soaps and lifted a white cake of it to her nose to enjoy the delicate scent of rose. Though more expensive than what she would have paid in Connecticut, she felt it was worth it and chose several bars which she carried to the front counter. Amanda and Phoebe were looking at dress fabrics while Susan searched through stacks of ladies' boots for a size to fit her tiny feet.

After making their purchases, the women walked further up the street to a tea room for lunch. While the décor seemed rather crude in comparison to eastern establishments, the food was good and the ladies enjoyed lingering over cups of tea before returning to the confines of the boat.

Some of the men among their party had walked down the

wharf to the Chouteau fur warehouse. Governor Clark had assured them that Auguste Chouteau was in town and would welcome a visit. He had shared with the missionaries the history of the Chouteaus in Missouri.

Auguste Chouteau was the son of Jean Pierre Chouteau, one of the founders of St. Louis. The elder Chouteau, with his brother Rene, had built a fur trading empire in the French held territory before Napoleon had sold it to the United States. The Chouteaus had outfitted the Lewis and Clark expedition sent out by President Jefferson to explore and map the territory he had purchased.

President Jefferson had offered free tuition to the Army Academy at West Point to several young Frenchmen of the Louisiana Territory. Auguste Chouteau had been one of these West Point scholars.

Now at age 34 he was retired from the military with the rank of colonel though he still served in the local militia. Chouteau had aggressively expanded the family's fur empire into western Arkansas Territory.

In particular, Colonel Chouteau had worked to expand the family's fur business into the Three Forks region where the mission was to be built. He had located his own home at a large salt spring near the Neosho River some miles north of the mission site. His home was called Grand Saline.

Rev. Chapman led Will and George Requa, John Spaulding and Abraham Redfield to the Chouteau fur warehouse at the St. Louis wharf. A low-slung log building, it sat within a short distance of their keelboat's berth.

The interior of the building was dimly lit with lanterns and seemed piled to the low rafters with furs and hides of every description. The smell was a bit overpowering at first, but the men adjusted to it as they politely waited for the proprietor to finish haggling with a trapper over a good sized pile of beaver pelts he had brought in for trade.

When this transaction was completed and the trapper left with a voucher to be exchanged for goods at the Chouteau General Mercantile, the missionaries approached the rough-sawn counter.

"Would you be Colonel Chouteau?" Rev. Chapman asked.

"I am," the colonel responded.

"I'm Rev. Epaphras Chapman with the United Foreign Mission Society of New York," the minister said, extending his hand. "My associates and I are going to be establishing a mission near Three Forks and we wanted to meet you."

"But of course," said Chouteau his French heritage apparent as he grasped Chapman's hand. "You are the talk of St. Louis. I heard about you from my father when I arrived on Monday." The colonel was a slight man with a thin, beaky nose and dark hair that he wore swept forward around his face. But he held himself in the erect posture of the military man that he was.

"Your father has been most helpful in introducing us around the region," Chapman explained. "But we've been told by him and by Governor Clark that you are the best man for helping us when we settle near Three Forks." Then he introduced Chouteau to the other men.

"I will be happy to assist you in any way I can," Chouteau stated, leaning forward on his counter. "Will you be continuing your journey by river or will you travel overland on the Trace?"

The Osage Trace was an unimproved, but much traveled, trade trail used by the Osages to travel between Missouri and Three Forks.

"We're continuing on with Captain Douglas on the river," Chapman explained. We have our wives and children with us and felt that would be the best means of travel for them."

"With children, yes," the colonel agreed. "I, myself prefer the Trace, but that is because I have never learned to swim," he smiled somewhat ruefully.

The other men grinned and for the next half hour they plied Colonel Chouteau with questions about the Osages and the land where they would build their mission outpost. Chouteau informed them that Chief Cashesegra – or Big Tracks – had already returned to Three Forks.

As the hour approached noon, the door to the warehouse opened, sending a bright slat of sunlight into the room. In the doorway stood a woman, blonde and petite, and a boy about age nine.

Colonel Chouteau immediately glanced at a pocket watch he pulled from his vest. "Well, gentlemen," he said. "I am late for a dinner appointment with my lovely wife." Then gesturing the young woman forward, he introduced her. "This is my wife Sophie and my son Pierre."

The missionaries all turned to greet her and doff their hats.

"*Bon jour*," Sophie Chouteau returned the greeting with a small curtsy. Her son, who shared her blond curls, made a stiff little bow at her nudge.

Rev. Chapman said, "We won't keep you further, Colonel. You've been most helpful in answering our questions."

"It was my pleasure," Chouteau responded. "Please call on me at Grand Saline when you arrive at your mission. My associate, Joseph Revoir, will be happy to assist you, if I am not there."

"Thank you, Colonel," Chapman said and bowing to Mrs. Chouteau, he led the men out of the warehouse.

As they made their way down the wooden wharf toward the keelboat, George turned to his brother. "I thought you said the colonel's wife was Osage."

Will coughed into his hand and glanced at Rev. Chapman. "We said he had an Osage wife."

"But she didn't look Osage in the least," George said. "She appeared to be French."

"His Osage wife lives at Grand Saline," Rev. Chapman said quietly as they reached the gangplank and made their way aboard the boat.

"But that would mean . . ." George began but stopped as the situation became clear.

"He has two wives," John Spaulding finished his sentence.

"But that's not. . ." George stammered, his surprise rendering him almost speechless.

"It's not Christian," Chapman said, his jaw tight. "But unfortunately it's also not uncommon among the fur traders on the frontier."

George gave a low whistle. "Wait until the women learn about this."

"Are we going to tell them?" Will asked.

"I won't keep it a secret," Chapman answered. "We all knew we were coming to an untamed and uncivilized land. The Indians often take many wives. It's part of their ways. We didn't come to judge or condemn. We came to teach them and bring them to Christ."

"Yeah," George grinned. "But wait until the women hear about this."

"He has two wives!" Rachel Chapman exclaimed at the dinner table that evening. They were dining aboard the boat because they would be leaving St. Louis very early the next morning and would retire early that evening. "Mr. Chapman!"

"Rachel, do not blame me for this practice. I didn't marry him to either of his wives."

"He really has two wives?" Susan whispered to Will Requa. Will nodded, trying to school his face to appear very disapproving. In fact, he wanted to grin at the shocked look on all the women's faces. George had been right about their reaction.

Clarissa exchanged a look with her cabin mate Amanda Ingles while Phoebe tsk tsked the news of Colonel Chouteau's vagaries. She wondered if either of the Mrs. Chouteaus knew about the other one.

"If this is intolerable to any of you," Rev. Vaille interrupted the buzz of conversation around the dining tables, "you might reconsider your decision to work at our mission." He spoke quietly but his words were forceful. "We will no doubt encounter many such indelicacies on the frontier. We must not let our shock or disapproval offend those we hope to reach with the gospel."

"But surely we must teach a better way," quiet Abraham Redfield stated.

"Yes, certainly," Rev. Chapman agreed. "But how we teach will determine how well the message is received."

He looked around at all the missionaries who had grown quiet. "Rev. Vaille is right. If anyone cannot tolerate frontier conditions now is the time to decide whether you will continue on with us or will return home." He gave an almost pleading glance at his wife Rachel who closed her mouth and said nothing more.

Clarissa and her cabin mates were still discussing frontier conditions, however, as they prepared for bed that evening. The young teacher sat on her bunk, brushing out her chestnut hair, a task she had neglected too often on the journey. Susan, who occupied the bunk above her, sat with her bare feet dangling over the edge.

"Will . . . I mean, Mr. Requa . . . says he's known for some time about the colonel's wives," she told the other girls. "I don't think the men seem at all disturbed by this."

"They probably think it's a fine idea," Phoebe interjected. "Men, even good Christian men, think women were put here purely for their convenience and pleasure."

"Oh, I don't think all men feel that way," Susan objected. Her little girl voice made the statement sound particularly naïve and Phoebe snorted her opinion of Susan's opinion.

"Well my husband shall not feel that way," Amanda stated in a matter-of-fact tone as she climbed into the bed Mrs. Woodruff had once occupied.

Phoebe leaned over her bunk and looked down at the red-haired cook. "You're sure of that are you?" she asked. "And what if he does feel that way?"

"Then he won't be me husband," Amanda laughed. "We have the choice of whom we shall marry you know."

Clarissa was silent. The bitterness she thought she had tamped down in her heart reared its head once again. *Not everyone has a choice*, she thought. She remembered overhearing the headmistress at the Colchester school discussing her broken engagement with another teacher. "Such a shame," the woman had said. "Her chances are ruined now."

"I supposed we do at that," Phoebe surprisingly agreed. "None of us will have folks arranging a marriage for us where we're going."

"And there are some fine men going to the mission with us," Susan said, her voice even more dreamy than usual. She was clearly smitten with Will Requa.

The other girls giggled at their young friend as Amanda reached over to turn down the lantern light.

"Aye, we all know you've settled your cap," Amanda said, her lilting Irish accent seeming more pronounced in the cabin's darkness. "And what of you, Miss Phoebe?" she asked. "Who among our fine men has caught your fancy?"

"I'll not be choosy," Phoebe stated, her practical nature always present. "I've no expectation of a flock of beaus. One good man who'll have me is all I expect and all I need."

Clarissa tried to lie very still hoping the others would think she had already drifted to sleep. This discussion was too uncomfortable to want to be a part of it. Such gossipy talk of men and marriage reminded her of her young students in Colchester.

"What about you, Miss Johnson?" Susan asked.

A sigh escaped Clarissa's lips before she could stop it. What could she say? The only unmarried man of her station was Dr. Palmer and he was clearly taken with Miss Cleaver.

"I didn't set out on this mission endeavor to find a husband," she finally said, hating that she sounded haughty. She only wanted to pretend an indifference to marriage. "For some there is no greater calling than the work of the Lord. We don't all have to be married."

A choked back "harrumph" came from Phoebe's bunk, but the other women were silent.

Setting out the next morning, the journey toward their mission began anew. All of the missionaries remained on board, none having chosen to return to New England.

The rowers pulled the boat from the St. Louis wharf out into the strong Mississippi current.

The river level was high with spring rains, and the water ran muddy and fast. What took a week to travel from Cape Girardeau to St. Louis only took two days on the return voyage.

Traveling the Mississippi River seemed very different to Clarissa, though the teachers tried to re-establish their school routine. The river was much wider than the Ohio and seemed much more littered with debris. She learned a new vocabulary from Mr. Pennywit who warned them of "sawyers" and "planters," the floating or stationary logs that were abundant on the river. Either could rip a hole in the side of a boat and cause considerable damage. Avoiding such obstacles was a chief concern for any pilot.

Dozens of islands, large and small, proved to be obstacles as well. They passed more than one rotting boat stranded on some sandy shore, abandoned by her crew because she could not be returned to the river's flow.

The abandoned boats caught debris floating in the river and a pile of driftwood would gather around them, and any other stationary object, creating further obstacles for travel. Mr. Pennywit now rarely had time to visit with the passengers as they continued south. He and Captain Douglas were kept busy in trying to plot the best course through the labyrinth of river debris.

On occasion they would even order one of the small lifeboats lowered and would send a few men to row ahead and scout the conditions of the river. Captain Douglas had earned a reputation for never having stranded a boat and this cautious approach was one of the reasons he had been so successful in navigating the Mississippi for over 20 years.

One afternoon just before supper, the captain and his steward had been conferring in the pilot house for some time. Clarissa and her students sat at the oarsmen's benches while she read a Bible story to them in the warm afternoon sunshine. A group of the men soon gathered at the pilot house door and Clarissa found herself distracted in wondering what their conference was about.

When she finished her reading, she dismissed the girls and gathered up her books. Abigail, Elizabeth and Leah were eager for their play time and ran off in search of their favorite entertainment – a game with Phoebe Beach. Mr. Spaulding's class of boys was soon romping after the girls.

Sauntering by the pilot house, Clarissa caught the eye of Abraham Redfield. Keeping her voice low, she asked, "Is there a problem, Mr. Redfield?"

He shook his head. "No, but there's some debate about which course to take around a large island up ahead. Wolf Island, I think Mr. Pennywit said. We'll reach it just before nightfall and Captain Douglas wants to be certain we take the right course."

"Wolf Island," Clarissa repeated and just the sound of it seemed rather frightening.

"Timber wolves," George explained, turning from his place at the door. As always, he was eager to display his knowledge of the river. "The island's full of eastern timber wolves. Or so they say."

"We won't dock there, will we?" Clarissa asked.

"No, it's not a port of call," George answered. "We'll pass it through the night. So we might hear the wolves howling at the moon," he quipped. It seemed he couldn't help but tease the young teacher just a bit.

Clarissa widened her eyes at the thought of hearing wild wolves howling at midnight and she barely suppressed the shudder that coursed up her spine.

George gave her elbow a squeeze. "We'll likely never see a single wolf, Miss Johnson. No need to fear."

Clarissa felt a warmth rush through her at George's expression of concern. For all his youthful exuberance at their river adventure, he could be a thoughtful young man.

"Well, then I'll not worry," Clarissa smiled. "I'll see you gentlemen at supper." She nodded at Mr. Redfield and the other men and then made her way below to the cabin deck to freshen up for the evening meal.

CHAPTER ELEVEN

Wolf Island
June 3, 1820

The missionaries were lingering over a last cup of coffee with their dried apple cobbler later that evening. The mothers of the group – Rachel Chapman, Asenath Vaille and Alice Spaulding – had just returned from getting their children tucked into bed.

Rev. Vaille opened his Bible for their evening reading and had only begun on the first verse when the boat gave a sudden lurch. It was only a quick jolt as if they had bumped against something in the water, but it was enough to cause Mrs. Woodruff to spill her coffee on the dining table.

While she and Rachel dabbed at the spill with the plain cotton napkins, a screeching sound came from below. Everyone froze in place for a moment. Lydia Fuller grasped her husband's arm. Lydia had a terrible fear of water and had often expressed her concern about the boat's safety. Amanda, who sat next to her, reached over and gave the woman's shoulder a reassuring pat.

There was silence for another moment as everyone waited to see if there would be any further disturbance. Hearing nothing, Rev. Vaille again began his reading. He had covered several verses when the sound of footsteps hurrying along the outside corridor again interrupted him.

This time, Rev. Chapman stood and walked to the dining

hall door. Seeing Mr. Pennywit at the end of the passage, he hailed the steward.

"Is there a problem, Mr. Pennywit?" he asked.

Philip hesitated a moment. He seemed torn between stopping to explain the situation to his passengers and obeying an order to follow the other boatmen below.

"A slight problem," he drawled. "We've encountered a submerged planter, it seems. Gouged the side of the boat. Nothing to be alarmed at."

"Do your men need assistance?" Chapman asked. "We'd be glad to help."

Again Philip hesitated and the moment seemed filled with unspoken danger. Clarissa saw the Requa brothers exchange a look. A quirk of his eyebrow seemed to say that Will was ready to jump to assistance if called upon. George nodded his agreement.

"I'm sure we'll have everything set to right quickly," Pennywit finally said. "We'll shore up the wall tonight and if need be we'll put into the next port to make repairs." He turned to continue down the stairs, but Rev. Chapman wasn't satisfied with the information the steward had given.

"Will we put to anchor here tonight, then?"

Philip turned back again. "Yes, the anchors have been lowered." Then he added, "You do recall where the lifeboats are located?" he asked.

"Oh, no," Lydia moaned. Stephen Fuller slipped his arm around his wife and pulled her close.

"Yes," Rev. Chapman responded. "Should we be prepared to board them?"

"I don't expect we'll need the boats, but Captain Douglas is a cautious man. He likes to be prepared for every contingency," Philip explained. "Now, I really must get below."

As Mr. Pennywit clambered down the stairs to the lowest deck of the boat, Rev. Chapman returned to be seated by his wife.

"Do you think we should get the children up and dressed?" she asked. "In case . . ."

Chapman looked around the room at his fellow missionaries. While most seemed calm, Lydia was visibly trembling and Martha Woodruff had turned very pale. Clarissa felt nervous, but not upset. She, at least, had been around water enough not to be terribly frightened of it. She knew many of her fellow passengers, however, did not feel the same way. Very few of them could swim.

"I think it might be a good idea to get them up," Rev. Chapman said. "But let's try not to frighten them. This is only a precaution."

Rachel nodded to the other mothers and then asked Phoebe and Susan to come assist with dressing the eight children. The other missionaries remained in the dining room.

"Perhaps a moment of prayer might give us all some assurance," Dr. Palmer suggested.

"You're certainly right," Rev. Vaille agreed. "Shall we stand for prayer?"

The scraping of chairs against the wooden floor filled the room for a time, but when silence reigned, the family bowed their heads and Rev. Vaille offered a simple prayer for safety for everyone on board the vessel, for strength to the boatmen and wisdom to Captain Douglas.

He had just concluded with a solemn "Amen," when the children trooped into the dining hall. Alice carried Billy who clearly had not awakened even while being dressed. His blond head was draped over her shoulder and his thumb was firmly planted in his mouth. Little Sarah Vaille too seemed barely awake in Phoebe's arms, but the other children were alert and excited at this unexpected adventure.

Thomas and James Chapman immediately ran to their father. "We heard an awful noise, Papa," Thomas said. "What was it?"

"I believe we've bumped into some driftwood," Rev. Chapman explained in simple terms. "And with the boatmen all running around we thought you might have a hard time sleeping so you might as well be up and in here with us."

"Why are the boatmen running around?" Abigail asked her father. She was standing behind her mother's chair while four-year-old Leah crawled into Rachel's lap.

Rev. Chapman was quiet for a moment. "They have to check the boat out and make sure everything's all safe and sound," he said. "Captain Douglas runs a tight ship, you know."

"Governor Clark says Captain Douglas is one of the best men on the river," Thomas said in his clear piping voice. He frequently quoted the famed explorer as proof of his visit to the man's home.

Somehow his simple, child's confidence in the good captain gave Clarissa a stronger sense of assurance. Josiah Douglas was a capable captain who had never stranded a boat. Even if this boat had been damaged by a "planter," they were surely not in any danger.

"Why don't we sing a bit," suggested Alexander Woodruff. The burly blacksmith was fond of singing and had a surprisingly good baritone voice.

"Let's sing about the 'rattlin' bog'," Elizabeth Vaille quickly suggested.

And so Amanda Ingles started them off in the lively Irish folk song that soon had the children squealing with laughter and all the adults gasping for air. They had just started on the hymn, "A Mighty Fortress Is Our God," when Captain Douglas appeared at the dining hall doorway.

The singing trailed off and all eyes turned to the portly man who seemed uncharacteristically disheveled. He cleared his throat as if trying to locate his voice.

"I don't wish to alarm you," he said as quietly as his booming voice would allow. "But we're taking on water and I've made the decision to put the boat aground on Wolf Island. I will not strand her, but it will take some rough maneuvering to get her on the sandbar. I think it best if all passengers de-board to the lifeboats. I assure you this is just a precaution."

"Oh heavenly days," Lydia Fuller moaned. "I knew something like this would happen."

Rev. Chapman stood with one hand on the shoulder of each of his sons. "We'll cooperate fully, Captain," he said, nodding to Rachel. She stood beside her husband, setting Leah down between them. Abigail slipped her hand into her mother's.

The other missionaries stood and began to make their way out of the dining hall to the upper deck where the lifeboats awaited. Clarissa heard Mr. Fuller and Amanda trying to reassure Lydia as they walked to the rail where the boatmen were putting down the boats. A rope ladder would enable the passengers to reach the boats once they were settled in the muddy river.

Looking over the rail, Clarissa felt her first sensation of fear. The light was growing dim as the sun was just now sinking to the horizon. Managing the sturdy but very mobile ladder would not be easy for any of the women in their long skirts.

Four boats were lowered to the water; each could hold ten people. There was more than adequate room for all the missionary passengers so two boatmen were assigned to the oars to keep the boats as steady in the water as possible.

It had been agreed that the women and children would go first and the men last for each boat. The unflappable Rachel Chapman agreed to be the first missionary overboard. All eyes were on her as she carefully moved down the ladder. At each rung she was forced to lift her skirt to ensure she had a good foothold so her progress seemed extremely slow. When Rachel was within a few feet of the lifeboat, one of the boatmen grasped her at the waist and carefully lifted her into the boat.

There was an audible exhaling of breath among the passengers in relief. "Nothing to it," Rachel called up to the mission family. "Now it's your turn, Leah."

Rev. Chapman knelt before his little daughter. "You think you can go down by yourself?" he asked. "I can carry you if you want me to."

"I can do it, Papa," Leah lisped. "Just like Mother did."

"Yes," her papa agreed. "Just like your mother."

"You can do it, Leah," Thomas encouraged his little sister.

Leah started slowly at first, but with a shorter skirt she found it much easier to manage the ladder. She picked up speed as she descended and squealed in delight when the boatman lifted her off the ladder and settled her in her mother's lap.

"If Leah can do it, anybody can do it," James Chapman said.

Abigail, James and Thomas quickly followed their sister. Susan Comstock then made her way down followed by Rev. Chapman and Will Requa. Their boat pulled away and a second one was maneuvered into place at the ladder.

Into this boat went the Vaille family. Rev. Vaille carried

little Sarah. Phoebe and Abraham Redfield were also in this boat. The Spauldings with Eliza and the Woodruffs were in the third boat.

By now dusk had settled in and the island sitting slightly to the port side of the boat loomed over the water like a black hulk. While the others were making their way to the lifeboats, Mrs. Fuller had worked herself into a state of tears. "I can't do it," she sobbed against her husband's chest. "Oh, why did we have to come out here?"

"You know why," Stephen responded in a quiet voice against her ear. "We had no choice. Just like we have no choice now." He felt alarm at his wife's reaction.

"Why don't you go down just before her," Amanda suggested, trying to find a solution to her friend's fear. "She'll feel more confident if she's not on the ladder alone."

"We'll all help her get out on the ladder," George offered. "You go first and wait for her to step out just after you. Then you can guide her down."

"Can you do that, Lydie?" Stephen asked. "I'll have hold of you the whole time."

Lydia looked over the rail at the ladder and squeezed her eyes shut. "I'll try," she whispered.

It took a while for Mrs. Fuller to get the courage to actually place her foot on the ladder. George and Dr. Palmer each stood by to assist her. The first three boats had already been rowed to the island and their passengers were waiting on the sandy shore. Their oarsmen had rowed around the bow of the boat and re-boarded by hauling themselves up a rope. All hands had been ordered to the lower deck to help in shoring up the damaged hull.

Slowly Stephen and Lydia made their way down the ladder. When they reached the lifeboat and were safely seated, Amanda and then Clarissa went down. Dr. Palmer followed and George was the last of the missionary passengers to leave the keelboat.

Their boatmen had just lowered the oars to the water when George's prediction of howling wolves came true. Apparently the light from the boat's lanterns had stirred the island's inhabitants. A pack of seven or eight of the timber wolves set up a terrible racket of howls and snarls that would send a shiver up the spine of even a hardy riverman.

Mrs. Fuller, already in an agitated state, now was completely panicked. She began to flail against her husband, her screams adding even more noise to the surreal scene.

"No, no," the woman wailed as she tried to stand in the boat as if she might escape the horrible noise by fleeing from it.

"Lydie, sit still," Stephen cried grabbing at his wife as she continued to flail about in fear.

The boat rocked dangerously in the water. Clarissa felt herself sliding across the bench where she sat with Amanda. The cook followed her path and their shift in weight tipped the boat precariously.

Mrs. Fuller, half standing and unbalanced, went over into the water. Her husband made a grab for her and his movement completely turned the boat. All its passengers joined Lydia in the muddy Mississippi.

Clarissa surfaced quickly, sputtering to remove the awful water from her nose and mouth. While she was by no means an expert swimmer, she knew enough to be able to tread water and keep her head above it.

In the darkness, confusion reigned. The oarsmen were struggling to right the lifeboat while on shore the other missionaries watched in frightened concern. Will Requa, Mr. Redfield and Rev. Chapman waded out from the shore to try to be of assistance but none could swim so they were forced to wait in the chilly water, hoping to lend a hand to the others as they tried to reach the island.

Clarissa felt a steady arm encircle her waist. She turned, expecting to see George, but it was Dr. Palmer who had reached her.

"Are you alright, Miss Johnson?" he asked.

"Yes," she said, though she was starting to shiver in the cool night air.

"Can you swim?" the doctor asked.

"A little," Clarissa nodded, her teeth chattering.

"Will you be alright while I assist with Mrs. Fuller?" he then asked. "I'll come right back for you."

"Yes," Clarissa assured him. "Help Mrs. Fuller. I'll be fine."

The doctor nodded and then swam away from her with

strong, steady strokes. Clarissa immediately missed his reassuring presence and regretted that she had sent him away. It seemed like a lifetime while she waited in the darkness. Her skirts grew heavier and heavier and felt as if they would drag her to the bottom.

A rim of light on the western horizon and the glow of the lanterns cast strange shadows on the water. Floating debris in the river kept bumping against Clarissa causing her to start each time. She could tell that Dr. Palmer and Stephen Fuller had managed to get Mrs. Fuller to the waiting men and they were helping her to the shore.

Some distance away, the boatmen had righted the lifeboat and were searching for the lost oars. George and Amanda were clinging to a drift of wood a good distance from her. Neither of them could swim. For a brief moment, Clarissa feared she would be forgotten and left in the cold water. She had drifted into the shadow of the keelboat. She felt a sense of panic for a moment and her heart began to pound.

"Lord, help me," she softly prayed, forcing herself to stay calm. "Help us all."

The rivermen had secured the oars and were now rowing toward George and Amanda. George helped the girl climb into the boat and then he clambered in after her. Both collapsed in the bottom of the lifeboat, relieved to be out of the water. The rowers started toward the island.

Clarissa watched as they pulled away from where she struggled to keep her head above the water. Her arms were tiring and she didn't know how much longer she could stay afloat. Should she try to paddle toward the shore? She was finding it harder to keep her fears at bay. They howled around her mind like the timber wolves on their island.

"God, God, please," was all she could whisper.

Her thoughts were growing muddled and she was losing the feeling in her feet. Her arms felt like lead and she realized she had waited too late to try to get herself to the island. It was too far for her tired body.

Would nothing save her now? She could see nothing in the darkness that settled around her like a tomb. Her face slipped beneath the water.

Again she felt a strong arm circle around her pulling her upward.

"I have you, Miss Johnson," Dr. Palmer said.

Clarissa was so relieved a sob escaped her lips.

"I've removed my coat," the doctor said. "Take hold of it and I'll pull you to shore."

Clarissa grasped the sodden coat he thrust into her hands. Carefully Marcus began to swim toward the waiting group on Wolf Island. While they were still many yards out, the tall doctor gained his footing on the river's bottom.

He now reached back and again slipped his arm around her waist, pulling her forward until her own feet could feel the sandy beach of the island. Such close intimacy would have been scandalous under normal circumstances, but Clarissa found herself clinging to the doctor. She was shivering uncontrollably.

As they reached the shore, Will Requa and Rev. Chapman reached out to both of them and helped them trudge up the sand toward a waiting fire. Mr. Woodruff had used one of the lantern candles to start the blaze. It had driven the wolves back into the shadows.

Mrs. Fuller sat at the fire, nearly collapsed in her husband's arms. Rachel Chapman pulled Clarissa to sit on a large piece of driftwood at the fireside. Mr. Spaulding offered Clarissa his coat. She smiled her thanks and gratefully drew it around her shoulders.

Clarissa looked at Mrs. Fuller over the fire and felt a spasm of resentment. It was because of Lydia she had nearly drowned as had George and Amanda. But then her eyes fell on Dr. Palmer who had dropped to the sand by the fire. He had drawn up his knees and rested his arms across them. He looked completely exhausted.

"*Dear, Lord,*" Clarissa thought. "*He saved my life.*" She felt tears sting her eyes and she looked away from him to the crackling fire, afraid her emotions could be read on her face.

CHAPTER TWELVE

Mississippi River
Early June, 1820

Clarissa awoke the next morning in her bunk on the keelboat. Her body felt sore and she ached with fever. She could barely remember boarding the boat after Captain Douglas had successfully brought it ashore on the island.

She vaguely recalled George helping her walk up the steep gangplank that had been lowered to Wolf Island. Then Phoebe and Susan had helped her and Amanda remove their wet, muddy clothes. She had toweled her hair dry but this morning it felt stiff and smelled of fish and mud.

Clarissa turned her head and saw sunlight streaming through the small porthole. It must be mid-morning.

"Oh, you're finally awake," said Susan Comstock who sat on Amanda's bunk across the small room. "How are you feeling this morning?"

"Tired," Clarissa croaked. Her mouth felt dry and gritty.

"Would you like some tea?" Susan asked, coming to the teacher's bunk and laying a practiced hand on her forehead. Though Susan was the same age as Clarissa, she had worked for years as a governess and was quite competent in caring for others. Her tiny voice might match her tiny waist, but she was not nearly as immature as she appeared.

"I would like some tea," Clarissa said, trying to sit up in her bunk. Her arms felt wobbly. Surely she wasn't so weak just from a dunk in the river. But she could not shake her weariness.

"I'll run quick and fetch it," Susan said. "And some dry toast. Dr. Palmer says to be careful of what you eat for awhile. "In case you swallowed too much of that dreadful river water."

With a swish of her green muslin skirt she was out the door to bring breakfast. When she returned just a few minutes later, she had brought Dr. Palmer with her.

"Look here who's come to check on you," Susan said as she entered the cabin. Dr. Palmer followed Susan into the room, carrying his black medical satchel, and ducking to enter through the low door.

Clarissa felt her cheeks flush and knew it wasn't from the fever. *Don't be silly,* she scolded herself, but even as she thought it she worried about how terrible her hair must look.

Susan set the tray of tea and toast on the cabinet between the bunks and stepped back so Dr. Palmer could sit on the brassbound trunk to examine Clarissa. He felt her forehead, noting the flushed look of her cheeks. Then he took her wrist to measure her pulse.

"Heart rate seems a little elevated," he said more to himself than Clarissa. She knew her heart was pounding at the nearness of the doctor.

"How are you feeling this morning?" he asked, looking at her closely.

"A little tired," Clarissa responded, finding it hard to meet his gaze. "And feverish, I guess."

"You took a chill in the night air, I'm afraid," Dr. Palmer said. He realized he was still holding her hand and quickly placed it down on the bedcovers. "A few days of rest should be all you'll need to fully recover."

"I want to thank you, Dr. Palmer," Clarissa spoke barely above a whisper. She was very aware of Susan standing behind Dr. Palmer and watching their exchange with interest. "You saved my life last evening."

"Nonsense," Marcus shrugged. "You were amazing. Had you panicked in the water, matters would have turned out much worse than they did."

Clarissa lifted her eyes to the young doctor's and thought she saw admiration there. But it was she who had much to admire in her rescuer. A silence stretched between them.

"Poor Mrs. Fuller," Susan said, interrupting the moment. "She has fared much worse."

"Yes," Dr. Palmer agreed as if he were suddenly aware of

Susan's presence. He stood and picked up his satchel, but his eyes never left Clarissa's face. "I'd better go check on her. I'll let you get to your tea before it grows cold. Should you need anything, Miss Johnson, please send for me."

"I will," Clarissa said. "Thank you, Doctor."

Marcus nodded and then ducked out the door. Susan moved around the trunk and sat to pour tea from the small pot on the breakfast tray. She handed the cup to Clarissa, eager to share with her the all the news of the boat that she had learned during breakfast in the dining hall.

"Amanda says Lydia has taken quite ill again," she began. "She says she's coughing up blood." The girl feigned a shudder, but it was clear she enjoyed sharing the gossip. "And Captain Douglas is being a bear with all his crew. Mr. Pennywit says he's only had to run a boat aground once before and he hates doing it."

"Can the boat be repaired?" Clarissa asked as she took a bite of the dry toast. It had little flavor, but she was hungry so she ate steadily while Susan talked.

"Oh, yes," she answered. "The boatmen have already repaired it. They had to pump out the water too. Thank goodness it only got into the lower deck." She handed Clarissa the cotton napkin from the tray.

"Mr. Pennywit says the difficulty will be in getting the boat back into the water. Captain Douglas may have to hire some of the local men to help. Rev. Chapman says the men who live along the river won't be of much help. He says all of them are inclined to drink too much. Captain Douglas will probably have to pay them in whiskey. Can you imagine?" Susan's eyes were big as she rambled on.

"Is everyone else well?" Clarissa asked when she'd finished her breakfast. "Mr. Requa and Amanda, Mr. Fuller?"

"Oh, yes, all are well. The children were in quite the dither last night, I can tell you. We had a time getting them all back to sleep. We finally convinced the cook to allow us some warm milk for them." Susan replaced Clarissa's breakfast dishes on the tray.

Clarissa suddenly felt very tired and though she longed for a bath to wash her hair, she wasn't sure she could stay awake long enough to indulge in one. She covered a wide yawn with her hand.

"Looks like someone still needs her sleep," Susan tsked as if she were speaking to one of the children. "I'll just take these things away and let you rest. That will be the best thing for you after your ordeal." She picked up the tray and made her way to the cabin door. Clarissa was asleep almost before it closed behind her.

A few hours later, Clarissa awoke to a gentle hand shaking her. She opened her eyes to see Mrs. Vaille standing over her.

"I'm sorry to have to wake you, dear," she said. "But Captain Douglas has managed to hire the crew of a passing keelboat to help in moving our boat. He's asked us to de-board again to Wolf Island. Mrs. Fuller will remain on the boat with her husband. She isn't well enough to move, poor dear. Do you feel up to it?"

Clarissa sat up, trying to shake the heavy feeling of her eyelids. "Yes, if you can help me dress," she said, pulling herself from the fog of sleep. With Mrs. Vaille's assistance she quickly donned her clothes and pulled her hair into one long braid down her back.

Then they joined the other passengers as they made their way to the gangplank. Though steeply angled to the sandy shore, they would all be able to walk off the boat to the island.

"Feeling better, Miss Johnson?" Dr. Palmer asked her as they all queued up at the gangplank.

"Yes, much better," Clarissa said. The fever had left her while she slept so except for some stiffness in her neck and arms, she felt fine.

"We were worried about you," George Requa said, coming up on the other side of her. "Glad to see you up and about. Can I assist you down?" he asked waving toward the plank.

Clarissa glanced at Dr. Palmer but could think of no reason to refuse George's proffered arm so she slipped her hand around it and thanked him.

Behind her Eliza Cleaver was waiting in turn. "You can assist me, Dr. Palmer," she said. The two of them followed George and Clarissa.

Wolf Island in the light of day seemed far less frightening than it had last evening. It was basically just a very large sandbar though numerous trees grew on it. The island's inhabitants – the timber wolves – were nowhere to be seen or heard.

Watching the re-launch of the boat proved interesting. The two keelboat crews used their long poles as fulcrums to slowly lift and inch the boat backward into the water. Captain Douglas roared orders and had to apologize to the ladies on two occasions for his language. Finally the boat was far enough out that the river could lift it off the sand.

Then, again using the lifeboats and rope ladder, the passengers boarded the keelboat. There were no problems this time around.

Douglas paid the other keelboat crew for their assistance, all the while grumbling about "piracy" as he counted out the gold coin. His own crew took to the long oars and soon had cleared Wolf Island and set the boat back into the main current of the river. By supper they had covered several miles and Wolf Island disappeared as they left their only river mishap behind.

Over the next few days, progress down the river seemed slow. Always cautious, Captain Douglas took his time to plot a course through the increasing river debris. After another two weeks, the captain announced at breakfast that they were approaching the Chickasaw Bluffs of Tennessee. A series of rapids, referred to as "The Devil's Race-ground," would make for some rough travel over the next hour.

By now the missionary passengers had grown accustomed to the many moods of the river, but as the boat began to move rapidly through the white water, most were on the upper deck to watch. Mrs. Chapman had insisted on the younger children remaining below on the cabin deck, but Thomas Chapman and Richard Vaille stood at the starboard rail with George and Will Requa enjoying the boat's dance through the white water.

Clarissa sat with most of the other women on the oarsmen benches. All the boatmen were manning their long poles at the rails to keep the boat on course through the rapids.

Lydia Fuller was much improved in health by this time, but

she rarely left her cabin. She expressed to her husband shame for her panic at Wolf Island, knowing she had put others in danger.

Stephen tried to encourage his wife to join the others up top, but she declined. "I can't face them, Stephen" she said. But finally he convinced her to join Susan, Phoebe and Mrs. Vaille in the dining room with the children.

Now Stephen stood with Rev. and Mrs. Chapman at the port rail not far from where Clarissa sat. Once past the worst of the rapids, he plunged into an apology to the mission director.

"Lydia feels real bad about what happened at Wolf Island," he said, as he gripped the boat's rail. "She wanted me to let you know that." His nod toward Clarissa let her know that he was including her in the apology.

"That's all behind us, Mr. Fuller," Rachel Chapman said, laying a reassuring hand on his arm. "We just hope she's fully recovered."

"Oh, yes, ma'am," Fuller assured her. "She's much better now. Hardly coughs at all since the doctor fixed up that sarsaparilla tea for her."

Rev. Chapman looked at his farm director with concern on his face. "Fuller, tell me honestly," he said, "will your wife feel comfortable at the mission? Is this endeavor too much for her?"

"Lydie will be fine," Stephen answered with determination. "She's as hard a worker as any woman I've ever known and she won't be no burden to anyone once we reach the mission. She just had a bad scare as a child – nearly drowned in a pond once. It's made her real fearful of water ever since."

"But what of her health, Mr. Fuller?" Rachel continued. "She's struggled with illness for most of the journey."

"She'll be fine," Stephen reiterated. "Her lungs bother her some, but the doctor back home told her a drier climate would help. That's partly why we decided to join the mission." He glanced away from the Chapmans, an inscrutable look of pain on his face.

Clarissa noted the look and wondered what the other part of their reason for coming on this mission might be. She felt more sympathy towards Lydia, knowing all about having painful reasons for leaving home.

She glanced toward Dr. Palmer at the starboard rail. He was laughing with George, Will, and the two boys about something. She was considering joining them now that the boat was steady, but before she could, Eliza Cleaver strolled up to the men and they immediately turned their full attention to her. Eliza's golden hair glistened beneath her straw bonnet and even from this distance Clarissa could see her bat her eyes with great effect. Clarissa sighed and turned her eyes to the bluffs hemming in the river and forcing its passage through the rocks below. She felt like the river, driven by elements beyond herself and outside her control.

The rapids were soon passed through and the river slowed once again. By the next day they had reached Fort Pickering which sat high on the last of the bluffs. A new little community called Memphis had been laid out near the fort by the famous general, Andrew Jackson.

The boat would stop here for supplies at the Chickasaw Bluffs Trading House. The Trading House offered little to appeal to the New Englanders. Its trade focus was primarily on offering goods to the Chickasaws who lived in the area. But they found it interesting to look over the items the Indians brought in for trade. Besides the furs and hides they took in the hunt, they also traded beeswax, pecans, medicinal plants, rabbit fur gloves and deer hide moccasins decorated with intricate beadwork.

The missionaries saw little to purchase at the log trading post except for Rev. Chapman who gave into his children's pleading and purchased some molasses candy for everyone. But they lingered in the dark interior of the store, reluctant to return to the boat until the call for boarding came.

The clerk at the store, whose name was Charlie, seemed quite interested in hearing the missionaries' news from back east and in turn shared information about the frontier. He spoke around a chaw of tobacco that made his whiskered jaw bulge. He carelessly aimed at a spittoon beside the store's counter, missing as often as he hit it. The ladies moved their skirts out of range of the brown tobacco juice.

"Wooee," the clerk exclaimed when he learned the

missionaries were journeying toward a new mission on Osage land. He scratched his head, which seemed none too clean. "The Osages are a fearsome lot. Course now, I'm sure they won't give you no trouble. They mostly tussle with other tribes."

Clarissa wondered again about the wisdom of their mission. They had been assured by the mission society that the Osages were at peace with the United States and their citizens. But they seemed to be at war with all their Indian neighbors.

"Have you had many dealings with the Osages?" Rev. Vaille asked.

"Not much," Charlie admitted. "They don't venture into Cherokee or Chickasaw land too often. But when they do . . . wooee, the feathers fly!" He punctuated his words with a ping of tobacco juice into the spittoon. "Them Osages and Cherokees is always swappin' lead."

"Surely with the new fort at Belle Point the tribal conflict has died down," Rev. Chapman said. He had motioned for Rachel and the house mothers to take the children out of the store when the clerk's talk had turned to Indian warfare.

"Fort Smith ain't done much to keep the Osages in check," Charlie responded. "Their villages are too far upriver from Belle Point. What the army needs is some rangers on horseback to patrol the area. The Third Infantry tries to keep the peace, but without horse soldiers, it's a losin' battle sometimes."

"Now, Charlie," Mr. Pennywit's voice at the door caused them all to turn. "Don't be telling your tall tales. You know you only have a passing acquaintanceship with the truth. You don't want to frighten the ladies."

"Oh, no, no," Charlie said somewhat sheepishly. "I didn't mean to frighten anyone. Just jawin' ya know."

"If ya'll are finished with your purchases," Pennywit addressed his passengers, "Captain Douglas would ask that you return to the boat."

Clarissa joined the others as they once again boarded the keelboat. River travel had grown wearisome and talk of Indian warfare made her wonder what their journey to this untamed land would really bring to them.

CHAPTER THIRTEEN

Arkansas Post, Arkansas Territory
June 17, 1820

In another week, the keelboat reached the mouth of the
Arkansas River. As the rivermen poled the boat into its waters,
the missionaries were at the rails to mark the occasion. They
were at last entering Arkansas Territory and from this point on in
the journey would be traveling through this western region
carved out of south Missouri Territory.

By late afternoon they had docked at the capital of the
territory, Arkansas Post. This village, though small in
comparison to St. Louis, was larger than Memphis and had
operated as a fur trading post since the time of French control.
After supper, while most of the missionaries went to the upper
deck to catch a breeze from the river, Captain Douglas called a
meeting of Rev. and Mrs. Chapman and William Vaille. They
gathered in his office which adjoined the captain's living
quarters.

Josiah Douglas sat behind his desk on which were scattered
the various charts he relied on to navigate the sometimes
quarrelsome rivers. In deference to Mrs. Chapman, he remained
wearing his navy uniform jacket, but he had loosened the top
button of his shirt and seemed more relaxed than he had ever
been during their journey.

"Well, we have made our destination," the captain said,
leaning back in his leather chair. The well-appointed furnishings
of his office were the only luxury on the keelboat. There was no
need for excessive refinement in a boat that would be sold for its
lumber when it arrived in New Orleans.

"This was perhaps your destination, Captain," Rev. Chapmen countered. "But we still have many more miles to travel. We were hoping you might be favorable to carrying us at least to Belle Point."

"I've never managed to get a keelboat to the Point," the captain grunted, looking longingly at the decanter of sherry on the side table, but refraining from reaching for it. "The Arkansas is too shallow for our draught. You'll be better served hiring a flatboat to take you the rest of the way to Three Forks."

"Are flatboats readily available here at Arkansas Post?" Rev. Vaille asked.

"The river's usually thick with them," Douglas responded, "though at this time of year even flatboats can struggle in the low river levels. I was surprised to find the Arkansas as high as it is. July is normally so dry as to stop most river traffic until the fall rains return."

"As you are aware, Captain," Rev. Chapman said, "we are traveling to a mission that has yet to be built. We're naturally reluctant to take the women and children to the site before we have shelter for them established. This means we'll need for them to remain behind somewhere while most of the men travel on and construct our housing."

The minister looked at his wife who nodded. They had obviously discussed their situation before bringing it to the captain. "Arkansas Post, from what I've seen of it, seems a rather rough place for them to remain. We were hoping to get them to Belle Point where there would be some assurance of protection from Fort Smith."

"Are there any boarding houses here at Arkansas Post?" Mrs. Chapman asked.

"None of any repute," Captain Douglas admitted. "From this point on, you'll find accommodations anywhere along the river to be rather simple, though not inhospitable. Even Belle Point caters more to the trapper and soldier than to women and children."

"So you'll not consider attempting travel any further up river?" Rev. Vaille asked.

"We're prepared to make it worth your while," Rachel said.

Captain Douglas leaned back in his chair, steepling his

fingers over his massive chest. He gave the question some
thought before answering.

"As I said, the river seems high for this time of year. I
might be able to get you to Petite Roche -- the Little Rock – but I
sincerely doubt I could get you any further than that. I'm afraid
that is the best I can do."

"And what sort of town is Little Rock?" Rachel asked.

"Clean, just surveyed, laid out on the south bank of the
river," Captain Douglas supplied. "It's already clamoring to be
the territorial capital since it's much more centrally located than
Arkansas Post. Actually has a few families and professional
businessmen. It might have the best accommodations you'll find
in the territory."

"How many days' journey by river is Little Rock from
Three Forks?" Chapman asked. "When we traveled out here last
year, we went by land from Belle Point."

"Depends on the river level," the captain replied. "Could be
anywhere from three weeks to two months or longer. The falls
above the Illinois River are a low-water obstacle. No way to get
over them unless the water's running high enough."

"So you'll carry us to Little Rock?" Rachel sought to clarify
the captain's commitment.

Douglas looked at Rachel for a long moment. Though a
pleasant, attractive woman, she clearly was strong willed and
determined. From the financial arrangements that had been
made for the journey he knew she controlled much of the
financing for this missionary endeavor.

"Yes, to Little Rock," he finally agreed, naming a price for
the effort that would be worth the two extra days of travel. Then
he added, "Just say your prayers that I don't get stuck there for
the summer."

The keelboat would take on its last load of furs for the New
Orleans market while docked at Arkansas Post. This gave the
missionary family time to explore the young territory's capital
city. The weather was humid and by 10:00 in the morning the
air was thick and hot. The many dogs that wandered at will
about the town had all sought shade under the boardwalks.

By noon they had toured most of the town and agreed to

return to the one hotel and restaurant the town boasted. The 28 members of their group filled all the tables in the small establishment, but the owners took it all in stride having often served guests who had just arrived by riverboat.

The meal was served on plain china at unadorned, scarred wooden tables and was a simple fare of brown beans with a bit of ham, corn pone and dried fruit pie. The coffee was fresh and strong, but was too hot to appeal to the visitors so they all chose glasses of cider instead.

Though the interior of the restaurant offered shade from the sweltering sun, the room was by no means cool. Still the missionaries did not rush through their meal, knowing their cabins on the keelboat would be unbearably warm. Finding a shade tree near the river to rest sounded appealing and they were just discussing a move to the waterfront when a gentleman stepped into the diner.

He stood in the door for a moment, letting his eyes adjust from the bright sunshine. He was of average height with dark hair and he wore a leather apron over his white shirt and linsey-woolsey trousers. Doffing his hat he made his way into the room, stopping at the table where Rev. and Mrs. Vaille sat with their children.

"Good afternoon, folks," the man said in the western drawl of the frontier. "My name is William Woodruff. I'm publisher of the *Arkansas Gazette*. I happened to see you folks as you walked by the newspaper office and I thought I might catch you here having your dinner. I wonder if I might talk with you a bit."

Rev. Vaille stood and shook hands with the man whose fingers were stained with ink, a hazard of his trade. The pastor introduced himself and Rev. Chapman as the leaders of a group of missionaries headed toward the Osage lands.

"You don't say," Mr. Woodruff said. "Now that's news my readers will want to hear about. I thought you'd likely have a story for me."

Then with a somewhat dramatic flourish, he pulled a small note book and pencil from his pocket while taking a seat in the only available chair. Wetting the pencil lead, he made a brief notation in his book, and then for the next half hour, he questioned the missionaries about their plans.

Mr. Woodruff had been in Arkansas Territory for less than a year, but he was knowledgeable about the region. The missionaries plied him with questions about the Indians. Was it true that warfare was a constant problem?

"Well, I wouldn't say constant," Woodruff replied. "Things have been fairly quiet for the last several months. Fort Smith has helped some, though there's talk of needing a fort further up river. And it's not all the tribe who's inclined to making trouble. Just a few young bucks with something to prove. They're always looking for a fight."

"We were told there was a peace treaty in place," Rev. Chapman said. "Don't the Indians honor it?"

"In their way, they do," Woodruff smiled. "Chief Pawhuska visited President Jefferson back in '08 and signed a treaty with the United States. But there's no such treaty between the Osages and the Cherokees, or the Pawnees for that matter. The Pawnees don't have a treaty with anyone."

"So the Osages won't harm American citizens?" Rev. Vaille pressed.

"Not deliberately," Woodruff replied. "But now if a white man gets in the way of one of their bullets, well then it's his own fault if he gets hit."

"But can't the chiefs control their warriors?" John Spaulding asked. "Isn't this Pawhuska able to keep the peace?"

"Well, old White Hair – that's what Pawhuska means in their language – is already gone to the 'happy hunting ground.' He was very much venerated by the tribe and he was able to control the young ones fairly well. But his son, also called White Hair, doesn't have the same control. In fact the tribe is more or less split into three groups with three chiefs. Big Tracks is the youngest but it's Claremont's son that is most likely to stir up trouble."

"Big Tracks' village is at Three Forks," Rev. Chapman said.

"That's right," Woodruff agreed. "Claremont's is further up the Verdigris River and Pawhuska's is in Missouri on the Osage River."

"We met Pawhuska when we visited the Osage River village in Missouri," Chapman said. "He's a fairly young man himself. I thought his name of 'White Hair' seemed odd when

Chouteau told us that. But I suppose he was named for his father."

"Well, he probably chose the name himself as his adult name," Woodruff answered. "Males of the tribe usually have a birth name and then an adult name – something that is significant to them." He chuckled and leaned back in his chair.

"Pawhuska, the elder got his name because of the white wig he wore," he said, then waited for everyone's reaction.

"I didn't know the Indians were inclined to wear wigs," Rev. Vaille said.

"No, normally they're not," Woodruff answered. "But Pawhuska took a wig off an American officer in a battle in Ohio back in '91. Since it saved the man from being scalped, he thought it had magic – or 'good medicine' as they say. So he wore that wig for the rest of his life believing it would keep him from being scalped. And I guess it worked, because he never was."

Amanda's eyes grew big as the printer spoke. Then she snorted with laughter and as the other missionaries realized what she was laughing about, they joined her. Chief Pawhuska had worn Benjamin Knowles' white wig! The story the captain had told them in Cincinnati had been a true story after all.

Of course, Mr. Woodruff as well as the men who had met them in St. Louis had not heard Benjamin Knowles' war story so with everyone talking as once those who had heard it explained their sudden laughter.

"Well I'll be jigged," Mr. Woodruff laughed. "I've never heard that one. I'll have to ask Hugh Glenn about it when next I see him. You've just given me another article for the *Gazette*. I thank you kindly!"

The printer was still chuckling about the white wig as he bid the group goodbye and returned to his newspaper office.

CHAPTER FOURTEEN

Little Rock, Arkansas Territory
June 23, 1820

The following day, the keelboat crew hauled in its anchors
and the rowers pushed the boat against the current of the
Arkansas River. Despite the continued heat, the passengers felt a
sense of excitement as they neared the Little Rock. They were
now within just days of their final destination.

Passing through the low-lying delta lands, they witnessed
slaves working in the rice fields. The institution of slavery
would require another cultural adjustment for the New
Englanders. Since reaching Louisville, their encounters with
slavery had increased as they journeyed further south.

Negro stevedores were common along the waterfronts of
the small river towns and though Captain Douglas owned no
slaves, other riverboat captains did. Clarissa had noted many
Negroes manning the oars of the keelboats and flatboats they
passed in the southern waters of the Mississippi.

Still, it was not a practice any of the missionaries expressed
comfort with and some, such as John Spaulding and William
Vaille, were quite vocal in their opposition. Mr. Spaulding had
turned away in disgust after watching a group of Negro children
working alongside adults in one field. Alice had seemed
alarmed at his reaction.

"John, please," she said softly as she followed him from the
boat's port rail. "Don't stir things up again."

Clarissa and Amanda watched them cross the boat's deck to
the starboard rail, their heads together in conversation. Clarissa

looked at the young cook and raised an eyebrow in a question mark. Amanda was an extremely gregarious girl, much more so than Clarissa, and she often knew things about her fellow missionaries that Clarissa wouldn't have dared to ask about.

The red-haired cook leaned closer to Clarissa and said in a quiet voice, "Miss Eliza told me that Mr. Spaulding was dismissed from a school in New York because he was caught teachin' three Negro students. Even though he had separated them from the other students, many of their parents were quite alarmed about it. When he refused to remove the Negro children from his class, he was fired."

The two women watched as Mr. Spaulding slipped an arm around his wife's shoulder. Such contact was not considered appropriate in public, but Alice was clearly distressed.

"Apparently Mr. Spaulding gave the school officials a good piece of his mind," Amanda went on. "They in turn vowed to keep him from findin' another position anywhere in New England. The Spauldings were quite desperate by the time Rev. Vaille offered him a job at the mission."

"Given Rev. Vaille's inclinations toward slavery, I'm sure he was eager to hire Mr. Spaulding," Clarissa said.

"As sure as certain," Amanda agreed. "Mrs. Chapman has said that Rev. Vaille may endanger the mission if he is too insistent on resistin' slavery. They say even the Cherokees here in Arkansas Territory hold Negro slaves."

While Rev. Vaille had insisted upon acceptance of the Indian's cultural differences, he was less inclined to take such a tolerant attitude toward slavery. A staunch abolitionist, he expressed his anti-slavery beliefs strongly after his scripture reading that very evening.

His comments sparked a debate among the men of their group. The ladies were not expected to hold, and certainly not to express, views on such issues. But they listened with interest after they had seen the children put to bed. No one defended slavery, but there were differing opinions about involving themselves and their mission in this national debate.

"We'll likely encounter slavery among the Osages," Rev. Chapman stated. "Though the slaves they hold are usually Pawnees or Comanches they have captured in battle. Slavery is

an old and pernicious institution. As much as we abhor it, it's
unlikely we shall change it."

"But surely education will make a difference to the
Osages," Abraham Redfield argued. Though the 21-year-old had
been hired as the mission buildings manager, he often expressed
a passion for educating the Indians.

"Education will hardly suffice," Dr. Palmer countered.
"Most of the slaveholders of the South are educated men. It's
Christianity that will change the heart and ways of the Indian."

"And many of those Southern slavers are pillars of their
church," Rev. Vaille returned sharply, "and they will quote the
Apostle Paul to justify their actions."

"The best course for us will be to tread lightly in this area,"
Rev. Chapman interrupted. "We must not jeopardize our
mission by involving ourselves in political issues."

"It's not political," John interrupted, his face growing red.
"It's a moral issue. We must speak out against it."

"It'll be seen as meddlin' by our neighbors," Alexander
Woodruff put in with a shake of his head. "Best stay out of it."
A man of few words, it was rare for Woodruff to enter into any
conversation. The thin set of his lips told Clarissa he found the
discussion upsetting.

The blacksmith's words seemed to surprise the other men,
given his usual reticence to offer his opinion. Rev. Chapman
nodded to the burly man and again stated, "We will not
jeopardize this mission before it has even begun. Our calling is
to bring the Osages to Christ. And that is what we will work to
do. Is that understood by all?"

All the missionaries, including the women nodded. Clarissa
looked around the room at the others. It was a rare occasion for
them to have such a strong difference of opinions. Most of the
time, their interaction was amiable and relaxed.

She noted that only one of them seemed rebellious toward
Rev. Chapman's decision. Only John Spaulding refused to nod
his agreement. And that left Alice with a very worried look in
her eyes.

Captain Douglas' keelboat reached Little Rock the
following afternoon. His passengers found Little Rock, like

Arkansas Post, to be a town with growing ambitions. Its founders were determined to make it the territorial capital and eventually the state capital.

The streets, though dirt, were laid out in neat grids leading away from the river and many business establishments lined them. As the keelboat docked, the passengers scanned the south shore of the river and noted more than one hotel and a few boarding houses. The sound of construction vied with the usual waterfront noises.

Mr. Pennywit informed them at dinner that they would need to quickly make arrangements for their accommodations in Little Rock. The captain would offload their trunks and supplies as soon as possible. He would not risk being caught upriver with water levels dropping in the rainless heat.

The Chapmans and the Vailles went ashore directly after their meal in search of room and board for their group. The other missionaries set about to get all their belongings packed. Clarissa and her three roommates could barely move about their small cabin as they worked to fill their opened baggage. Though she had bought only a few items along the journey, Clarissa struggled to get all of her belongings back into her brassbound trunk. Within just a few minutes Mr. Pennywit arrived with a couple of roustabouts to carry their baggage up to the dock.

In a matter of two more hours, the keelboat was preparing to pull away from the Little Rock wharf. Captain Douglas truly wanted to spend no more time than necessary this far upriver. As the anchors were lifted, the missionaries were laughing among themselves at the rather unceremonious way that they had been deposited at the waterfront.

Rev. Chapman had hired stevedores to unload the tools they had purchased in St. Louis to use in building the mission. He had secured warehouse space to store these items until they set out by flatboat for the Three Forks area. It had taken some effort to move the large anvil Mr. Woodruff would use in his blacksmith forge at the mission.

Mr. Pennywit had taken a moment on the wharf to shake hands with all of them, even the children, as he bid them goodbye. He had been a good and helpful friend to them on their journey and the missionaries expressed their thanks and their regrets that he could not go with them all the way to their final destination. But he promised them that someday he would own one of those new steamboats and he would come to visit them in it. They all wished him well.

Clarissa watched as the keelboat pulled away. It was almost as frightening as when this same boat had pulled away from the dock in Pittsburgh. That seemed like a lifetime ago and felt just as final. They were cast upon the edge of the wilderness, losing this one last familiar thing – Captain Douglas' keelboat – and the last connection to home.

CHAPTER FIFTEEN

Little Rock, Arkansas Territory
July, 1820

It took over a week for the missionaries to secure two flatboats for the men and their supplies and even then their journey onward could not begin. River levels were so low now that few boats would venture further upriver. It was too easy to get stranded on one of the many sandbars in the Arkansas River. Though the Arkansas was the largest of the Mississippi River's western tributaries, it still went almost dry in some locations during the late summer.

The family had taken rooms at a respectable looking boarding house built of rough-hewn lumber not far from the river. The woman who ran it was a widow with two young sons who kept the place scrupulously clean and served decent meals.

For the first few weeks of their stay in Little Rock, the missionaries had enjoyed exploring the town and had engaged the services of a laundress to clean their clothes. Cleanliness had been woefully difficult during the long journey.

The heat continued unabated into their third week and they would often sit in the rocking chairs out on the wide front porch in the evenings, for sleeping was difficult in the warm rooms on the second floor of the house. Clarissa was still sharing a room with the other single women. The small rooms of the boarding house were almost as cramped as their cabins on the keelboat, but they were used to it by now.

At least the boarding house had a bathing room with a full size tub where the women could have a bath. The men took to visiting the local barber who offered hot baths as well as a shave and haircut. Mrs. Woodruff jokingly said that she had forgotten what a fine looking bunch of folks they all were. Clarissa felt truly clean for the first time in a long time and that made her dread what living conditions at the mission might be like.

By the third week in Little Rock, the men were growing restless and eager to be on their way to the mission grounds. During many of their evenings they gathered around the large dining room table where their meals were served, studying crude maps of the Three Forks region or drawings that Mr. Redfield had made for how the mission would be laid out and constructed.

They spent hours calculating how much lumber would be required. There were no sawmills in the area so they would be felling the timbers themselves and building basic log structures. Redfield, Mr. Fuller, Mr. Woodruff and the Requa brothers all had construction experience and would be invaluable in getting the mission built from the ground up.

Rain fell at the end of August and gave them a break from the incessant heat. It also brought a rise in the river level. At last, after a month in Arkansas Territory, the crew and pilot they had hired for the journey to Three Forks were ready to pole their flatboats upriver.

The entire mission family gathered at the waterfront to see the men off. Rev. Vaille and John Spaulding would remain in Little Rock because they did not want the women and children left without some male protection.

John Spaulding had ruefully volunteered to remain behind. "I would be little good with an ax or cross saw," he explained as he pushed up the spectacles on his nose. "Dr. Palmer would be sorely taxed to keep me pieced together with such tools in my hands."

Rev. Vaille had built a church in New England, but only by raising the funds and supervising the progress. He had no real construction experience either and so he also had been selected to remain in Little Rock. Rev. Chapman's knowledge of construction was rudimentary, but he was simply too eager to see the mission started to remain in Little Rock. And Dr. Palmer would make the journey because there would likely be no physician in the area and the rough conditions might make his medical assistance necessary.

The two flatboats they had secured were vastly different from Captain Douglas' keelboat. True to their name, they were squat and simple in construction with only a single deck. The mission's goods and supplies were stacked on the flat deck, covered in canvas to protect them from the weather and secured tightly with ropes. There were no cabins for sleeping. Generally a flatboat was tied up at the shore each evening and the passengers and crew either stayed in an accommodating cabin or hostelry or they camped out on the river's edge or on one of the many sandbars in the river.

The idea of camping out made Thomas Chapman and Richard Vaille beg to be allowed to travel with the men. They were sure they could be of help in building log cabins. "Please, Papa," Thomas begged one last time, grasping his father's hand in both of his.

The Chapman parents exchanged a look over the boy's head. Mrs. Chapman shook her head slightly, but the message was clear.

Rev. Chapman knelt down on the wooden planks of the wharf so that he was eye to eye with his son. "Thomas, your mother will need you here to help look after your brother and sisters," he explained. "I'm depending on you to take care of things while I'm gone."

Thomas hung his head. He was clearly torn between the idea of camping in the woods or being the man in the family while his father was away. "Yes, Papa," he said.

He looked up at his mother through his lashes and she smiled and gave him a conspiratorial wink. His head came up. His mother made life seem like a grand adventure. Maybe it wouldn't be so bad to stay in Little Rock.

Stephen Fuller had led Lydia a little apart from the rest of the group. "Will you be alright, Lydie," he asked her, dreading the separation from his beloved wife.

"Yes, Stephen, don't you worry none for me," she responded as she clasped his strong, work-worn hand. "You just be taking care of yourself out there in the wilderness."

"We're going to get through this, Lydia," he whispered, leaning closer in to her and smelling the clean soap of her skin and hair. "You'll be better and we'll have a fresh start."

Lydia nodded, her eyes filling with tears. Stephen's eyes filled as well and he couldn't say anything more. Another few months apart from his soul mate seemed almost more than he could bear.

Clarissa watched the exchanging of goodbyes with tightness in her chest. She remembered when her intended, Robert, had come to tell her goodbye – at her mother's insistence she was sure. He had tried to make it sound as if he was bowing out of their engagement because he felt he wasn't good enough for Clarissa. But she had already heard the rumors about him being seen with wealthy Mary Anderson after church on Sunday.

The pain of his betrayal was made all the more acute because Clarissa really had loved him. It had been more than an appropriate match agreed to by their parents. At least for her it had. Now watching the husbands and wives say goodbye brought it all flooding back to her. And it hurt all over again. Had she truly lost all hope of marriage and motherhood?

Even Will Requa and Susan seemed to be spending a little extra time in their goodbye. Susan had never hidden her interest in the older Requa brother, though Clarissa couldn't see much difference between him and George. Certainly nothing that would recommend him over his younger brother.

As she watched Mr. Requa and Susan, George was suddenly at her elbow and she started and blushed because he had just been in her thoughts.

"Well, we men board another boat, Miss Johnson," he said. "Hopefully we won't be taking any dunks into this river. And I haven't *The Navigator* to tell me what lies ahead."

Clarissa turned to smile at him. He wore a lighter coat on this hot summer day than when they had set out from Pittsburgh, but otherwise it was almost exactly the same as when they had talked on that chilly day last April.

"This may be the most interesting leg of the journey then," she said. "For you won't know what lies just around the bend."

"Yes, you're right," he nodded. Then he offered her his hand. "Well, take care while we are gone," he said.

Clarissa shook his hand. "You also," she replied. She almost said she would miss him, but that would not have been appropriate.

She watched him walk down the wharf toward the flatboat with the other men. She was confused in her feelings toward George. He was not of her station, had little education and was not in any way an appropriate match. But "appropriate" had only brought her heartache. Perhaps she should consider something totally inappropriate.

"I will miss you, Miss Johnson," Dr. Palmer's quiet voice interrupted her reverie. Clarissa looked up at the doctor standing beside her. She hadn't realized he had not boarded with the other men. Marcus seemed to realize his words were too personal so he stammered, "I mean, we shall miss all of you and the good fellowship we have had in the Lord."

Clarissa was so astonished that for a moment she was speechless. And considering where her thoughts had just been going, she hardly knew what to say in response to the doctor's words.

"Well," she said, trying to make her brain work. "You all must be careful out in the Osage lands. Don't get in the way of one of their bullets." Immediately she regretted her words. *What a stupid thing to say*, she scolded herself.

But the doctor smiled. "I'll do my best." He tugged at his hat brim and gave a brief bow. And then he turned and walked toward the boat. Clarissa stood with her mouth open, watching him. She couldn't for the life of her remember what she was thinking about before the doctor spoke to her.

Poling the two flatboats upriver awakened muscles that had known little activity while the men had been on the keelboat. Rev. Chapman had hired only a small crew and a pilot for the boats, planning for the missionaries themselves to help in moving the boats upstream.

The current of the Arkansas River was lazy and slow and didn't create much resistance for the boats. They had to be wary of running onto the many sandbars in the river. Their pilot, a wizened little Frenchman, stood at the bow of the first boat and kept them in the main channel of the river, calling out directions in a sing-song voice.

Within the first hour, the men had all shed their coats which were required attire in polite society. Then they were quickly rolling up their sleeves and bending their backs into the rhythmic movement of their paddles and poles. They quickly devised the best arrangement of poles and paddles and the varying strengths of each man.

Though Alexander Woodruff was the oldest of the men, he was also without doubt one of the strongest. Long used to pounding out metal tools on his anvil, he had developed the strength of an ox. He was placed at the bow of the front boat on the starboard side and could easily do the work of Mr. Redfield and Rev. Chapman on the opposite side.

They let the boats drift to shore for a lunch break and a brief nap for each of them in the shade of towering cottonwood trees. When they resumed their work, Mr. Woodruff started a song, Elizabeth Vaille's favorite Irish tune. The other men joined in and they moved from folk songs to majestic hymns as they moved steadily up the river. Their river crew suggested a bawdy bar tune at one point, but a disapproving look from the missionaries squelched the song before it began.

By nightfall, they were tired and sore, but satisfied with their progress. They were a good 20 or 25 miles upriver from Little Rock and were on pace to reach Fort Smith in another few days.

For the missionaries who remained in Little Rock, the much discussed question was how to occupy their time while the men were gone for several weeks, perhaps even months building the mission. Not wishing to be idle – idleness being a tool of the devil – each had looked about for an occupation while in Little Rock.

Amanda had been the first to find employment, taking a job as cook at a hotel near the waterfront within a week of their arrival in Little Rock. She was pleased with the chance to work in a kitchen. It was truly a pleasure for her.

Rev. and Mrs. Vaille met with a young Presbyterian minister who was trying to establish a church in town. They offered to assist him in his endeavors. This was the type of work William Vaille apparently thrived on. He told the young minister that he loved starting a work from nothing and seeing it grow. This was why he had found the mission such an exciting venture.

Little Rock had only a small one-room school and had no need for teachers and could not accommodate more students. So it was agreed that Clarissa and John would continue to teach the children at the boardinghouse. The children had spent the month of August running barefoot and free and it would prove difficult to get them to settle again into a school routine.

The widow who ran the boardinghouse, Mrs. Steadman, offered to allow school in her back parlor in exchange for her seven-year-old son being included in John Spaulding's classes. Joshua Steadman was a bright boy with blonde, almost white, hair and two missing front teeth. His younger brother, three-year-old Gideon, was a good companion for Billy Spaulding, who had turned four in August, and for little Sarah Vaille. Phoebe and Susan kept the younger children occupied during the day, allowing Alice Spaulding to take a job at a milliner's shop just up the street.

Susan had gone nearly every day to the largest general store in town which also served as the post office. Here was where folks sometimes posted job notices. She was hoping to find a position as governess, but there was little demand for such work among the frontier families.

Rachel Chapman was using the time to search for additional supplies for outfitting the mission. They would need furnishings, linens, crockery and cookware and a whole host of sundries to make the outpost livable. She and Martha Woodruff and Lydia Fuller spent much of their days cutting and hemming bed and kitchen linens.

The day after they had seen their men off, the three women sat around the dining table stitching bed sheets. "How I miss Sally," Martha said. "She was a most excellent seamstress. She showed me some of her embroidery once and the work was beautiful. My stitches are shameful in comparison."

"Such a pity that we lost her," Rachel replied. "She would have been a great help to us and I know from interviewing her that this was what she wanted."

"I always thought that she knew, somehow, that she would not arrive at the mission with us," Lydia put in. "She seemed almost satisfied with that or at least accepting of it."

"Yes, there was always a melancholy about her," Martha

agreed, as she stitched slowly. "Sometimes people know when it is their time to meet God."

"Yes," Lydia said softly, her eyes holding a far-away look. "Sometimes you know."

Martha looked at her sharply but before she could ask about Lydia's comment, Thomas Chapman burst into the room.

"You'll never guess who's here to see us," he said to his mother, excitement making his words come out in a big gulp.

"And who would that be?" Rachel asked, reaching up to smooth down her son's rumpled hair.

"It's Mr. Woodruff," he said. "I mean, the Mr. Woodruff from Arkansas Post," he explained, turning to Martha. "Not your Mr. Woodruff."

"Mr. William Woodruff," Rachel said. "And why is he coming to see us?"

"I don't know," Thomas answered. "But he's out on the front porch talking to Mr. Spaulding. He asked about all of you so I said I would come and get you."

"Well, then let's go and visit with him," Rachel said.

The women set their needles in their work and stepped out onto the front porch of the boardinghouse. Mr. Woodruff stood to greet them, doffing his hat at the same time. He did not wear his leather apron but was dressed in a wool suit and looked quite dapper.

"Ladies," he greeted them. "I hope I find you all well."

"We're quite well, thank you, Mr. Woodruff," Rachel answered. They all took seats on the porch rockers and visited for a while. Mrs. Steadman brought out lemonade for everyone and seemed quite impressed that the newspaper editor was visiting her home.

Woodruff explained that he frequently visited Little Rock as it vied to become the territorial capital. His readers were very much interested in the goings-on in town. "I like to keep an eye on things up here," Woodruff said.

He set his empty glass on a low table beside him. "But I came by to see you because I remembered these two fine young men," he said, indicating Thomas and Richard who were seated on the front steps to the porch. "I'm in need of a couple of newsies and I wondered if you two would like the job."

"What's a newsie?" Richard asked.

"He's an enterprising young fellow who will sell newspapers for me," Woodruff replied. "You'd buy my papers from me and then sell them on the street corner at a profit. Whatever you make is yours to keep."

"Can we, Mother?" Thomas asked eagerly.

Rachel looked hesitant. "We'll see," she said in a noncommittal way. "I'll need to speak with Richard's parents first. This can't interfere with your school work."

Thomas looked disappointed that he couldn't start immediately as a "newsie," clearly not really having a true concept of what the job entailed.

"There's no need for it to interfere with schooling," Mr. Woodruff assured Rachel. "Most folks want their paper as early in the morning as possible. And since we're only a weekly right now, it would only involve one or maybe two mornings a week. The boys can sell as many or as few papers as they have time for before the school session begins."

"Well, we'll see," was all Rachel would say.

In the end, the Vailles and Mrs. Chapman agreed to let the boys try their hand at selling papers on the opposite corners of the street where Mrs. Spaulding worked. She could keep an eye on them that way. And so two more of the mission family found employment and the boys took great pride in the 15 to 20 cents they earned each week.

Eliza Cleaver was the only one of the family who did not seem inclined to find an occupation. She was too old for school and she had no desire to be a clerk and no interest in hemming sheets.

Most days she read one of Clarissa's books in the morning and then carried lunch to her sister at the millinery. She would browse the shops around town for awhile and then return to the boardinghouse, bored and pouting because she had no money with which to buy anything.

"She'll not be able to buy anything until she gets a job," Susan whispered to Clarissa when the girl had sighed and headed upstairs to her room. Even though Susan herself had not yet found work, she showed little sympathy for Eliza.

The family in Little Rock had settled into a routine by the

time the men had been gone a few days and part of that routine was to pray for their safety each evening before the children were put to bed.

John had found a map of the territory which prominently marked the Arkansas River. The boys especially liked to study the map and imagine how far the flatboats might have traveled that day.

CHAPTER SIXTEEN

Arkansas River
Late August, 1820

A week out from Little Rock, the men encountered a thunderstorm that brought jagged streaks of lightening, deafening peals of thunder and a hard, driving rain. Jean Baptiste, their pilot, urged them to quickly move their boats to shore and seek shelter off the water.

They were near a tiny settlement called Dardanelle, established by early French settlers and more recently inhabited by a number of Cherokee families. They had stopped at the community trading post that sat near an outcropping of rocks over the river. Here they had purchased supplies and posted letters to the family in Little Rock.

The men pulled their boats into a small tributary known as the Illinois Bayou, tied up the boats to an overhanging tree and sought shelter in a nearby barn. The rain was coming so heavily that they were soaked to the skin by the time they made their way into the dim interior of the wooden structure. It was a small outbuilding, empty of animals at the time, but a couple of stalls filled with fresh hay told them it was still in use.

The main homestead was not in sight of the barn. Jean Baptiste assured them he knew the Cherokee family who inhabited the land and knew them to be friendly and hospitable. They would not mind the use of their barn.

The rain lasted for over an hour and after the storm had passed the woods still dripped as they made their way back to their boats. The heavy smell of the watered earth and the slap of wet leaves under their boots gave the walk back to their boats a somber feel.

The water of the bayou was flowing fast, too fast to try to maneuver the boats through the swirling eddies where it joined the Arkansas.

They decided to camp for the night, trusting the water level to have dropped by morning. It was an evening meal of cold, hard cornbread bought from the trading post at Dardanelle and cloudy water from the bayou. All the wood was too wet to get a fire going for their usual fare of coffee, biscuits and beans.

Thankfully the rain had cooled the air to make sleeping a little more bearable, but the whine of mosquitoes continued unchanged. The men had learned from the first day out of Little Rock to wrap themselves in their wool blankets to keep any exposed skin from being covered with bites that would itch and fester in the daytime heat.

Such uncomfortable conditions made reaching Fort Smith a few days later a welcome relief. The missionaries chose to break their journey here and pause for some rest. Moving the flatboats upriver had proved a daunting task. At times the river was so shallow the boats dragged the sandy bottom and the men were forced to get off the decks and with ropes wade through the water and mud to haul the boats forward.

The missionaries had insisted on keeping the Sabbath, so they had not traveled on Sunday. Yet they were quite weary when they called upon Major William Bradford, the commander of Fort Smith. When he offered accommodations in the barracks they gratefully accepted his hospitality. A troop from the Third Infantry was out surveying for a supply road and their beds were available.

"What a welcome thing a real bed is," Rev. Chapman said as the men prepared to retire that evening. The minister had struggled of late with fever and chills. Having the least amount of experience with physical labor, the work of the journey had taken its toll upon him.

Dr. Palmer and the other men had tried to get him to rest on one of their boats while they moved them upriver, but he had refused to be added weight for them to bear. Wrapped in his blanket he had walked along the shore for the last two days, keeping up with their steady but slow progress. The mission leader would have a chance to rest and heal while at the fort.

"And please keep my papa safe," lisped Leah Chapman as she knelt in a row with her brothers and sister at their bed they shared in the boarding house in Little Rock. It was a nightly prayer for the children and their mother smiled at the earnest faces bowed over hands pressed tightly together.

"Amen," all four chorused and then there was a scramble to get into bed before Rachel dimmed the oil lantern on a table between their bed and hers.

"Sleep well," she said as she made her way to the bedroom door.

"Goodnight, Mother," another chorus of voices said, followed by a ferocious yawn from young James.

Rachel closed the door and made her way downstairs to the front parlor. Most of her companions were either out on the front porch, watching a new moon rise or playing a game of whist at the dining table.

She settled into a wing chair and drew from her apron pocket the letter she had received that day. Rev. Chapman had posted it at the mercantile near Dardanelle and she had read it twice already but would savor it one more time before retiring for the night herself.

The children had expressed their excitement when Miss Comstock had brought the letter after her morning visit to the post office. There had been letters for Mrs. Fuller and Mrs. Woodruff, as well as one from Will Requa addressed to Susan herself. She had been teased quite a bit by Amanda and Phoebe about that and had blushed prettily over it, but had willingly shared the contents of the letter just as the other women had. Whether a few personal comments were left out in the sharing of letters was unknown by any of the others.

Rachel had read every bit of the letter from Papa to the children and then had watched as Mr. Spaulding helped them find on the map where Dardanelle was located. How it helped to trace a finger over the spot and know their men had made it safely that far.

She pulled the letter once again from its envelope and

opened the carefully folded pages. Her husband's florid script brought a smile to her face. It told of his bold, but impatient temperament, and his sometimes reckless determination.

"It was sure good to hear from our men," Martha commented from where she sat on a nearby settee in the parlor. She too had the open letter from her husband on her lap.

"Yes," Rachel agreed. "If I know my husband, he is pushing those men up that Arkansas River. If anyone can build a mission compound in the wilderness it is Rev. Chapman."

"He seems quite a determined man," Martha agreed. "I can tell you like that in him."

"It was what attracted me to him," Rachel confessed. "My parents did not approve of the match, of course, he being a middle-class minister. But he had my heart from the first hello. I would follow him anywhere."

Martha nodded as if she understood the sentiment perfectly. The two women sat in companionable silence, once again perusing the love letters they had received.

The glow of the candle lamp in the parlor cast a square of color through the window onto the porch outside where dusk was falling. Alice and Eliza were seated together on a wicker settee working to refashion one of the girl's bonnets with bits of ribbon left over from the millinery shop where Alice worked. John sat on the steps reading a book, a favorite pastime for him, and Rev. and Mrs. Vaille sat together in the swing at the other end of the porch.

Behind them in the shadows, Clarissa sat in a rocker, observing the other missionaries but not taking part in their conversation. She had halfway hoped there might be a letter for her when Susan distributed them this morning. But neither George nor Dr. Palmer had written and she chided herself for expecting it.

She had posted letters to her family in Connecticut when the keelboat had stopped at Cincinnati, St. Louis and Arkansas Post. And since they would be in Little Rock for a few months, she had also written to let them know that they could respond to her here.

She had missed her family as they had journeyed west, but tonight seemed particularly lonely, knowing it could be a few more months at least before she would receive a letter from anyone back home.

She refused to let herself imagine that Robert might write. Her mother would never share her address with him. She had tried not to indulge in the fantasy that he had realized in her absence that he really loved her and would follow her out to the wilderness to win her back. Knowing that would never happen made her even more melancholy on this fall evening and a tear slipped down her cheek. She wiped it quickly away, hoping the watchful eye of Asie Vaille had not seen her.

Clarissa sat quietly for a moment, composing herself so she could say goodnight to her companions and make her way upstairs to bed. She trapped a sigh before it could escape. She had fled her hometown and the wagging tongues of gossip to escape her past, but now her future stretched out before her like an expanse of untamed prairie and it seemed lonely indeed.

After their rest at Fort Smith, Rev. Chapman was recovered enough from his fever that he was ready to press on upriver. Major Bradford assured them that travel would be much easier to the mouth of the Illinois River, for he had a corps of his men working to clear the river of debris.

It was his goal to clear the Arkansas all the way upstream to Three Forks and downstream to Little Rock. By next year he hoped to have made the river passable for keelboats or even the new steamboats that were beginning to ply the rivers.

The men restocked their supplies from the fort's sutler and set out at dawn almost a month after they had left Little Rock. Passing the mouth of the Poteau River which joined the Arkansas below the bluff where Fort Smith sat, they now entered the least inhabited section of Arkansas Territory.

The Poteau was a clear and fast flowing river, unusual in that it flowed from south to north out of the Ouachita Mountains which Jean Baptiste pronounced Wash-i-tah. The old mountain range rose to the south in undulating folds of multiple shades of blue. The morning was cool and progress was made easier with the river cleared of debris.

For the next few days, they passed few inhabitants as they ventured further into the land of the Osages and the Wichitas.

Occasionally they would see a small hunting party on a trail that followed the river. Their pilot told them that most of the Indians would be hunting further west at this time of year. The migrating buffalo of the plains would have ventured into the region as they moved southward for the winter.

After a week they reached the falls on the Arkansas which Jean Baptiste called "La Cascade." In times of low water, the almost seven foot descent of the river was completely impassable. Small craft could be carried around the falls on shore, but large craft would be stranded at the falls until the river level rose.

When the heavy mission flatboats reached the falls, water levels were high from recent rains. The men checked that their supplies were well secured and then pressed into the white water, working hard against the rushing current. They were soaking wet with water and sweat from the effort, but grinned at each other at the thrill of working through the rough stretch of the river. Exhausted from the effort, they cut their day short and sought shelter and supper around a campfire on shore above the falls.

The next day they arrived at Three Forks. Here the Verdigris and Neosho Rivers flowed into the Arkansas within a mile of one another making the area a natural rendezvous and gathering place. A number of fur trading outfits lined both sides of the Verdigris which was the middle river of the three.

Jean Baptiste told them Three Forks was about the only American settlement on the Arkansas west of Fort Smith. Still the domain of the fur trapper, few farmers had yet moved into the region. It remained a land of the Indians disputed over by the Osages, Cherokees, Chickasaws, Wichitas and Pawnees.

Though the mission was to be built along the Neosho River, the missionaries pulled their flatboats into the mouth of the Verdigris and pushed upriver to a rock ledge where boats could be tied to metal stakes driven into the soft sandstone. Above the landing site stood the trading post of Nathanial Pryor. Rev. Chapman planned to meet with Pryor before going to the mission site.

The men stepped from their boat onto the river bank and climbed a short distance up the shore. It was mid afternoon and the fur trading community was alive with activity. Besides Pryor's post, there were several other trading outfits strung along the riverbank.

Rev. Chapmen led the way to Pryor's log warehouse. Like Chouteau's in St. Louis it was a low-slung building with few windows, making it dark and gloomy with the heavy smell of the hides that were stacked to the ceiling. Light from a few lanterns, burning smoky bear oil with its own unpleasant scent, illumined the interior.

As the missionaries stepped inside, their river crew made their way further up the shoreline to Colonel Hugh Love's post where they knew whiskey was one of the trade commodities available. Dr. Palmer watched them hurry toward their goal, shaking his head over their eagerness to indulge their appetite for alcohol. If this stop was like their week in Fort Smith, the men would beg him for a cure for a massive headache the next day.

Inside the warehouse a young clerk sat perched on a stool behind a long counter. He appeared to be working on a ledger, a guinea feather pen in his hand. He wore a chambray shirt, open at the throat. His dark hair was cropped close as if he were trying to keep it from curling and making him looking even younger than he was. He looked up at the men when they entered.

"May I help you?" he asked.

"We're here to see Captain Pryor," Rev. Chapman said. "Is he in?"

"Yes," the young man answered, looking the men over for a moment. Then turning to the back of the warehouse he called out, "Captain, you have guests."

After a few moments, the captain stepped out from behind a deer-hide curtain that separated the two rooms of the warehouse. He was pulling on a coat of black wool as if he were preparing to greet important company. He stood about six feet in height and was himself fit and trim. His dark hair, graying only slightly at the temples, and his deeply tanned skin told of his Native American ancestry for Governor Clark had told them Pryor was a descendent of the great chief Powhatan of Virginia.

"Gentlemen," he greeted the mission brothers. "We've been expecting you. You've made good time." He extended a hand and greeted each man as Rev. Chapman made introductions.

"But how is it that you were expecting us at this time?" Chapman asked.

"Ol' Bogey knew you were at Fort Smith and heading upriver. He just arrived himself two days ago after a run to Little Rock. He was probably just a day or two behind you and then passed you at the fort," Pryor explained.

"Nothing gets by Joseph Bogey," he went on. "He operates the post right at the mouth of the Verdigris. Been here the longest of any of us. Came back in '06, I believe. Isn't that right, Samuel?" He turned to his trade partner who nodded.

"I think we did meet him at Fort Smith," Rev. Chapman stated. "He made good time to get here two days before us."

"Bogey's a master of the river," Captain Pryor agreed. "He makes a regular run to Little Rock for supplies and news. He could probably navigate the river in his sleep. Some say he does!" Pryor laughed at his own joke and Samuel grinned.

"Are you heading right up to the site?" Pryor then asked.

"We'd like to," Rev. Chapman answered. "But we've heard there have been some troubles between the Osages and Cherokees. We thought we'd stop in and check with you first. See if there were any problems we should know about."

Pryor hesitated for a moment, exchanging a look with Samuel. "No, it's been quiet for a while," he said. Dr. Palmer had the impression there was more that Pryor wasn't saying.

"Would you like me to travel up to the site with you?" Pryor asked. "We could leave first thing in the morning."

"That might be a good idea," Rev. Chapman said. "If there are Osages in the area, I'd like to have you with us. We were wondering, too, if you would travel with us to Claremont's village. We know he trusts you and since you helped negotiate with him to allow the mission, we'd like you to introduce us. We don't want to raise any suspicions among the Osages."

"Be glad to go with you," the captain agreed. "Shall we leave at first light tomorrow? You're welcome to bed down out back this evening. And Miz Bradshaw will likely offer you some supper. Her husband's a trapper and they have a cabin just up the way."

The missionaries agreed to Pryor's suggestions. They walked for about two miles before finding the Bradshaw cabin. But the meal Mrs. Bradshaw served – fried prairie chicken, biscuits with freshly churned butter, and peas from her garden – was worth the walk. They slept well under a crisp fall sky with stars that seemed almost close enough to touch.

Rounding up their crew the next day from the various locations where they had dropped from drunkenness took some time so it was past first light when they set out the next morning. Pryor laughed at the uselessness of the crew for the first hour of travel for they could barely hold up their heads. Dr. Palmer was disgusted by the sight of them for he knew what the excessive consumption of alcohol would eventually do to their health.

The Neosho River was true to its name for as Pryor explained the word *neosho* in the Osage language meant clear water. It flowed out of the Ozark Mountains over a rocky bed and its water was far more drinkable than that of the very muddy and salty Arkansas.

They reached the mission site late in the afternoon as the shadows were stretching across the land. The crew secured the boats, and then with the missionaries and Captain Pryor they scrambled up the rocky riverbank. Thick cane, standing as tall as the men, lined the shore and Jean Baptiste had to pull out his long knife and hack through it. They walked single file through the cane for about 100 feet before coming into the open prairie.

The tall prairie grasses waved gently in the breeze. Dried to the color of ripe wheat, the grass was tipped in orange and stretched out as far as the eye could see.

Stephen Fuller squatted down and dug his fingers into the soil. He pulled up a clump of rich black dirt and hefted it in his hand. "Good soil, but a little heavy," he said. "Should be adequate for crops."

"And there's a sweet water spring not too far," Rev. Chapman said. "So we'll have good water as well."

"There seems to be one thing missing," Abraham Redfield stated, looking out across the land where they planned to build the log cabins for the mission compound.

"What's that?" Chapman asked.

"Trees," Redfield responded.

George and his brother Will began to laugh. On the 1,000 acres of land granted to the mission, only a thin line of small trees along the river could be seen. They would surely have their work cut out for them.

CHAPTER SEVENTEEN

Little Rock, Arkansas Territory
September 22, 1820

"Mother," Thomas Chapman called as he entered the door of the boarding house. He was returning from his morning work of selling the *Arkansas Gazette*. The screen door slammed behind him as he hurried into the dining room where Rachel sat visiting with Mrs. Steadman.

"There's someone here to see you!" The boy skidded to a stop by her chair.

"Don't let the screen door slam, young man," Rachel scolded gently with an apologetic look toward their landlady. "And did you shut the main door or leave it standing open?"

Thomas briefly rolled his eyes, but stopped immediately at his mother's frown. "I left it open because the man who wants to see you is standing on the porch. It would be rude to close the door in his face."

"It would have been more polite to invite him inside," Rachel responded. She stood and turned to Mrs. Steadman. "Please excuse my son," she said.

The landlady chuckled. "No need to apologize," she said. "I have sons. I know how it is."

Mrs. Steadman and Rachel followed Thomas to the front door where a bear of a man stood waiting with a grin on his leathered face. He had a full head of white hair and a long white beard and wore the clothes of a trapper.

"He looks like Father Christmas," Thomas whispered.

When the ladies came into view, he pulled off the beaver

hat he wore and gave a polite bow. "I am seeking Mrs. Epaphras Chapman," he said in an odd combination of a backwoods twang with a French accent.

"I'm Mrs. Chapman," Rachel said as Mrs. Steadman opened the door and invited the man inside. Rachel clutched at her stomach as if she feared hearing bad news.

"I am Joseph Bogey of Three Forks," the man said as he stepped into the front parlor of the boarding house. "I bring news of your husband and the other men of his party."

"Have you seen our men?" Rachel asked as she moved to take a seat.

"May I serve you tea, sir?" Mrs. Steadman interrupted.

"Tea, no," Mr. Bogey replied, taking a seat where the women indicated. He made the chair seem small. "But perhaps some coffee, eh?"

"Certainly," the landlady responded. "I'll bring it right out."

Mrs. Steadman alerted her other guests of the arrival of Mr. Bogey as she made her way to the kitchen. Curious, they all moved toward the front parlor. Clarissa and John had been preparing for class in the back parlor, but allowed the children some play time with Phoebe while they went to visit with their guest.

Martha, Lydia and Susan hurried from the kitchen where they had been clearing away the dishes from breakfast. Martha turned back to assist Mrs. Steadman with the refreshments. Eliza had just come in from a visit to the outhouse and quickly removed her cloak to join the other ladies as they made their way to the front room. Rev. and Mrs. Vaille were away, calling on a sick parishioner of the church and Alice and Amanda had already left for their jobs in town.

When all were seated in the parlor, Joseph Bogey resumed his news. He seemed to love an audience and was pleased with the interest his visit had stirred.

"I met your men at Fort Smith," he told them as he perched on the edge of the dainty chair as if he was afraid to put his full weight on it.

"Did you find them well?" Rachel asked quickly.

"As well as could be expected," Bogey responded, but

quickly amended his statement when he saw Rachel's look of alarm. "They was just plum tuckered out. It ain't easy pushing two flatboats upriver."

The group pressed Bogey for details and he shared his meeting with the men at Fort Smith and then assured them that they had arrived safely at Three Forks. Mrs. Steadman and Martha brought in refreshments and the conversation turned to conditions in the Osage lands. Joseph Bogey was a wealth of information about the frontier.

Bogey told them he had been the first to establish a trading post at the junction of the three rivers though the French, when they held the territory, frequently used the point as a rendezvous place for trading with the Indians.

"Place is crowded now," Bogey stated, accepting another cookie from Mrs. Steadman. "Mighty fine cookin' ma'am," he grinned, unabashed by the fact that he had already eaten five of her molasses cookies.

"What is the population at Three Forks?" John asked.

"Must be 40 or 50 people there now," Bogey said, shaking his head. "When Big Tracks returns from the hunt, there'll be another three -- four hundred Osages at their village. I'm thinking to move further west if it gets any more crowded."

The missionaries gave each other looks of amusement. Such sparse population could hardly be called crowded by New England standards, but they were quickly learning what a different perspective existed out in the wilderness.

"Does Big Tracks have 300 hunters?" Susan asked, her eyes big with wonder.

"Oh, no," Bogey said. "That's the whole village. They all move west for the buffalo hunt this time of year. The men kill the beasts, but the women skin them and clean them. Pick the bones clean and use the bones too."

Clarissa's stomach turned at the thought and she set down the cookie she was about to bite.

"We've heard there has been some fighting between the Osages and other tribes," John said.

"The Osages love a good fight," Bogey said, rubbing his hands together as if he loved a good fight too. "But it's been quiet through the summer. Nothing much happening since Mad

Buffalo attacked a group of Cherokee hunters down on the Poteau River last winter. Pryor paid for that one, he did."

"You mean Captain Pryor?" Rachel asked. "How was he involved?"

"Well Pryor, he's some kin by marriage to Mad Buffalo. The Cherokee call Mad Buffalo Skiatook, which means 'big man.' Pryor's wife is Osage, you see, and she is from the same clan as Mad Buffalo."

Clarissa and Susan exchanged a look. Was this Mrs. Pryor the only Mrs. Pryor or was there another one in St. Louis?

"Mad Buffalo is Chief Claremont's son and rather a hot-tempered one. There's been bad blood between him and a Cherokee named Walter Webber for some time. It flares up now and then. Mad Buffalo and a group of Osages encountered a Cherokee hunting party down on the Poteau. Since the Osages consider that their hunting ground, they attacked the Cherokees. Killed three of them."

Lydia gasped and covered her mouth with her handkerchief. Fighting was one thing, but killing was another. Clarissa felt a shiver run up her spine.

"Was Pryor with them?" John asked.

"No, but the Cherokees wore the red paint for sure after that. Vowed to get revenge on Mad Buffalo," Bogey explained. "Pryor helped him escape being captured . . . or so that's the talk. Pryor never has admitted to it."

"When the Cherokees couldn't find Mad Buffalo, they took their revenge on Pryor. Cleaned out his warehouse of furs. Would have done worse if the captain weren't such a good friend of Governor Clark. But the Cherokees let it be known that Mad Buffalo was a marked man. He hasn't been seen in the area since then. Most believe he's gone to Pawhuska's camp in Missouri. If he ever comes back . . . well, I wouldn't want to be him. The fightin's liable to start all over again." Bogey smacked his lips in satisfaction, whether from the story or from the sixth molasses cookie was hard to say.

The missionaries were quiet as they pondered Bogey's tale. He took such relish in telling it, Clarissa wondered if he was stretching the facts for the sake of a good story. But even if he was, she knew they all felt concern for the seven men who were building their compound just a few miles from Chief Claremont's village.

The men had spent the first day after their arrival in cutting a trail from the river through the dense cane to the area where the mission buildings were to be constructed near the natural spring. Then for another two days they had unloaded all their supplies from the flatboats.

Jean Baptiste showed them how to use the thick river canes to build a shelter for their supplies and for sleeping. They set the cane in a large circle and used a sapling driven into the ground for a center lodge pole. They covered the cane, bound by dried vines, with the large canvas tarps that had protected their gear during their travel upriver.

After their river crew had helped haul their supplies to the shelter, they were dismissed and headed back to Three Forks with the boats. Until the mission could acquire horses, the men would be limited to travel by foot.

Captain Pryor had offered to procure horses from the Osages who were savvy traders in horseflesh among the tribes of the plains. Pryor and his family lived in a cabin on a creek north of the mission site about half the distance to Claremont's town. Pryor had set out the next day for his home, promising to return shortly with the horses.

In the meantime, the men spent the next few days scouting the area to familiarize themselves with the resources available to them. Will Requa found the river bank revealed a layer of rock that could be used for foundations and fireplaces. Stephen Fuller and Abraham Redfield paced off areas for a barn and corral and George and Alexander Woodruff worked to get their tools sharpened and ready for use.

They chose to burn off the dried grass where they would build their log cabins. Abraham had made the decision to borrow from the Indians the concept of the longhouse. They would build the cabins all attached together under one roof. The married couples and families would have a cabin each. The single men would share a cabin at one end of the longhouse while the four single women would be at the other end for propriety's sake. This would cut down on the number of walls and fireplaces they would need to build and would decrease the amount of wood the construction would require.

The lack of trees on the property would be their first great challenge to overcome. In their scouting forays, Stephen and Abraham had spotted a grove of trees further up the Neosho on the east bank. It was a fairly new stand of pine, just the right size for the logs they would need. But it was not on mission property so they would need to secure permission from the Osages before they could begin to fell the trees.

A few days later Captain Pryor returned on horseback, leading three other mustangs. These were all the horses Claremont was willing to spare to the missionaries. His village had just returned from their fall buffalo hunt and had lost a few horses in the wild melee that a stampeding herd of bison could become.

In the spring, they would forage the prairie for the wild herds of horses that roamed at will across the sea of grass and would replenish their stock then. Or they would simply steal them from the Pawnees, something Pryor said they took great delight in doing. But for now, the Osages, along with most of the plains tribes, were settling into their winter camps and would not venture out into the trackless prairie until spring.

"We're grateful to get these," Rev. Chapman told Pryor when he apologized for not returning with more horses. "Is Chief Claremont open to receiving a visit from us? We want to establish a friendship and trust with the Indians. We also need to secure permission to harvest some trees for our cabins."

Pryor smiled. "The Indians love to receive company just as everyone else does out here in the wild country. They're very hospitable and will put on a feast of fresh buffalo for you. They had a very successful hunt this fall. We can set out tomorrow if you like."

"That would be wonderful," Chapman agreed.

Pryor, Chapman and Dr. Palmer made the journey to Claremont's village. The two New Englanders were unused to riding without saddles and their horses seemed skittish. Marcus was sure he would be thrown before they reached the village, but after a few miles the mustangs settled down.

Coming upon the village, they first saw the smoke rising

from its lodge fires. Claremont's camp was set among a series of ancient mounds. The lodges were set in two half circles on either side of a path that ran east to west. The homes were made from small saplings driven into the ground and bent together at the top. These were covered with small branches, grasses and hides. A hole in the center of the roof allowed smoke to escape from the fire pit below.

The Osages welcomed Rev. Chapman and Dr. Palmer with gracious curiosity. The men were given a place of honor in the lodge of Chief Claremont. Many members of Claremont's clan crowded into the lodge to meet their visitors. Just as the captain had predicted, a lavish feast was spread out before them.

The missionaries recognized some of the foods from what they had tasted at Governor Clark's home in St. Louis. Besides the buffalo, they were served a soup made from pumpkin and roasted pumpkin seeds. The pumpkin was a staple crop for the Osages, along with beans, corn and squash, and had just been harvested from their gardens.

With Pryor acting as interpreter, Rev. Chapman thanked Claremont for allowing the mission and explained their purpose in coming.

Claremont listened politely, but seemed unimpressed with Rev. Chapman's offer to teach the Osages about God or about farming. They already knew about God – *Wa-Kon-Tah*, the Great Creator – and they had no interest in becoming farmers.

"Would you be willing to send your children to our school?" Rev. Chapman asked the chief.

Claremont sat cross-legged across the fire from Dr. Palmer and the minister. Like his people he was tall and lean with a proud, even haughty, visage. He wore the traditional breech cloth and leggings made of deer hide, and moccasins decorated with intricate beadwork. His tattooed chest was bare but he draped a blue and yellow woven blanket across one shoulder. The blanket served as both coat and bedroll. His head was shaved except for the scalp lock that ran from his forehead to the base of his neck.

"My children study with the Little Old Men," he answered and Pryor conveyed his words to Rev. Chapman. "They learn the ancient ways of our people. They have no use for your white talking leaves." Pryor explained that the Little Old Men were the keepers of the oral history and traditions of the Osage.

Claremont paused and took a draw from the long-stemmed pipe he was smoking. "My people are free to choose for themselves. If they want to send their children, I will not stop them."

While not a ringing endorsement of the mission school, Rev. Chapman expressed his gratitude to get this small commitment from Claremont. At least he would not fight their efforts.

Having gotten this concession from the chief, he boldly pressed forward.

"We hope also to see peace in the Osage lands," he stated. "Surely your people want peace as well, for your wives and children. We hope that we can live always in peace together."

Claremont's eyes narrowed as he listened to Pryor translate the minister's words. His smile seemed a little mocking but his words were polite. "You need not fear war from the Osage," he said. "But do not trust the Cherokees."

As the supper continued, the mission director listened closely to his Osage hosts as they conversed among themselves. His stated goal was to learn the Osage language, recognizing that this would not only greatly aid their work but would also create a sense of trust and fellowship with the Indians. He hoped, in time, to translate some children's primers, hymns and passages of Scripture into the native tongue of the Osage people.

Two women, one older and one quite young, waited on Claremont and his guests. Pryor explained that they were both wives of the chief. The older woman was first wife, named Yellowbird, and was Osage. The younger woman was a Pawnee named Whitestar and was a slave-wife. She was very petite, in contrast to the tall Osage women. She rarely raised her eyes while serving the men and clearly took her orders from Yellowbird.

Marcus felt pity for the young woman. He wondered how common the practice of having a second wife was among the Osages. He knew that however much this was a part of the Osage culture it would meet with disapproval from many in their mission party. He did not feel comfortable with it himself.

Captain Pryor seemed quite accepting of the practice, but he virtually ignored the girl as did everyone except Yellowbird. Marcus could not tell if she resented Whitestar or if she was glad to have someone to order about.

The meal had drawn to a close, the missionaries having tried to politely eat at least a little of everything served to them. Chief Claremont offered them his pipe, something Pryor told them was the ending of any important meeting or meal. Rev. Chapman, having experienced the same ritual with Chief Pawhuska in Missouri, bowed his thanks and took a draw on the richly decorated pipe. Then he passed it to Marcus.

The doctor hesitated. Something about drawing the smoke from a burning tobacco leaf into his lungs seemed very unhealthy to him. Though smoking was quite the fashion in New England, even considered a "health" remedy by some, he found it unpleasant. Nevertheless, he did not wish to offend their host so he took the pipe from Chapman and pulled a very shallow draught into his lungs. Then with a cough he passed the pipe to Pryor.

Claremont and the other Osage men in the lodge smiled mockingly at the doctor. The paleface was turning green. With the strange foods in his stomach, Marcus indeed did feel rather sick. He breathed a prayer that he would not embarrass himself and his hosts by losing the contents of his stomach.

Pryor clearly enjoyed the smoking ritual for he leaned back and took several puffs on the pipe before passing it along around the circle. Only the men smoked. The women sat outside the main circle always at the ready to serve the men.

The meeting was drawing to a close when a tall, young Osage man entered the lodge. Yellowbird stood quickly to greet him and pull him into the circle of the firelight. Chief Claremont also seemed very pleased to greet the man.

"This is my son," Chief Claremont explained through Pryor's translation, "Mad Buffalo."

CHAPTER EIGHTEEN

Union Mission, Osage Lands
October, 1820

After two more days at Claremont's home, the men set out
to return to the mission site. Claremont had bestowed upon them
a gift of several buffalo hides which Pryor told them would be
welcome for sleeping under in the coming winter months.

"Hardly need a fire when you have a good buffalo robe to
keep you warm . . . or a good woman," he winked at the other
men.

Rev. Chapman smiled, clearing thinking of his good woman
Rachel. He had often expressed how much he missed her when
they were apart. Few others would follow him out to a mission
outpost, he knew.

"Is it common for Osage men to take more than one wife?"
he asked as they maneuvered their horses across a small stream
lined with cottonwood trees.

"Yes," the captain smiled ruefully. "It's a bit shocking to
you, I suppose. I've gotten used to it myself." Seeing Dr.
Palmer's raised eyebrows he quickly added, "But I don't hold to
it as Colonel Chouteau does. Catherine is my only wife."

"My wife will be glad to hear it," Chapman returned. "I am
worried about how Rachel will react to the treatment of Osage
women."

The men stopped for dinner alongside a creek they had been
following toward the compound. They made their meal from the
dried buffalo meat Yellowbird had given them. They reached
the mission as dusk was falling and the temperature dropped

quickly. The buffalo robes would be good for sleeping under this night.

Having received permission to take logs from the "*spa-vi-nah,*" the men wasted no time in getting started. Abraham notched the trees he had already chosen while waiting for Chapman and Palmer to return. George and Alexander Woodruff made quick work of bringing them down. As on the boats, the strength of the blacksmith proved invaluable. He could bring down two trees to every one that George and Abraham felled.

After the trees were down, Will and Marcus trimmed the limbs. When they had several trees ready, Mr. Fuller and Rev. Chapman lashed them together with ropes then all the men maneuvered them into the river. The horses pulled the raft of logs from the shore downstream to the mission site.

Despite an occasional day of cold rain, the men made good progress on the longhouse. While all but Stephen worked to raise the walls, the farm director split large limbs for a corral fence. A barn would be the next construction project and he was eager to get started with it.

When the exterior walls were halfway up, Will and Alexander began the work of laying stone for the fireplaces. The men had much debated following the Indian method of laying a fire pit in the center of each cabin and leaving a vent hole in the roof, but they had concluded that the women would not like such an arrangement.

About a month after their arrival at the site, the men were finishing their noon day meal when a rider came into view from the north, following the road known as the Osage Trace. With no trees to block their view they watched the man's progress as he slowly approached. He was leading a cow by a tether.

"Hello the camp," the man called rather unnecessarily. The men were already walking towards him, curious about this unexpected visitor.

"Good afternoon," Rev. Chapman greeted him when he reached the compound. He dismounted his unsaddled horse in the manner of the Indian, but he was clearly not a full-blood native.

"*Bon jour*," the man responded with a bow. "I am Joseph Revoir, partner of Auguste Pierre Chouteau. He asked me to pay a call and bring you a gift from his home at Grand Saline."

With that he turned and loosened the tether of the cow, pulling it forward. "She will drop her calf soon and you will have milk," he explained. "I understand you have children with you."

Stephen reached for the cow's rope and rubbed his hand over the docile creature's flanks. His expert eye told him the calf would arrive soon. They'd need to get started on the barn right away.

"We thank you," Chapman said. "Our children aren't here yet, but we will be grateful to have milk for them."

"Butter and cheese will be good, too," Stephen said. "My Lydia's a good hand at making cheese."

Marcus' stomach rumbled hungrily at the thought of fresh butter and a sharp wheel of cheese. The steady diet of beans and buffalo jerky was growing tiresome. The men had taken little time yet to hunt though game was abundant in the area.

Abraham invited Mr. Revoir to their fire for a cup of coffee. For over an hour they visited with the French-Osage trader, eager to learn any news he might have. They were learning that the isolation of their outpost made them as eager as others in the "neighborhood" for outside contact.

"Chouteau returned from St. Louis at the Pumpkin Moon," Revoir said, reckoning time as the Indians did. "He generally spends the winter months here."

"Are the winters cold here?" George asked. "Will we need a good supply of firewood?"

"Not so cold as you are used to I am sure," Revoir responded. "Snow is usually light, but ice can be treacherous. The signs say we will have a mild winter this year though."

Before leaving to continue on to the Chouteau trading post at Three Forks, Revoir promised to add a sow and some chickens to their livestock supply. He mounted his horse, but hesitated for a moment before starting the animal forward. "You might want to keep a watchful eye out," he said. "Mad Buffalo is back. He stopped by Grand Saline a few days ago."

"Yes," Chapman said, "we met him at Claremont's village."

He clearly did not understand the significance of Revoir's words. "The Cherokees will hear of it soon," Revoir said, "if they haven't already. If you see them pass by on the Trace, keep your heads down." Then, as if he had said more than he should, he heeled his horse's flank and started out at a quick trot down the Osage Trace toward Three Forks. The missionaries watched him go, unaware of what his enigmatic warning meant.

Clarissa pulled the gray knitted shawl she wore closer over her shoulders as a draft of cold air blew into the back parlor where she and John were conducting class. Though this room was smaller than the formal front parlor, the two teachers had created two separate classrooms divided by a screen of painted silk. They considered it inappropriate for girls and boys to attend class together.

Clarissa sat in a wing chair while her three girls – Elizabeth Vaille, Abigail Chapman and Leah Chapman – occupied a small settee near the fireplace. John's four students sat cross-legged on the floor, bent over their slates and books. Thomas and James Chapman, Richard Vaille and Joshua Steadman were more willing students today since a cold mist hung in the air outdoors making play outside unpleasant.

The Negro man who delivered firewood for Mrs. Steadman was bringing in a load of wood to stack in the long hallway between the back parlor and the kitchen. He made a regular delivery with his son each week. They were free Negroes of African and French Caribbean ancestry, the missionaries had learned, who lived at the outskirts of town and supplied many residents with wood.

The son, whose name was Louis, looked to be about ten years old. His father always sent him into the back parlor with an armload of wood to stack in a bin beside the brick fireplace. This day, Clarissa noticed that Louis seemed to dawdle at his task. Elizabeth was reading a simple Bible story – David and Goliath – and Louis was quietly listening where he knelt by the wood bin. Elizabeth was the best reader of the three girls and loved to add drama to the stories she read.

"Do you know this story, Louis?" Clarissa asked when

Elizabeth had finished. The girls turned to look at the boy and he seemed embarrassed.

"Yes, miss," Louis answered in an exotic accent that always made the girls giggle. "My granny tells me dem good stories."

Clarissa reached inside her bag of school supplies and pulled out one of the extra readers she had brought from Connecticut. "Would you like to read more stories?" she asked, offering him the book.

Louis stood and appeared ready to reach for the book, but then hesitated. He put his hands behind his back. "I thank you, miss," he said, "but I cannot read."

"Would you like to learn?" John asked, popping his head around the screen before Clarissa could say a word.

And before Louis could answer his father Bertrand stepped into the room from the hallway. "I sure would wish for my boy to learn," he said in that same melodic Caribbean accent.

Clarissa felt a shiver of alarm run through her. If Mr. Spaulding found trouble in teaching Negro children in New York, what would happen here in the South? She wished he wasn't so eager to push against societal boundaries. Rev. Chapman had warned against endangering their mission, yet Mr. Spaulding seemed driven to do exactly that.

"Perhaps we should consult Mrs. Steadman first," Clarissa suggested timidly, hoping their landlady might overrule the plan before it could begin.

"Of course," John agreed, though he looked none too happy about it.

"Yes, miss," Louis' father agreed.

John wasted no time in going in search of Mrs. Steadman. He was explaining his desire to teach Louis as they walked together back into the parlor.

Mrs. Steadman twisted the dish towel she held in her hands and seemed flustered by the situation. "Well," she said with a great bit of hesitation, "I suppose it would not hurt."

Clarissa wished John would realize he was placing Mrs. Steadman in an awkward position – one she was obviously not completely comfortable with. But in his eagerness to challenge convention and his passion to educate any student who wanted to learn, he ignored her discomfort.

Without consulting either Rev. Vaille or Mrs. Chapman, John arranged for Louis to come to the Steadman Boarding House each morning for class. He did agree to have Louis sit at a small work table in the kitchen for his lessons.

Clarissa felt her heart thumping with a nervous sense of alarm at the situation. But realizing that the three girls were looking at her in wide-eyed curiosity, she tried to keep her concern from showing on her face. What would the community of Little Rock think about this school situation? It worried her to think of wagging tongues again directed her way.

As Clarissa expected, Rev. Vaille was heartily in favor of the arrangement while Mrs. Chapman expressed reservations over the noon meal.

"Mr. Spaulding," she said, carefully choosing her words in the presence of the children. "You are aware of my husband's wishes with regard to Southern sensibilities."

"Yes," John said, his voice tight and his jaw set stubbornly.

"If we should have any problems," she went on, "I will expect you to do what is best for the mission."

Neither John nor Rev. Vaille looked happy that Mrs. Chapman was presuming to take a leadership position on this issue. Societal structure said it was not her place as a woman. None of the other women at the table spoke and their opinion was not sought. Clarissa kept her eyes on her soup bowl, trying to appear unconcerned with the matter. Yet she could not help wondering what Alice Spaulding would think of this turn of events.

The subject was not broached by the adults at the supper table that evening. It was Richard Vaille who brought it up, expressing his hope that Louis would bring his slingshot when he came to class the next morning. He had shown it to the boys earlier and they all were envious of his "frontier" weapon.

Both Alice and Eliza shot a look of alarm at Mr. Spaulding.

"Louis?" Alice asked through tightened lips. "The son of the man who delivers firewood?"

"Yes," John answered.

"He's coming to your class?"

Yes." John's clipped answers told everyone at the table that he had no intention of being questioned by his wife – at least not in front of the rest of the mission group.

Alice did not pursue the subject, but she exchanged a look with her sister. Clarissa saw the look and so did Amanda who nodded at the teacher over her teacup. The tension at the table was as thick and steamy as Mrs. Steadman's hearty bread pudding. But no one said another word about it.

Later that evening, Clarissa, Susan and Phoebe climbed the stairs to their room to retire for the night. They parted with Amanda who had moved into the room across the hall and shared the space with Lydia Fuller and Martha Woodruff.

When the women stepped into their bedroom, they could distinctly hear the voice of Alice Spaulding through the thin walls. The Spaulding family occupied the room beside their own.

"How could you, John?" Alice was saying. "You never seem to think about your family when you make these decisions. Do you want to lose your job again? Do you want us near destitution again?"

John's lower voice made his words indistinct, but there was clearly the sound of anger in them.

"I'm of a mind to take Eliza and Billy back to New York," Alice retorted. "Then you can have your precious class with no thought of me or your responsibilities."

"Oh, dear," Susan whispered. None of the women wanted to overhear the conversation taking place next door. In her usual no nonsense manner, Phoebe walked to their door, opened it and shut it forcefully.

Silence fell in the other room. The young mission sisters undressed in the quiet that now reigned on the floor and crept into their beds without saying a word. Clarissa pulled the patchwork quilt on her bed up to her chin and whispered a prayer. "God, help us all," she said, and she felt as if she were drowning again.

CHAPTER NINETEEN

Union Mission, Osage Lands
November 8, 1820

Marcus paused in swinging his ax at the limb of the tree that Abraham Redfield had just brought to the ground with a crash. Only a few more trees would be needed to complete the longhouse. The walls of their snug little barn were also rising steadily. Abraham moved on to the next tree and Marcus and Will worked to clean off limbs.

The weather had turned cooler and autumn's colors were just beginning to transform the land. All seemed well as the men notched the logs and rolled them toward the river, yet Marcus felt uneasy for some reason. His thoughts turned to the young schoolteacher, Miss Johnson, back in Little Rock. He hoped all was well with her . . . and the others of the mission family.

Overhead, the quacking of ducks drew the attention of the missionaries. For the past few days they had seen large flocks of geese and wood ducks as they flew southward. Today, the flock overhead was enormous and filled the sky, almost blocking out the sunlight. Marcus and Will paused their wood chopping to watch in awe as the hundreds of birds flew overhead.

George and Stephen Fuller had chosen to take the day to go hunting and with such an abundance of wild game available, the hunting foray would surely be successful. The down from the birds would make warm mattresses and pillows and the meat would be a welcome break from the supply of pemmican Captain Pryor had provided them.

The men had just turned back to their work when they heard a rifle blast. Before Will could comment to Marcus, however, they heard a cry of pain from Abraham Redfield. Thinking at first that he might have been struck by a bullet they turned to see him fall to the ground, grasping at his leg.

Alexander Woodruff reached the young man first where he writhed on the ground. Blood poured from a wound just above his boot top. But it was not from a bullet. The head of his ax protruded from the wound, its splintered wooden handle still in Abraham's hand. He was clutching it in a white-knuckle grip from the pain.

"Palmer, come quick," Alexander called as he knelt over Redfield.

Marcus dropped his own ax and ran to join the blacksmith. The ax head was deeply imbedded in Abraham's leg, and it looked to have reached the bone. Alexander was about to reach for the splintered end, but Dr. Palmer stopped him.

"No, leave it," he said. "We'll need to pack the wound first." He was already pulling off his coat and lowering his suspenders to pull his muslin shirt out of his waistband. Will did the same as Rev. Chapman came running from the river.

"Get the horses," Will called to him. Chapman turned back to bring the horses up from the riverbank.

Dr. Palmer was tearing his shirt into strips. "Hold him still," he instructed the burly blacksmith. Then, working carefully, he began to gently pack the strips of muslin around the ax head. They were immediately soaked with blood. Will handed him the strips of cloth from his own shirt.

"Do you need more?" Alexander asked.

Palmer shook his hand. "This will do for now," he said. The three men waited for Chapman to bring the horses, their breathing heavy with worry and tension. Abraham was shivering uncontrollably where he lay on the cold ground and low moans escaped through his gritted teeth. Marcus covered him with his own coat.

After what seemed like an interminable length of time, Rev. Chapman arrived, leading the two horses they had been using to haul the logs downriver.

"Should we make a travois for him?" Will asked.

Marcus considered it for a moment, but finally shook his head. "It will take too long and would be useless in crossing the river. Better to get him up on one of the horses."

"I can lift him," Alexander offered. "You should ride with him."

With a nod of agreement, Marcus motioned for Chapman to bring one of the horses as close as possible to where Abraham lay. Then he grasped the mane of the horse and hoisted himself onto its back. The animal was used to the men by now and stood patiently while Chapman held its reins.

"Ready, Abraham?" the blacksmith asked. The young man nodded and set his jaw. His sandy hair fell into his eyes, but the pain he felt was clearly visible in them.

Alex and Will carefully helped Abraham to stand. The blacksmith lowered his shoulder and with a grunt grasped the gangly young man under his knees and arms and as gently as possible lifted him to the back of the horse. With Will's help on the other side of the animal, they managed to get Abraham to straddle the horse.

Marcus saw that the injured leg was still bleeding. "We'll need to move as quickly as possible without jostling him too much," he said. Chapman led the horse while Will and Alexander walked beside it to keep Abraham steady. Will gave a sharp whistle and the other horse followed behind them.

They reached the river and followed the bank to a spot where a wide island filled most of the riverbed. This was the location the men had discovered was shallowest and easiest to ford.

By the time they reached the mission compound, the horse's flank was covered in Abraham's blood. The men helped him from the horse and carried him into the central cabin in the longhouse. They had completed the fireplace and a soddy roof on this cabin. There was no bed, but Will quickly gathered several buffalo robes for Abraham to lie on.

Marcus raced to their supply shelter and frantically searched for his medical kit. They had all had a few minor scrapes and bruises that had required his attention over the last six weeks, but he couldn't recall where he had last stored his bag. It took him a few minutes to locate it, and all the while the doctor's mind ran through a checklist of items he would need to care for Redfield's injured leg. He feared the injury might require that he amputate Abraham's foot. He prayed that would not be necessary.

When he reached the cabin, Will was working to start a fire in the fireplace he had completed only a few days earlier. The blacksmith had left to fetch a bucket of water from the spring. Rev. Chapman was tearing strips of muslin from another shirt to serve as bandages. The quiet competency of his companions helped to steady Marcus and he breathed a prayer of thanks as he knelt beside his young mission brother.

After helping Abraham take a few swallows of whiskey to dull the pain, he set to work on the leg. He removed the man's boot that was soaked with blood and carefully cut away his pant leg. For over an hour, he worked to gently remove the ax head, cleanse the gaping wound and stitch it closed with his long, curved needle. Alexander assisted him by holding the leg still.

Except to cry out in pain when the doctor had poured whiskey over the wound to sterilize it, Abraham bore the procedure in the silence of gritted teeth. He was still shaking from the shock and as soon as Marcus felt he had done all he could to clean and close the wound, he covered Abraham with one of the buffalo robes.

"Will, make some coffee," Palmer instructed the stone mason. "He needs something warm inside. We'll add some more whiskey to help with the pain."

Will nodded and he and Rev. Chapman worked to quickly grind the beans and set the iron kettle over the fire. Marcus was assisting Redfield in sipping the hot coffee when George and Stephen arrived back at the camp, loaded down with both duck and quail from their hunt.

On discovering Abraham's accident, George immediately volunteered to ride to Three Forks for any supplies the doctor might need to care for the injured man.

"We could use more whiskey and cloth for bandages," the doctor said. "And we've used all the liniment I brought with me. Get more of that."

George nodded and was about to leave when Marcus said, "What we really need is ice. It will help the swelling. I don't recall seeing an ice house at Three Forks, though."

"There was ice on the pond where we hunted today," Stephen said. "We can chop some from it and then haul it back here."

"I'll help you with it," Alex volunteered, appearing anxious to be able to do something more. He had often expressed a fondness for all the young men of the mission and told them he thought of them as sons.

"Let's get to it then," Stephen said and the two men bundled back up in their coats and headed out. George took the third horse from the barn and directed it toward the Trace which ran through mission land to the fur trading community. He promised to return as early as possible the next day.

Through the night the men took turns keeping a watchful vigil at Abraham's side. Will had prepared a meat broth after hastily cleaning some of the quail his brother had brought in. Abraham had eaten some of it, but had little appetite. He had developed a fever and his eyes were glazed.

Marcus checked the wound frequently through the night, worried that the swelling was increasing despite the ice packed around it. The wound was an ugly red and continued to seep blood. If gangrene should set in, he would have no choice but to amputate.

The doctor shuddered at the thought. Of all the medical procedures he had undertaken in his short career, amputation was one of the most difficult for him.

His thoughts turned sadly to Sally Edwards. He still felt responsible for her death; a fever should not have taken one so young. It made him doubt his abilities once again. Would everyone he treated die under his care? Why had he chosen medicine instead of the ministry, as he had originally planned? The pressure from his father and his brother to continue the "family business" seemed a poor reason for his choice as he kept his vigil through the night.

An hour later, Rev. Chapman came to take his turn at watch. He laid a hand on Palmer's shoulder, as if reading the doctor's thoughts. "We'll pray," he said quietly so as not to waken Abraham who had fallen into a fitful sleep. "You've done a good job in caring for the wound. The rest is in God's hands."

Marcus nodded. As much as he wanted to have faith right now, his fear of failure made believing for a miracle almost impossible.

In Little Rock, the mission family was dealing with another medical emergency. Lydia Fuller had taken a fever again and was coughing blood. Rev. Vaille had brought the local doctor in to examine her, but he could offer little to help.

"It's consumption," he said quietly to the Vailles and Mrs. Chapman in the hall outside Lydia's room.

"What can we do for her?" Rachel asked.

"There is little known to treat the disease," the doctor stated. "We don't really even know what causes it. A drier and warmer climate can help, but . . ." his voice trailed off.

It was common knowledge that many died from the disease which attacked the lungs of its victims. Consumption was prevalent in the dark and crowded tenements and factories in New England.

"Yes, she was much better during the summer months," Asie Vaille mused. "It's only since it turned so cold that she has struggled with a fever and cough again."

"Keep her as warm as possible," the doctor advised as he snapped his medical kit closed. "Plenty of hot liquids to drink."

"The disease is contagious, is it not?" Rachel asked.

"Yes, but not highly so," the physician replied. "Keep the children away. Any healthy adult should be fine around her. But maintain a clean environment."

"We'll need to inform Mrs. Steadman and everyone in the family," Rev. Vaille stated. "I wonder that Mrs. Fuller wasn't aware of what illness plagued her."

"I believe she knew, as did Mr. Fuller," Rachel commented. "He said as much on the keelboat. But I am surprised that Dr. Palmer didn't recognize her symptoms."

"I think he did," the doctor explained. "Mrs. Fuller probably asked him to keep the matter private. She asked the same of me, but I convinced her that it was necessary to inform you in order to take the proper precautions. She was reluctant to give me permission to tell you. She seems to feel a burden of guilt for it."

"Poor dear," Asie said. "She can hardly be blamed for succumbing to a disease that is so common, especially among the lower classes."

"Will she recover, doctor?" Rachel asked.

He seemed reluctant to answer. Keeping his voice low, he said, "I won't deny that the disease seems fairly advanced, given the amount of blood she is coughing up. But if you get her out on the arid prairie, it may prolong her life." He shook his head sadly. "Eventually she will die from it." At that he took his leave and made his way downstairs.

Rev. Vaille held a meeting of the mission group that evening after the children had been put to bed. Explaining Lydia's situation, he asked first that they join together in prayer for her. Clarissa bent her head and closed her eyes, and saw the dying form of Sally Edwards in her mind. She shuddered with the thought of another of their family dying. A sense of fear could not help but creep into her prayer for Lydia.

"We'll want to take turns in sitting with her," Rev. Vaille said when the prayer concluded. "If we are here in Little Rock for only a brief time longer, we will hope she will improve once we get to the mission site. The doctor seemed to feel it would help her."

Encouraged by his words, the group devised a plan for Lydia's care. Martha, Asie and Rachel would assist her during the work day. Amanda and Alice volunteered to help in the evenings after their workday was completed. Alice, who sat on the opposite side of the parlor from her husband, seemed pointedly eager to spend her evenings at Lydia's side. The others pretended not to notice. John said nothing, but he looked miserable.

That evening Amanda sat beside her bed and helped Lydia sip some hot broth Mrs. Steadman had prepared for her. Lydia ate with little appetite. Her cough was better, but she seemed resigned to her illness and made little effort to fight it.

"Come now," Amanda cajoled her friend. "I know Mrs. Steadman's cookin' is not nearly as good as me own," she said with a wink. "But you best be eatin' every bite or you'll hurt her feelin's."

Lydia smiled wanly and took another sip of the broth. "It doesn't matter if I eat or don't," she sighed. "I'm not going to get any better."

"Now don't talk so," Amanda scolded gently as she took the now empty cup and set it on the bedside table. "You have to get better. Your husband is waitin' for you to join him."

Lydia's eyes welled with tears at the mention of her husband's name. "Stephen will be better off without me," she said with a catch in her voice.

"Lydia!" Amanda reacted. "How can you say such a thing? Stephen would be lost without you. I've rarely seen a man so devoted to his wife."

Lydia dabbed at her eyes with her handkerchief. "He's too devoted," she sighed. "He's given up everything for me and I've given him nothing but worry and medical bills. He longs for a son, but I cannot even give him that."

"You know you are better than ten sons to Stephen," Amanda argued.

"No," Lydia shook her head. "He might say so, but that is only because he has such as good heart. He mortgaged the farm trying to get a doctor to find a cure for me. And when we couldn't make the payments, he was forced to sell it. That farm had been in his family for three generations." She buried her face in her hands, sobbing quietly.

Amanda was silent. She knew the Fullers had sold their land to come on the mission, but she had not realized the desperateness of their situation.

Finally Lydia's tears subsided. "I tried to leave him," the distraught woman confessed in a whisper. "But I lost my courage. I couldn't bear to live without him. But I know . . ." She stopped herself and shook her head sadly. "I know."

Amanda reached for her friend's hands that twisted the sodden handkerchief in her lap. Grasping those hands firmly she said, "Lydia, what I know is that Stephen needs you. Please don't give up. The last letters from the men said they'll be comin' for us soon. The doctor here says you'll be better out on the prairie. You'll start a new life there with Stephen."

Lydia shook her head. "I don't believe I'll ever see the prairie. It's too late." She broke into a deep, hacking cough as if to emphasize her words. Turning her head away, she struggled to regain her breath.

Amanda watched silently. Lydia's resignation seemed as deep and entrenched as the cough that wracked her body. What would encourage her friend and strengthen her faith?

Before she could speak, Lydia turned back to her. Gripping the cook's hands she spoke urgently. "Promise me that you'll look after Stephen," she said. "He'll not eat properly if you don't stay after him. He'll work too hard. He nearly killed himself trying to save me."

"Oh, Lydia," Amanda shook her head.

"Promise me," Lydia pleaded.

"I promise," Amanda agreed. But as she watched her friend drift off to sleep, she felt a sense of dread at what the promise meant.

CHAPTER TWENTY

Little Rock, Arkansas Territory
December 19, 1820

The front door to the Steadman Boardinghouse slammed
shut as Thomas and Richard rushed through the front parlor with
James, Joshua Steadman and Louis following at their heels. Asie
Vaille was just coming down the stairs with Lydia's breakfast
tray and stopped her son in his tracks with three words, "William
Richard Vaille."

"Sorry, mother," he said, skidding to a stop. But his
contrition was short lived for he had exciting news to share.

"There's a keelboat pulling into the wharf," he said.
"Everyone's going down to see it. The barber says it'll be
carrying a crate of oranges!"

The young newsies had in the past two months become a
good source of information about the goings on in Little Rock
and all of Arkansas Territory. Their classmate Louis would
often meet them in town when his father was delivering wood
and walk with them back to the boardinghouse for his lessons.
All five of Mr. Spaulding's students were excited about the
prospect of seeing the cargo unloaded from the keelboat,
especially if it included oranges.

Not since Captain Douglas had brought the missionaries to
Little Rock this summer had a large keelboat made it to the soon-
to-be capital of Arkansas Territory. It was an event that would
bring everyone in town down to the wharf to get the news from

eastern cities, to see the passengers who were arriving and to pick up any cargo and freight they might have ordered.

The general mercantile had placed an order for oranges for Christmas and they were arriving just in time for the holiday.

"Can we go to the riverfront?" Thomas asked the adults who were gathering in the dining room after hearing the boys' news.

Mr. Spaulding smiled at his students' enthusiasm. It surely arose just as much from a desire to get out of their studies as a desire to see a keelboat. After all, Thomas, James and Richard had spent months aboard just such a boat.

"Why don't we all bundle up in our coats and go downtown," he suggested.

Everyone except Mrs. Woodruff, who offered to stay with Lydia, was eager for the diversion. Even Mrs. Steadman, who had just finished setting bread to rise, joined with the missionaries to get their coats for the walk down to the wharf.

They joined with neighbors and others from town who were all making their way toward the port. There was a holiday atmosphere along the waterfront as folks gathered in groups, talking and laughing and enjoying the show of watching the boat's crew pole it up to its pier.

Clarissa found it interesting to be on the other side of watching a boat dock. She now understood why such large crowds had gathered whenever Captain Douglas had stopped at a river port along their journey. The boat represented a connection to folks in the states. Clarissa hoped this boat carried letters from her family back home.

How long ago it seemed since she had waved goodbye from the stage as it pulled away from its stop in Colchester. It was a lifetime ago in some ways.

As she and Susan tried to keep the girls still and out of the way of the crowds, she was swamped with a feeling of homesickness like never before. What had she been thinking to come to this untamed land, leaving behind all that she held dear? For a brief moment she toyed with the idea of buying passage on the keelboat's final leg to New Orleans and then taking a sailing vessel around the coastline back to New England.

But the thought of traveling alone for months was too

daunting even if she had the money to pay for the journey. And would she really want to go back to Colchester to the same wagging tongues and cruel reminders of her failure to secure a suitable marriage? How she had hated the pitying looks from her mother's friends at church or social occasions. The whispers behind her back had been almost unbearable.

As the gangplank was lowered from the keelboat, the crowd grew quiet, waiting with curiosity to see who would de-board and what cargo would be unloaded.

"Girls, be still now," Susan admonished the three young female students. They were dancing in place in excitement, though Clarissa wondered if they really knew what they were excited about. It was simply fun to be away from the boarding house and enjoy a new experience.

From behind her, Clarissa heard the stage whisper of a woman in the crowd. She was speaking to another woman who stood beside her. "Them's those missionaries staying with Mrs. Steadman," the woman said. "Do you know they're teaching the woodcutter's boy – right there in the house with them girls? It's shameful."

Clarissa felt her face grow hot whether from embarrassment or anger even she wasn't sure. *"O, Lord, no,"* she thought. *"Don't let the whispers start here too."*

"Well, what can you expect?" the woman's companion replied. "I hear they're going to try to teach the Osages, too. Everybody knows you cain't learn an Indian nuthin'."

Now Clarissa knew the emotion she felt was anger. Talk about ignorance and being unteachable! Clarissa thought about turning around and saying something to the two gossips, but her natural timidity kept her silent. Her face felt flush and she bit her lip.

"Well, all I can say is they better not be staying around in Little Rock much longer," the first woman added. She seemed to want Clarissa and Susan to hear her words.

The two young missionaries exchanged a look, but neither spoke, not wanting to say anything in front of the girls. Clarissa felt the same heart-pounding dread she had felt when Mr. Spaulding had first offered to teach Louis. *"Oh, please let the men get here soon,"* Clarissa prayed silently.

Dr. Palmer carefully pulled back the bandages from Abraham Redfield's leg while Rev. Chapman held a lamp beside him. For eight days the young man's fever had raged and the ugly wound festered with blood and pus. Marcus had opened the wound and drained and cleaned it again hoping to stave off the threat of gangrene. Today as he checked the wound, he found no seepage. The skin was dry, though still red and puckered. It was the first hopeful sign in the long battle and the doctor felt great relief.

"So am I going to live, Doc?" Abraham asked as he watched Marcus work.

"I think you just might," Marcus grinned.

Will and George turned from the fireplace where they were working to prepare a breakfast of cornmeal mush and fried rabbit, glad to hear the doctor's prognosis.

"It's about time you stopped laying around," George joked. "We're tired of doing all your work."

In the last few days, they had managed to get all the walls and roof completed on the longhouse despite a light nighttime snowfall and unrelenting cold temperatures. They all slept in the snug central cabin, kept warm by a constant fire in the stone fireplace.

Abraham's design had made building the seven adjoining cabins quick and efficient. Just two months after arriving at the mission grounds, they were ready to bring the rest of the mission family to the site.

And now that Abraham seemed truly on the mend, they could get back to Little Rock.

Stephen stepped into the cabin, returning from the barn with a pail of frothy warm milk.

"Sun's out finally," he said. "Might warm up today." He set the milk on an upturned half barrel the men used for a table. Furniture was still lacking in the cabins though they had fashioned a rope strung bed to get Abraham off the cold dirt.

"Let's hope it does," Woodruff stated. "I'm tired of this dreary weather."

The men were helping themselves to breakfast when a voice called outside.

"Hello, the house!"

George stepped to the door to look out. Tying his horse to their corral fence was the fur trader Joseph Bogey. George and Stephen had met him when they had gone into Three Forks to order supplies two weeks earlier.

Bogey was dressed in a massive buffalo robe, leather breeches with fringe and moccasins. He carried the pack of supplies.

"Welcome," George called to him. "You're just in time for breakfast."

"Well that's good timing, indeed," Bogey responded with a grin. "I've brung the supplies you ordered."

His pack was large and clearly weighed much, but Bogey carried it easily. Though nearing 70 years of age, he moved with the quiet ease that characterized the Indians. Long years of "running the woods" as a trapper had given him the grace and stealth of the occasional panther or mountain lion seen in the area.

George opened the door wider to allow him entrance. Bogey stepped inside, lowered his pack and pulled off the beaver cap he wore. "How's the patient?" he asked, nodding to Abraham.

"Much improved today," Marcus answered. "But how did you know we had a patient?"

George had gone straight to the Pryor trading post for the medical supplies the week before and had spoken only to Samuel there.

"I know everything that happens in the neighborhood," Bogey replied, accepting a tin plate of food from Will and wasting no time to sit on the floor and dig into the hot breakfast.

"I know that you've finished your cabins," he stated around a mouthful of mush. "They seem right snug too," he said looking around with approval.

"And who reported on our cabins?" Rev. Chapman asked from where he sat near the fireplace.

"Some from Claremont's town brought a load of furs in two days ago," Bogey explained. "Said you had smoke rising from every lodge. I think they were impressed with the place, though they'll likely not let you know that."

"We saw them on the Trace," Will stated. "We invited them to stop in on their way back home, but they didn't."

"They'll watch you for a while," Bogey nodded. "Make sure they can trust you. Don't take offense. It's just their way."

The missionaries had watched the Osages too as they made their way single file down the road towards Three Forks. The men were on horseback. The women walked with packs of furs on their back. Marcus had noted the Pawnee woman, Whitestar. Her petite frame stood out from among the taller Osage women. Yet she seemed to carry as much as they did.

"They work their women like slaves," Stephen said in a low growl to Marcus and George where they worked on the roof of the last cabin. They were overlapping thick squares of sod cut from the prairie. Captain Pryor had shown them how to cut the sod and he promised such a roof would be watertight.

"So now that your cabins are complete, what's next for you?" Bogey asked while helping himself to more mush from the frying pan on the hearth.

"We'll head back to Little Rock to bring the rest of the family here," Chapman answered. "Would you be able to help us get a flatboat for the journey?"

"You won't need a flatboat," Bogey responded, "unless you're going to haul something to Little Rock. We can take a couple of my pirogues. I'm heading to Little Rock myself in a few days."

The missionaries had learned from Captain Pryor that a pirogue was a hollowed out log that was paddled like a canoe. Lightweight and agile, these boats were the fastest means of travel on the frontier.

"We've heard from Pryor that keelboats have made it to Belle Point," George said. "Is that true?"

"*Oui*," Bogey responded. "Your supplies came on a keelboat as far as the fort. First one to make it past Little Rock. I expect I'll be seeing a keelboat tying up at Three Forks before the winter is out. Major Bradford has done a good job getting the river cleared."

"It would be wonderful if we could travel by keelboat all the way to Three Forks," Chapman mused, rubbing at his beard. "I have dreaded making the trip with the women and children on a flatboat. Not that Thomas and James would mind camping out in the woods."

"How long to Little Rock by pirogue?" Will asked.

"Depending on the weather and river conditions, maybe eight to ten days," Bogey answered. "Will ya all be going back to Little Rock?"

Everyone looked at Abraham and Marcus who sat on the floor beside the bed. Clearly the young man would not be able to travel any time soon and Marcus would want to stay behind as well to be sure his healing continued.

"How many men will we need for the pirogues?" Chapman asked.

"Your three strongest will get us there quickest," said the fur trader. "More men than that just becomes added weight."

"Well, I'm by no means the strongest," Rev. Chapman said ruefully, "but I'll need to go so I can make arrangements for purchasing our furnishings. What about Woodruff and Will as the other two? You'll paddle circles around me and I've no doubt you'll get us there fast."

Both men were agreeable to paddling the pirogues to Little Rock. Both had someone who was waiting for them there.

CHAPTER TWENTY-ONE

Little Rock, Arkansas Territory
December 22, 1820

Clarissa stood at the window of the front parlor watching Susan entertain their students with a sketch she was completing of the boardinghouse in Little Rock. Susan was quite an accomplished artist and all her young charges, both boys and girls, were huddled around her where she sat on the front lawn facing the house.

Though she couldn't hear their conversation, Clarissa knew Susan was also keeping the students entertained with one of her fanciful stories while she sketched the house. With her soft childlike voice, she could capture their attention with a story far better than either Clarissa or Phoebe. The children would not have sat so quietly during their recess period otherwise.

The weather had turned unseasonably warm just a few days before Christmas and the children were eager to be out of doors whenever possible. It gave the adult missionaries a few minutes to secretly work on small gifts for the children's stockings that were already hung on the mantle in the back parlor. Mrs. Chapman had secured for each stocking one of the precious oranges brought by the keelboat.

The keelboat had pressed onward toward Fort Smith and the missionaries had sent hastily written letters with it. Clarissa had considered writing to George Requa, but in the end had decided against it. From Fort Smith the letters would be carried to Three Forks, perhaps by the keelboat, if river levels allowed, or by one of the flatboats that regularly carried supplies to the fur trading outpost.

The keelboat had also brought letters from back east as Clarissa had hoped. How eagerly she had opened the envelope bearing her mother's delicate script after Susan had distributed them. Inside was a brief note from her brother George and longer missives from her sisters Millie and Jerusha.

Her mother's letter had been filled with admonishments to take care not to contract any of the dread diseases of the wilderness or be taken captive by hostile Indians. Clarissa could tell that her mother had spent the months since her departure in wild and fearful imaginings, no doubt fueled by the chattering tongues of her friends in the Ladies' Aide Society.

It was Jerusha's letter that told her what she really wanted to know about life in Colchester. Not unkindly, she had informed Clarissa that the banns had been read in church for Robert and his fiancée Mary Anderson, just two weeks after Clarissa's departure from Connecticut. At least they had had the decency to wait until she was gone.

Clarissa had waited for the tears to start falling as she read Jerusha's letter. But she found that she was tired of the self-pity she had indulged in over the last ten months. Now she only felt anger at the betrayal and with it came the resolve that she would not allow herself to be in such a position again. As the other young women on this mission had pointed out, there would be no one arranging a marriage for them on the frontier. They could marry whomever they would choose. But would anyone choose her?

Clarissa sighed as she stepped to the front door to call the children in. As she opened the door she saw two rough looking men approach Susan and the children. Fearing trouble, she hastily stepped out onto the front porch and called to the students.

"Girls, it's time to return to class," she said. "And boys, Mr. Spaulding needs you in your classroom right away."

She hoped to communicate that the boys and girls were not sharing a classroom space, even though in reality they were.

As the children moved with their usual reluctance to return to their studies, Clarissa had to resist the urge to hurry them along.

Susan stood and casually brushed away grass from her

brown wool skirt. Clarissa noticed that Susan made sure to stand between the children and the two men who were now turning into the yard of the boarding house. For all her appearance of sweet fragility, Susan had the mothering instincts of a she-bear. She would not allow anyone to hurt one of her students.

"How cum yo're teachin' that boy?" the shorter of the two men asked, pointing a dirty finger toward Louis as he made his way inside with the other students.

"We're teaching several young men," Susan answered, managing to inject steel into her reply.

"Ain't right, him being in the house with them girls," the man contended. "Shouldn't be mixin' the races. The Bible says so."

With trepidation, Clarissa stepped off the porch to join Susan. She slipped her arm through the other young woman's, hoping to present a strong, united front, all the while praying that either Mr. Spaulding or Rev. Vaille would become aware of the situation and come to their rescue.

At closer inspection, Clarissa could tell that the two men were typical of many they had seen in the river towns of the west. Unkempt and unshaven, with the soured smell of whiskey or rum about them, they were hardly in a position to be misquoting the Bible or making pronouncements about propriety.

Rev. Chapman had commented once during the journey, that there was as great a need for a mission to these men as to the Indians. For whatever reason, they had wandered from home and society and had lost themselves in the bottom of a bottle of rotgut alcohol. They survived by begging for food or by doing day jobs that paid just enough to buy their next bottle. Clarissa felt a mixture of pity and disgust as she stood before the men.

"You folks are wasting yo're time teachin' a boy like that," the taller man slurred.

He took a step closer to the young women and Clarissa felt a familiar tremor of fear run up her spine. But her newfound anger was looking for a target and this man would do.

"It is never a waste of time to teach a child," Clarissa countered, even as she pulled Susan into a step backward toward the house. "Not even for your teachers," she added, "though I'm sure they would be saddened at the poor use of the education they provided you."

Susan glanced at Clarissa, surprise showing on her face. She'd never seen the timid schoolteacher take such a forceful stand on anything.

"Humph," one of the men grunted, unable to respond to Clarissa's barb. In truth, it was clear they had received very little education and the quick retort of the school teacher had left them nonplussed.

"You teachin' that boy yourself?' the taller man finally asked.

Clarissa opened her mouth to say, "No, of course not," but she stopped. What business was it of these two men? "Yes, I am," she responded, though all she had actually done was to loan him a copy of a child's primer.

And for the first time since Louis had become a student at the boarding house, she no longer felt afraid of what others would think . . . or say about her . . . or do to the mission. A child needed an education and wasn't that what she had come on this mission for?

No, actually she had come to escape gossip and pity. But now she was here to teach and she would stand up to anyone who tried to stop her. The courage she suddenly felt was invigorating.

All the while, Clarissa and Susan had continued their gradual steps backward toward the house. The children were all safely inside now and the two young women did not want to linger in the presence of these two uncouth ruffians.

When they reached the porch steps, they turned to go inside. "Good day to you, sirs," Susan said in a dismissive voice.

The men stood for a moment with their mouths hanging open before turning and ambling off down the road.

"Stupid men," Clarissa muttered under her breath as she and Susan mounted the stairs to the boarding house. Susan cut her eyes toward Clarissa and then the two young women gave in to a fit of nervous giggles as they entered the front door. Clarissa continued on to the back parlor, a smile still on her face. She felt as if she had just won a great victory.

Three days later, the family gathered around the large table in the dining room of the Steadman boarding house to enjoy a bountiful Christmas dinner. The children had spent the morning enjoying the small gifts they had discovered tucked into their stockings on the schoolroom mantle.

The boys had already eaten their Christmas oranges but the girls had declared they would save theirs for after dinner. The Christmas feast consisted of baked ham, candied yams, Amanda's special yeast rolls, dried peas, apple cobbler and a new dessert to the missionaries – pecan pie.

Mrs. Steadman made it with pecans Joseph Bogey had brought her on his last visit to Little Rock to thank her for the constant supply of molasses cookies she provided when he called on the missionaries. The Osages gathered pecans in the late fall and brought pounds of them to Bogey's trading post to barter for the goods he stocked there.

They were just pushing back from the table with a comment by Rev. Vaille that they were all going to have to ask forgiveness for the sin of gluttony. Even Lydia Fuller had been able to join them for dinner and had made an effort to eat a little of each dish. Still pale from her illness, she sat quietly amidst the chatter of the children who were excited about their Christmas gifts.

They heard a pounding at the front door of the boarding house. Thomas jumped up from his seat, but a look from his mother brought him back into his chair. "It's Mr. Bogey," he said in a stage whisper for he could see him through the lace curtains in the door's oval window.

"Oh, dear," Mrs. Steadman said as she rose to answer the door. "I'm all out of cookies. Do you think he'll be content with a piece of pie?"

"I doubt that he'll turn down anything you offer him," Rachel said wryly.

The missionaries all rose from the table and followed Mrs. Steadman into the front parlor. A visit with the fur trader was always welcome for he invariably brought news from their men and from Three Forks.

The big man filled up the doorway when Mrs. Steadman opened it so it took a moment for everyone to realize that others were with him. Rev. Chapman, Mr. Woodruff and Will Requa were also waiting on the porch.

"Papa!" James Chapman yelled, dropping his carved wooden Christmas horse and rushing to grab his father by the legs. Thomas, Abigail and Leah all followed and quickly surrounded him. Rachel stood gripping the back of a chair, refraining from a public show of affection as if by the sheerest of willpower.

Mrs. Woodruff seemed less concerned with propriety for she met her husband at the door and took his hands as he stepped inside behind Rev. Chapman. The two exchanged a look in the way that two people who have been married long years can – speaking volumes just with their eyes.

As Will Requa entered the parlor, Clarissa noticed that he immediately looked around for Susan. Giving her a nod, he removed the beaver cap he wore. Susan smiled at him and looked very happy. Clarissa felt a little pang in her heart. Was it jealousy? She was disappointed that only three of the mission brothers had made the return trip to Little Rock.

The men were all helped out of their coats then and urged to have a seat at the dining table where Christmas dinner was still spread out in a welcoming feast. They needed little urging to fill the plates that Mrs. Steadman and Amanda brought them. For a time, everyone seemed to talk at once, trying to answer questions and catch up on what had happened in the four months since the men had been gone.

When Rev. Chapman mentioned Abraham Redfield's injury, Phoebe gasped and covered her mouth with her hands. "Lawsey," she breathed, "is he alright?"

"Yes," Chapman answered. "Dr. Palmer, with the Lord's great assistance, worked a miracle. There were moments when we all feared he would lose his leg. But he was up and walking with the aid of a crutch when we left."

"Thank the Lord," Martha murmured. "And all the rest of the men are alright?"

Clarissa was glad she asked the question, for she wanted to know but was hesitant to ask.

"All are well," Chapman stated. "Mr. Fuller was already breaking ground for corn when we left. George was helping with that. Dr. Palmer and Abraham were laying in more firewood for all the cabins."

"We hope you'll be happy with the way we set the mission up," Will Requa said, working hard not to look directly at Susan when he spoke. Clarissa noticed that after their initial greeting the two had studiously tried not to look at each other.

"I'm sure we'll be quite happy," Rachel said, "just to be all together again. Though we've enjoyed Mrs. Steadman's hospitality, I cannot wait to arrive at our new home."

It was another ten days before the family was ready to make the final leg of the journey to the Union Mission. Clarissa found herself getting excited about reaching the mission grounds. This journey which had begun with so much fear and pain now no longer seemed like an escape. It now truly was a mission and she couldn't wait to begin teaching the Osage girls who would be her students.

She said a prayer of thanks for the change of heart as she worked to pack her clothes into her trunk. Odd that it seemed much harder to fit everything into the trunk now than it had when she packed nine months earlier. She had only added several bars of soap and two heavy full-length muslin aprons that she had stitched while in Little Rock.

Martha Woodruff had suggested they all create the aprons with roomy pockets in front. "They protect your dresses," she said, "and give them longer wear." They all knew there would not be the chance to purchase much in the way of dress goods out in the wilderness.

Thinking about that, Clarissa planned to buy some lengths of fabric to take with her. She could stitch new dresses once they were at the mission. With a pang, she thought of Sally Edwards. If she had lived, she would have given birth to her baby while in Little Rock. And she would be helping them all with the sewing. Clarissa was a fair hand at embroidery, but she had less skill at actually sewing garments. Fortunately, Mrs. Vaille and Mrs. Woodruff were better at it than Clarissa was.

Rev. and Mrs. Chapman had spent the days making purchases of furnishings for the mission. These, along with the linens and enamel dishes Rachel had already secured, were stored in a waterfront warehouse until they could be loaded onto the boat that would carry them on to Three Forks.

The same keelboat that had brought the Christmas oranges was docked again at the Little Rock wharf. It was a great relief to all the women that they could take this boat at least to Fort Smith rather than having to travel on the open flatboats.

The winter weather was much milder in Arkansas Territory than in New England, but even so it would have been a daunting journey in the cold. Several days of icy rain had ushered in the year 1821, raising the water level of the Arkansas River. This might allow the keelboat to travel all the way to Three Forks. They were certainly praying this would be the case.

It was sad to say goodbye to Mrs. Steadman and her sons and to their new friend Louis. Clarissa told the boys to keep the readers she had loaned them. She would write to her mother and ask her to send more books if they were needed. Both Louis and his father had expressed their thanks for the opportunity for schooling. It was likely Louis would have little chance at formal study after the missionaries were gone.

The day of departure dawned cloudy and overcast, not unlike the morning they had left Pittsburgh. The Steadmans accompanied the mission family to the waterfront and others in the community were there to see them off as well. Friends they had made at the little Presbyterian Church were on hand to offer a parting prayer for their safety.

The keelboat was smaller than the one they had spent so many weeks on when coming to Arkansas Territory. All the men would have to sleep in hammocks on the lower deck among the boatmen who worked on the river.

The boat seemed not as well built as the one owned by Captain Douglas and Clarissa wondered about its soundness. A dunk in the cold Arkansas in January would be far worse than the mishap they had experience at Wolf Island. She hoped this final leg of their journey passed quickly and safely.

CHAPTER TWENTY-TWO

Dardanelle, Arkansas Territory
January, 1821

Their passage up the Arkansas River was cold and damp. A steady rain for the first two days kept the missionaries huddled below deck in their cramped cabins. The dining area was so small they could only eat in shifts and they could only pass each other in the dark narrow hall by turning sideways. All expressed the hope that the time would pass quickly. They were eager to be settled in their new home.

It took only three days to reach Dardanelle. They arrived mid-morning as the sun was finally breaking out from the dreary clouds. Eager to be out of their cabins, the missionaries were glad to learn that the captain planned a layover at the Dardanelle trading post.

The missionaries trudged up the muddy path that led to the mercantile overlooking the river. A scattering of other buildings made up the settlement of Dardanelle, including a blacksmith shop, grist mill and livery.

Lounging on the front porch of the trading post were several Indians, looking quite different from the Osages they had seen in St. Louis and the Chickasaws at Memphis. Their brightly-colored clothing and the turbans they wore gave these Cherokees an oriental look and Rachel had to work hard to keep her children from staring. Truthfully, even the adults seemed to struggle not to gape in curiosity. These Cherokees looked very different from the drawings of be-feathered native people they had seen in eastern newspapers.

As the mission family entered the trading post with its dim interior and cacophony of smells, one of the young Cherokee men rose from the porch, leapt over its low railing and ran up the one dirt street leading away from the river.

His movement startled Clarissa who was one of the last of their group to climb the porch steps. She imagined the Cherokee running to alert others of the tribe. She could picture them gathering under the council oaks and taking up arms to force the white intruders off their land. She felt a shiver run up her spine and she stepped closer to Susan and Will Requa who were strolling among the incredible array of trade goods that had been packed into the small building.

No one else seemed to share Clarissa's concern, or perhaps they had not noticed the young man's flight. She was just scolding herself for her own flight of fancy when the same man suddenly appeared in the door of the mercantile.

Somewhat out of breath, the man paused for a moment before speaking to the clerk behind the counter in a language Clarissa presumed to be Cherokee. His words were rhythmic, but somewhat guttural and all the missionaries listened to the exchange in fascination. Clarissa wondered if her own eyes were as big as the children's.

Despite having spent a few months in Arkansas Territory, most of them had experienced little interaction with the native people in the area. Clarissa felt nervous, and it occurred to her that from here on in their journey they would be more likely to encounter Indians than the few settlers who had ventured this far west.

The man behind the counter spoke in broken English, addressing the mission family. "You be the water-sprinklers who come with talking leaves?" he asked.

"We are Christian missionaries," Rev. Chapman answered, careful not to mention that they were planning to work among the Osages. "We have come to build a school and teach from the talking leaves."

Clarissa understood that "talking leaves" meant the written word on paper, but the term "water-sprinkler" puzzled her. She could tell that the others were also trying to understand the man's words.

Finally, John Spaulding whispered where most could hear him. "Baptism," he explained. "It's how we baptize."

The light dawned on their faces. Clarissa supposed water baptism did seem an odd custom to those who were unfamiliar with the sacraments of the church.

"Tahchee bring word from Walter Webber," the merchant said. "He ask you to dine with him at his wigwam this evening. Tahchee will guide you to it, if you please."

Rev. Chapman exchanged a look with Rachel and then with Rev. Vaille. "We would be most pleased to dine with Mr. Webber," he said carefully.

Rachel caught her breath and threw a look at Rev. Vaille. Apparently her husband did not know about the feud between Webber and the Osage warrior Mad Buffalo whom they called Skiatook.

The two Cherokee men exchanged more words, then the tradesman said, "Tahchee meet you here at sundown. He will guide you."

"Thank you," Chapman said, turning to give a slight bow to the man named Tahchee. "We will return here at sundown."

"Uh," Tahchee said. The missionaries would later learn that the Cherokees had no words for "you're welcome" and thanks were usually acknowledged in this way. Tahchee turned from the door and settled back at his post on the porch of the mercantile.

After much discussion back at the boat, it was decided that they would limit the number who would call upon the Cherokee leader Walter Webber. Rev. Vaille shared with the mission director the information Joseph Bogey had given them about the Cherokee-Osage conflict.

Would Walter Webber have issued the invitation if he knew the missionaries planned to establish a school for the Osages? Was there something sinister in the invitation? Many of them expressed a measure of uneasiness at the prospect of dining with a declared enemy of Chief Claremont and his son.

"Perhaps you should send our regrets," Rachel said to her husband as the group sat at the oarsmen benches on the upper deck of the keelboat. It was the only area where the whole family could gather.

"I think it's too late for that," Epaphras countered. "We don't want to give offense."

"And don't forget that Governor Clark urged us not to show favoritism among the tribes," William Vaille said. "The Cherokees will learn soon enough about the mission. If we refuse to dine with a Cherokee leader, they may see that as having chosen sides in the conflict. We can't afford to do that. It could put the mission in danger."

It was decided that only the men would accept Mr. Webber's invitation to dinner. Alexander Woodruff, at first sought to excuse himself from the group. "I'm a simple man," he said. "Won't be much good at diplomatic relations."

"I'd feel better if you were with them, Mr. Woodruff," Rachel said. "We don't know what the men might be walking into."

"You're our strongest man," her husband agreed. "Your presence alone may keep the evening quiet and peaceable."

Alex and his wife Martha exchanged a look that Clarissa found interesting. His look seemed almost desperate; hers gave quiet reassurance.

Finally the blacksmith nodded. "If I can be of some help," he said with a sense of resignation.

The five men made their way back to the trading post as the sun was setting. The air was chilly and they all wore their heavy coats. They entered the store and immediately gravitated to the little pot-bellied stove in the back corner. All the men who had been sitting on the porch earlier that day were now sitting around the fire. Obviously this was a community gathering place.

Tahchee was not among the Cherokees in the mercantile and the missionaries waited about fifteen minutes for him to arrive. As before, he appeared silently at the door and spoke to the tradesman who was seated with the other men around the stove.

The shopkeeper, who had introduced himself as Absalom Simms, translated again. "Tahchee asks where are your women?"

Rev. Chapman hesitated for a moment. Had they risked

offending their host by not including at least their wives in their party?

"They were tired from our journey and begged forgiveness for not attending," Rev. Vaille stated. Chapman threw him a look of gratitude.

One of the men sitting at the fire muttered to the others and they laughed. John caught the words, "weak white women." The men exchanged looks of concern.

"Come," Tahchee said. Apparently he could speak at least a little English. He turned and picked up a glowing lantern he had set on the porch of the mercantile. Without a backward glance he took up a brisk pace down the dirt path that led through the little village.

The missionaries hastened to follow him. Without the aid of the lantern, the trek would have been difficult. There were only a few homes in the town proper; most of the Cherokees in the area lived on small farms as Jean Baptiste had told them. The gathering shadows danced in the moving lamplight held by Tahchee.

They walked for about twenty minutes before reaching their destination. The "wigwam" of Walter Webber was quite a substantial home by frontier standards. Though constructed of logs, the house was whitewashed and curtains hung at the glass windows. The home consisted of two cabins connected by a single roof with a "dog trot" between. A wide front porch was graced with hand-carved rocking chairs and a bright braided rug sat before the front door.

It was such a contrast to the traditional Plains lodge of the Osages that Rev. Chapman expressed astonishment under his breath. "Amazing."

Tahchee tapped at the front door and it was opened almost immediately by a Negro woman with rich, dark skin. She greeted Tahchee in Cherokee and then opened the door wide and gestured for all the men to enter. Tahchee did not stay, but nodded to the woman and then returned down the path they had just taken.

"Welcome to the home of Mr. Webber," the woman said in English. "My name is Etta. Let me take your coats and then ya'll can warm up by the fire."

The missionaries stepped into a small parlor where a cheery fire blazed in the stone fireplace. Before the hearth stood a man in the traditional Cherokee dress, his long dark hair pulled into a braid down his back. He turned from the fire and spoke to them in his native tongue.

"Mr. Webber say hello and welcome to his home," the woman translated. "Why did you not bring your women? Tahchee says there be lots of women from the boat."

"Please accept our apologies, Mr. Webber," Rev. Chapman said. "The women chose to remain at the boat with the children."

With Etta acting as translator, Webber invited the men to sit. The furnishings were of plain wooden construction, but bright pillows with beaded designs adorned the chairs. Etta stood a respectful distance behind Webber's chair.

A plump and attractive Cherokee woman entered the parlor. Her dress was that of the latest Eastern fashion, but she wore her hair in two long, thick braids.

"*Osiyo*," she said.

"Hello," Etta translated. "This is Mrs. Webber."

The men all stood and bowed their greetings to their hostess. Webber watched them from his seat, an amused look on his face.

Mrs. Webber and Etta spoke quietly for a few moments then Etta turned to the missionaries. "Mrs. Webber will serve supper in just a while," she explained. "Please have a seat."

All were seated again, except for Etta who remained standing behind Webber's chair. Their conversation consisted of the kind of polite small talk that might have taken place in any parlor in New England, though it was somewhat stilted since Etta had to translate what everyone said.

The Webbers asked about their journey west and their impressions of Arkansas. Will, Alexander and John Spaulding kept quiet, leaving the talking to the two ministers. Rev. Vaille seemed the most comfortable of all of them, chatting easily as if he were visiting a parishioner from his church.

Soon another Negro woman stepped into the parlor and said to Etta. "The food's ready to be served."

Mrs. Webber indicated they all should move to the dining

room. The missionaries took their seats at a long oak table set with fine china and linen napkins. Etta and the other woman, perhaps the cook, followed Mrs. Webber's direction in serving her guests. The men noted that neither of the Webbers offered to say grace over the meal.

As they enjoyed the first course of a nutty flavored soup, Mr. Webber began to steer the conversation toward the mission. Etta, who now stood behind Mrs. Webber's chair, translated, "Mr. Webber asks why you have come to Arkansas Territory? The Cherokees don't need no church."

Rev. Chapman took a deep gulp of air before answering, showing his nervousness. "We believe all people need to learn about God and we seek to bring His message of love to the people of Arkansas. That is why we are building a mission here," he said.

"Where you gonna put this mission?" Etta translated Webber's question.

"It will be located about 25 miles north of Three Forks," Rev. Chapman responded. This would make clear that their mission was near Chief Claremont's village.

"Osage," Webber said with an obvious look of disapproval on his face. His spat out a rapid tirade in Cherokee that Etta seemed reluctant to translate.

Mrs. Webber spoke to her husband in a gentle but firm voice. The mission brothers sat quietly, staring at their plates during this moment of anger.

"Mrs. Webber say please excuse her husband. He lose his cousin to an Osage arrow. Cherokee law says such a death must be avenged."

"We seek to be at peace with all people," Rev. Chapman said. "Chief Claremont assured me personally that he desires peace for his village. We hope the Cherokees will desire peace as well."

"The Cherokees always seek first the path of peace," Webber answered through Etta. "But do not trust the Osage."

Conversation was even more stilted as the supper continued. The men breathed sighs of relief after they politely thanked their hosts and then excused themselves to return to the keelboat.

Two days later, the mission family arrived at Fort Smith. The keelboat carried a large cargo of supplies for the garrison which would take the better part of a day to unload. The boat's captain planned a layover of two days at Belle Point.

Major William Bradford, the fort commander, invited the missionaries to dine with him in the officers' mess. Phoebe and Susan kept the children at a table apart from the adults at one end of the mess hall.

Amanda and the Vailles had accompanied Lydia Fuller to the fort hospital. She was having difficulty breathing and her cough had grown worse again. Major Bradford sent food to the four of them at the infirmary.

The officers' mess was a smaller dining hall than that provided for the enlisted troops and was appointed with three long tables and straight-backed wooden chairs. Two privates acted as servers for the meal. Major Bradford apologized for the simple fare of venison stew and fresh bread from the post's bakery.

"Don't apologize, Major," Rachel reassured him. "The food is hot and hearty and you'll hear no complaints from us on such a cold night as this."

Clarissa watched in amusement as the two young enlisted men, barely more than boys, would almost trip over each other in their eagerness to serve pretty Eliza Cleaver. The girl had grown rather quiet and withdrawn over the last few months, but the attention she was getting from the men at the garrison had turned her back into the flirtatious coquette she had once been.

Clarissa might have been annoyed with the display had she herself not drawn the attention of a handsome lieutenant who had managed to get a seat beside her at the dining table.

He told her his name was Benjamin Bonneville and like Colonel Chouteau, he was of French descent and a graduate of the Military Academy at West Point. He seemed quite interested in hearing about Clarissa's journey from Connecticut, but Clarissa was even more fascinated with his life for he casually mentioned that his family was connected with the famous Marquis de Lafayette.

Lieutenant Bonneville was very attentive during the meal,

but Clarissa knew it was most likely because females were so scarce on the frontier. And since she and Eliza were the only two single women dining with the officers, both of them were receiving their share of attention. Still, it was flattering to Clarissa and not a little soothing to her still hurting heart after Robert's betrayal.

The conversation at the table turned to the Osage-Cherokee conflict and Rev. Chapman asked Major Bradford for his opinion on the matter.

"Will we see trouble between the two tribes?" the minister asked.

"It was the Secretary's hope that placing Fort Smith here between them would be a deterrent to the fighting," the officer responded, leaning back in his chair. "And our presence does give some assurance to the American settlers in this area. But we aren't mobile enough to forestall trouble. The Third Infantry is the best on the frontier, but what is needed out here is a ranger company. Or perhaps another fort further upriver – maybe at Three Forks itself."

"We've met with both Chief Claremont and Chief Webber," Chapman said. "Both seem like reasonable men and both say they want peace. Yet the conflict continues."

"We found Webber's home and manner of living to be quite civilized, except for owning slaves. He seemed to be a man of some means," Rev. Vaille interjected. "Yet, he was very set on avenging the death of his cousin at the hands of Mad Buffalo. He seems to live in two worlds."

"You'll often find that among the Cherokees," Bradford said. "Webber is the son of a Scotch immigrant and Cherokee mother and he's a canny businessman. And the Cherokees, like the Scots, are strongly loyal to their clan and have very long memories when it comes to an offense against them."

Lieutenant Bonneville added, "The feuds can go on for generations."

"Then we can expect Webber to continue to seek revenge against Mad Buffalo?" Will Requa asked.

"I hope not," Major Bradford replied. "I've spoken to Webber and have asked him to bury his hatchet on this. But he made me no promises."

"Will we be in danger at the mission?" Rachel asked, throwing a glance across the room to where her children sat with Phoebe and Susan.

"No," Bradford shook his head adamantly. "The Indians know they'll bring the full force of the army against them if they harm an American. Besides, Webber is a principled man – he'll follow Cherokee law and seek his vengeance only against those he believes are responsible for his cousin's death. Besides, Skiatook . . . er, Mad Buffalo . . . hasn't been seen in the area since last fall."

"Well, he's back in Arkansas Territory, for we met him at Claremont's village," Rev. Chapman told the officer.

"I hadn't heard that," Major Bradford said, exchanging a look of concern with the lieutenant. "I'll send out a patrol when the weather improves. If Mad Buffalo stays in Arkansas, our peaceful winter may be over."

CHAPTER TWENTY-THREE

Union Mission, Osage Lands
February 1, 1821

The men at the mission compound were lingering over a last cup of strong, hot coffee following their morning breakfast. A light drizzle of freezing rain that had begun sometime in the night made none of them eager to head outdoors for their routine chores. The cold weather that had set in after Christmas kept them inside much of the time, except for caring for the livestock, chopping firewood or going on hunting forays across the prairie.

Abraham Redfield was much improved from his accident and was able to walk now with a cane that George Requa had fashioned for him. But the cold weather made his leg ache and he winced now as he hobbled to the fireplace to pour himself the last of the coffee.

"I guess we've put off the chores for as long as we can," the sandy-haired young man said as he sipped the dark brew while standing close to the fire. As if in agreement, their cow in the barn bellowed her insistence on being milked. Stephen Fuller sighed and reached for the milk pail before shrugging into his heavy coat that hung on a peg by the door.

He reached to open the door, but it would not budge. "I think it's frozen shut," he said. George set down his tin coffee mug and went to help the farm director. Together they managed to tug the door open.

The world outside that greeted them took them by surprise. A thin coating of ice covered every blade of grass and every branch of the scrubby trees and cane that lined the river bank. Heavy clouds blocked the sun, but what little light reached the landscape made the ice glisten. It was a strange wonderland and all the men gathered at the cabin door to marvel at the change that had taken place overnight.

Tiny pricks of ice tinkled and pinged as they hit the ground and when Stephen stepped outside to make his way to the barn, his footsteps crunched across the glassy grass.

"I've never seen such weather as this," Marcus Palmer stated as the other men watched Stephen pick his way carefully to the barn.

Suddenly the crack of what sounded like musket fire made all of them jump. With Abraham and George, the doctor quickly pulled on his coat and they made their way around the longhouse to determine where the sound had come from. The limbs of a lone cottonwood tree near the river were bent downward by the weight of the ice. While the men slipped and slid on the frozen ground, a limb loudly snapped and fell with a crash. The sound they had heard had been that of a falling tree limb.

"We won't have to chop trees for firewood for a while," Abraham observed, as they heard another distant snap upriver. "Nature is pruning the trees for us."

The falling ice made doing their chores uncomfortable for it bit into any exposed skin. "Get inside," Marcus told Abraham. "I don't want you slipping on this ice and re-injuring that leg."

Abraham opened his mouth to argue, but saw that George was looking at him with the same stubborn determination that the doctor wore on his face. "I'll start a stew for dinner," he said with a sigh and hobbled back to the cabin.

After helping Stephen water and feed the horses, hogs and chickens, and bring in more wood as well as water from the spring, the men settled into the central cabin for a dreary day inside. All of the men were working on small projects that kept the boredom at bay when the weather held them inside.

George Requa was carving a set of wooden spoons. Each time he completed one he would jokingly predict what delectable dish Miss Ingles would prepare with it when she arrived. His elaborate description of each dish told just how tired he and all of the men were of their own cooking.

"No offense to you, Abraham," Stephen said, "but I'm getting mighty anxious for some of my Lydia's cooking. I'm thinking she'll give Miss Ingles a lesson or two in fine fare."

Stephen was pulling thick, leathery strips from the cane he had harvested along the river bank. He would use the strips to weave seats for the chairs Abraham had fashioned from sturdy tree limbs he had planed and sanded smooth.

"No offense taken," Abraham responded as he absently rubbed his aching leg. "I'm sick of my cooking, too. The women can't get here fast enough for me. I'm sure every one of them is a better cook than I am."

After their dinner of quail stew, the men set aside their work for a time of scripture reading. With the absence of both ministers from the mission site, Abraham had taken to reading their daily scripture and sometimes commenting on the passage. He had served as a lay preacher back home in New York and was very knowledgeable of biblical truths.

"Blessed be God, even the Father of our Lord Jesus Christ, the Father of mercies, and the God of all comfort; who comforteth us in all our tribulation, that we may be able to comfort them which are in any trouble," he read, but then paused before continuing on through the chapter.

"I have found this to be true in my own life," he said quietly. "When my parents died, I knew the Lord's great comfort. It was all that sustained me for a time."

"I didn't know your parents were deceased," Dr. Palmer said. "Was it a recent loss?"

"No," the gangly young man said. "I was just 15 when they died. I've been on my own since then, but they left me a good foundation of faith. It truly has kept me saved and sane."

"Sane?" George quipped. "I wouldn't go that far. You're out here in the wilderness with the rest of us. My folks questioned my sanity for wanting to come out here."

The other men laughed, but then sobered quickly as each seemed to think about their reasons for traveling so far from home.

Marcus thought back to wrestling with his decision to come to the Indian country. He wished he had known the comfort Abraham spoke of. It was the loss of three patients within a week that had almost driven him from the medical profession. He'd only entered it at the insistence of his father and brother, both themselves doctors. Marcus would have preferred to go into the ministry and like Abraham had done some lay preaching as a young man.

But when the opportunity arose to join the mission, he had struggled with the choice. Was he fulfilling his desire to work for God, or just fleeing the sense of failure heaped on him by his brother? Even today, he wasn't sure what truly motivated him.

"Well, it's a comfort to have you here with us, George," Abraham said to the younger Requa brother. "You see there is comfort from the Lord in every situation," he smiled.

Stephen joined in the jovial laughter, but his eyes turned back to the Bible passage.

From the moment Abraham had begun to read it, the young farmer had felt a sense of dread inside him. He had worried constantly about Lydia since they had been apart. Would he need the comfort of God when the rest of the mission family arrived?

Lydia was his soul mate. He had given up everything to bring her out to the drier climate of the prairie . . . to save her life. Yet he feared they had waited too late. He could not imagine living without her.

He silently breathed a prayer for his wife as he had every hour since her cough had begun three years ago. But deep in his heart he knew . . . suddenly at that moment he knew.

"She's gone," Rev. Vaille said quietly as he joined his fellow missionaries in the mess hall at Fort Smith the afternoon following their arrival. "Dr. Russell says Mrs. Fuller passed away some time this morning. She went peacefully."

Dr. Thomas Russell was the post surgeon who ran the small hospital where Lydia had spent her last few hours on earth.

The group was silent for a moment, stunned by the minister's words. For a time, the only sound was from a shower of ice falling on the roof of the building. Then Amanda began to cry softly. She and Lydia had grown very close during their long journey. Mrs. Vaille moved to sit beside the red-haired girl and drew her into an embrace.

"Her husband will be devastated," Amanda said as she fumbled in her skirt pocket for a handkerchief to mop her eyes. She remembered the many conversations she had shared with her friend about her devoted husband. Amanda's words brought tears to almost everyone's eyes then. Clarissa dreaded seeing Mr. Fuller's reaction when he learned of Lydia's death. Oh why did another of their family have to die? Was this the way it was going to be for all of them out here in the wilderness? Looking around at the faces of the other young members of their group, she knew they all were thinking similar thoughts.

"It's a blessing that she can be buried at a civilized place," Rachel Chapman murmured softly. "At least her grave will be close enough that Stephen can visit it. I hope that will be some comfort to him."

"I doubt that anything will comfort him," Amanda said. She remembered her promise to Lydia and wondered if there was any possible way that she could keep it.

The sleet and freezing rain continued through the rest of the day, but the clouds had cleared by the following morning. A weak sun did little to warm the ice-crusted landscape or to cheer the missionaries as they prepared to bury another member of their family.

Alexander and Will had set out to fashion a coffin for the woman who had struggled with her health for the entirety of their journey. Martha lined the simple pine box with a pretty length of dress goods she had purchased at Little Rock. Asie Vaille and Mrs. Chapman prepared Lydia's body for burial.

Major Bradford had assigned a group of soldiers to dig the grave in the cemetery near the fort. Rev. Chapman conducted the funeral service in the post chapel, speaking passionately about the rewards that their faithful sacrifice would bring them. Clarissa knew he believed it sincerely, but she wondered if the cost to flee from the gossips of her hometown would be far greater than any reward she would find out here in the Indian country.

As the group passed before the coffin where Lydia lay, Clarissa was surprised to see Eliza Cleaver tuck a bit of greenery into the folded hands of the woman. She gave Eliza a quizzical look as they followed the men who carried the coffin out of the chapel.

"It was mistletoe," Eliza explained quietly. "One of the soldiers climbed a tree to get it for me. There's not another green thing to be found anywhere and I couldn't bear to think of Mrs. Fuller having nothing of beauty at her grave."

Clarissa was so astonished at the girl's thoughtfulness that she could think of nothing to say. Eliza had spent the last few months pouting and sighing in exaggerated martyrdom, though she rarely complained out loud. Had she made this gesture to truly honor Lydia or had it just been a way to get one of the soldiers to do something for her?

Immediately Clarissa felt guilty at her thoughts. She had spent enough time in self-pity over the last few months that she had no right to judge Eliza. So she smiled at the girl and said, "That was very thoughtful of you, Miss Eliza. I'm sure Mrs. Fuller would have appreciated that."

The mission group shivered at the graveside while Rev. Vaille read Psalm 23. When Clarissa looked up after the final prayer, she was surprised to see Joseph Bogey and another man standing at the back of their group. She had not noticed the arrival of the old trapper who walked with the silence of an Indian hunter. The tall man with him looked to be Indian though he was dressed like a trapper as well.

"Mr. Bogey, how kind of you to join us," Mrs. Chapman said as the group made their way carefully across the ice-crusted ground back to the officers' mess.

"I was sorry to learn of your loss," Bogey replied. "The major told me when Mr. Revoir and I arrived just now. We wanted to pay our respects."

The missionaries had left Little Rock before Mr. Bogey but he had caught up with them at the fort. He had met Joseph Revoir, the partner of Auguste Chouteau, in town and they had joined together in bringing a load of trade goods upriver to Three Forks.

Rev. Chapman invited the two traders to join their group for coffee in the mess hall where the warmth of a crackling fire drew them all close to the big stone fireplace.

"Will you wait out this miserable cold here at the fort?" Will Requa asked Mr. Bogey while he gripped a hot mug of coffee in both hands, trying to warm them.

"Nah," Bogey responded, as if the ice were only a minor inconvenience. "You'll learn that the cold doesn't last very long this far south so there's no point in sitting around. It'll be balmy and spring-like in just a few days."

The New Englanders found such a claim hard to believe. It was just February and they would expect at least two more months of cold weather back home.

"Willow is swelled and ready to green," Joseph Revoir agreed. "The Redbud Moon will be early this year. The ice breaks open the sky for the sun to return strong. You see . . . spring will be soon."

Clarissa found his way of speaking fascinating. His English was quite good even though laced with an accent, but it was as if he were speaking another language altogether. She hoped his words were true. This journey to an untamed land had been difficult and full of sorrow. She was ready to reach their new home and welcome spring.

CHAPTER TWENTY-FOUR

Three Forks, Arkansas Territory
February 18, 1821

Several days later, the crew of the small keelboat carrying the mission family poled the craft into the mouth of the Verdigris River at Three Forks. As the two traders had predicted at Fort Smith, the weather had warmed considerably following the ice storm. It was as if nature was trying to make amends for its fit of winter like a capricious child apologizing for a tantrum.

The missionaries were on deck in the pleasant sunshine watching the boatmen secure the keelboat by ropes to the heavy metal stakes driven into the soft sandstone of the river bank. They were at the Bogey trading post beyond French Point, the jut of land that divided the Verdigris from the Neosho River.

Rev. Vaille explained to those new to the area that the mission was actually on the Neosho River, but it was barely navigable even by flatboat. The keelboat would not attempt to reach the mission. They would have to secure wagons to reach the compound where they were to live.

Clarissa and the others who had never been to Three Forks looked around in curiosity as the boatmen prepared to lower a gangplank so they could debark. The village was small and more crudely constructed than any other they had visited in Arkansas Territory. It was clear to see that they were indeed at the very edge of civilization.

Three Forks was primarily a fur trading community strung out along both banks of the Verdigris River from its mouth where it joined the Arkansas River to its falls a few miles further north. The Falls of the Verdigris were considered the end of navigation in the region.

The trading houses were all of log construction, some with canvas lean-tos attached. On the west bank stood the Bogey post and to the north stood Colonel Chouteau's post and a boat building enterprise. While lumber was not abundant on the prairie, the Verdigris and Arkansas were lined with trees and cane. Chouteau employed a small crew of mostly Negroes to build his flatboats which he loaded with furs and then floated downriver to New Orleans where he sold both the furs and the lumber from the boat.

Bogey's trading outfit was the oldest at Three Forks and showed signs of having been in a fire. Several small additions had been tacked onto the main building as proof that Bogey's was a successful outfit that continued to grow.

Nearby a blacksmith shop, little more than a three-sided shed, had two horses waiting to be shod. The burly Negro blacksmith was pounding a horseshoe on his massive anvil. Mr. Woodruff wandered over to speak to the man while the other missionaries made their way to Bogey's post.

The smell that greeted them at the door nearly made Clarissa gag. How could Mr. Bogey work among the stacks of hides and furs? She looked down to see Leah Chapman holding her nose and her sister Abigail wrinkling her freckled face in agreement.

"I believe the other women and I will wait out here with the children," Rachel said to her husband.

"We'll not be long," Rev. Chapman nodded. "Mr. Bogey said he would have wagons arranged for us. We'll just check to see where we are to meet them."

The women and children wandered toward a well that sat only a few yards from the riverbank. While the children gathered around the stone lip of the well, the women discreetly looked around the little community that would be the closest supply post to their new home at Union Mission.

A group of Osages lounged around the door of the Chouteau trading post. The nine women tried not to stare, but the Indians felt no such reluctance. They openly appraised the group which was probably the largest assembly of white women ever seen in the region.

Clarissa felt a little shiver run up her spine. She exchanged a look with Susan who winked at her. It was if she were saying they had no need to be afraid of a group of men. Clarissa felt a little secret smile spread across her face. No, she would not be afraid.

"I think those must be our wagons," Martha Woodruff said and they all turned to see three wooden carts hauled by mules pulling up to the Glenn post across the river. They would have to re-board the keelboat which would then be poled to the east bank of the river.

Though Clarissa was desperately tired of travel by boat, those wagons looked very uncomfortable. But she supposed it would be the best they could hope for in such primitive surroundings. At least they would soon be home.

The children had chattered excitedly for the first ten miles of travel up the Osage Trace. The prairie grasses, not yet green, rose higher than the wagons and seemed to undulate like ocean waves in the cool breeze. The children had eventually grown tired though and most dozed against one of the adults in the group. Clarissa could not see how they could sleep as they bumped along the rutted trail.

"I'll be bruised black and blue before we get there," Amanda observed to no one in particular in the wagon she shared with Clarissa, Phoebe, Susan, the Woodruffs, and Will Requa. Elizabeth Vaille and Abigail Chapman were using the two housemothers as pillows, both sound asleep in the rocking wagon.

As with their river travel, the landscape that had seemed very interesting as they started out had quickly become boring and Clarissa felt her own eyes getting heavy. If it were not for the bouncing of the wagon she might have slept as well. Instead she felt the beginnings of a headache in the tightened muscles at the back of her neck.

"Almost there," Will Requa finally said. Clarissa leaned forward to look around Susan and over the rumps of the four mules that pulled the wagon. Still a half-mile distant, the mission complex could be seen rising above the flat prairie. It seemed very small and lonely on the vast stretch of tall grass.

As they drew closer, Will whistled shrilly to alert the men at the mission. The two eight-year-old girls awoke with a start and even Clarissa jumped at the sound. The mules picked up their pace a bit.

"Sorry," Will apologized with a grin. 'Didn't mean to scare anyone."

"Well, everyone's awake now," Martha Woodruff laughed. All the children were indeed awake and some even standing in the wagons. Thomas and Richard would have scrambled over the side had not their mothers stopped them.

Excitement rippled through the group as they pulled into the mission grounds. The four men who had remained at the mission made their way toward the wagons. George Requa laid down the ax he had been using to chop wood and pulled on his coat.

Abraham Redfield and Dr. Palmer exited a cabin and hailed the new arrivals. Mr. Fuller stepped out of the barn and quickly pushed through the corral gate, his eyes already scanning the wagons for a sight of his wife.

As the men began to help the women and children climb out of the carts, it became clear to Stephen that Lydia was not among the group. He bent nearly double as if the truth had punched him in the stomach. "Lydia," he moaned.

Everyone stopped as if frozen for a moment, feeling the sorrow afresh. Dr. Palmer rested his head on his arms against the side rail of one of the wagons. He knew the devastation he felt could not match that of Lydia's husband, but his stomach too felt assaulted.

"Did she succumb to her illness?" Abraham asked Rev. Vaille quietly. The minister nodded briefly and then made his way toward Stephen.

"Mr. Fuller, I'm so sorry," he began.

Stephen waved away his condolences and turned on his heel. By the time he reached the barn door he was practically running, chased by the phantoms of sorrow and guilt. He clutched his stomach as if he was going to be physically ill.

Rev. Vaille followed him inside the barn. He paused a

moment for his eyes to adjust to the dim interior of the building and he finally located Mr. Fuller where he sat on the dirt floor with his back against a stall door.

His quiet sobs filled the small structure. Rev. Vaille waited quietly for the emotion of the grief-stricken man to subside so that he would be able to hear what the minister had to say.

Finally Stephen became aware of Rev. Vaille's presence. "It's my fault," he said, his voice still choked with sobs. He scrubbed his eyes across his shirt sleeve. "I waited too long to get her out here."

"No, Mr. Fuller," William countered. "There was no way anyone could know how much time she had."

"I was stubborn, prideful," Stephen went on, as if not hearing. "I didn't want to give up the farm. Kept hoping she'd get well back home. We should have left as soon as the doctor told us what was wrong."

"I'm thinking Mrs. Fuller didn't want to leave any more than you did," Rev. Vaille stated quietly, coming to sit down beside the young farmer.

"She didn't," Stephen agreed. "But I should have made her. I should have insisted we sell the farm and move to this desert. She'd still be alive if it weren't for me."

Rev. Vaille waited a moment before speaking. "I've never known anyone who lost a loved one to death who didn't feel some guilt about it," he finally said, stretching out his long legs and settling back against the stall. "We all think we should have done something more or something different. But, the truth is, we all just do the best we can with the knowledge and strength that we have. We're none of us God. The power of life and death is not in our hands."

Stephen let out his breath half in a sigh, half in a sob. "What will I do without her?" he asked.

"Take it a day at a time, Mr. Fuller," the minister advised. "We will all do everything we can to help you. Healing from grief is a slow process, but it does come."

The sadness of the moment made it difficult for the missionaries to take pleasure in looking around their new home. Though they all complimented the men who had built the longhouse, it didn't seem appropriate to celebrate their long last arrival at the mission. After a tour of the compound, careful to avoid the barn, the group all gathered inside the central cabin. Though this was the largest cabin, intended for the Chapman family, they all could barely fit inside.

"Our plan is for the three families to have the three center cabins," Rev. Chapman explained the layout of the longhouse. Then the two couples . . ." he stopped at that moment. Clearing his throat, he said, "We'll allow Mr. Fuller the privacy of his cabin, if that is agreeable to everyone."

"Certainly," Mrs. Vaille agreed and all the others quickly nodded.

"Then the four single women will occupy the cabin closest to the center of the compound and the four single men will have the outside cabin. We hope this will afford everyone with a sense of safety."

Clarissa wondered at his words. They had received constant assurances from everyone they asked that the Indians would never harass the mission. Was the cabin arrangement simply a matter of decorum and caution, or did the leaders of the mission truly fear there would be trouble? She wondered how well she would be able to sleep this first night at Union Mission.

After their meeting, the women gathered at the wagons where a limited amount of food and linens had been included among their baggage. The remainder of their furnishings and supplies would be hauled to the mission tomorrow by these same mule skinners. Once they had emptied the three carts of their belongings, the men who had driven them out turned their mules back toward Three Forks.

Amanda had gone to the Chapman cabin to help Rachel and Alice Spaulding begin supper. Clarissa, Phoebe and Susan set about folding the linen sheets they had stitched in Little Rock over the buffalo robes that covered the rope strung beds in their cabin. Stitching heavy canvas ticking into mattresses and filling them with the down and feathers the men had saved from their fruitful hunts would be a first order of business.

While they worked, Abraham Redfield knocked at their door. Phoebe opened it to admit the mission superintendent who had a load of firewood in his arms. He blushed slightly as he stepped inside, as if he felt awkward about entering the ladies' quarters.

"I thought you might like me to get a fire going in your fireplace," he said.

"That would be wonderful," Phoebe responded. "We haven't wanted to take our coats off in here because of the chill."

The three women continued to unpack and arrange their belongings as Abraham limped across the cabin. He knelt and shaved a small pile of kindling in the fireplace. As soon as a spark flickered to life from his flint, he added more wood until he had a nice blaze going.

"Ah," Susan exclaimed. "That feels wonderful. Thank you so much, Mr. Redfield."

"My pleasure," he nodded toward Phoebe who smiled at him in an odd way. "Please let me know if there's anything else I can do to help you settle in. If there's something you want changed about your cabin, just let me know."

Clarissa thought it was the most words she'd ever heard from the quiet young man. She had been surprised when Phoebe told her he was a lay preacher. He seemed far too shy to stand before a congregation and deliver a sermon.

Phoebe walked him to the door and he moved on to the Woodruff's cabin next to theirs. Abraham was taking his job as mission superintendent seriously to be sure that everyone was comfortable in their new home.

A short time later, Amanda called everyone to supper by banging one of George Requa's carved wooden spoons on a tin pan. They gathered again in the Chapman cabin, though George, Will and Abraham took their plates outdoors to eat as soon as they had filled them. With only a couple of chairs available for seating, most everyone sat on the hard-packed dirt floor to eat.

Perhaps it was because she was especially hungry, but Clarissa thought the soup that Amanda had prepared was quite tasty. The Irish lass was as good a cook as she had proclaimed herself to be. She could bring a touch of civilization to this rough environment.

Without realizing it, the schoolteacher breathed a sigh of relief. She was sitting on the bare ground, eating from an enamel bowl with a crude wooden spoon. But at least the food was good. If she had to be out in this wilderness so far from her home and family, at least she knew she wouldn't starve. It was a small reassurance, but nevertheless made her feel somehow more confident about this venture into Indian country. She might just survive it after all.

As everyone ate, mostly in tired but companionable silence, George came in to dip a second helping of soup and take another slab of the thick corn bread Amanda had prepared. He paused at the open door before stepping back outside, looking around the cabin.

"Where's Mr. Fuller?" he asked.

His question made everyone realize the farm director had not joined them.

"I'll check his cabin," Will volunteered, setting down his own bowl and spoon. In a few minutes he returned. "He's not in his cabin, nor in the barn," he said.

Amanda remembered Lydia's words to her back in Little Rock. *Promise me that you'll look after Stephen. He'll not eat properly if you don't stay after him. He'll work too hard. He nearly killed himself trying to save me.*

Were they in danger of losing another member of their family? Amanda silently prayed that it wouldn't be so.

CHAPTER TWENTY-FIVE

Union Mission, Osage Lands
February, 1821

The wagons carrying the remainder of their supplies arrived
the next afternoon. Loaded from the keelboat at Three Forks, the
wagons were piled high with chairs and tables, more bed linens
and towels, pots, pans and metalware, barrels of molasses, corn
meal, flour and dried peas and beans, two precious loaves of
sugar, casks of nails, plus their trunks and more bags holding
their personal belongings.

It took all afternoon just to unload the wagons and deposit
everything in the cabins or barn. It would take another week to
sort through everything and divide the supplies among the living
quarters. Until the men could complete a kitchen and dining
hall, food stuffs were divided and stored in all seven cabins.
Clarissa felt as crowded as she had aboard the keelboats with
little room to walk among the trunks, barrels and furnishings.

The weather had remained mild and by late February bits of
green were peeking through the dried grasses and thick river
cane. It seemed incredible to the New Englanders that it did
indeed feel like spring was about to lay claim to the land.

Joseph Bogey traveled up from Three Forks for several
visits, usually timing his arrival to allow him to sit down to a
meal with the missionaries. He warned them that nature could
be capricious and more winter would be felt, but they all reveled
in the sunny, warm days.

One day in late February, Amanda stepped out of the central
cabin to call everyone to dinner. The men had been setting
stones for the huge fireplace going up in the kitchen, but were

quick to put down their tools and answer her call after a stop to wash up at a pitcher and basin set on a wooden stool outside the Chapmans' door.

The children came running from the barn where they had been playing with a fat gray mouser Joseph Revoir had brought them just the day before. Most of the women had been stitching mattresses in the Vaille's cabin, but set their needles in a seam and joined the group to fill their plates with thick slabs of meat pie.

Amanda shaded her eyes to look out to the west field where Stephen continued to push his plow. Most days, he did not come in from the fields to join the others for the noonday meal.

Everyone had tried to be considerate and respectful of his grief, but all were growing concerned as he drove himself relentlessly to finish breaking 40 acres of the land the mission owned. He rarely spoke and only picked at his food, if he didn't skip the meal altogether.

Amanda tightened her jaw in determination. She had made a promise to Lydia and she was going to do her best to keep it. She stepped into the cabin and took up one of the enamel plates and filled it with a generous portion of the pot pie she had baked in a flaky flour crust. She poured some steaming coffee into an empty sorghum tin and secured its tight fitting lid. Then grabbing a fork and napkin, she made her way to the door.

Rachel stopped her. "Is that for Mr. Fuller?" she asked.

Amanda nodded. "I'll send it by one of the men, if you think it more proper," she offered.

Rachel thought for a moment. "No, I think it best for you to take it," she said. "Mr. Fuller may be grieving and think he's not hungry, but he is still a gentleman. He would not refuse food from your hand because he wouldn't wish to offend you since you prepared it. My husband and Rev. Vaille have tried repeatedly to get him to eat. You may be the only one who can succeed."

"I'll do me best," Amanda said, feeling even more responsible for Stephen's care.

She made her way carefully across the mission compound toward the freshly turned earth where they would all work to plant corn soon. The mission had purchased a pair of oxen for plowing since the horses Chief Claremont had given them were untrained for such work.

As he turned the plow at the end of a row, the farm director noticed Amanda's approach. He whoa'd the oxen and waited, prepared to politely decline her invitation to dinner.

"Since you won't come to me food, I've brought the food to you," she said with what she hoped was a disarming smile.

"Thank you, Miss Ingles," he said, tugging at the knitted, wool cap he wore. Lydia had made it for him. "But I'm not really hungry. I'll just keep at the plowing."

"Oh, but I made so much," Amanda said. "And this flaky crust won't keep well; it will become soggy and I'll just have to throw it to the sow. And as much as I like the old gal, I'd rather not be givin' her me special meat pie." And she smiled again appealingly, hopefully.

Stephen was torn between sending the cook away and the fear that he would hurt her feelings if he did. He hesitated for a long moment and Amanda held the plate a little closer to him, hoping the fragrant steam would entice him.

He looked at the plate and then at the hopeful freckled face of the pretty cook. "I suppose I could eat a little something," he sighed.

Amanda's smile was genuine and bright. "I'll keep you company while you do," she said, wisely knowing that he would not eat more than a bite or two if she didn't remain.

Stephen took the plate and forked a small bite into his mouth. To his surprise, it tasted good, not like sawdust as his own cooking had this morning. He found he was hungrier than he thought and while Amanda chattered on about the weather and her plans for a big kitchen garden, he finished every bit of her savory meat pie.

She was opening the sorghum tin for him when she looked up toward the Osage Trace off in the distant west. "Oh, me," she said and Stephen turned to follow her gaze.

A long line of Osage warriors on horseback could be seen in the distance. They were coming south from the direction of Claremont's town and were turning off from the trail and heading toward the mission.

Stephen took a long swallow of the coffee and then handed

the tin and his plate back to her. "Better get back to the cabins," he said quietly, not wanting to alarm the young woman. "Looks like we're going to have visitors. Let Rev. Chapman know."

Amanda nodded silently, her chatter stilled at the sight of some fifteen Osage men approaching. She turned and as quickly as possible made her way back to the mission compound. She had to resist the urge to run the last few yards.

She stopped at the half-high walls of the kitchen where all the men had returned to their work after their meal. Intent on their work, none had noticed their approaching visitors.

"Rev. Chapman," Amanda called, somewhat out of breath. "We've company comin'," she said.

The men paused from their work, all catching sight of the Osage warriors at the same time.

The warriors rode across the just-plowed field, heedless of the havoc they made of Stephen's neatly turned rows. He tightened his jaw, but said nothing. He noticed that Joseph Revoir was among the group.

The leader of the Osage men halted his horse beside the oxen and they snorted and sidestepped in agitation. Stephen tightened his grip on the reins and the plow handle to keep from being jerked sideways.

The warrior spoke in Osage, his voice dripping with disdain.

Revoir translated his words. "Mad Buffalo asks why you work in the fields like a woman?"

Stephen understood that there was both an insult and a challenge intended with the man's words. Demonstrating the value of farming to the Indians was a goal of the mission, however, so the farm director sought to make that point. "My work alone will feed a hundred people," he said. "No woman could do that."

Mad Buffalo listened to Revoir's translation and then gave a begrudging nod of respect toward Stephen. His point had been made.

"Chief Claremont has heard that all your people have arrived at the mission," Joseph explained. "He sends his son to welcome them to his lands."

Another point being made? Stephen wondered. Were his

words a reminder that the mission was here only with the permission of the Osage leader and that permission could easily be revoked at any time?

"We are glad to receive your visit," the farmer said, feeling inadequate for the task of host. "Please come up to the cabins."

Then he backed up the oxen to be well away from the prancing mustangs the warriors rode. Revoir nodded and then translated Stephen's invitation. The Osage men made their way across the rest of the field and approached the mission compound.

By this time, Amanda had alerted all the missionaries to their unexpected visitors. Most had gathered at the half-finished kitchen, but Mrs. Chapman had asked Susan and Phoebe to take all the children to her cabin. They left the door open, though, so they could watch the Indians approach.

When Mad Buffalo halted his black mustang before the group of missionaries, Rev. Chapman greeted him in the Osage language. He had been working hard to learn some basic phrases in Osage from Pryor, Bogey and Mr. Revoir.

From the smiles on the faces of their visitors, the warriors were either pleased with his effort, or amused at his difficulty in pronouncing the words.

Clarissa eased closer to George Requa as they stood and waited for the Osage warriors to dismount their horses. She felt nervous and uncertain about how she would be expected to interact with the dark-skinned, blanket-clad men.

Three of the warriors were appointed by Mad Buffalo to hold their horses' reins, a practice that kept the barely tamed animals under control, but also was a defensive move in case they chose to make a quick exit. The rest of the men waited for no invitation to begin inspecting the mission buildings. They wandered about the half-completed kitchen, curiously looking up the chimney of the large fireplace.

Rev. Chapman eagerly tried to engage Mad Buffalo in conversation, but Clarissa could tell that he felt nervous too for he stumbled over his words. Knowing the children were being kept in his cabin, he invited the Osage leader and Mr. Revoir to the Vailles' cabin.

Rev. and Mrs. Chapman and Rev. and Mrs. Vaille followed

Mad Buffalo and Joseph Revoir through the door. The remaining missionaries and other Osage men were left outside to try to politely stay out of each other's way.

Conversation was impossible without Revoir to interpret, though Clarissa knew some of the Osages spoke French. She was fluent in French as were Will and George Requa, but none of them ventured to start a conversation in that language. They simply didn't know what would be appropriate to say. How ill-prepared they were for this moment.

Clarissa was astonished to see the Indians enter some of the cabins and look around. She held her breath as two stepped into the rooms she shared with Phoebe, Susan and Amanda.

"Well, I never in all me born days," Amanda quietly sputtered in Clarissa's ear. "Should we stop them?"

"How?" Clarissa responded. "Do you want to tell them it's rude to enter a lady's quarters without an invitation?"

Amanda gave Clarissa a look that said she wouldn't and clamped her mouth shut.

"I'll ask them to leave, if you wish me to," George offered.

Clarissa considered his offer. "I'm sure they're just curious," she finally said. "Surely they mean no harm."

Dr. Palmer stepped a little closer to their group. "I don't think they will take anything. Like Miss Johnson said, they are mostly curious about our way of life."

Shortly the two men who had inspected the women's cabin then wandered into the Chapman's cabin where Susan was reading a story to try to keep the children occupied. They all looked up as the Osage warriors entered, a mixture of fear and curiosity of their own on their faces.

The shorter of the two men walked over to where Susan sat in a rocker with Billy Spaulding on her lap. He fingered Susan's honey blonde hair and said something to his companion. The other warrior laughed and responded with a leer on his face. The first man stroked Susan's silky tresses as if fascinated with their color and feel. Susan sat quietly and Billy buried his face against her shoulder. The other children and Phoebe sat frozen like statues, afraid to move or say anything.

Finally the Osage warrior patted Susan's head and then Billy's, as if to assure her he meant her no harm. With another comment to his companion they both left the cabin. Everyone in the room exhaled their held breath.

Thomas Chapman jumped up from where he sat by Susan's chair and went to the door to watch the men as they went next door to the Vaille's cabin.

"I would have stopped him if he tried to hurt you," Thomas said, turning back to look at Miss Comstock.

"Me too," Richard Vaille said, not to be outdone by his friend.

"I know you would have, boys," Susan said, "but you see that the Indians don't mean to hurt us. They're just interested in what we are like. Just as we are about them. Hopefully, we'll all become friends after this and you'll make even more friends when school starts this fall."

"Will they teach us to shoot with a bow and arrow?" James Chapman asked, joining his older brother at the cabin door.

"That will depend upon what your mother says," Phoebe answered.

"Oh," James' face was crestfallen. "Then I guess not."

Phoebe and Susan exchanged a smile.

CHAPTER TWENTY-SIX

Union Mission
Early Spring, 1821

Before their Osage visitors left, Rev. Chapman invited them to share a meal with the mission family. To have enough room for everyone, they gathered in the unfinished dining hall, with everyone seated on the ground. Amanda and most of the other women had worked to prepare a meal of venison steaks, boiled potatoes and the dried peas she had been simmering throughout the day.

Amanda had quickly prepared a dried apple cobbler in the large oven she had brought with her from New England. Clarissa had thought the oven much too large to be useful when she had seen the cook unpack it, but it looked small sitting among the coals in the massive kitchen fireplace. The Osage warriors made appreciative gestures as they ate the cobbler and didn't hesitate to help themselves to the scrapings from the bottom of the pan.

When the men departed, Rev. Chapman invited them to return with their wives and children. He explained that they would be welcome to a Sabbath service each week. Mad Buffalo gave no commitment that he or his people would participate in either the church or the school they would begin in the fall.

The missionaries watched the men ride north on the Trace back toward Claremont's town. While the visit had been friendly, none of the missionaries could assume that the Osages welcomed or even felt any interest in education or the gospel. They clearly saw no need for what the missionary society hoped to accomplish among the native people. Clarissa went to bed that night wondering if there would be a single Osage girl in her class come fall.

But though they all had felt the uncertainty, no one spoke of it in the days ahead. They continued the work of building the dining hall and Stephen Fuller took a few days from his field work to plow the kitchen garden Amanda wanted.

The women finished the mattresses they had sewn and then had stuffed with goose and quail feathers and soft down. The children settled into their own chores – the boys gathered the hundreds of dried buffalo chips scattered across the prairie for the fires and the girls were responsible for feeding the chickens and gathering the eggs.

A cold snap welcomed March but within a few days of it the trees in the *spa-vi-nah* were unfurling tiny leaves of delicate green. Joseph Bogey paid the mission a visit, bringing up a load of supplies hauled to Three Forks by keelboat.

"Would you be needing a young apprentice for your work?" Bogey asked over a cup of coffee in the now completed dining hall.

"Perhaps," Rev. Chapman said thoughtfully. Indeed, they had quickly discovered that there was more than enough work at the mission for everyone the Society had hired and more besides. The women in particular were in need of more help, having lost Sally and Lydia on the journey. But women were scarce on the frontier.

"A Negro lad showed up at my door last week," Bogey said, helping himself to another of Amanda's cookies. "Looks to be about 13 or 14 in age, though he claims to be 16. Says his parents died in a keelboat accident. He needs work and a place to stay. I thought of you here and wondered if you might have need of him."

"I should think we could take him in," Rev. Vaille answered, throwing a look at Rev. Chapman for his confirmation. The other minister nodded.

"We can't pay him more than room and board," the mission director stated. "But we certainly have plenty of work for him. What of you, Mr. Woodruff? Could you use a hand at the forge?"

"I can always use someone working the bellows," the older

man replied. "I always had an apprentice working with me in my shop back home."

"Send him up the Trace if you think you can trust him to find the way," Chapman said to the trader. "Or bring him with you the next time you come out for a visit."

"I'll do it," Bogey agreed, slapping his leather britches as he stood to go. He pilfered another cookie from the plate on the long wooden table. With a twinkle in his eye, he smiled at Amanda. "Mighty good cookies, Miss Ingles," he said.

"It's Mrs. Steadman's recipe," she replied.

"I thought I recognized it," Bogey declared. "I'll stop in to see her next time I'm in Petite Roche and give her your regards."

"Please do," Rachel Chapman said, smiling at the incorrigible tradesman.

Within a week, Bogey was back with not one, but two young apprentices for the mission. The Negro boy was named Paul Gillard and did look younger than the 16 years he steadfastly claimed. The other boy was Robert Bake, a tow-headed lad who plainly acknowledged he was only 14 and also an orphan. Robert, or Robbie as he preferred, said he had farm experience.

The boys were settled into their quarters – Paul in the back of the forge where he would be responsible for starting the fire each morning, and Robbie in the loft in the barn. He would assume responsibility for feeding the stock and milking the cows as well as helping Mr. Fuller with the field work.

The new additions to the mission crew quickly fell into the rhythm of life at the frontier outpost. John and Clarissa had resumed classes for the children as soon as the dining hall had been completed.

The women all took turns helping Amanda with preparing meals as well as seeing to the regular household chores. Eliza and Susan also watched after Billy Spaulding and Sarah Vaille. There was so much work, it never seemed to all get done and there was little time for the kind of social niceties they had known in New England.

Rev. Chapman, Will Requa and Abraham Redfield made frequent journeys to Chief Claremont's village, hoping to learn the language and begin to commit it to writing. Occasionally Dr. Palmer would accompany them and he tried to discreetly assess the medical needs of the Osage people. While their native neighbors were always hospitable to their visits, it was plain to see that they felt no need for the mission's evangelism or education.

The missionaries soon discovered that the Osage Trace which connected Missouri to Three Forks and Spanish-held Texas saw a surprising amount of traffic for such a remote region. Mule whackers hauling freight passed by often and with the coming of spring Indian hunting parties frequently used the Trace to access the many game trails leading to the rivers. Besides the Osage, Cherokee and Chickasaw hunters also passed through. The missionaries watched the spring ritual with interest, but the Indians showed little regard for the mission.

Will and George Requa reported at supper one evening that they had caught a glimpse of a panther along the river while they were out hunting.

"Was it a big one?" Robbie asked, suddenly alert. He had been shoveling in the venison stew on his plate as if it was his last supper, but his attention quickly diverted from his food with the mention of the wild cat.

"Oh, it was a big one alright," George said dramatically. "Wouldn't want to run into that fellow after dark. All you would see would be those glowing yellow eyes."

Clarissa shuddered at the thought even though she suspected George was exaggerating the cat's size.

"I'm sure we need not fear the cat entering the mission though," Mrs. Chapman stated.

"Wild animals are going to naturally stay clear of humans," Will said. "But everyone should keep a careful look out just to be safe. Especially if you're working outside the mission."

"You hear that boys?" Rev. Chapmen asked. "Keep a watchful eye and let an adult know if you see anything."

"We will, Papa," Thomas said and the other boys nodded solemnly.

From the look on Robbie's face, Clarissa thought the youth was eager for a glimpse of the cat. She hoped he wouldn't wander off looking for it.

A few days later, Stephen was plowing the south field which ran along the river. The day was bright and warm and the small native trees known as redbuds were in full bloom along the banks of the Neosho.

Swarms of bees in the thousands were busily working among the buds. Stephen watched them as he worked, wondering where their hive was located. Some fresh honey would be a nice addition to their limited diet and he knew Miss Ingles would be happy if he could find it.

Amanda delivered his noon meal to him as she did every day. Stephen found that he looked forward to this break in his work day, enjoying the cook's cheerful chatter as well as the tasty dishes she brought him. Her eyes lit with pleasure when he told her about his intent to find the honey tree.

"Ooh, I'll be forever in your debt, if ye do, Mr. Fuller," she said, her Irish brogue thickening in her excitement. "I've had to be awful sparin' with the sugar for Mrs. Chapman says it must last me this entire year. Some honey would do fine for sweetenin' up some pies and cobblers."

For some reason, Miss Ingles' pleasure made Stephen glad. Her smile over so simple a gift as wild honey brought a bit of brightness to his spirit that had known only a dark sadness for the last month. He was determined to find the bee hive and resolved to start his search after he finished his chores today.

Amanda came back to the dining room with a happy smile on her face which Clarissa noted as she looked up from the book she was reading to the girls. She wondered what had brought the cook such pleasure. Amanda had a generally sunny spirit, but she seemed especially buoyant today. She hummed the rousing Irish folk song she had taught them as she joined Phoebe and Mrs. Vaille in washing up the dinner dishes.

Later that day, it was Clarissa's turn to help with the dishwashing after a fine supper of stuffed quail and dandelion salad. Mr. Fuller had joined the group for the meal, something he rarely did and for the first time since learning of his wife's death, he entered into their conversation and even stayed for the evening devotions led by Rev. Vaille.

While Martha Woodruff cleaned the dining tables and
chairs, Amanda shaved thin curls of soap into a pan of warm
water and began to plunge the enamelware dishes into the suds
she stirred to life.

Glancing over to see that Mrs. Woodruff was out of hearing,
the cook leaned close to Clarissa as she handed her a mug to dry.
"I'm thinkin' we may be havin' a weddin' here at the mission ere
too long," she whispered conspiratorially.

Clarissa raised her eyebrows in surprise. "You're getting
married?" she asked.

"No, not me, silly." Amanda laughed.

"Susan?" Clarissa guessed next. Susan and Will had been
circumspectly flirting with each other since the men had joined
the keelboat in St. Louis. The blond housemother had never
hidden her admiration for the older Requa brother, but Clarissa
had not thought their relationship had reached the stage of
marriage.

"No, though I daresay Susan would be quite happy if it were
she who was gettin' married," Amanda countered.

Then who? Clarissa wondered as she wiped the plate
Amanda handed her. "Not Eliza, surely," Clarissa said with a
sinking feeling in the pit of her stomach. Eliza too had never
hidden her admiration for one of the mission brothers. She
seemed to invent excuses to rush her nephew Billy to Dr. Palmer
for care of a scrape or bruise just so she could spend time with
the physician.

Eliza had even taken to her bed with fever on two occasions
in the months since they had been at the mission. Though
Clarissa had never seen anything but a professional manner from
the doctor toward the seventeen-year-old young woman, she
could think of no one else who might be getting married.

"No, not Miss Eliza, though it's not for lack of trying on her
part," Amanda stated knowingly. Clarissa assumed the cook had
also noticed Eliza's attempts to gain the doctor's attention.

"Then who?" Clarissa finally asked.

"Phoebe," Amanda said, turning to take up one of the large
roasting pans to scrub clean.

"Phoebe?" Clarissa repeated in disbelief. "Surely you jest?"

"No," Amanda replied in a matter-of-fact tone. "She told

me herself, after a little coaxin' from me," the redhead winked. "Though it's nothing official yet, you understand."

"But who . . ." Clarissa stopped herself before completing the unkind thought, but it continued in her head. *Who would want to marry Phoebe?*

Instead she finished her words with ". . . who would Phoebe agree to marry?"

"Mr. Redfield," Amanda stated. "Haven't you noticed how he blushes to the roots of his hair every time Phoebe speaks to him? And how she goes all tongue-tied whenever he's around? It's a wonder they could have a complete conversation, but apparently they have. I saw them walkin' together down by the river the other day. That's when I pried the confession out of Phoebe."

It was hard to imagine shy Mr. Redfield and frumpy Phoebe Beach forming an attachment. Though it was true that they both loved children, they seemed to have little else in common. As she thought about it while drying the roasting pan, Clarissa did recall seeing the two of them often playing a game of hide-and-seek or keep-away with the children in the dusky hours after chores were completed and before their mothers called them in for bedtime.

"Have they actually reached an understanding?" Clarissa asked, feeling like a gossip, but still trying to grasp the idea that Phoebe would be the first among them to marry.

"I don't think Mr. Redfield has actually stated his intentions," Amanda answered as she prepared to take the dishwater out to her garden. "But he's hinted at it, accordin' to Phoebe. And she's prepared to agree if he does ask."

"Well, of course," was all Clarissa could say. How many times would Phoebe receive a marriage proposal? As she had pointed out herself, there were few prospects beyond the mission here on the prairie.

"It will be a welcome blessin' for her," Amanda said as she opened the kitchen door, "especially after such a sad endin' to her first marriage." Then she stepped outside, leaving Clarissa so shocked she nearly fell into one of the dining chairs.

Mrs. Woodruff looked at her oddly and asked, "Are you feeling poorly, dearie?"

Clarissa looked up at the motherly woman and had to swallow hard not to confess that she was suddenly not feeling well. But her complaint was not a physical malady. She could hardly confess that she was feeling a pang of jealousy that Phoebe . . . plain, uneducated, ordinary Phoebe . . . was about to embark on a second marriage. And she, Clarissa, had been unable to secure even a first marriage.

Not that she considered herself to be a great beauty – like Eliza – but she would certainly have thought that she had better prospects for marriage than Phoebe. She knew her muddled thoughts were less than kind and certainly not those that should be entertained by a Christian, but she felt herself on the verge of tears.

"I'm just a bit tired, I guess," she stammered. "I think I'll retire for the evening."

"Yes, get some rest, dear," Martha said, giving Clarissa a kindly pat on the shoulder. "It will all look better in the morning."

In the morning, Clarissa found herself watching for the signs of a romantic attachment between Phoebe and Abraham Redfield, half expecting to discover that they were nothing more than Amanda's imagination. However, the subtle looks that passed between the two during breakfast and morning devotions confirmed Amanda's report.

The following Sunday, after the hymns were sung for morning worship, Rev. Vaille announced that there would indeed be a wedding on the following Sabbath. Abraham turned to smile at Phoebe from where he sat on the men's side of the dining hall which was also serving as their chapel.

The blush of pleasure on the young woman's face made Clarissa feel ashamed of her earlier thoughts. When Susan and Amanda offered to spend the afternoon helping Phoebe plan her wedding, Clarissa joined in and was soon caught up in the joy of the occasion. With laughter, and some tears, the four mission sisters discussed her plans for a simple ceremony.

"I don't want no great fuss," Phoebe declared. "I don't want or deserve some big, fancy wedding. If we were back in New England, my marrying again would be a scandal."

"Now why would that be?" Susan asked, her childlike voice reflecting her ignorance of Phoebe's past.

Phoebe and Amanda exchanged a look. "'Cause I'm divorced," Phoebe stated in her blunt manner. "Abra . . . Mr. Redfield . . . had to do some mighty talking to convince Rev. Vaille to marry us. If there had been a civil authority anywhere nearby, he probably would have sent us there instead."

Clarissa knew the truth of Phoebe's words. Divorce was scandalous and nearly an unforgivable sin in the staid New England churches they all had attended. Murder was almost more forgivable than divorce, she thought with bitter irony. Even her broken engagement had seemed tantamount to some great moral failing.

She wondered that the mission had accepted Phoebe's employment. She supposed they had received few applicants willing to make this journey west to serve the Indians in such primitive environs. Still the willingness to accept a divorced woman made her half seriously wonder who among them had committed murder. What worse could be forgiven?

Susan's eyes were large as she considered Phoebe's admission. She seemed to hardly know how to respond. "Oh, I didn't know," was all she could find to say.

"I ain't proud of it," Phoebe stated softly, tears filling her eyes. "My father arranged the marriage with a man much older than me. He weren't happy with me when I didn't produce a son for him. To get the divorce, he told the church that I was unfaithful to him. But it weren't true! He was the one who was unfaithful." She pulled a handkerchief from her apron pocket and dabbed at the tears that spilled down her cheeks.

"Of course it wasn't true," Amanda said hotly as she circled Phoebe with her arms. "Men!" she huffed. "Always think it's the woman's fault if there are no children."

Clarissa hoped for Phoebe's sake that it was not her fault that she had borne no children for her husband. For someone who clearly adored children as she did, the prospect of never having any of her own must be a very sad one.

Phoebe continued to dab at her eyes. "I've confessed to Mr. Redfield my situation," she said, "and he assured me it don't change his feelings toward me." Then she broke down and sobbed into her handkerchief. The other two sisters joined Amanda in a group embrace.

"God is truly good to me," Phoebe said when she had composed herself. "I don't deserve a man the likes of Mr. Redfield."

"Nonsense," Amanda said. "You treat yourself too meanly. None of us deserves love. It is always a gift."

How true, Clarissa thought with a pang. *It cannot be bought with a handsome dowry and certainly can't with a meager one.* But she kept her thoughts to herself and joined her mission sisters as the wedding plans continued.

The women looked over Phoebe's limited and somewhat drab wardrobe and declared that she would have to borrow a dress from one of them for the wedding. Clarissa proved to be the closest in size so she swallowed her feelings and offered the scarlet faille that she had worn to Governor Clark's home. With her dark hair, the dress was quite becoming on Phoebe and brightened her complexion.

When Phoebe stood before Rev. Vaille a week later, her eyes bright and a wide smile on her face, Clarissa had to acknowledge that all brides are indeed beautiful. Susan had tucked a sprig of redbud blossoms in her hair and she carried a tiny nosegay of wild prairie flowers that Amanda and the girls had gathered for her.

Abraham looked handsome in the suit he had borrowed from Rev. Vaille, but he appeared very nervous. As he repeated his vows, he kept clearing his throat to cover his emotions, making his Adam's apple bobble noticeably.

When Rev. Vaille pronounced the couple "man and wife," the group swarmed them with handshakes, hugs and good wishes. Amanda and the other women had created a veritable wedding feast to follow the ceremony, including a lovely cake made with the precious sugar.

The newlyweds would even travel for their honeymoon, taking the Trace up to the Harmony Mission in Missouri. Joseph Revoir was to be their guide. Rev. Chapman had long wanted someone from Union Mission to visit Harmony. He wanted them to learn all they could about what successes or failures the Harmony missionaries had experienced.

While the Redfields were gone, the men helped Mr. Fuller move his gear into the bachelors' quarters. When they returned, Abraham and Phoebe would occupy the cabin built for the Fullers.

At the same time, the women helped Eliza move into the ladies' cabin. She had declared that she was old enough to leave the Spaulding family quarters. As she settled her things in the space that Phoebe had once occupied, sighing over the limited area, Clarissa had to swallow her feelings once again.

CHAPTER TWENTY-SEVEN

Union Mission
Spring, 1821

"We've got visitors," Robbie Bake called from his perch on the partially completed roof of the chapel which would also serve as the schoolhouse. The men had been working steadily on the structure despite Mr. Redfield's absence. The mission superintendent had left them detailed plans for the work while he and his bride were away.

Robbie's call made everyone at the mission stop their chores and turn toward the Trace to see who might be paying a visit. It was the Redfields returning from Missouri, along with Joseph Revoir, the Osage leader Mad Buffalo, and three others that they did not recognize. Redfield turned the mission wagon, pulled by their team of oxen, off the road and into the mission yard. Revoir and Mad Buffalo followed on their mustangs.

Everyone gathered around the wagon, eager to meet their guests and welcome the Redfields home.

"Well, you made it back," Rev. Chapman greeted Abraham, shaking his hand after he had helped Phoebe from the wagon.

"And we've brought the Austin family with us," Redfield explained. "Mr. Austin is the millwright at Harmony Mission. I asked him to come and help us work up a design for our mill."

"We're pleased to have you pay us a visit," Mr. Chapman stated as he extended his hand to Mr. Austin. The men had often discussed the need for a mill if they were to put most of their land into corn production.

"Daniel Austin," the man said, to introduce himself. "This is my wife Martha and my daughter Mary."

Mr. Austin was a stout man with a balding head and meaty hands. His wife was taller than him by an inch or two, very thin and with a dour look on her face. Clarissa supposed she was tired from the long journey. Their daughter looked to be about ten years old. She wore her auburn hair in two long braids and had a spray of freckles across her nose. She hopped from the wagon and openly appraised the mission children who were also gawking at her.

While everyone greeted their visitors, Amanda, Susan and Asie Vaille hurried to the dining hall to complete supper preparations for the group. Mad Buffalo declined to stay, turning his mustang quickly and trotting down the Trace towards Three Forks. But Revoir joined everyone in the dining hall.

The adults talked long into the evening, comparing the efforts of the two Osage missions and making plans for exchanging preaching dates. The children were asked to show young Mary Austin around and Phoebe and Abraham along with George Requa took charge of the children. The young couple seemed very happy, their fingers intertwined as they strolled with the youngsters around the mission compound.

The Redfields graciously gave the Austin family use of their cabin for the three days that they stayed at Union Mission. The young newlyweds slept on a pallet laid out in a room at back of the kitchen where supplies were kept.

After a night's sleep, Mrs. Austin seemed in a much better mood, though she was quiet and spoke very little. Her daughter Mary, on the other hand, chattered like a little magpie. She and Elizabeth Vaille and Abigail Chapman became best friends for life during the three-day visit.

The three girls shed tears as they bid each other goodbye when the Austins' visit ended.

In a borrowed wagon provided by Mr. Revoir, the Harmony missionaries set out to return to Missouri.

George had helped Mary Austin into the back of the wagon. The girl placed her hands on the young man's shoulders and in a perfectly serious voice stated, "I'm going to marry you someday." George seemed taken aback by the declaration, but finally said with a grin and slight blush, "Well, I guess I'll have some waiting to do for you to grow up."

"Oh, just four or five years," Mary assured him.

"Mary!" her mother scolded. "Sit down and don't talk such nonsense."

Mary quickly sat down in the wagon but seemed not at all chagrined at her mother's remonstration. She grinned and waved as the wagon pulled out.

Clarissa smiled at the girl's boldness as did all the adults who had heard her stated intentions. Oh, if only she could be so bold.

The young teacher cast a shy glance at George, but his eyes were on the wagon, a thoughtful expression on his face. She sighed and turned to go back to the school room but caught a quick glimpse of Dr. Palmer. He was looking at her with the same thoughtful expression and it was now Clarissa's turn to blush.

"Mama, Mama," Leah called as she entered the Chapman cabin the following morning. The five-year-old was clearly upset and tears filled her eyes.

"What is it, dearest?" Rachel asked, quickly setting aside the sewing she had been working on.

"One of the chickens was killed," the little girl said, climbing up into her mother's lap. "All that is left is feathers and blood."

"Oh, dear," Rachel soothed. "A fox or a hawk must have gotten it," she explained, hugging her daughter close. "It's the way things are out here in the wild."

"I know," Leah sighed, "but it frightened me. That old fox won't eat me will it?"

"No, no, honey," her mother assured her, but her voice held concern as well. "Foxes don't eat people. You don't have to be afraid."

She quietly mentioned the killed chicken to Mr. Fuller at breakfast and he promised to check into it. Their horses had seemed nervous yesterday evening and though Fuller and Redfield had checked the perimeter of their compound and found nothing amiss, it still made all the adults wary.

Stephen and Will walked out to the coop when breakfast was finished. The gate was secured, for the girls had been strongly admonished to never leave it open. They found the feathers scattered at the back corner with spots of blood splayed about.

"Look here," Will said, squatting down to examine a paw print in the soft earth. He whistled softly at the size of it. "That's no fox or opossum," he told the farm director.

"It's a cat of some kind," Stephen agreed. "A big cat."

"Could be that panther George and I saw," Will said. "But why would it come so close to a human camp? There are plenty of prairie chickens and other easy game."

"And why didn't we hear the chickens put up a ruckus?" Stephen responded.

"Must have struck so fast that the other hens weren't even aware."

"We'll have to try to track it," Stephen said. "Can't have it thinking it can find a ready meal here. It will only grow bolder."

"George, Woodruff and I will head out and see if we can find its trail," Will said.

"I'd join you, but I found a honey tree I've been searching for," Stephen said. "I promised Miss Ingles I'd bring her the honey today."

"We'll all be grateful for that," Will grinned. "Her description of scones dripping with butter and honey had me dreaming last night."

Stephen laughed. "Food is definitely Miss Ingles' gift."

"Watch your back," Will warned as the two parted, Stephen heading to the blacksmith forge to get his newly sharpened ax and a bellows and firebox he had asked Paul to fill with coals. He would use smoke to quiet the bees before taking down the hollow tree where the hive was located.

When he arrived at the site close to the river about a half mile from the mission compound, he took the time to tuck his pants legs firmly into his boots, draw on a pair of gloves and slip a bandana high around his neck and up under his cap to limit any exposure to bee stings. The busy creatures were working industriously, their steady hum giving Stephen a shiver. He'd never liked the sound of swarming bees.

He worked carefully to build a small fire in the box adding some damp wood to create more smoke than flames. Then he slowly pumped the smoke into a rotted opening at the base of the tree, allowing it time to drift upwards to where he knew the queen was probably located. When he felt he had settled the bees as best he could, he took his ax and began to hack at the base of the tree.

The bees grew agitated as their hive vibrated. Stephen stopped when he had made it about halfway through the softened trunk. He bellowed more smoke into the tree, feeling a sting on his forehead. He swatted the bees away and hastened to finish the job. With just a few more whacks at the trunk, the tree came crashing to the ground. It split like a ripe melon exposing the golden honey and honeycomb.

The angry buzzing intensified as the bees darted in and out of the hive in search of the cause of the disturbance to their home. Stephen stepped back several paces and bent close over the firebox, pumping the bellows to push the smoke toward the fallen tree. He never saw the cat before he felt the panther's claws rip into his back.

At first his mind could not register that he was being ripped by the big cat. He thought it was the bees. By the time he realized the true danger, his back was nearly in shreds. He was too late and too weak to grab the musket he had brought with him. All he could do was fall to the ground and try to protect his throat and head.

He wondered if he was about to die and did not feel fear. He would join his Lydia now, something he had often wished for in the days after he had learned of her death. "God," he prayed as the pain intensified. "God, help me." The last sound he heard was the buzz of angry bees.

At the mission compound, Robbie Bake was again working on the roof of the chapel. He paused and ran his eyes along the tree line of the riverbank. In the distance he could see Mr. Fuller chopping down the honey tree. And then he saw the panther, a sleek, black, sinewy blur leap upon the farmer's back.

"Cat!" Robbie yelled at the top of his lungs. The men

working below stopped to look up at him. "The panther's on Mr. Fuller," he said, pointed toward the river.

Abraham lunged for the loaded musket the men always kept within reach of their worksite. He began to run toward the river. Rev. Chapman darted toward his cabin to pull down his own gun from its peg high above the children's reach. He was joined by William Vaille and they followed after Abraham. Dr. Palmer had the presence of mind to grab his medical kit and quickly pull a sheet from his bed. Then he too ran for the river.

The women and children gathered in the mission yard, fear upon every face. Sarah and Billy were soon crying, sensing the fear even though not completely understanding it.

"Come let's gather in the dining hall and pray," said Mrs. Chapman. As the children entered the hall, she turned to Clarissa, Martha and Amanda. "Get a bed ready for Mr. Fuller. Heat plenty of water. We'll start tearing bandages." The women nodded and set about to follow her instructions.

By the time the men arrived to where Stephen lay in his pooling blood, the panther had fled, driven away perhaps by the still angry bees.

Abraham fired a shot toward the river just to ensure the cat kept running. He dropped to his knees beside the farm director. His back was in bloody ribbons and the bees were still darting about. He grabbed the bellows and pumped smoke vigorously toward the fallen tree, sending the bees inside the hive.

The three other men arrived shortly and Dr. Palmer knelt to feel for a pulse at Stephen's throat. "He's still alive, but barely. We have to get this bleeding under control." While he worked to check Fuller's wounds, Abraham began to tear the sheet into wide bandages.

Shortly, Will, George and Alex came running up from the river's edge. They had heard Robbie's warning cry and had followed the sound of Abraham's shot.

"Father God," Will breathed in prayer, horror on his face as he saw the extent of Stephen's wounds. "We should have found that cat before it could do this."

George gripped his brother's shoulder. He felt responsible too. They had been the first to sight the panther. They should have pursued it from that first moment.

217

Dr. Palmer was working to press the bandages against the worst of the wounds trying to stanch the flow of blood.

"Can we move him?" Alexander asked. "I think I can carry him."

Marcus considered the options. He would most certainly need to stitch the wounds and it would be best to do that back at the cabins. Mr. Fuller was a small man and Alexander probably could carry him, but how to manage it without doing further damage was the question.

"I'll lift him across my back," Alex stated, demonstrating with a gesture how he would complete the task.

"Alright, we'll try it," Dr. Palmer agreed. Quickly he and Abraham worked to wrap more cloth strips around their brother. Carefully the blacksmith hoisted Stephen onto his shoulders and began the slow trek back to the mission. As he walked slowly, George noticed that there were tears streaming down Alexander's face.

Before they reached the compound, the older man's steps faltered. His breathing was heavy.

"Here, let me take him the rest of the way," Will offered and as gently as they could they transferred the man to Will's shoulders.

He carried Stephen into the men's cabin and with George's help carefully laid him face down on the clean sheets Mrs. Woodruff had spread across the bed. Stephen groaned, but mercifully remained unconscious.

"Get me some light," Palmer instructed as he rolled up his blood-stained sleeves. Rev. Chapman quickly lit a candle and placed it in a lantern, bringing it to Stephen's bedside.

The cabin door opened and Clarissa and Amanda entered, carrying two heavy kettles of hot water, using their long aprons to hold the pot handles. They were followed by Rachel and Martha whose arms were loaded with wash rags, towels and strips of bandages.

Dr. Palmer laid out the surgical tools he would use – a scalpel, scissors, the long curved needles and the catgut suturing. Once again he was grateful that his mission family kept calm and anticipated what would be needed to save Mr. Fuller's life. He wished he felt as calm and competent as they.

"Mrs. Chapman, will you pour some of the hot water in a basin for me to wash up?" he asked.

"Certainly," Rachel said. She dipped out some of the water and laid a bar of lye soap and a clean towel by the basin.

As he washed his hands and forearms, the doctor continued with his instructions. "Miss Ingles, please get some of the bison pemmican boiling to make a broth. Mr. Fuller will need it when he regains consciousness."

"Aye, I'll start it immediately." She left the cabin and hurried to the kitchen, barely able to suppress the tears that threatened. She knew Stephen had been trying to harvest honey for her when he was attacked. *If he died because of her . . .* she couldn't continue the thought. "Oh, please, Father," she prayed. "Don't let him die. Please . . . I need him; we need him."

She mopped the tears that now broke free as she worked to begin the broth. She could hear the other women and children in the dining area, joining her in praying for Mr. Fuller.

Dr. Palmer dried his hands and looked around the cabin. "George, please take hold of Fuller's legs to hold him still. And Miss Johnson, wet those wash cloths and ring them out thoroughly for me."

Clarissa nodded and set to work. She handed the rags to Martha who was assisting the doctor in cutting away the temporary bandages and Stephen's bloody and torn shirt. Together they worked to gently wash away the still flowing blood until there was a terrible, awful pile of red-stained rags on the little wash stand.

"I'll take these out and bring more," Rachel said, gathering up the bloody cloths. She shuddered as she carried them out. The blood loss alone might take Mr. Fuller's life.

"Mrs. Woodruff, if you'll continue to sponge away the blood, I'm going to try to suture the wounds," Dr. Palmer stated as he carefully sterilized his instruments with whiskey. "Miss Johnson, can you assist me?"

"Me?" Clarissa asked with a quiver in her voice.

"Your hands are clean," the doctor explained. "I need another pair of hands to hold the wounds closed while I stitch."

Clarissa closed her eyes momentarily. She who gagged at the thought of making soap was being asked to assist with surgery? How could Dr. Palmer possibly think she could do this?

She opened her eyes and took a deep breath. Dr. Palmer, Mrs. Woodruff, Rev. Chapman and George Requa were the only ones in the cabin and all were watching her, waiting for her to come and help.

Clarissa swallowed down her fear and stepped closer to the bedside. Breathing a prayer, she nodded to the doctor. "If you'll show me what to do . . ."

Marcus looked her in the eye and knew she was afraid, but he also knew the woman who survived Wolf Island had a greater strength than she realized. "You'll be fine," he assured her quietly.

He pulled together the ripped flesh at the center of Stephen's back and showed her how to hold it in place while he stitched. They would work outward, closing each slash carefully.

Clarissa felt her stomach roll as she touched the skin and gently held it. She found that she could not watch the doctor pull the needle through the flesh or Mrs. Woodruff wipe away the blood.

She made herself look instead at the back of Dr. Palmer's head bent over his patient. She noted that his dark hair was curling around the collar of his shirt. He needed a haircut. It was a silly thought in such a serious moment, but she needed to distract her thinking from the task at hand.

It seemed like hours before the doctor took the last stitch and declared, "It's done."

Everyone in the room breathed a sigh of relief. It felt as if they all had been holding their breath during the entire procedure.

Clarissa felt her legs were about to give out so she moved to the cabin's small breakfast table and sat in one of its chairs. Mrs. Woodruff crossed the floor to stand behind the chair and put her arms around the young woman's shoulders, laying her cheek against Clarissa's. "You did good," she said. Dr. Palmer looked at her and nodded his agreement before turning back to the task of wrapping bandages around Stephen's torso.

The farm director had not stirred since being laid in the bed.

His skin was a ghastly gray and his breathing was shallow. Rev. Chapman left the cabin to let the rest of the family know that the surgery was complete. Their prayers had brought Mr. Fuller through thus far, but many more prayers would be needed.

Later in the day, after the surgery had been completed, Will and Abraham had returned to the spot where Stephen had been jumped by the panther. They found that the bees had abandoned their ruptured hive so they returned to the mission and brought back two of Amanda's largest pans. Filling both to almost overflowing, they carried the golden sugar to the cook. What would have brought her joy earlier now caused her tears to flow again.

Abraham motioned for Phoebe who sat with the children in the dining hall and she came to embrace her friend. "Don't blame yourself," she wisely whispered in Amanda's ear. "It's no one's fault."

"How unimportant honey seems now," Amanda said, as she wiped her tears. "I wish I'd never said I wanted it."

George and Alexander had set off with their guns to try to track the panther, but by the fall of dusk they had not sighted it. They returned to the mission and joined the others for a quiet supper, heavy with concern and grief.

Later that evening, Marcus sat on the floor beside Stephen's bed. With Amanda and Will's help they had managed to spoon a bit of broth into his mouth and thankfully he had swallowed reflexively. The doctor knew this deep sleep was better for the man for the pain from his wounds would surely be nearly unbearable if he had been conscious.

Across from him on the other side of the bed, Rev. Vaille sat in a chair, joining the doctor in a night's vigil. He held his Bible open and read by lamplight. The Requa brothers lay quietly in their beds at the opposite wall of the men's cabin but neither slept. Quietly all the men lifted prayers through the night for their sleeping brother.

Dr. Palmer closed his eyes and leaned his head back against the log wall. He ran through the events of the day in his mind, meticulously judging whether he had done everything possible to save Stephen's life. His self-doubts were never far away at moments like this.

As he recalled the hours-long surgery, the details stood out vividly in his mind – the crimson cloths, the glint of his needle in the candlelight, the softness of Clarissa's hands next to his, the smell of blood and sweat and fear . . . and the faintest hint of roses. Despite his worry, the memory made him smile.

CHAPTER TWENTY-EIGHT

Union Mission
Spring, 1821

Marcus woke to a rooster crowing in the yard. He had not expected to sleep after the tense day, but exhaustion had eventually claimed him. He rolled his head to work the kink out of his neck and then straightened up and turned to Stephen's bed. Feeling for a pulse, he breathed a sigh of relief to find the man still alive.

"Did he make it through the night?" Rev. Vaille asked quietly from his chair.

"Yes," the doctor confirmed. "But he's not out of danger. He has a fever."

William nodded as the Requas stirred in their beds. "We'll work in shifts to care for him. With God's mercy we'll see him through this."

"I would advise that your wife not be involved with changing his dressings," the doctor said quietly. "In her delicate condition, well, she'd best not be exposed to something so upsetting."

"Thank you for your concern," William smiled. "I'll see that Asie helps only with other duties. But I can assure you that my wife will insist on taking her turn with nursing Mr. Fuller back to health. She has borne three children with no problems and with your excellent care we don't anticipate any with this fourth child."

Dr. Palmer nodded. Asenath Vaille had only recently informed him of her pregnancy. Remembering Sally Edwards, the doctor was concerned about childbirth out on the frontier, but he had seen many women at Claremont's town carrying healthy children in the cradleboards on their backs. So he would try not to borrow trouble for Mrs. Vaille. Right now, he would need to concentrate all his efforts on helping Stephen Fuller.

While Dr. Palmer and Mrs. Woodruff took their breakfast at Stephen's bedside, the rest of the mission family met in the dining hall to pray together for their farm director and work out a schedule for his care.

As they changed his bandages later that morning, Stephen groaned in pain. It was a hopeful sign to Dr. Palmer, but also a concern. Managing the man's pain would be a challenge. He would need to send George or Will to Three Forks to replenish the supply of whiskey he kept for medicinal purposes and hopefully they could purchase more laudanum as well.

Supplies were always somewhat limited at the trading posts, though whiskey was never lacking. And with the soon approaching summer, the keelboats would have a harder time reaching the trade community. They'd need more cloth for bandages too.

Stephen hovered between consciousness and sleep for days, able to take a little nourishment, groaning through gritted teeth with constant pain, close to delirium from fever. As the missionaries worked to help him through his recovery, there was hardly a moment both day and night that prayer was not being lifted on his behalf.

Mr. Bogey paid the mission a visit several days later, bringing more laudanum and other supplies, the last few issues of the *Arkansas Gazette* and a satchel of letters from their families back in New England. As always he had timed his arrival to enjoy a meal with the missionaries, but they were glad to share their dinner for he always brought news from Three Forks and beyond.

Dr. Palmer pulled out the small brown bottle of laudanum from the burlap sack filled with supplies.

"Is this all you could get us?" he asked the tradesman.

"Sorry to say it is," Bogey replied. "Dr. Russell at Fort Smith gets first priority with medicinals. We're lucky to get what we do."

"Well, keep an eye out for any more that might come in," Palmer said.

"Aye, I will," Bogey agreed. "You might try what the Indians use too," he said. "They steep the bark from the willow tree for a pain reliever."

"Does it work?"

"Seems to help some," Bogey said. "I used it when I had a toothache. Kept me from too much pain until the barber at Fort Smith could pull it for me."

"The *Arkansas Gazette* reports that there's a steamboat making a regular run to Arkansas Post now," the tradesman said as he stood to leave. "But I don't expect we'll see one at Three Forks anytime soon. La Cascade will put a stop to them this far up the Arkansas."

Bogey had almost reached the door of the dining hall when he stopped and turned back. "I almost forgot," he said, but then hesitated. Turning to the children's table, he said, "Thomas, I brought some of them molasses candies you like so well. What say you take the other children out to my wagon and you'll find them in my leather pouch on the seat."

"Can we . . . I mean, may we, Mother?" Thomas asked as he jumped eagerly from his seat.

"Yes, you may," Rachel answered. "But don't be greedy. Only one piece for each of you."

She'd barely finished speaking when all the children were out the door and racing to the trader's wagon waiting by the corral fence.

Mr. Bogey returned to the long dining table and resumed his seat. "I wanted the children out for a moment," he explained in a quiet voice.

"Is there a problem, Mr. Bogey," Rev. Chapman asked.

"Walter Webber was at Three Forks two days ago," Bogey replied. "He stopped at my post to ask if I had seen Skiatook in the area."

"What did you tell him?" William Vaille asked, as everyone in the room leaned forward with concern.

"The truth," Bogey responded. "I told him I knew he was back in Arkansas."

"Mr. Bogey, you know of the feud between Webber and Mad Buffalo. Could you not have declined to answer?" the pastor asked.

"Nothing worse to an Indian than to tell him a lie," Bogey responded forcefully. "And you never take sides in their fight. I answered Webber truthfully and if Mad Buffalo asks if I've seen the Cherokee, I'll tell him the truth as well. I've paid for taking sides in the past and I won't do it again. Back in '07, the Choctaws didn't like that I was trading exclusively with the Osages. They cleaned out my warehouse and then set it afire. I still haven't received the compensation the government promised me for that."

The missionaries hardly knew how to respond to the normally affable trader. There was worry in his tone and that worried them.

"Do you expect trouble now?" Chapman asked.

"You can count on it."

"Should we warn Mad Buffalo?" Will Requa asked.

"Stay out of it," Bogey responded. "It's not your fight and you'll not be wanting Walter Webber or Mad Buffalo to have a reason to set your fine new buildings on fire."

"Is there not something we can do to stop this feud?" asked Abraham Redfield.

"No," Bogey said. "It's a matter of honor for both of them and you'll not persuade either side to back down. You'll just end up getting caught in the middle."

"How do you see this ending?"

"If he's smart, Mad Buffalo will go back to Missouri and when Webber can't find him, then he'll return to Dardanelle. I'd advise you not to visit Claremont's town for awhile. Keep close to your camp and keep an eye on the Trace."

"We could get word to Major Bradford at the fort," John Spaulding suggested. "Perhaps a troop of soldiers at Three Forks would keep a lid on things."

"I'll say something to him when next I travel to Petite Roche," Bogey said. "I could be wrong about the trouble," he acknowledged as the children returned. "I hope I am."

He stood to go.

"Children, what should you say to Mr. Bogey?" Asie Vaille prompted.

"Thank you, Mr. Bogey," they all responded around bulging cheeks and sticky smiles.

"You're more than welcome," the white bearded man smiled in response. "I'll keep you abreast of things," he said to the men.

"We appreciate it," Rev. Vaille said, rising to walk the man to his wagon.

No one said anything more about Bogey's warning with the children present, but all returned to their daily chores with much to think and pray about.

The following Sunday, the mission family was gathering in the dining hall for their Sabbath worship. Alexander and Martha were caring for Stephen, and Asie was keeping Sarah in because she had a cold, but all the rest of the family were preparing to begin the service.

"Hello, the camp." They heard the friendly call from of an approaching visitor. Paul stopped his chore of handing out the hymnals and hurried to the window. "It's Mr. Revoir," he announced.

George was closest to the door and went to open it to their neighbor. More than just Joseph Revoir were dismounting from his wagon. A woman, clearly Osage, and two children were with him.

"It's the Revoir family," George said. He and Will had called upon the Grand Saline trading post when out on a hunting foray in the *spa-vi-nah* and had met Mrs. Revoir and her two children. She was dressed in an interesting combination of French and Osage cultures – a bright calico skirt was topped by a buckskin shirt trimmed with ribbons. She wore her jet black hair in a chignon held in place by a beaded snood and long polished bone. The children, a boy and girl, were both under eight with bright inquisitive eyes.

"Come in and join us," George welcomed the family. "We were just beginning our worship service."

"We stopped to see how your Mr. Fuller was faring," Revoir explained as they all stepped into the dining hall. "Bogey told me of his encounter with *inlonka*. That cat was protecting a female with two cubs. Claremont's men have been tracking him."

"We thank you for your concern. Mr. Fuller is showing some improvement," Rev. Vaille explained. "Will you join us for worship? Mr. Redfield was just about to lead our singing."

"We can stay," Joseph replied. He and his family settled into the chairs George and Will had quickly set in place for them.

Clarissa noticed that Mrs. Revoir was singing along, though she did not look at the hymnal Paul had given her. She wondered where the Osage woman had learned an English hymn.

Rev. Chapman could barely hide his pleasure at having an Osage family join them for church. They had extended numerous invitations to Claremont's village, but had yet to see any from that town come to a service. After his hour-long sermon, the minister invited the Revoirs to join them for dinner as well.

Over the noon meal, the women tried to draw Mrs. Revoir into conversation, but she seemed shy. Usually Mr. Revoir answered for her when a question was posed to her. They learned that her Osage name meant Little Fawn in English, but she had taken the Christian name of Teresa.

To the missionaries' surprise, they learned she had been baptized several years ago by an itinerant Jesuit priest who also ran beaver traps on a bayou that fed the Arkansas River near Three Forks. Father Pierre Menard held services every Pumpkin Moon when trappers and traders would rendezvous at French Point for a week of swapping furs for trade goods and telling tall tales.

"Teresa belongs to the Arkansas Band led by Cashesegra -- Big Tracks," Revoir explained. "She grew up at Three Forks. We met at the annual rendezvous ten years ago when I brought trade goods from Colonel Chouteau. She was happy to learn that there was to be a permanent church in the neighborhood."

"We hope you can come and worship with us often," Rachel

smiled at the woman. "And your children will certainly be welcome when we start school this fall."

"I am glad for school," Teresa said, her voice husky and low. Then she quickly looked to her husband as if to check that she had said the right thing.

He smiled at her. "It's a long ride from Grand Saline to come to school," he said to the Chapmans. "We will see."

"We will provide room and board for students who have a long distance to travel," Rev. Chapman explained. Since this would include any child from Claremont's or Cashesegra's towns, they had plans to add a dormitory when needed.

"You'll want your children in school," John Spaulding said.

Clarissa watched Teresa's face and saw a conflict of emotions cross her features. She could understand the woman's dilemma. The desire to have her children receive an education would certainly battle against sending them away to school. She wondered again how many Osage or frontier parents would be willing to trust the mission with their children.

Revoir looked over at his two offspring where they played with their new friends among the mission children. Beyond them, out the window of the dining hall, he caught a glimpse of the sky. Alarm showed on his face.

"Looks like a storm builds on the horizon," he said. "We must begin the journey home or the clouds will catch us."

"You're welcome to stay and ride out any storm," Rev. Vaille offered.

"We have time to make it home if we leave now," Revoir responded.

Teresa stood and called for Jean and Louisa in Osage. They quickly joined their parents at the door.

Will walked with the family to their wagon at the corral fence.

"Thank you for your fine meal," Revoir told him as he helped Teresa into the wagon. Jean and Louisa scrambled into the back and onto a pile of hay covered with a massive buffalo hide.

"You're welcome any time," Will said and then with a glance back at the mission he added in a low voice, "I think you ought to know that Walter Webber's been seen in the neighborhood recently. He's looking for Mad Buffalo."

"Mad Buffalo knows of the Cherokees' presence in the Osage land," Joseph replied, also in a low voice.

"Perhaps he should pay another visit to Missouri," Will suggested.

"He left for Missouri last fall at Yellowbird's insistence," Revoir explained, "but he is not likely to leave again. He cannot lead his men if they believe he is afraid of Walter Webber."

"He's your friend," Will said. "Perhaps you could convince him that it would be best for everyone . . . everyone in the whole area . . . to avoid a conflict that could lead to bloodshed."

"It will lead to bloodshed," Revoir said in the fatalistic way of the Indian. "But Mad Buffalo will not leave his people. The Cherokees attacked Claremont's village three summers ago at the Strawberry Moon. The men were out on a hunt and all that remained in the village were children and women, and the Old Men. Mad Buffalo will never let that happen again."

Will could offer no other argument. It was a man's duty to protect his family, his people.

"Mad Buffalo never stays in one place two nights in a row," Revoir said. "Perhaps Webber will grow tired of chasing a shadow and will go back to his farm." He said the word farm with disdain.

The tradesman climbed into the wagon and sat beside his wife. "I thank you for your concern," he said in parting. "But stay out of this matter. It doesn't concern you and you cannot change the way of warriors."

CHAPTER TWENTY-NINE

Union Mission
June, 1821

A few weeks later, the children and Robbie were all helping Amanda and Rachel weed the garden. Amanda was explaining to the girls what dishes she would prepare from the beans, peas, carrots and other vegetables they had helped her plant. The boys were gleefully gathering the slithering red worms they uncovered with their hoes and planning a fishing trip for later in the afternoon.

"Billy, no!" Mrs. Chapman grabbed for the four-year-old in time to keep him from placing one of the worms in his mouth. "The worms are for the fish to eat, not you." She laughed at the surprised look on the boy's face. He had rarely heard the unflappable preacher's wife raise her voice.

"Mother," James said, a tone of concern in that one single word.

"What now, James?" she asked as she turned to her youngest son.

James pointed to the Osage Trace. "I don't think those Indians are Osage."

Rachel and Amanda both raised a hand to shade their eyes and looked past the cornfield toward the trade trail. A long line of horses, carrying warriors, were walking in single file north along the road.

These were not Osage for they used saddles and their dress

was very different from the men from Claremont's village. Instead of blankets, they wore calico shirts and turban-style hats. Their faces were painted with streaks of red – the war color. They were Cherokee.

"You're right, James," Rachel said as calmly as she could. "They aren't Osages."

"I don't think they are coming to see us," Abigail said. All the children had ceased their work and were watching the Indians with interest.

"Perhaps they are going to hunt the buffalo," Amanda said, a little too brightly. She looked at Rachel to ask what they should do.

"Well, since they aren't coming to visit us," Rachel said, "we should all get back after these weeds." She put her own hoe to work though she kept glancing toward the Trace. "Thomas, why don't you go tell your papa that the Cherokees are heading north on the road. He might not have noticed them since the men are working inside today."

"Yes, Mother," Thomas readily agreed, glad to drop his hoe. "Can I show him how many worms we have?"

Rachel smiled at the ordinariness of the boy's question. "Certainly," she replied. "He'll want to know how many you've collected since it will mean fresh fish for supper tonight."

Thomas grinned and grabbed up the molasses pail where the bait was being held. "I'll be right back," he called as he hopped from row to row over the pea patch.

He dashed toward the classroom/chapel where all the men were working today except for Stephen and Dr. Palmer. Using a cask that had once held nails, Paul was mixing the mud mortar for chinking the logs of the building. Will and Alexander Woodruff were laying rocks in place for the fireplace while the two ministers, John, and Abraham were filling the gaps between the logs of the wall with the sticky mortar.

"Papa," Thomas said, as he rushed through the doorway of the building. "Mother sent me to tell you that the Cherokees are going north on the road right now."

"The Cherokees?" Chapman said, setting down his trowel and walking to the window to look out toward the Trace.

The other men also ceased their work and walked to the

west-facing windows. In the distance they saw the last of the Cherokee warriors pass the mission compound.

"I guess we know where they are going," Abraham said.

"Where are they going?" Thomas asked. "To find Mad Buffalo?"

"Why would you say that, son?" his papa asked, turning to look at him.

Thomas shrugged. "I don't know," the boy responded. "Just stuff people have said. The Cherokees don't like Mad Buffalo."

"No, they don't," his father agreed, but chose not to say more. "But we can't stand around watching them. We best get back to work."

"Yes, Papa," Thomas assented. "But I brought the bait bucket for you to see. We have lots of worms for fishing. Can we go this afternoon? After we finish our chores?"

The minister looked at the other men before nodding. "Sure," he said. "In fact, some of us men will go with you. We need a break and it will be cooler down at the river."

"Really?" Thomas' face lit with happiness. It was rare that his father took time from work. "Can we ask Miss Ingles to pack a picnic?"

George laughed. "I'm for that. Looks like we'll all be going down to the river."

"I think a few of us will need to stay at the mission," Rev. Vaille countered. "To keep a watch . . . I mean . . . to stay with Mr. Fuller."

"Oh, sure," George said.

Thomas looked from his father, to Rev. Vaille to George, curiosity on his face and then sudden understanding. "I won't tell the children," he said, as if he suddenly wasn't one of them. Then he turned and hurried out the door and back to the garden.

"Your son is a smart boy," Alexander remarked. "Growing into a fine young man."

"Yes," Chapman smiled. "I just hope he isn't forced by circumstances to grow up too fast."

"We will want to set up some type of watch," Abraham said. "I don't believe the Cherokees will molest the mission, but we can't be too careful."

"One of us is awake with Fuller both day and night," William Vaille said. "That should be adequate. I think the Cherokees know we are not hiding Mad Buffalo here or they would not have simply passed by."

"I had wondered why Mad Buffalo had not been to the mission for some time," Chapman said, as he returned to his trowel. "I was afraid he was sending a message of disapproval of our work here. But I think now he may have been protecting us. He wanted Webber to know he would not take refuge here."

"You think the Cherokees know that?" John asked.

"I wouldn't be surprised if they have been watching us for the last few days . . . at least since Bogey's visit."

"Then it's good we haven't had any contact with the Osages of late," Will observed.

"Except for the Revoirs," Paul said.

"What's happened?" Stephen Fuller jerked upward off his pillow as if awakening from a nightmare.

"Steady, man," Dr. Palmer said, placing a hand on the farmer's shoulder. "You were jumped by the panther. He ripped your back to shreds. You must lie still and not pull at the stitching."

Stephen groaned, but put his face back to the pillow. "I thought it was the bees," he said. "The honey tree," he suddenly remembered, jerking up again. "Send someone to get the honey for Miss Ingles."

"Requa and Redfield harvested it days ago," Dr. Palmer assured him. "Miss Ingles is making wild strawberry preserves with it. And if you'll lie still, I'll be sure she brings you some for breakfast tomorrow morning."

"How long have I been abed?" Stephen asked.

"It's been ten days."

"The fields," Stephen groaned again for a different reason now. "I meant to finish seeding the west twenty acres in corn."

"Don't trouble yourself about it," Marcus said. "Robbie and Redfield finished it. The corn is up and nearly knee high already. The rows aren't very straight, but the corn doesn't care."

Stephen smiled faintly, then grimaced as he became aware of his pain.

"Miss Ingles has gone to bring you some willow bark tea," Marcus said quietly, noting the tense shudder that passed through his patient. "It will help with the pain."

Only a few moments later, Amanda and Martha entered the cabin after knocking briefly. They carried a pot of tea and a bowl of soup for Stephen.

"Well, you're awake at last," Martha said as she approached Stephen's bedside. She set the teapot on the table and then gently squeezed the farmer's hand. "We've been very concerned about you."

"I'm sorry to have been a trouble to everyone," Stephen said, his voice husky as he tried to hide his discomfort from the women.

Amanda's face clouded with concern as she poured the bitter tea into a tin cup. "You must drink all of this though I'll take no blame for how bad it tastes," she said, trying to smile.

Together the three of them helped Stephen to sit on the side of his bunk. "I've never known you to make anything that tastes bad," he said to Amanda, but grimaced again when he actually took a sip of the tea.

"It's medicine," Amanda said, pretending to be offended. "It's supposed to taste bad. But I could add a bit o' honey next time. Perhaps that would make it go down better."

Stephen shook his head. "Save the honey for the children," he said.

"If anyone should have it, you should," Martha replied as she brought the bowl of soup to Stephen.

"You paid a high enough price for it," Amanda said softly, tears springing into her eyes as they so often did when she thought about his suffering.

The cook had pulled up a chair to the bedside to spoon the broth for Mr. Fuller. Any movement of his arms was discouraged by the doctor.

"I was glad to do it for you," Stephen told her, looking briefly into her eyes then he dutifully opened his mouth for the spoonful of broth.

"And I thank you for it," Amanda whispered with emotion.

Her hand trembled a little as she offered him a bite of the cabbage and beef soup. It was her first opportunity to express her gratitude to him.

Mrs. Woodruff smiled knowingly as she bustled about the cabin, straightening bed clothes and gathering up soiled bandages. Marcus watched the exchange with curiosity, sensing an undercurrent of meaning that he didn't understand.

"I'll take these rags out to the rubbish pile," Martha said. "I'll not be gone long." She left the cabin, careful to keep the door open for propriety's sake.

Stephen was only able to swallow a few spoons of soup before weariness overtook him. Dr. Palmer helped him settle back into bed with several feather pillows gently supporting his back. Within a few moments he was asleep.

Amanda gathered her dishes to leave, but turned back at the door to speak to the doctor.

"Is he on the mend?" she asked.

"I believe he is," Marcus answered. "He still has a long recovery and may not get his full strength back for some time. He will survive . . . though not without scars."

"Well, we all have our scars, don't we," Amanda said thoughtfully. "Most of us came here with some burden to bear."

"Do you think so?" Marcus asked, rather surprised at Amanda's observation.

Amanda looked at Stephen's still form, but she seemed to be seeing something far removed from the mission cabin. "Our past can make it hard to trust again."

"Or to take risks," Marcus said softly, almost to himself. He wore a pensive look on his face.

"Yes," Amanda agreed thoughtfully and then turned to go.

Neither of them knew for sure if they were talking about Stephen or themselves or someone else.

Later that evening, Marcus snuffed out the candle beside Stephen's bed after he had checked on his patient. The compound was quiet as the evening darkness had brought everyone into their cabins after a splendid afternoon of fishing and a feast on the catch of tender crappie for supper. Night sounds filled the air – the bass thrum of tree frogs, the pulsing rhythm of cicadas and locusts, the soft murmur of the river current in the distance.

Dr. Palmer had just settled on his bunk when the night was suddenly disturbed by the distant pounding of horses' hooves.

Marcus and the Requa brothers rose from their bunks at the noise. "What is it?" George asked, even as he reached for his britches and hastily pulled them on.

Will opened the cabin door, just as the other men in the family cabins did also. Coming from the Trace was a single horseman at a gallop, his dark face barely visible in the shadows.

"There be trouble at La Saline," the rider called without ceremony, while trying to steady his prancing horse. "Mr. Joseph been shot by the Cherokees. Miz Teresa asks can the doctor come."

"What happened, Monday?" Will asked the Negro slave whom he had met at the Chouteau post. All the men gathered around his now quieted mustang while the women watched from the cabin doors. Rev. Vaille carried a hastily lit lantern and its light threw strange shadows on the log walls.

"They come just at supper," the man answered Will. "'Bout thirty of them. Looking for Mad Buffalo. When Mr. Joseph wouldn't say where he was, they shot him!"

Marcus had already rushed back to his cabin to collect his medical bag from Stephen's bedside. "How bad is it?" he asked when he returned. Abraham headed toward the barn where Robbie helped him quickly saddle a couple of their horses.

"He's bleeding bad," Monday responded with a shake of his head. "Can't say even where the bullet hit him there's so much blood."

"Sounds like a gut shot," Marcus said, mostly to himself. He knew full well that if the bullet had entered the abdomen, the damage to internal organs would mean almost certain death.

Abraham came from the barn leading two horses. He was preparing to mount one of them, when Will Requa stopped him. "Stay with your wife," he said. "I'll go with Palmer."

Abraham hesitated then looked to where Phoebe stood in the doorway of their cabin. With a nod, he handed the reins to Will.

Marcus and Will mounted their horses and then joined

Monday in a quick trot up the Osage Trace toward Grand Saline. The doctor dreaded what he would find at Colonel Chouteau's home.

The remaining missionary family slept little through the night, concern for Marcus and Will and the Revoir family driving rest away. Susan cried quietly on her bed and Clarissa felt sick to her stomach with fear.

Somewhere in the darkness, the Cherokee war party searched for their enemy. They had already shot one man; would they shoot those who tried to help him? All the warnings of staying out of the feud rang in Clarissa's head.

Amanda rose to begin the day before the rooster's crow as the darkness was just fading to gray. She dressed quietly and then peeked out the door, fearful of making the trek to the outhouse. She listened for any unusual sounds, but heard nothing except the birdsongs. Surely the birds wouldn't be trilling so cheerfully if a danger lurked about.

She stepped out quietly and crossed the compound yard to the outbuilding set downstream from the spring. As she approached the dining hall, she saw the outline of a man with a musket in his hands, leaning against the wall facing the Trace. She stopped suddenly, not knowing if she should run or scream, and feeling as if she could do neither. Then he turned toward her and she saw that is was Rev. Vaille.

"Oh, Reverend," she said breathlessly, laying a hand upon her heart.

"I'm sorry, Miss Ingles," he said. "I didn't mean to startle you. It's been my watch since four o'clock."

The men had held a hasty meeting after Will and Marcus left and established a schedule for each to take a two-hour shift through the long night. Mr. Woodruff would relieve the minister soon.

"Have Mr. Requa and Dr. Palmer returned yet?" Amanda asked.

"No, not yet," Vaille responded. "If they're not back by afternoon, some of us will set out to check on them."

"Has there been any movement of the Indians?"

"Not as far as I know," the minister said. "At least Mr. Redfield reported nothing when I took the watch."

"Do you think we will see trouble?"

"It's hard to know what is in the mind of the Indians," he said. "Both the Cherokees and the Osages know that to molest the mission would bring a troop from Fort Smith. I don't think they want that."

"But the fort is so far away," Amanda worried. "Can they really provide us protection?"

"We will trust the Lord for protection and hope we won't need to rely upon Fort Smith."

While they spoke, the first rays of the sun had lightened the landscape. Robbie came from the barn, carrying the milking pails to the springhouse. Others of the mission family were stirring about to begin their morning chores.

Paul walked toward them with an armload of firewood from the stack by the forge. "Got your kindlin', Miz Ingles," he said. "You want me to start the breakfast fire?"

"Yes, Paul," she said. "Thank you."

Then to the pastor she said, "Well, I best be about me business."

"Try not to worry, Miss Ingles," Vaille said. "The Lord is with us."

"Aye," she said, but she wasn't sure she could follow that advice.

When they all sat down to breakfast about an hour later, the doctor and Will still had not returned. After prayer, they ate quietly, no one feeling like making conversation. The children solemnly spooned their porridge and watched their elders with concerned eyes.

They were clearing away the breakfast dishes when George glanced out a window.

"Osages on the Trace," he said with a hint of steel in his voice. All of them hurried to the west facing windows and watched as a line of about thirty Osage warriors passed, heading south toward Three Forks. They wore their war paint and each had a feather plume stuck into their scalp lock.

"I don't think Mad Buffalo was among them," Rev. Chapman said.

"We can hope that the Cherokees have left the area," Abraham Redfield stated. "At least the Osages believe they are no longer around Grand Saline."

It was early afternoon when Robbie sounded a joyful cry from the hay mow in the barn. "They're back," he shouted and raced down the ladder into the mission yard. In the distance two riders made their way south on the road.

Martha, Alice Spaulding and Eliza finished wringing out the garments they had been washing and joined Amanda, Rachel, and Clarissa who were picking peas in the garden. The men left their work on the chapel and the Vailles stepped out from Stephen's cabin. All gathered at the garden's edge waiting for Marcus and Will to reach them, eager to know the results of their night's ministry to Joseph Revoir.

Upon a closer view of the two men, Phoebe and Susan hurried the children back to the dining room. Dr. Palmer was covered in dried blood and Will was much the same. They both slumped in the saddle as if deeply tired and burdened with sadness. However, neither appeared to be injured.

"What of Revoir?" Chapman asked without prelude as Abraham and Robbie took charge of the horses after Marcus and Will had dismounted.

Dr. Palmer shook his head. "He didn't make it. We could never stop the blood loss." He had started to say more, but refrained in the presence of the women.

"Have you had breakfast?" Amanda asked. "Can I get something for you?"

"Coffee would be most welcome," Will answered.

"I'll set some to boilin'," Amanda said, turning toward the kitchen.

"Come rest at the table," Chapman said, reaching for Dr. Palmer's medical kit which also had blood upon it.

"Perhaps they would like to clean up first," Rachel suggested.

"Yes, of course," her husband agreed. "I'll have Paul draw you some water."

The two weary men made their way to the bachelor's cabin to remove their soiled clothes and wash away the reminder of the lost battle for a man's life. When they returned to the dining hall, they seemed almost to be in a daze from the weariness and strain of the long night.

"Was anyone else harmed?" Rev. Vaille asked quietly as Will and Marcus ate the scrambled eggs and biscuits Amanda had set before them. The Redfields and Spauldings had taken the children down to the river on the pretext of gathering cane for baskets. Both men carried their muskets.

"No one else was hurt," Will answered. "According to Monday, the Cherokees left as soon as the one shot was fired."

"Webber was responsible?" Chapman queried.

"He was leading the war party," said Will. "But Monday didn't know who actually fired the shot."

"Mrs. Revoir wants a Christian burial for her husband," Dr. Palmer interjected.

"How is she?" Rachel asked, showing a great sympathy for the young woman.

"Stoic," said Marcus. "In shock. It will take time for the grief to come."

"Did you see any signs that the Cherokees are still in the neighborhood?" George wanted to know.

"We didn't see anyone on our ride back," Will told his brother. "Even Captain Pryor and his wife were not at their cabin. They probably went to Three Forks."

"Let us hope the captain or someone from Three Forks can get word to Major Bradford at Fort Smith," Rev. Chapman said. "If we don't soon have a military presence here, I am afraid more blood may be shed."

Dr. Palmer stared into his coffee cup. The thought of more blood made him shudder.

CHAPTER THIRTY

Union Mission
June, 1821

Early the next day, Will and George drove a wagon to Grand Saline to bring the body of Joseph Revoir to the mission for burial. Mrs. Revoir wanted a Christian service for her husband and did not want him buried at Chouteau's post, saying her Osage relatives would insist on following the mourning traditions of their people.

Rev. Vaille conducted the funeral service the following afternoon. Colonel Chouteau and his Osage wife Rosalee attended as did Captain Pryor and many of the other traders from Three Forks. Joseph Bogey was absent for he had undertaken the journey to Fort Smith to alert Major Bradford of the situation. A small handful of Osages from Big Track's town were also present.

Mrs. Revoir sat quietly through the sermon; her eyes dry but with a look of tragic pain upon her face. Clarissa found herself having to dab at the tears that threatened to spill from her eyes. She hadn't known Joseph Revoir well, but the circumstances that Teresa and her children were now facing created a great sadness for the teacher and all the other missionaries as well.

Asie Vaille seemed almost distraught and cried quietly throughout the funeral. Rachel put an arm around her shoulders to comfort her, assuming her pregnancy accounted for the overflow of emotion.

Lacking a coffin, the body had been wrapped in an Osage blanket sewn shut. Several of the men, lifted Revoir's remains onto a wagon after the service and the entire group followed it solemnly to the site chosen for the mission cemetery. Alexander, Will and Abraham had dug the grave early that morning. Following Captain Pryor's advice, they had chosen a location that was at a high point above the river where flooding hopefully would never threaten this grave, or any future graves that might fill the cemetery.

After Rev. Vaille had read a scripture at the graveside, the group returned to the mission dining hall for a quiet meal. Mrs. Chapman invited Mrs. Revoir and her children to stay at Union Mission for a few days to give them time away from the place where her husband had been killed.

Clarissa helped Amanda clear away the dishes after the meal. Most of the men had gone back to the gravesite to complete the burial, but had admonished Dr. Palmer to remain behind and rest. He still seemed quite weary as he sat at one of the dining tables, lost in thought. As he always did, he was re-examining his last medical procedure, a task his father had always insisted upon.

"Could I get you more coffee, Doctor?" Clarissa asked.

He looked up as if surprised to see her there. "Yes, I would appreciate that," he said.

She took his cup and filled it from the pot that sat on the grate in the fireplace. The dying coals had kept it warm.

"Here you are," she said, handing the enamel cup to him. She wanted to say something to cheer him for he looked so tired and discouraged, but she could think of nothing that seemed appropriate. She was never one to offer trite platitudes.

"Miss Johnson," Dr. Palmer said, as she started to turn away.

"Yes?" Clarissa asked. "Can I get you something else?"

"No," he said, "I mean, this is fine." He took a sip of coffee. "I just wanted to say thank you."

"You're welcome."

"No, I mean for helping with Mr. Fuller's surgery," Marcus explained. "In all the confusion, I never had the chance to thank you."

Clarissa hardly knew what to say. "I was glad to help," she finally murmured, though she felt a prick of her conscience for she really had not wanted to be a part of the operation. "I'm afraid I'm not a very good nurse."

"You did an excellent job," the doctor stated, but saw the doubt in the young teacher's eyes. "You are stronger than you think you are. Few other women would have had the courage to come out here to the wilderness to teach."

Her conscience truly flared now. If he only knew why she had chosen to come, he would hardly think she was strong or courageous. She had fled disapproval and gossip and now she fearfully found herself on the edge of an Indian war. And she had only kept her stomach through that long, bloody surgery by studying the back of the doctor's head while conjugating French verbs in her own head.

Clarissa had a sudden urge to tell Dr. Palmer the truth of why she had come on this mission to the Osages. His apparent admiration of her was undeserved and she was tired of keeping her secret. She had never wanted to tell anyone before and had steadfastly resisted Amanda's curious questions. But now, looking into the tired eyes of the doctor, she thought he might understand.

"I'm not courageous," she began, but before she could continue, she was interrupted by Amanda who had been working to clear the other dining table.

She came over to Clarissa and slipped an arm around her waist.

"You'll not convince me of that," she stated. "I'm ever so grateful to the both of you for helping save Mr. Fuller's life. It would have haunted me conscience forever if he had died tryin' to harvest that honey."

"Your conscience should not be seared by the actions of a panther, Miss Ingles," the doctor argued.

"Well, I'm just glad we have you here, Doctor," she replied. "And you, too, Miss Johnson. I admire your dedication to teachin', even to the point of denyin' yourself marriage and children. We are fortunate to have you."

Clarissa now felt like a total hypocrite. "You give me too much credit," she tried to protest.

Dr. Palmer was looking at her in an odd sort of way . . . as if he were disappointed in her.

"Yes, Miss Johnson," he said, sounding sad. "We are fortunate to have someone so dedicated."

Later in the afternoon, the women were working in the kitchen to prepare supper for the mission family as well as the Revoirs and the Chouteaus who had spent the day at Union.

"What is that noise?" Martha Woodruff asked looking up from the biscuit dough she was rolling out.

The other women ceased their work to listen.

"It sounds like sleigh bells," Susan said. "Who would be using a sleigh out here in the middle of summer?"

Wiping damp hands on their long aprons, the women stepped into the dining hall where they could look out the building's windows.

The men were gathering at the door of the chapel, having also heard the unexpected jingle of bells.

Teresa Revoir had been seated at a dining table with Rosalee Chouteau and Rachel Chapmen.

"No, no, no," she said emphatically as the sound of the bells grew closer. She rose and went to a window. "I said to them I do not want a scalp at the grave of my husband."

Mrs. Chouteau patted her arm to comfort her. "It is the tradition," she said. "They feel they must honor the dead this way."

"But someone had to die for this tradition," Teresa said through clenched jaw. For the first time today, there were tears in her eyes.

"What is it?" Rachel asked. "What is going on?"

"It's the mourning party," Rosalee explained. "They lift a scalp from someone to place in the grave of a warrior to prove what a great fighter he was."

At this time a line of Osage men on horseback appeared, slowly making their way toward the cemetery. Woven into the tails and manes of their mustangs were scores of small metal bells that sounded with each step of the horses. Were it not for their gruesome intent, the sound might have seemed cheerful. Colonel Chouteau explained to the men the ancient mourning tradition of the Osage.

"There is Mad Buffalo," he said in a low tone. The Osage leader was among the warriors who rode toward Revoir's grave.

None of the warriors even glanced at the mission compound though they were surely aware that they were being observed. Only Mad Buffalo looked in their direction. He must have seen Mrs. Revoir at one of the dining room windows for he turned his mount and made his way toward the mission compound.

Drawing an arrow from a quiver on his back, he hurled it into the ground and then nodded toward the Osage woman. Pausing only another moment, he then rejoined the other warriors. The bells could be heard even after the horses were out of sight.

"What was the meaning of the arrow?" Rev. Chapman asked the colonel.

"It was Mad Buffalo's way of telling Mrs. Revoir that he would avenge her husband's death."

"Even if she doesn't want vengeance?" Will Requa asked.

"Avenging a murder is a law among the Indians," Chouteau said. "For the Osages and for the Cherokees."

"But how does the killing ever stop?" asked Abraham.

"It sometimes goes on for generations," Chouteau replied.

"We shouldn't be surprised by it," Rev. Vaille stated. "It is the practice of all ancient peoples. It was addressed in the law of Moses."

"We need a city of refuge," Rev. Chapman agreed, referring to the Mosaic command to provide refuge for those fleeing from the avenger until a court of law could settle the matter.

"Perhaps our mission will be called upon to be just that," Vaille mused.

"Do not wish for it," Chouteau said. "It is better to let the forts be the places of refuge. They represent the law here on the frontier."

"You're right, of course," William Vaille said. "We will not be a city of refuge, but perhaps we can be a place of forgiveness . . . and hope."

The Chouteaus took Teresa and her children back to Grand Saline the following day. The missionaries tried to get back into their normal routine, but they could never quite shake the uneasiness that hung over the whole neighborhood. The Cherokees had not been seen since Mr. Revoir's death. The Osage war parties passed by frequently, keeping everyone praying that new fighting would not break out.

A week after Revoir's burial, Captain Pryor, Joseph Bogey and Major Bradford from Fort Smith called upon the mission. With them was the government agent to the Cherokees, a man named David Brearley. The men were on their way to meet with Mad Buffalo and his father Chief Claremont to try to work out a truce between them and the Cherokees.

"Do you think a truce is possible?" Rev. Chapman asked, as the men sat around one of the dining tables.

"Mr. Webber is open to something being worked out," Major Bradford answered. All the men were enjoying a slice of Amanda's blackberry pie.

"Then you have spoken with him?"

"He came to the fort after the incident at Grand Saline," Bradford responded. "He claimed his men acted in self defense. Said that Revoir was armed and threatened to shoot."

"Do you believe him?" Will asked.

"I don't know what to believe," Bradford said. "We only have the word of a woman and a slave to say otherwise."

From the door to the kitchen, where the women stood listening, Phoebe bit back a retort. Mrs. Chapman's jaw tightened visibly at the disparaging words of the officer. Amanda rolled her eyes at Clarissa and Eliza and they both stifled giggles.

"The Cherokees don't want a war with the Osages," David Brearley stated. "They know the territorial governor has made promises that he will crack down on Indian depredations. The whole of western Arkansas is upset by this feud; folks are clamoring for the fort to put a stop to it."

"We're authorized to use force if it's called for," Bradford said. "But I believe Captain Pryor and Colonel Brearley will be able to work out an agreement between Mad Buffalo and Webber."

"We will certainly pray for God's speed in your endeavor," Rev. Vaille said.

"We appreciate your prayers," Brearley said. "We'll let you know what is worked out."

The military presence at Three Forks seemed to bring a sense of calm to the area. Besides Major Bradford, Lieutenant Bonneville and a small contingent of troops were camped at Pryor's trading house, while the two Indian agents met with the Osage leaders. Though the agents could elicit no actual peace treaty between the two tribes, they were assured by both parties that they would not act as aggressors in the future. It was the best Pryor and Brearley felt they could do, though Major Bradford had strongly urged them to get a treaty signed.

At the mission, the men completed the chapel/schoolhouse and now awaited the desks and other school supplies they had ordered while in Cincinnati. Clarissa and John met with Rev. Chapman to discuss the school layout and the schedule of classes they hoped they would be able to offer come fall. It was still uncertain whether they would have any students other than the children of the mission family.

When three weeks had passed without further incidents between the Osages and the Cherokees, the Fort Smith troops returned to their garrison at Belle Point. Late one hot afternoon, most of the women were working in the kitchen canning beans. The steamy work was made worse by the sultry day.

"I'm thinkin' we'll just be wantin' buttermilk and cold cornbread for supper tonight," Amanda said as she wiped her face with the tail of her apron.

"Anything cold will be good," Clarissa agreed.

"I wish Mr. Bogey would bring us another bushel of peaches," Martha Woodruff said from the table where she snapped a lapful of string beans. "Those last ones were sure good."

"We haven't seen Mr. Bogey for a while," Susan responded. "He must have made a trip to 'Petite Roche'," she said, trying to capture his French accent. The other women smiled.

Rachel glanced into the dining hall where Abraham Redfield sat with Stephen Fuller. It was the first day that the farm director had been out of his cabin. Though still weak, he was feeling well enough to take the short walk to the dining hall.

He and Redfield were discussing plans for a smokehouse. They'd need one completed before butchering this fall.

"It's good to see Mr. Fuller up and out," Rachel said to no one in particular.

"Amen to that," Phoebe replied.

Before anyone could say more, a voice called from the edge of the mission compound.

"Hello, the camp!"

"Well, speak of the devil," Martha said. "I believe that's Mr. Bogey."

"He's early," Amanda smiled. "It's not time for supper."

"Must be something important to bring him out before a meal," Alice Spaulding agreed.

"Oh, dear," Rachel said, smoothing down her long muslin apron. "I hope a problem has not arisen. I was just thanking the Lord this morning that everything seemed back to normal."

Her words caused a small ripple of concern to pass among the women. They all stepped from the kitchen into the dining hall to await the trader's arrival. Most of the men had been harvesting corn in the south field, but they halted their work at Mr. Bogey's call.

"Welcome, Bogey," Rev. Vaille called as the men reached him as he dismounted his horse. "What brings you by?"

"Brought you your mail pouch from the keelboat that just landed," the trader responded, handing the leather satchel to Rev. Chapman. "You've a pile of supplies at the dock, too."

"We had hoped the keelboat would bring them up the Neosho for us," Chapman said.

"Those storms last week put the river too high and fast," Bogey explained. "Guess the captain's the cautious sort for he chose the Verdigris landing instead."

"Who's the captain?" John asked.

"Name's Douglas," Bogey said with a twinkle in his eye.

"Captain Josiah Douglas!" George exclaimed.

"The same," Bogey said. "First time he's ventured up to Three Forks. He's anxious to see you so I told him I'd alert you to his arrival. I'm on my way to Grand Saline."

"We'll get a wagon down to the Point first thing tomorrow," Will said as he glanced at the sun. It was too late in the afternoon to set out today. "Perhaps we can persuade the captain to return with us for a visit before he heads back down river."

"You'll want to take both your wagons," Bogey advised. "And all your oxen. There's a mighty pile of desks and chairs at the landing."

"Thanks," said Rev. Chapman, "we will." Then he added with a smile, "Can you stay for a cup of coffee and something sweet from Miss Ingle's larder?"

Bogey looked tempted but shook his head. "Need to get on to the Grand Saline before nightfall," he said. "I'll be sure to stop in on my way back."

George and Will set out at sunrise the following morning, hoping to arrive at Three Forks before the hot July sun made their Saturday unbearable. They located their supplies easily for the great pile of school furnishings and boxes of books sprawled around the landing. They found Captain Douglas visiting with Colonel Hugh Glenn at his trading post. The boatmen who had manned his keelboat were enjoying a day off and were deep into several rounds of rum at the Love trading house.

The Requa brothers were faced with a dilemma. It would take them more than a few hours to load their supplies into the two wagons they had brought and that would make it too late to return to Union Mission. They would have to spend the night at Three Forks as well as the following day for they would not travel on the Sabbath. And with two keelboats tied at the Verdigris landing, the trading center was overrun with boatmen, most in some stage of inebriation.

Three Forks wasn't a very hospitable place, even when not hosting two drunken keelboat crews. Will made the decision that they would have to return to Union and come back on Monday, load their supplies and then make the return trip on Tuesday. It would mean Captain Douglas would not be able to call upon the mission as they had hoped. He informed them that he intended to haul anchor early Monday and begin the final leg of his journey to New Orleans.

The mission family was disappointed that the good captain had not called upon them, but they were consoled with the enjoyable task of unloading the supplies the brothers brought from Three Forks. There were seed potatoes to delight Amanda who had long wanted some for her garden. Two casks of salt pork were welcomed by them all for they were growing tired of the gamey venison and prairie chickens that had been the bulk of their diet for so many months.

For Clarissa, there was nothing as wonderful as lifting a new primer to her nose to enjoy the scent of the fresh ink upon clean white paper. It made her long for classes to begin and she lifted a prayer and a hope that some young Osage girls would want to learn from these "talking leaves," and that she really would make a difference in their lives.

CHAPTER THIRTY-ONE

Union Mission
August, 1821

Rev. Chapman and the two teachers set a date in mid-September for their school year to begin. With visits to the villages of Claremont and Big Tracks, the Union missionaries let the Osages know school would open at the time of the full Persimmon Moon.

Clarissa asked Elizabeth, Abigail, Thomas and Richard to help her print some handbills announcing the date for the school's commencement. George promised to post them in all the trading houses at Three Forks.

"Do you think anyone is going to come, Teacher?" Elizabeth asked, as she and the other students sat at their new desks copying the school announcement that Miss Johnson had written on the blackboard.

"I hope they will, don't you?" Clarissa responded from her desk at the front of the room.

Elizabeth merely shrugged with a look of uncertainty on her face.

"What will it be like to go to school with Indians?" her brother Richard asked.

"I don't know," Clarissa answered honestly. "It might seem strange at first, since they may not speak English very well. But we must all work very hard to make anyone who comes to our school feel welcome."

"If they don't speak English, why are we writing the handbills in English?" Thomas then asked.

"Mr. Bogey says there are a few American families who live around Three Forks. We want them to know that their children can come to school too."

Given the fact that the Union Mission school would be the first one opened in all of western Arkansas Territory, the missionaries were hopeful any child in the region might board with them and attend classes. Realistically, they knew it might take time to grow their enrollment, but there was space for six girls and six boys to sleep in the divided loft above the classrooms. If more students than that came, they would have to build a dormitory.

The students were just finishing the handbills when George opened the schoolhouse door and cautiously stuck his head inside. It was almost as if he were afraid to enter the classroom.

"Excuse me, Miss Johnson," he said. "We have a visitor in the dining hall. Mrs. Chapmen asked me to let you know."

"Why thank you, Mr. Requa," Clarissa said, smiling at the young man's awkward appearance. Having received a limited education, George always seemed a little uncomfortable around the institution. "I'll be right over." George nodded and quietly closed the door.

"Does that mean we're done?" Richard asked. He was none too comfortable with education himself, and eager to be outside.

"Yes, Richard," the teacher said. "You are all free to go. I thank you for your assistance."

The students piled their handbills on the teacher's desk and all but Abigail wasted no time in taking their flight to freedom.

The girl lingered for a moment, clearly wanting to ask her teacher a question.

"Yes, Abigail?" Clarissa prompted as she stood and prepared to leave for the dining hall. She was curious about their visitor and eager herself to quit the classroom.

"You like Mr. George, don't you?" Abigail asked.

Clarissa was taken aback by the question. Was it just an innocent query, or was the girl already engaging in the kind of gossipy boy-girl speculation that had constantly swirled around the School for Girls where Clarissa had taught in Colchester. Not wanting to fan such speculation to flame here, she hesitated before answering.

"Certainly I like Mr. George," she finally said in a nonchalant tone. "I like everyone here at the mission." But then her curiosity got the better of her. "Why do you ask?"

"'Cause you always smile at him," Abigail observed. "You know . . . like this." Then she batted her eyes, tilted her head and smiled dreamily.

Clarissa felt alarm at the girl's demonstration. Surely she did not behave is such an obvious school-girl fashion. Oh, surely. And if Abigail had noticed, had anyone else?

"Nonsense," Clarissa responded a little more quickly this time. "You imagine things. I don't smile at Mr. Requa any differently than anyone else."

"You smile at him like Miss Eliza smiles at Dr. Palmer," Abigail reiterated.

Oh that was a sad indictment indeed. Eliza made no attempt to hide her smiles directed at the doctor. Susan and Amanda teased her about it often and she'd never denied her interest in their kind physician.

"Well, that's different," Clarissa lamely argued. "Dr. Palmer smiles at Miss Eliza too."

"No, he doesn't," Abigail said, knowingly. By this time, she had lost interest in the conversation and was already skipping toward the door. But as she opened it she looked back at her teacher and threw one last flame. "He smiles at you."

Then she was gone, leaving Clarissa with an odd sensation in her stomach. My goodness, what a revelation this bit of girl talk had been.

Collecting herself took a moment; then Clarissa gave herself a mental shaking and walked over to the dining hall. She had no chance in competing with beautiful Eliza for any man's attention, so she would just put such an idea out of her mind.

She stepped into the dining hall to find most of the adults gathered around a trapper who sat at one of the tables enjoying a cup of coffee and piece of peach cobbler.

He was a big man with tanned, leathery skin and a long dark beard, streaked generously with gray. He wore the usual trapper's garb -- leather britches, beaded moccasins and a fringed jacket that had been trimmed with the tails of some of his catch. A beaver pelt cap sat on the table beside him.

"His name is Pierre Menard," Susan whispered to her in answer to Clarissa's questioning look as she took a seat beside her. "He's a priest; can be you believe it?"

Clarissa remembered the name mentioned by Joseph and Teresa Revoir. He was the Pumpkin Moon preacher who had led Teresa and others from her village to Christ. But she agreed with Susan's assessment. He hardly looked like a Catholic priest.

"Got a cabin down on the bayou near Three Forks," Father Menard was saying. "I've come back from checking my summer traps and will settle down here for the winter."

"Where do you run your traps?" George asked, eager for this type of education. Clarissa studiously avoided looking at him.

"Got a line along most of the Arkansas," Menard answered in a gravelly voice that seemed rusty from lack of use. "I've been out as far west as the Great Mountains."

For a time he shared stories of his adventures further west which the missionaries found of great interest. He told of his encounter with a mother bear protecting her two cubs and described the mountain vistas, and the boulder-strewn, ice cold, Arkansas River in western Kansas Territory. It was hard for the mission family to imagine the sand-choked Arkansas they had traveled starting out as a tumbling mountain stream.

"We understand from the Revoirs that you hold church at Three Forks," Rev. Chapman said. "Have you had much success in making converts among the Indians?"

"The Pumpkin Moon is the time for rendezvous at Three Forks," Father Menard said. "All the trappers in the area come in from the summer hunt. They gather at French Point to trade their furs, swap tall tales about mama bears, buffalo stampedes and the like. I always set up an arbor and offer communion, listen to confession, and try to encourage the faith, so to speak. The Osages like the music and come around when we start to sing. They like hearing the Bible stories. Some have been baptized."

"So they can be receptive to the gospel?" Rev. Vaille asked.

"I will share with you the secret I have learned in my dealings with the native people," the priest said, leaning back in his chair. "Don't come at them saying you're bringing them a new religion. Tell them it's an old religion, passed down to you from your elders."

"Why is that?" Redfield inquired.

"You Americans love anything that is new. But most Indians love anything that is old. They are taught to respect their elders, to follow the old traditions. They're suspicious of anything new. So tell them you're bringing an old, old story about the great God of the universe and his Son. They'll listen. They'll respect that."

"Thank you for telling us that," Chapman said. "I'm afraid I have been guilty of using the word 'new' when talking about the faith with the Osages. No wonder they seemed to have no interest."

"I've observed that they'll listen to stories better than scriptural exposition, if you know what I mean," Menard winked. "They come from a tradition of oral learning and their Old Men teach them their values from the stories of the past. A good story is as much appreciated among the Indians as among us."

Clarissa made a mental note of this information. She had long worried in her mind how she would teach girls who came from a different culture. Any advice was welcome and she could tell Mr. Spaulding felt the same way. He was leaning forward in his chair, unmindful of his spectacles that had slipped to the end of his nose.

"I was sorry to hear of Revoir's death," Father Menard was now saying. "He and Teresa were good friends to me. I hate to see that Mad Buffalo and Walter Webber have been at it again."

"Their feud is a long one?" Dr. Palmer asked.

"Not so long as some have been," Menard said. "But long or short, it's a sad business, this need to avenge a death. Revoir was a good friend to Mad Buffalo too. I'm afraid he'll be determined to take a scalp over this."

"Captain Pryor and David Brearley have gotten assurances of peace from Mad Buffalo and Chief Webber," Rev. Chapman said. "We haven't had any trouble in over two months."

"Well, I hope it lasts," Menard said, slapping his hands against his leather britches and starting to rise. "I thank you for the sweets," he nodded to Amanda. "And I'll expect to see you all at French Point in about a month. Rendezvous is a good time to meet all your neighbors, learn all the goings on."

"And a good time for a little preaching?" Rev. Vaille asked.

"Yes . . ." Menard pulled on his beaver cap. "Once they all sober up." He winked again and headed for the door. His pack mule waited patiently at the corral fence to carry him to his cabin near Three Forks.

The day set for school to begin dawned clear and fresh. The weather would not keep students away and Clarissa didn't know how she felt about that. She was more than a little anxious about facing her new class. She dressed with care, feeling a flutter of nerves building in her stomach.

She joined Amanda in the kitchen to help get biscuits in the fireplace oven. Phoebe shared kitchen duties today and was slicing ham and humming a tune -- a bit off key, but happy sounding nonetheless. Since her marriage, Phoebe had lost much of her dark, fatalistic point of view.

Clarissa was preoccupied after all the mission family had sat down to morning devotions and breakfast. She was rehearsing in her mind the welcome speech she planned for her students. She would have to use a combination of the few Osage words she had learned along with French and English. It was going to be a challenge to keep it all straight and she hoped that she would adequately communicate with her new students.

Rev. Chapman had made learning Osage a priority for himself and had through the past months traveled often to Claremont's town to try to capture a language that had yet to develop a written form. Then Rev. Chapman would share pertinent words with the whole group after evening devotions most nights.

Hello and welcome were words easy enough for Clarissa to learn, though she was a little uncertain of her pronunciation. But the word teacher from the Osage referred to the Little Old Men and she knew she could not use that word to refer to herself. She could just imagine the girlish giggles that would bring. She would have to use the French word *professeur*, and hope they would understand.

Many evenings during the prayers following devotions, Clarissa had prayed that at least one of her students would be conversant in either English and Osage or French and Osage and could thus act as an interpreter for her. She had considered asking Rev. Chapman if Teresa Revoir might serve in that capacity, but was waiting to learn about her students first. Perhaps Teresa's daughter Louisa might be able to help.

At least Clarissa was conversant in French; Mr. Spaulding was fluent in Latin and had a great understanding of Greek, but not French. George or Will Requa would be assisting him since both had learned French from their Huguenot grandparents.

"Well are you ready for the session to begin?" Dr. Palmer interrupted Clarissa's reverie.

"What?" she said, feeling foolish as she looked up to find him standing across the table from her. Most everyone else was leaving to begin their day's work.

The doctor smiled at her. "I asked if you were ready for the school session to begin. It's a big day for the mission."

"Yes, it is," Clarissa agreed. "But I'm not sure I am ready. I don't think I fully grasped how difficult it might be to communicate with my students when I volunteered to teach."

"Do you regret coming?" Marcus asked.

Clarissa thought for a moment. "No," she said, rather surprised that this was her honest answer. Despite the less than noble reason for taking the position, she really didn't regret it. "I just hope I can do a good job."

"You'll be fine," Marcus sought to assure her. "I know your girls love you as their teacher."

"As long as they don't have to stay in class a minute past three," she laughed.

"Well that is the universal stipulation for teachers everywhere," the doctor agreed. "Don't keep us in class a moment longer than necessary."

"Yes, I suppose I felt that way as a student."

"I wish you a successful first day then," Dr. Palmer said. "Please call upon me if I can be of any assistance."

"Thank you," Clarissa said, feeling a sudden spring of tears to her eyes. How nice of the doctor to make such an offer. "I will."

Dr. Palmer nodded and then crossed the dining hall to help Mr. Fuller rise from the table. The farm director was making good progress in regaining his strength, but still found it hard to push himself up from a sitting position.

Clarissa finished the last of her coffee and then quickly rose to make her way to the school building. As she walked across the mission yard, the never absent prairie wind teased at her skirts. She could hear it whispering through the dried cornstalks stacked in the fields between the mission and the Trace. She looked around the schoolyard, but saw only the eight mission children there. There were no children from the neighborhood or either of the Osage villages.

The Chapmans and Rev. Vaille were on hand to greet any students who might show up. Mrs. Vaille, now several months into her pregnancy, kept more and more to her cabin. The ministers, along with Clarissa and John, stood for a while outside the school watching the road, making small talk. Everyone seemed to feel disappointment but they tried not to show it.

Finally John rang the school bell and the students, teachers and ministers filed into the boy's classroom. Rev. Vaille led a brief devotion then they sang a hymn. After prayer, Clarissa led her girls into their classroom.

She felt a mixture of guilty relief along with the disappointment. To have not one neighborhood child come was disheartening. But they had known it would be a challenge to interest the Osages in their school. They would just have to keep trying.

Clarissa was giving the girls a reading assignment about mid-morning when she happened to look out the west facing window. Teresa Revoir was approaching the mission compound on horseback. Louisa rode behind her and Jean rode a second horse, with a girl behind him.

The four dismounted at the corral fence, secured their horses and walked toward the classroom building. Clarissa felt her heart rate increase in nervousness. John must have also seen the Revoirs for he exited his classroom and called a greeting to them. Clarissa took a deep breath and joined him outside.

"Welcome," Mr. Spaulding greeted Teresa and the children. "We're glad to have you join us."

"Yes," Clarissa added, smiling brightly at the two girls. Louisa was probably six years old and the other girl looked to be ten. "We thought no one was coming."

Teresa glanced at the sun. "You said the morning after the full Persimmon Moon. It is morning."

"Yes, we did," John responded, exchanging a glance with Clarissa. In their minds, morning meant by 8:00 a.m., but to the Indians it meant any time before the sun reached its zenith. They would need to get better at communicating time.

The Chapmans approached from their cabin and greeted the new arrivals. Rev. Chapman could not hide his delight that three students had chosen to come. They settled the children into their respective classes and Mrs. Chapman invited Mrs. Revoir to join her for tea.

Teresa had introduced the second girl as Marie Lombard, the daughter of Teresa's sister who had also married a French fur trader and lived in a cabin on a creek the Osages called the Flat Rock. Marie was nine, but had never had any schooling.

"*Parlez vous français?*" Clarissa asked Marie after the girls had taken their seats.

"*Oui*," the girl responded and Clarissa felt great relief. Her welcome speech in Osage had completely fled her mind.

She spent the rest of the morning giving instruction in both French and English, since the mission girls had received only very basic lessons in French. By the time Amanda rang the dinner bell, Clarissa was beginning to feel a headache form at the base of her neck. She felt as confused as the girls sometimes looked as she tried to conduct the lessons in two languages.

The classes walked to the dining hall and Mrs. Chapman engaged Teresa, Louisa and Marie in conversation while they ate. Rachel had received part of her education in France and was even more proficient in the French language than Clarissa.

In the afternoon session Mrs. Revoir asked if she could sit in on the class and Clarissa readily agreed. It was Teresa who finally shared with her that while Marie was not proficient in English, she could understand it. This made everything simpler for the teacher.

Still she felt exhausted by mid afternoon and felt little guilt for letting the girls out early. The Revoirs and Marie mounted their horses after Jean was set free and made their way to the Lombard cabin.

In the following weeks, a few more students, mostly French-Osage who lived in isolated cabins in the area came to school. Some walked and others came on horseback.

Attendance was spotty, however. None of the students came every day and they arrived at different times. There seemed to be a general indifference toward education among the children and their parents. All the missionaries could hope to do was make the school seem a hospitable and friendly place where all were welcome. Eventually they hoped to penetrate the darkness of illiteracy that existed among every group of people on the frontier.

For the Pumpkin Moon Rendezvous in October, school was dismissed for a week. Very early on Friday, all the mission family except for Rev. and Mrs. Vaille and Stephen Fuller loaded into their two wagons, and headed south on the Trace to Three Forks. It was the first time the women and children had left the mission compound since arriving in February and they were all excited about taking a holiday. The Redfields had agreed to supervise the three Vaille children since their parents were not able to travel.

Amanda packed an abundance of food for the journey in three big baskets Susan had woven from river cane. Always creative, making the baskets was just one of the ways Susan had contributed a little practical beauty to their prairie outpost.

They found Three Forks bustling with activity. Not only were there several fur traders present, but two keelboats were tied up at the Verdigris landing and boatmen joined in with the festive atmosphere. Many Osages and a few Pawnees and Wichitas had brought furs for trading as well.

The missionaries pulled up to Captain Pryor's trading house and quickly climbed down from the hard wagon beds.

"Children, you need to stay close to an adult while we're here," Mrs. Chapman told them as they looked around with open curiosity. They had been given little chance to explore the trade community when they arrived the past winter and now there was much to see. The weather was fine, the sights and sounds and

smells were enticing and they were all eager to experience
Rendezvous for the first time.

"Mr. George, can you take us to Mr. Love's post?" Thomas
Chapman asked. Whenever George came to Three Forks for
supplies, he always brought back horehound or molasses candy
from Hugh Love's trading house. The children imagined it
being a confectionery delight and wanted to spend the precious
coins they had been given.

George laughed at the children's eager faces, but looked to
Mrs. Chapman for permission before agreeing to take them to
the trading post.

Rachel nodded her agreement, but gave the children a
warning. "Don't spend all your money on candy," she said.
"Just a penny's worth for each of you."

"A whole penny?" little Sarah Vaille whispered, obviously
thinking that would buy a very great lot of candy.

"Can you come too, Miss Johnson?" asked Leah Chapman
who adored her teacher.

A little surprised at the request, Clarissa hesitated for a
moment, looking nervously at George. He seemed to be waiting
for her answer with as much interest as the girls.

"Well, I suppose I can," she said, being sure to smile at her
students and not at Mr. Requa.

"Might I accompany you as well?" Dr. Palmer asked,
directing his question to the boys.

"Sure, Doctor," Thomas said, "but you're not going to tell
us that candy is bad for us, are you?"

"No," Marcus laughed. "I promise I won't."

Eliza reached down to take Billy Spaulding's hand. "Well,
let's all go then," she said, inviting herself to the candy
rendezvous.

Susan and Amanda stood together watching the four adults
try to herd the children through the groups of men gathered
along the meandering trail that passed for a street.

"Well, that's a fine tangle of misguided interests," Amanda
observed into Susan's ear.

"Too bad everyone around here is blind," Susan agreed,
shooting darted looks at Will Requa who was deep in
conversation with Samuel Rutherford, Pryor's trading partner.

Amanda laughed sympathetically. "Ain't it so," she said.

They, along with the remaining women, made their way to the ferry that crossed the Verdigris. Mrs. Revoir had told them that Colonel Chouteau had bolts of dress fabrics available as well as ribbon and other sewing supplies. They would shop for their own goodies before meeting back at Pryor's for a supper of cornbread, cheese and boiled eggs. Then they planned to visit Father Menard's brush arbor at French Point.

French Point was the jut of land between the Verdigris and Neosho rivers where they flowed into the Arkansas. Long before the community of Three Forks had formed, French traders had used this familiar landmark as the point for the fall trading rendezvous.

These days the trappers and hunters took their furs to one of the six trading houses that lined both banks of the Verdigris, but Rendezvous was still a much-anticipated time of socializing before winter's cold kept everyone close to their cabin or campsite.

Set at a spot cleared of the thick river cane, Menard's "church," lit by lanterns, made a pretty site as they arrived near sunset. The fur trapper-turned-priest greeted the missionaries and seemed genuinely pleased to have them as guests. It seemed odd to Clarissa that they, as staunch Presbyterians, were attending a Catholic service but this was the frontier. As the priest at Cape Girardeau had told them so many months ago such distinctions didn't matter as much here on the edge of civilization.

There were a few log seats under the hide-draped arbor and these were offered to the ladies. But they frankly looked uncomfortable so the women chose instead to spread out the buffalo robes they had brought with them and sit on the ground.

The singing was surprisingly good. Father Menard chose some of the rousing Methodist hymns and these seemed to suit the setting and the audience. As he had predicted, several Osage families came when the singing began. Big Tracks' town was nearby on the banks of the Neosho.

Father Menard preached in his own concoction of English, French and Osage, using just enough of each language to get his message to his diverse audience. Clarissa admired the way he wove the languages together while colorfully telling the story of Zacchaeus from the Gospel of Luke.

After the service, the missionaries made their way to Mr. Bogey's trading post which was closest to French Point. Here they set up camp, spreading out the buffalo robes in and under the wagons for sleeping. The boys were ecstatic that they were camping out, and Richard and James declared that they were going to be fur trappers when they grew up.

CHAPTER THIRTY-TWO

Union Mission
Late October, 1821

Late Sunday evening after the Rendezvous holiday, the mission family had settled into their cabins following evening devotions. The nights were growing cooler, but the days were still warm and good for hunting. Teresa had told the teachers not to expect many students for a while as this was the time for the fall buffalo hunt. In fact, November's moon was called the Hunter's Moon.

Both Claremont's and Big Tracks' villages would all head west to where the massive herds had migrated. Even the Choctaws, Chickasaws and Cherokees made their way into western Arkansas Territory for this important hunting season. Just this morning, they had seen a group of Cherokees on the Trace.

"Get a good night's sleep," Amanda told her cabin mates as she blew out the last candle. "We start the hog slaughter tomorrow." She was actually looking forward to this fall ritual.

Clarissa was glad she would not have to participate in this annual farmstead activity. She would still be teaching the mission girls, even if no Osage students came to class. The teacher had no desire to make sausage or render hog fat for soap. It would be nice, however, to have a winter's supply of meat curing in their new smokehouse.

Amanda had just slipped into bed when they heard the sound of horses coming fast toward the mission.

"What is that?" Susan whispered, sitting up and reaching for her wrapper.

Eliza hurried to their window and lifted up a corner of the deer hide cover to peek out. Fortunately, they hadn't yet pulled the outside shutters closed so she could see the moonlit compound. "It's Indians," she said.

Quickly the other women had risen and huddled beside her, peering out into the shadows. Next door, Mr. Woodruff opened his cabin door slightly.

"They're women . . . and children," Amanda said in surprise.

By the time the riders had reached the center of the mission grounds, the men had thrown on clothes and were gathering outside the Chapman's central cabin. Abraham Redfield and the Requas held muskets.

Rev. Chapman stepped forward as one of the Osage women slid from her mount. It was Yellowbird, wife of Chief Claremont. She and the minister exchanged words in Osage then Chapman turned to the other men. "She says the Cherokees attacked the village at noon today. All the men, but the Old Men, were gone on a scouting trip to locate the buffalo."

"Was anyone hurt?" Dr. Palmer asked.

"Many hurt," Yellowbird stated in English. "We bring them. You fix."

"We saw the Cherokees this morning," Redfield said. "They were not a war party. They weren't wearing the red paint."

"Not war party," Yellowbird confirmed. "Hunting party."

"They must have realized the village was vulnerable and saw an opportunity to attack," Will observed.

"Was anyone killed?" Chapman asked.

"No killed," the woman said. "Lodges," she made a slashing motion with her arm, "down."

"Either harassment and intimidation or foolish mischief," Rev. Vaille said.

"You fix?" Yellowbird directed her question to the doctor. He had visited her husband's lodge several times and she knew that he was a medicine man. The doctor's reputation had risen much among the Osages after his valiant attempt to save the life of Joseph Revoir.

"Yes," Dr. Palmer agreed. "Let's get everyone in the dining

hall so I can assess the injuries." He turned to his cabin to get his medical kit.

By this time, the women who had been listening from their cabin doors were all hurrying to dress and offer what help they could.

Mrs. Chapman brought Martha, Alice and Phoebe to the single women's cabin to get them organized.

"Amanda, can you get some coffee boiling and perhaps start some soup?" Rachel asked.

"Aye," the cook agreed. "There's plenty of cornbread in the larder. I planned to make dressing with the hog cracklin's tomorrow."

"I can help Amanda," Phoebe volunteered.

"Me too," Eliza and Alice said in unison before Clarissa could. Frankly she was surprised that Eliza hadn't volunteered to be Dr. Palmer's assistant. She immediately felt guilty for the thought.

"Miss Johnson and I will help with cleaning and bandaging the minor wounds," Rachel was saying. "Susan will you help Mrs. Vaille watch the children. We'll send any of the Osage children who don't need medical attention to our cabin."

"Sure," Susan agreed.

"Martha, you're best suited to helping Dr. Palmer with any serious injuries."

"I'll do my best," the older woman agreed.

They all made their way to the dining hall. Amanda sent Paul and Robbie to the spring for several buckets of water. They would use some for cooking and some for cleaning wounds.

Everyone fell to the tasks assigned to them. The Requas and Redfield were walking the edge of the property to assist others from Claremont's town who Yellowbird said were following on foot. Stephen started grinding the coffee as Phoebe, Alice and Eliza cut vegetables for the soup. The ministers helped Dr. Palmer assess injuries.

Fortunately, most were simple cuts and bruises caused by the tumbling lodge poles. A few cuts were serious enough to need stitches so Dr. Palmer, Rev. Vaille and Martha set up a surgery area near the fireplace. One boy had a broken collar bone so Rev. Chapman set to work creating a sling for him.

Clarissa applied a cold compress to a bad pump knot on the head of Whitestar, the petite Pawnee wife of the chief. She appeared to be about six months pregnant. Dr. Palmer told Clarissa to watch her closely for any signs of a concussion.

Taking a chance that the girl spoke French, she asked if she had suffered any other injuries.

"No," Whitestar said, but she placed her hand protectively over the swell of her abdomen. The gesture made the teacher remember Sally Edwards. Sally had done that often. Clarissa hoped it didn't portend an equally sad outcome for Whitestar.

Robbie brought a cup of water to Clarissa and she handed it to Whitestar.

"*Merci*," the young woman said. There was a true gratitude in her eyes that made Clarissa wonder if the chief's second wife received much kindness in his lodge.

"You sit here and rest," she told Whitestar. "We'll have something for you to eat soon."

Paul and Alexander Woodruff had gotten a roaring fire blazing and the room was soon filled with warmth and the smell of the cooking soup.

The Osages were quiet, saying little except to explain their injuries to the doctor. They seemed stoic, even accepting of the violence that had brought them here.

Clarissa joined the other women in the kitchen after all the injured had been helped. "You don't know if they are sad or angry or just frightened," she said as they all stood watching Rev. Chapman speak to each one in Osage.

"I sure thought we were over this feud," Phoebe said. "I thought Mr. Webber and Mad Buffalo had buried the hatchet."

"It very well could be that Webber had nothing to do with this," Rachel observed. "Those Cherokees we saw today were hardly more than boys, probably looking to prove something the way young men always do."

"Just proves that men can be stupid sometimes," Susan said with all the vehemence her little voice could muster. She had joined them after getting all the children settled on pallets in the Chapman cabin.

Rachel looked at her and smiled for a moment. But then looking at Yellowbird, she said, "I fear that Mad Buffalo will not let this incident go unanswered, no matter what the motivation for it."

"Should someone alert Major Bradford at Fort Smith?" Alice asked.

"At the very least we must let Captain Pryor know," Rachel said. "Better get this settled as quickly as possible."

Others from Claremont's town arrived over the next few hours, but none of these were injured. Yellowbird had gotten all the injured to Union in the first group. In the early morning, everyone was settled to catch a few hours sleep before daybreak.

The following day, Yellowbird insisted that they all return to their village. They would need to restore their homes and clean up their household goods that had been tossed about in the melee. Dr. Palmer did convince her to let the boy with the broken collar bone stay at the mission for a few more days so he could monitor the healing process.

Rev. Chapman, Dr. Palmer and Will Requa accompanied them as they slowly made their way back to Claremont's town. Having received the Osages at the mission and given them assistance, there was little point in trying to keep out of the feud now. They would have to hope the Cherokees understood their work was Christian charity and not choosing sides.

George and Abraham rode to Three Forks to tell Pryor about the incident. As sub-agent to the Osages, it was his responsibility to deal with issues like these.

The children were too sleepy to absorb much from lessons, so they were dismissed at noon. Clarissa was grateful that the hog slaughter would be put off until the next day. Teaching was her excuse not to participate.

Even the older boys helped the following day and Clarissa felt just a little guilty that she had not volunteered to let the girls out of class as well. Glancing out the window, she saw Amanda, Susan, Martha and Phoebe all taking turns at stirring a large kettle over an open fire in the yard.

"I'm glad I'm not out there," Leah said as she followed her teacher's gaze. The wrinkling of her little nose said what she thought of grinding sausage and making soap.

Clarissa had to laugh. At least her choice had spared her girls getting their hands roughened with the wood ash lye. She would make a point of thanking all her sisters every time she enjoyed the fruit of their labor.

The next days were busy with the usual winter preparations as they awaited word from Pryor about the Osage-Cherokee incident. Amanda had Stephen and Robbie's help in harvesting the fall harvest of potatoes, turnips, beets and carrots and the other women helped her clean them and get them stored on burlap bags in the root cellar under the kitchen.

Amanda surveyed the harvest with satisfaction. The rich, river bottom land had produced a bounty and Stephen reported that they had taken about 120 bushels per acre of corn. Their corn crib, smokehouse and cellar were full and jars of canned vegetables lined several shelves that George and Abraham had constructed and installed in the kitchen.

"We ought to have a day of thanksgiving," Eliza suggested as she helped Amanda with dinner preparations.

"What a lovely idea, Miss Eliza," Amanda agreed. "I'll suggest it to Mrs. Chapman."

Both of the Chapmans were quite agreeable to setting aside a day for a Thanksgiving feast. It would create an opportunity to invite their neighbors to the mission for the occasion.

They set the date for the week after the Hunter's Moon and took word to Three Forks and the Osage towns. As the days grew shorter, the migration of birds increased and some days the sky would be darkened with the thousands of quail, ducks and geese moving south. The missionaries had never seen such an incredible bounty of game. The men easily brought back dozens of birds any time they went hunting and the women were kept busy dressing them out, saving the down and feathers for more pillows and mattresses.

Amanda planned her menu for the Thanksgiving meal and with the help of the other women began the cooking days in advance. Abraham, the Requas and the two apprentices had spent several days in the *spa-vi-nah*, felling trees for their winter supply of firewood. It became the job of Paul to keep the cabins, school rooms and the kitchen fireplaces all well stocked with kindling.

Two days before their Thanksgiving a visitor arrived from

Harmony Mission in Missouri. Rev. William Montgomery had come to Harmony in August with a party of workers from New England.

Always glad to have a visitor, the missionaries gathered with Rev. Montgomery for supper and peppered him with questions about events back home and the progress being made at Harmony.

"The school is growing there," Rev. Montgomery shared with them. "But we are desperate for workers. We lost seven members to the fever this summer, including my wife and little infant daughter." His voice caught as he spoke.

Stephen stared into his coffee, reliving the pain he had felt when losing Lydia. How terrible to lose both a wife and a child.

"Please accept our condolences, Rev. Montgomery," Rachel said. "I can only imagine how great your sorrow must be."

"Thank you, Mrs. Chapman," the minister replied. "My wife was deeply committed to the work we are trying to do among the Indians. She had no regrets for coming west and so I try to honor her by continuing the work."

"Can we help you in any way?" Rev. Vaille asked.

"Actually, I was hoping to get assistance," Montgomery confessed. "I was hoping I might persuade one of your housemothers to come to Harmony. We will have several winter boarders and need someone to help with their care."

Clarissa drew in her breath. She would hate to see either Susan or Phoebe leave; they were truly like sisters to her.

Rachel seemed reluctant to let either woman go as well and seemed to communicate that to her husband with just a look. "We'll have to give some thought to that," was all Rev. Chapman would say.

"The mission director at Harmony also wanted me to discuss another idea with you," Montgomery went on. "We believe the Plains Indians might benefit from seeing how a small homestead operates, instead of the large enterprises such as these missions are."

"How do you mean?" Chapman asked.

"It seems unlikely that the Osages or Sioux or Quapaws will ever be interested in working a 100-acre farm. They see no value in producing more grain than they can consume themselves. There's no market for it out here and we fear the tendency would be to convert any excess grain into liquor. We think showing them how to manage a smaller place might be more beneficial. Perhaps by setting up a five-acre 'demonstration farm,' if you will."

"I agree," Will Requa spoke up. "In talking with the Osages, I know they think what we're doing here is too ambitious for them to consider. Frankly, it seems like too much work and work is for women."

Rachel cleared her throat.

"Sorry, ma'am," Will quickly added. "That's not my sentiment; I'm just saying what the Indians think. Caring for the crops is the work of the women. They simply don't think their women could work such a large acreage or that they should. We need to show them that you can farm a small area and make a good life that way."

"I think he's right," Stephen said, to almost everyone's surprise. He rarely spoke at their meetings. "I love working a 40-acre field, but that's not practical for everyone. If showing the Indians how to farm is what we are about, then setting up a little homestead might serve that goal better."

"I myself would be willing to work such a demonstration farm," Montgomery stated. "That is partly why I was asked to pay you this visit. Perhaps, with Chief Claremont's permission we could establish a mission outpost nearby."

"I could help with that as well," Will volunteered.

Now it was Susan's turn to draw a startled breath, but she covered it quickly with a little cough. She exchanged a covert look with Clarissa and Amanda. Neither of them knew what to think about this turn of events.

Rev. Montgomery readily agreed to stay through their Thanksgiving. The women were all up early and in the kitchen to get started with final preparations. Slowly area neighbors began to arrive through the morning. The Revoirs and Lombards came first and the Pryors and Chouteaus followed shortly. A few Osages were present from Big Track's town, most were Teresa's relatives.

It was close to noon when a small group arrived from

Claremont's town, including the chief himself. It was the first time Claremont had visited and the missionaries realized that in doing so, the Osage leader was signaling a new respect and acceptance of Union Mission.

Yellowbird and several of the other Osage women carried packs on their back. They had brought buffalo hides, dried pemmican and a great many gourds and pumpkins to share with the missionaries. It seemed much like the Pilgrim Thanksgiving from 200 years earlier and provided the mission family with one more thing to give thanks to the Lord for on this day.

The women were just setting out the food in the dining hall when Thomas happened to look out the window from the children's table.

"I see smoke outside," he said. Paul heard him from where he worked to stack more wood by the fireplace. He had made numerous trips to and from the wood rick over the last three days. He went to the door and looked out.

"Fire on the roof!" he called.

There was a gasp from nearly everyone in the crowded dining hall. Quickly George and Stephen rushed outdoors to look up at the roof. Indeed, the dried grass of the sod roof around the chimney was in flames.

"Get the water buckets, boys," George called to the apprentices as he and Stephen raced to the barn for the ladder. Robbie, Paul and Thomas rushed to the spring house.

Acting quickly, Amanda ran for the empty soup kettle and other available pans in the kitchen. She handed these to Abraham who also raced to fill them at the spring.

The men formed a line stretching from the water source to the dining hall and began handing the buckets and pans from man to man. Traders, trappers, missionaries and Indians were all part of the effort. George and Will climbed to the roof while Alex stood halfway up the ladder to pass water to them.

Smoke from the chimney began to filter down into the kitchen and dining fireplaces that shared the same flue. The women hurried to open all the shutters and use towels and aprons to try to fan the smoke out of the rooms.

Though it seemed like hours, it took only a few frantic moments to douse the flames. But the dining hall was now so smoky it would take a while for it to clear. The food wasn't ruined, but was rapidly growing cold and Amanda felt near to tears. All their hard work now seemed in vain.

"We'll just have to move everything outside," the unflappable Rachel stated as they all surveyed the food-laden tables. "If you all will help us?" she asked their guests and Colonel Chouteau translated into Osage.

Everyone picked up dishes, tableware, chairs and tables and in short order everything had been reassembled out of doors upwind from the last wisps of smoke.

"Are we being Pilgrims?" James Chapman asked as he carefully set down a heaping bowl of mashed potatoes.

"Yes, dear, I think we are," Rachel smiled at her youngest son.

Rev. Chapman stood at the head of one of the tables and surveyed the group gathered for the Thanksgiving meal. To have the Osages join them was an answer to many heartfelt prayers and one that truly deserved their gratitude.

With Colonel Chouteau translating, he told their guests about the American tradition of setting aside a day of thanks to God for his blessings, being sure to tell them that it was a very old tradition.

"It is like the Green Corn Feast," Chief Claremont said and Chouteau conveyed his words to the missionaries. "We too give thanks to *Wah-Kon-Tah* for his gifts."

Rev. Chapman then asked for bowed heads for prayer. After he prayed, he asked Claremont if one of their number would also like to offer prayer. Claremont nodded to a silver-haired man with a beautiful, wrinkle-lined face.

He was Gray Wolf, one of the revered Old Men of the tribe. He stood and spoke an ancient prayer of his people and while the missionaries could not understand all the words, they sensed the reverence with which it was offered and found it very moving. It gave them hope that Gray Wolf and his people would not be long in embracing the Son of the Great God and joining them in a true fellowship of faith.

The missionaries and their guests visited around the tables while enjoying fresh quail and venison, ham and potatoes, turnips, peas and carrots, light bread and cornbread, berry cobbler and pecan pie. Those who didn't speak a shared language were easily helped by others who did so conversation was woven with English, French and Osage.

The missionaries were introduced to a young man from Claremont's town who had earned the name Panther Killer. He wore the claws of his prey in a beaded necklace. From his description of his kill, and the frightening size of the claws, the missionaries felt certain he had taken the panther that had attacked Stephen. It was a relief to everyone's mind for though none of them had sighted the cat in several months, the worry that it might return had been troubling.

Everyone ate until they could eat no more. Few of the serving dishes had any food remaining at the end of the meal. It gave Amanda a great feeling of satisfaction. She had always known that it would be food that provided the bridge between themselves and the Indians. Preparing food was her ministry, her gift, and she felt blessed for being able to offer it to the Lord.

The mission family bid goodbye to their guests in the early afternoon. Most would have a journey of several hours to return home. But all who had been a part of this Thanksgiving meal felt pleased with its success – despite the smoke that still lingered.

CHAPTER THIRTY-THREE

Union Mission
Late Autumn, 1821

The single mission sisters were readying for bed that evening when Susan interrupted their ritual hair brushing with a question.

"Do you think I ought to go to Harmony Mission?"

"Oh, Susan," Amanda immediately set down her brush and went to her sister. "We would all miss you terribly if you go."

Clarissa and Eliza nodded in agreement and turned their attention to the sweet young woman.

"But I'm not really needed here," Susan said. "Phoebe is more than able to keep the children we have. I came out here because I wanted to care for children who really needed it . . . who needed me. I think they would at Harmony."

"You've prayed about this, have you?" Amanda asked, taking both of Susan's hands.

"Yes," Susan said, but her childlike voice seemed uncertain.

"Isn't there someone here who needs you too?" Eliza asked. They all knew she was referring to Will Requa.

Susan sighed. "I've given him every opportunity to state his intentions . . . any intentions. We sat near each other during the dinner today, but he never once tried to talk me out of going to Harmony, even when I told him I was considering it."

Clarissa rolled her eyes. "Men," she said.

"He clearly likes you," Amanda smiled. "We can all see that."

"But not enough," Susan said.

Her words pricked Clarissa's heart. How well she knew how that felt. She could hardly blame Susan for wanting to go to the mission in Missouri.

"Have you spoken with Mrs. Chapman yet?" Clarissa asked. "I'm sure she would rather you stayed here. We don't know but what our school might grow quite a bit with boarders for the winter."

"Captain Pryor says it rarely snows this far south and the winters are usually mild," Susan countered. "We might not get any boarders. But they already have children staying at the school in Missouri."

"Don't make a decision without talking with Mrs. Chapman," Clarissa advised her friend. She was hopeful that Rachel would be able to convince Susan to stay.

"I'll speak to her in the morning," Susan agreed. "I think Rev. Montgomery plans to return to Harmony at the end of the week."

In the end, even Rachel could not convince Susan to stay. On Friday Rev. Montgomery mounted his horse for the journey back up the Osage Trace to Missouri, after thanking the Union missionaries for their hospitality. Abraham and Phoebe would travel with Susan in one of their wagons because it would be inappropriate for her to travel alone with the minister. The Redfields were familiar with the journey.

Will stood with the other missionaries watching the wagon head toward the Trace with a puzzled look on his face. "Why did she go?" he asked Amanda as they turned to walk to the dining hall.

Amanda made a disgusted noise in the back of her throat. "Because you wouldn't ask her to stay," she said quietly so only he could hear.

"Huh?" Will said, stopping in his tracks.

Amanda just shook her head and kept walking. Breakfast dishes were waiting and Stephen was filling her wash basin from the heated kettle at the fireplace.

A light snow fell in the first week of December but by afternoon it had melted away even with only a weak winter sun. The New England missionaries were amazed that snow could come and go so quickly, but the children wished for a chance to go sledding or ice skating.

One afternoon, Teresa Revoir arrived by horseback and sought out Mrs. Chapman. She wanted permission to set up her lodge near the mission so her children could continue their schooling through the winter. Granted permission, she chose a site near her late husband's grave. She pulled the materials for her lodge on a travois behind her horse and with Jean and Louisa's help quickly had established their winter home.

Teresa would occasionally join the missionaries for a meal, and attended Sunday services, but mostly she stayed close to her lodge working at the traditional women's crafts – turning deer hide to soft beaded moccasins or rabbit fur to warm mittens for herself and her children. She had told Mrs. Chapman that she would marry again in the spring. It was expected of her. But for now she would observe the time of mourning close to the husband she had clearly loved.

Christmas came and though Union Mission extended invitations for their neighbors to join them for a special service and share a meal, only Mr. Bogey, the Lombards and the Revoirs came. A brief but bitter cold snap kept everyone else close to their fires.

The children bemoaned the continued lack of snow for their first Christmas at the mission, but were still excited with the homemade gifts they received in their stockings. Mrs. Chapman had managed to get oranges delivered to Three Forks by keelboat and Joseph Bogey had brought them personally.

Dr. Palmer had half expected Mrs. Vaille to be delivered of her child on Christmas day. She was clearly near her time of birth. But when he visited with her the next day, she reported only a small twinge or two and assured him it would be at least another day before she would need assistance.

"I hope it won't offend you, Doctor," Asie Vaille said, looking up at him and her husband as they stood beside her chair. "But I'd rather have Mrs. Woodruff attend me for the birthing. She has midwife experience."

"No offense taken, Mrs. Vaille," Marcus assured her. He actually felt some relief. "Just know that I will be readily available should you need my assistance for anything."

"Thank you," Asie said, sounding weary. This was her fourth pregnancy so she well knew what to expect. As a small woman, birthing was never easy for her, but she was hopeful that the little brother or sister to Elizabeth, Richard and Sarah would arrive quickly.

Two nights later, Phoebe and Abraham had gathered the Vaille children in their cabin while Martha and Rachel assisted their mother. Dr. Palmer and Rev. Vaille paced so much in front of the cabins that Amanda took pity on them and got up herself to make coffee for them. She made them sit in the dining hall where Rev. Chapman joined them and offered a prayer for a safe delivery.

Stephen had just headed to the barn to help Robbie with the milking when the lusty cry of a baby broke the silence of the cold dawn. William Vaille jumped from his chair and hurried to be at his wife's side. Martha met him at the door.

"You have a son," she smiled. "Give us a few minutes more to get mother and child settled."

"And they're both doing well?" William asked, somewhat breathlessly.

"They are fine," Martha assured him. "You need to be thinking of a name. Mrs. Vaille tells us you have not settled on one." Then she closed the door.

The minister commenced pacing outside the cabin again, clearly trying to make his brain think about baby names, making no attempt to suppress the joyful smile on his face.

In short order all the others of the family, except the children who slept on, were gathered around the Vaille cabin. Congratulating the excited father, they spoke in quiet tones while blowing on their hands to keep them warm.

Martha opened the door and laughed to be greeted by a dozen anxious faces. "Just the father for now," she said, hurrying him inside to keep the cold out. "You will all get an introduction to the new little one after breakfast."

Having been properly dismissed by the woman who acted as mother to all of them, the missionaries headed to their regular morning chores. Phoebe and Alice helped get the children up and dressed and soon all were gathered for breakfast.

Rev. Vaille sat carefully on the bed beside his wife and new son who slept in the crook of her arm. Dark lashes fanned across his still red and wrinkled face and a black thatch of hair said he would have his father's coloring. William lifted one tiny hand, its fingers tightly curled, and marveled at the beauty of it.

"Ten of each," Asie smiled, indicating she had counted fingers and toes already. "I'm thinking we call him Joseph."

"That's a good name," William agreed.

"Do you think Teresa Revoir will mind?"

"I think she would be honored to have him named for her husband," William said.

"Mr. Bogey will think he's named for him," Martha observed as she gathered linens for the wash. Then she slipped out the door with Rachel and they headed to their own cabins to freshen up before going to breakfast.

After the morning meal, all the women gathered in the Vaille cabin to admire the newest member of the mission family and take turns holding him. Phoebe lifted his little face to hers and smelled the sweet baby scent. There was clear longing in her eyes and Clarissa felt her own fill with tears.

When it was the teacher's turn to hold Joseph, she felt a little nervous at first. She'd had little experience with babies so new, but as she dutifully admired the boy she felt a stir of longing in her own heart. Would she ever know the joy of holding her own child?

"Fine looking boy," Joseph Bogey said when he visited a few days later. He had indeed seemed pleased at the name chosen for the lad. The trader stood over the little cradle placed near the dining hall fireplace.

He had his hands wrapped around a tin of coffee, trying to warm them after his cold ride from Three Forks. He had arrived just as Amanda, Phoebe and Alice were setting out a supper of fried ham and potatoes with black-eyed peas and biscuits and wild plum pudding.

"Thank you, Mr. Bogey," Asie said from where she sat by the cradle, rocking it gently with her foot.

"We're pleased with him," Rev. Vaille added, sending a smile toward his wife. She had been rather weepy in the days since the birth and he wanted to encourage her.

"We thank you too for the letters from home," Asie said. She held two in her lap, already opened and read eagerly, just as the other missionaries had done. "But they do make me a little homesick," she added.

Clarissa was still perusing the three letters she had received. Jerusha and Millie both had written as well as her mother. As she turned the page of her mother's letter, she gasped quietly and raised her hand to her mouth.

"Something wrong, Miss Johnson?" George asked solicitously from where he sat nearby.

"My mother writes that her mother – my grandmother Thea – passed away this summer." Clarissa felt stunned. The last letter from home had said nothing about her being ill.

"I'm so sorry, Miss Johnson," Rachel said. "Were you close to your grandmother?"

"Yes," Clarissa said. "She lives in New Haven, but we visited her every summer and she always spent the holidays in Colchester with us." She felt the tears beginning to gather. It was certainly at news like this that she longed for home and to feel the comforting arms of her mother.

Instead, she felt the arms of Martha Woodruff around her shoulders. The older woman laid her cheek against Clarissa's in the way she did whenever the young women needed a motherly touch.

"She's living with our Father now," she said quietly.

"Yes, I know," Clarissa smiled through her tears. "But it's hard to think that I didn't have a chance to say a final goodbye."

"You shared good memories together," Martha comforted her. "I'm sure she knew of your love."

"Did she support your decision for missions work?" Rachel asked.

"Yes, very much," Clarissa responded, remembering her grandmother helping convince her parents to let her come west. "She approved more than my mother did," Clarissa gave a little laugh.

"So she's smiling her approval from above now," Martha stated. "Just remember that and remember all the wonderful times you shared with her."

"I will," Clarissa patted Martha's hand in thanks.

Everyone was now getting seated for supper so Clarissa tucked the letter back into its envelope and pressed the waxed seal closed. She would read it again in a quiet moment and take the time to grieve more properly then. She felt the sympathetic eyes of Dr. Palmer on her and she gave him a little smile to say she was alright.

During supper, Mr. Bogey told them Captain Pryor had returned to Three Forks after an absence. At Major Bradford's request, the former army officer had acted as a guide for a military expedition through western Arkansas and down into Spanish-held Texas. Upon his return he began to work with the Fort Smith commander on settling the running feud between the Osages and Cherokees.

"The Cherokees don't want a treaty with Claremont," Bogey said around a mouthful of fried potatoes. "They want Mad Buffalo himself to pledge peace. Pryor's just not sure he can get that to happen any time soon."

"Cannot the fort bring pressure on the Cherokees to keep their distance from the Osages?" John asked.

"There's only so much Bradford can do from Belle Point," Bogey said, spearing another slice of ham. "He's recommending to General Gains that another fort be built further west – maybe somewhere around Three Forks."

"I would certainly feel more secure with a fort closer to us," Rachel commented.

"Well, it likely won't be Bradford's decision to control," Bogey said, taking a large helping of pudding as it was passed his way. "He's being transferred next month to Fort Jessup in Louisiana. His replacement will be a Colonel Arbuckle, a veteran of the Seminole Wars in Florida."

"So he's dealt with Indian issues," Rev. Vaille observed.

"Yep," the trader replied. "He's supposed to be the expert. We'll just have to see if he agrees with Bradford about putting a fort near us."

Mr. Bogey stayed through their evening devotions that followed supper and then agreed to bunk down in the barn rather than go back to Three Forks in the dark.

Rachel and Martha rose to help Amanda with the supper dishes while Stephen, George and Abraham made a final walk around the mission compound as some of the men did each evening.

Clarissa was just getting ready to rise and go to her cabin when Dr. Palmer took the chair beside her. His nearness made her heart thump and she remembered the emotion she had felt after Wolf Island.

"I am sorry for your sad news from home, Miss Johnson," Marcus said.

"Thank you, Doctor," Clarissa replied. "It was a bit of a shock."

"Will you need something to help you sleep tonight?"

"No," Clarissa shook her head. "I'll be fine. But thank you."

"Call upon me if you should need something," Dr. Palmer said, wishing he could offer more than just medicine. This pretty teacher stirred his heart, but he did not feel at liberty to say anything.

"Well, I'll bid you good night then," he said and gently squeezed her hands where they sat folded on the table. He stood to join the two ministers and John who were deep in conversation near the fireplace.

"Good night," Clarissa said, wishing she could ask him to stay. She caught a glimpse of Eliza across the room, frowning her way.

Clarissa gathered her letters and also stood to leave. She would go to her cabin and have a good cry.

The remainder of January 1822 was cold as the Snow Moon waxed and waned. A few more students would show up on occasion now that the work from the fall hunt was complete. All total they had over 30 students on their roster, but usually only had ten to twelve present on any given day. John and Clarissa commiserated with one another on the difficulty of creating any continuity with their lessons. They wished they could convince parents to allow their children to board with them, but so far only Marie Lombard stayed at the Mission with any consistency and she spent her nights at the Revoir lodge.

Clarissa had her girls gathered close to the fireplace for their reading lesson one cold afternoon. A disturbance in the yard caused every head to turn toward the window, even though they could not see out because the shutters were closed. Someone was yelling and then they heard a muffled cry of pain.

Alarmed, Clarissa rose from her chair and all the girls looked ready to jump up too. "Stay seated, students," their teacher said and they slumped back into place, but with curious concern in their eyes.

Clarissa grabbed her wool cloak hanging on its peg and pulled it on as she stepped outside.

An Osage woman, riding astride, pulled a travois behind her mustang. On it, wrapped in a buffalo robe, was the young Pawnee woman Whitestar. She was clearly in labor and bearing much pain.

Rev. Chapman hurried from his cabin as Stephen and Alexander emerged from the barn where they had been working on the farm implements. Phoebe and Amanda looked out from the door to the kitchen. Most of the men were down at the river, looking for suitable stone for their gristmill. Clarissa wondered where Dr. Palmer was.

Chapman spoke to the woman in Osage, though it was quite obvious what the need was. The minister seemed to have trouble understanding everything the excited rider was saying. Clarissa had to fight the urge to say, "Stop talking and help this woman," but she kept her tongue.

Finally Rev. Chapman turned to the gathering group. "Buffalo Woman is Mad Buffalo's wife. She says Yellowbird sent Whitestar to us for help. She's been in labor for two days and the baby isn't coming."

"Could be breech," Martha stated as she knelt beside the travois and gently touched the woman's swollen abdomen. "We need to get her inside."

"You can put her in my bed," Clarissa volunteered. She felt a concern for the young woman since helping her last fall.

"Good," Martha said, standing. "I'll get things ready." Rachel and Alice hurried to help Martha.

Buffalo Woman dismounted and quickly untied the leather cords holding the travois in place. Stephen and Alexander grasped the poles and eased them to the ground while the Osage woman led the horse to the corral fence.

Then with Alexander carrying one end of the travois and Stephen and Chapman carrying the other end, they transported Whitestar to the women's cabin. Buffalo Woman followed in their wake.

Earlier Alexander had sent Paul to get firewood and he returned now with his arms loaded. He dropped it at the kitchen fireplace and came running at Rev. Chapman's call.

"Paul, see if you can find Dr. Palmer," the minister told him. "He should be at the river helping the other men."

"Yes, suh," Paul responded and took off in a run.

The women helped Whitestar into bed and then Martha shooed the men out the door. "Send the doctor to us as soon as he gets here," she told them.

"Well, we've been dismissed," Alex said. "Guess it's back to the barn for us."

"I think I'll see if Miss Ingles needs help with stacking that firewood," Stephen replied.

"Of, course," Alexander said, with a squeeze of Stephen's shoulder. "I'm sure she will need your help." He gave the younger man a wink.

Stephen felt his face flush a little that his motives were so obvious to this brother. But he didn't let that stop him from whistling a bit on his way to the kitchen.

All through the afternoon, Clarissa found her mind distracted from the lessons as she wondered about Whitestar. She assumed Paul had located Dr. Palmer and that he was working with Mrs. Woodruff to help the young Pawnee woman deliver her child.

When she dismissed class, the girls walked with her to the dining hall where Amanda always had a sweet treat and milk for the students. It was too cold to play outside today, so the girls were content to gather close to the fireplace with their dolls.

"Any word on Whitestar?" Clarissa asked Amanda and Phoebe quietly as she joined them in the kitchen.

"We haven't been told anything," Phoebe said, "but she must be bleeding bad. Mrs. Chapman has come for more towels twice."

Clarissa felt her concern deepen. She had little knowledge of childbirth but knew many women did not survive a difficult delivery. Her thoughts turned to poor Sally Edwards again and she wondered if Dr. Palmer was thinking about her too. Her death had shaken him so badly.

In the women's cabin, the doctor knew they were in a life-and-death struggle. They had worked all afternoon to try to turn the baby and Whitestar had struggled mightily through the ordeal.

Buffalo Woman sat cross-legged on the dirt floor, offering no assistance or even encouragement to the young mother. Her eyes remained impassive though she watched them closely.

The minister's wife was just lighting another lamp in the darkening cabin when at last a tiny baby girl slipped into the doctor's hands. Handing her quickly to Martha, he turned his attention back to Whitestar. They must stop the bleeding or they would lose her.

Martha and Rachel worked to clean the child who appeared not to have yet drawn a breath.

"Get some warmer water quick," Martha instructed. The basin they had filled earlier had grown cold. Rachel hurried to the kitchen, scolding herself for not having already taken care of this matter.

"I need a warm basin of water," she said without preamble when she reached the door. Amanda and Phoebe sprang into action and quickly had a basin filled from the kettle that always simmered at the fireplace and cooled with more water from the rain barrel outside the door.

"Miss Johnson, come with me," Rachel instructed as she picked up the basin. "Bring more towels."

"These are the last we have," Amanda said, as she placed a few in Clarissa's hands. "Should we tear sheets?"

Rachel looked ready to cry. "Yes, I think you will need to. And please find my husband and ask him to gather everyone for prayer."

Clarissa fearfully followed Mrs. Chapman back to the cabin. Martha was working to clear the baby's nose and when Rachel set the basin of water on the table, the midwife plunged the little one into its warmth. The shock of it made the baby jump and gasp for air. Then she gave an indignant cry. The women all released their breath and smiled in relief.

Buffalo Woman rose from the floor and walked over to look at the baby. "Girl," she said. Then she went back and sat down again in her solemn vigil.

Barely conscious, Whitestar stirred at the sound of the baby's cry and looked at her daughter, now being wrapped tightly in a blanket. Martha came to her bedside and lowered the infant for Whitestar to see. She was going to set the child beside her, but Whitestar gave a barely perceptible shake of her head.

"*Professeur,*" she whispered, pointing to Clarissa. The teacher moved toward her, thinking Whitestar wanted to tell her something in French. She was totally unprepared for her words.

"She is yours," the young woman murmured. Then she closed her eyes and was gone.

CHAPTER THIRTY-FOUR

Union Mission
January, 1822

Though Martha and Marcus worked for several minutes trying to revive Whitestar, they sadly could not. Stunned, Clarissa sat on Amanda's bed and rocked the infant she now clutched in her arms.

Across the room, Dr. Palmer sat on the floor with his arms resting on his knees and his head down on his arms. It was exactly the same exhausted posture he had taken after rescuing Clarissa at Wolf Island. But this time the outcome was far worse.

Martha and Rachel held each other in a comforting embrace for a moment, tears streaming down their faces. Whitestar had fought so valiantly to bring her daughter into the world. The sadness of losing her to death seemed crushing.

Buffalo Woman did not cry but she too seemed stunned. Then suddenly clutching her stomach as if she had been hit she gave a low keening moan. It startled the missionaries and they all turned their attention to the Osage woman.

Dr. Palmer rose and went to sit in a cane-bottomed chair near where Buffalo Woman rocked back and forth as if in great pain. He spoke to her in Osage, asking if he could help her.

Shaking her head, she shrugged off the comforting hand Martha laid upon her shoulder. Then she rose and walked out of the cabin toward the corral where Robbie had placed her horse.

Dr. Palmer started to follow, but Rachel stopped him. "You need to get some rest," she said. "I'll ask my husband to speak with her."

Nodding, the doctor sank back into the chair. Already his mind was replaying the day's events. If only the Osages had not waited so long to get help. It might not have mattered and he would never know if he could have made any difference.

Would the Osages and Chief Claremont blame the mission for his wife's death? It was the question clearly on everyone's mind later that evening as the adults gathered in the dining hall. Buffalo Woman had returned to her vigil in the cabin in the tradition of keeping watch through the first night after someone's death.

"Someone will need to travel to Claremont's town in the morning," Rev. Chapman was saying to the group. "I don't know their burial traditions under these circumstances, but I want to personally visit with the chief and assure him that we did all we could to help his wife and child."

"What about the child?" Rachel asked. "It seems too terribly cold to carry her all the way over there. Do you think they would allow us to care for her for a time?"

"She needs a mother," her husband countered.

"I can nurse her," Asie Vaille stated. "I already have once this evening."

It had been a great relief to Clarissa when Asie had come and taken the little girl who had begun to fuss and needed to be fed.

"We will wait about taking her to her village until I know what arrangements Chief Claremont wants," Chapman said. "We certainly don't want to risk her health in this cold. Hopefully the chief will understand that."

"I'll keep the baby tonight," Asie said. "She can share Joseph's crib until we can get her to her village."

Clarissa wondered how welcome the little girl would be at Claremont's town. Yellowbird had never seemed happy with Whitestar, though she had sent her to the mission to be helped. Clarissa hated the thought of the baby growing up facing hostility at the Osage village. The Osages were at continued war with the Pawnees as well as the Cherokees and this little baby was half Pawnee. Her prospects did not seem good.

After their meeting, Eliza declared that she did not want to sleep in the cabin where Buffalo Woman kept her death vigil over Whitestar. She asked if she could sleep in the lofts above the classrooms and she asked Clarissa and Amanda to keep her company.

Amanda rolled her eyes at the girl's squeamishness, but in the end agreed to the arrangement. They would respect the Indian woman's private mourning since she seemed little inclined to accept comfort from any of them.

Martha and Rachel had prepared Whitestar's body and wrapped it in a blanket. They would await Rev. Chapman's return from Claremont's lodge to determine what would be done for her burial.

"Mrs. Chapman said Whitestar gave the baby to you," Amanda said as the mission sisters carried their night clothes and bedding to the classroom building. "Will you keep her if the Osages don't want her?"

"Surely the chief will want his own daughter," Clarissa responded as they climbed the ladder to the loft. There were no beds set up, but down-stuffed mattresses would be comfortable enough for a night or two. They had learned from the Indians that buffalo robes were warm enough for sleeping under, even on very cold nights.

Before they left their cabin, they had urged Buffalo Woman to get some sleep on Susan's bed, but she was still sitting silently on the floor as they closed the door. At least she would not be cold for Paul had added wood to their fireplace that evening.

The following morning, Buffalo Woman was gone before any of the missionaries arose for the day. Stephen noticed her horse missing from the corral when he went to start the milking. "Did you hear the Osage woman leave?" he asked Robbie who was still rubbing the sleep from his eyes as he sat down to milk one of their cows.

"Didn't hear nothing," Robbie said. "Funny, ain't it, how even their horses know how to be completely quiet. Makes you wonder if the Indians have ever been through the compound and we never even knew it."

"Yes, it does," Stephen agreed and the thought gave his heart a little lurch. How safe were the single women in their cabin at night? The Indians had never made any threats against the mission, but there were all types of travelers along the Osage Trace these days. If anything were to happen to Miss Ingles . . . or Miss Johnson and Miss Cleaver . . . he would never forgive himself.

When Rev. Chapman and Dr. Palmer returned from Claremont's town late the next day, the missionaries gathered for another meeting.

"Claremont wants us to see to Whitestar's burial and Yellowbird is adamant that the little girl not come into her lodge," the minister said with a sigh. "If the baby had been a boy, I think the chief would have overridden her. But for now, at least, I think we should keep the baby here."

"But she ought to be with her own people," Rachel countered.

"Not if she would be treated as a slave," Rev. Vaille stated and John Spaulding nodded vigorously.

"What about the Pawnees?" Rachel argued. "Wouldn't they want one of their own?"

"But she's half Osage," her husband said. "She would face an equal prejudice among the Pawnee."

"At least here she would receive a Christian upbringing," Asie said.

Clarissa was holding the baby girl, having gone to the Vaille's cabin to get her for the meeting. Despite her qualms about knowing how to properly care for an infant, she was drawn to the child who looked up at her now with trusting black eyes. Perhaps she felt responsible since Whitestar had indicated she wanted the teacher to have her baby. What an incredible gift and awesome responsibility.

"Well, Miss Johnson," Rachel said, turning to look at the teacher rocking the little girl. "Whitestar trusted you with her child. Are you willing to care for her?"

Clarissa looked up to see everyone's eyes on her. Suddenly she felt very presumptuous to think she could rear a child. "I would be happy to," she said carefully, trying to think about what was best for the baby. "But perhaps Phoebe would be better suited to care for her. Or Mrs. Vaille." She knew how much the housemother longed for a baby of her own and hoped

Asie would agree to allow Phoebe and Abraham to rear the child even though she would have to nurse her.

"I can certainly watch her while you're teaching, Miss Johnson," Phoebe said. "But," she glanced at her husband sitting beside her. He gave her a nod and smile. "You see, Mr. Redfield and I will be having a little one of our own in a few months." Phoebe blushed slightly, but her face beamed with happiness.

"Oh, Phoebe," Amanda exclaimed, "Congratulations!" She reached across the table to grasp her sister's hand. "I knew it wasn't me cornmeal mush sendin' you to the outhouse."

Everyone smiled and offered their congratulations to the Redfields. It seemed as if this settled the question about Whitestar's baby in everyone's mind. She would be Clarissa's.

"What will you name her, Miss Johnson," Dr. Palmer questioned. They couldn't keep calling her Baby Girl which was the name the children had bestowed upon her.

Taken aback, Clarissa hesitated for a moment. Should she give her an Indian name? She quickly rejected that idea because she knew too little about the naming traditions of either the Osage or Pawnee. Then she smiled for she knew what she would name her. "Theodosia," she said. "That was my grandmother's name. We called her Thea though."

"What a lovely idea," Martha commented. "I'm sure your grandmother would be pleased."

"And Esther for a second name," Clarissa added. "It means star and that will be for her mother." She bent down and kissed baby Thea's downy black hair.

With some difficulty, Alexander and Will dug a grave for Whitestar in the cold ground some distance from the grave of Joseph Revoir. It was sad to the missionaries that their cemetery was proving to be so needed. After a brief graveside service, they all walked back to the mission compound. Mrs. Vaille had kept the babies in from the cold, but Clarissa promised herself that she would bring Thea to her mother's grave when she was older. She would be sure they placed prairie flowers there often.

Clarissa told herself not to become too attached to the quiet baby for Chief Claremont might change his mind and decide he wanted his daughter after all. But it was hard not to give her heart away. Thea rarely fussed or cried but she also seldom smiled. She seemed happy, but she kept the solemn facial expression that often characterized her people.

Phoebe and Asie Vaille kept Thea more than Clarissa did, but she made a point of spending time with her each afternoon when school was out. In reality, everyone grew to love Thea and she rarely was left in her crib. Someone always seemed to be holding her. Even some of the men were not resistant to the little girl's sweet appeal. In just a matter of weeks, none of them could imagine the mission without Thea. She had certainly become a part of their family.

It was late February, but they had already enjoyed a few warm days and the earth seemed to be waking up from its winter sleep. Clarissa had eight girls in class on a fairly regular basis and she was pleased with the progress they were making. Besides Louisa and Marie, two sisters whose parents were homesteading nearby also came regularly.

"Miss Johnson, Miss Johnson," Leah gasped excitedly as she entered the classroom one morning. She was returning from a trip to the outhouse.

"What is it, Leah?" Clarissa asked, looking up from where she knelt beside Louisa's desk to help her work her arithmetic assignment on her slate.

"It's snowing!" Leah squealed in delight. "See," she said, pointing to fat snowflakes still visible on her coat.

Instant excitement rippled through the classroom and all the girls were talking at once.

"Teacher, can we go see it?"

"Can we play outside?"

"Will there be enough to build a snowman?"

Clarissa held up her hand for silence and fought not to smile at their eager faces. She supposed she would not have the girls' attention for any lesson until their curiosity was satisfied.

"You must all put on your coats first." The words were barely out of her mouth before the girls were gathering their coats from the pegged rack by the door. Louisa and Marie kept the Osage tradition of using blankets for their winter wrap.

Clarissa couldn't help feel a little excitement herself. They had seen a few meager snowfalls this winter, but as New Englanders they had missed getting a true snow. Clarissa hoped they might enjoy one before winter was completely gone.

Gathering on her own cloak, she cautiously opened the classroom door. A lovely sight greeted their eyes. Fat fluffy snowflakes drifted across the landscape of orange-tipped prairie grass. The wind swirled the flakes in fanciful patterns and already it was collecting along the rock foundation of the building. If the snow continued at this rate for even a brief period they could get several inches.

The wind was cold, but not bitterly so. Without waiting for permission, the girls pushed past their teacher to twirl in the snowfall and try to catch flakes on their tongue. Their squeals of delight caused Mr. Spaulding to open his classroom door.

Clarissa smiled at the surprise on his face. "It's snowing, Mr. Spaulding," she stated the obvious. "Would your young scholars care to join us?"

Mr. Spaulding pushed up his glasses and nodded, then closed the door. Within less than five seconds his seven boys were out the door, joining the girls in romping through the quickly gathering snow. The two teachers stood and enjoyed the pretty scene.

Soon nearly all the other missionaries had also stepped outside to enjoy the rare winter snowfall. Stephen Fuller and Robbie walked over from the barn carrying several lengths of rope.

"Don't know how much we'll get from this," Stephen said, hefting the rope in his hand. "Think we should string some rope between buildings?"

"Probably wouldn't be a bad idea," John agreed. "Better safe than sorry, as they say."

The New Englanders had no idea if blizzard conditions ever occurred this far south, but they had heard of prairie blizzards and knew they could be quite dangerous if caught out in one.

Robbie and Stephen started the work of stringing rope from the classroom to the dining hall. The Requa brothers took a rope and strung it between the t-post of the clothesline and the barn, then on to the central cabin of the longhouse.

After Stephen secured the rope near the dining hall door, he sent Robbie to the springhouse to bring several pails of water to the kitchen. Meanwhile Alexander and Paul were restocking kindling at each fireplace. If they were to get stuck inside for more than a day or two they would need to be prepared.

Phoebe, Alice and Rachel brought bedding to the schoolhouse, in case they needed to keep their students through the night. All their families had been advised that students would be kept at the school in inclement weather.

Amanda had been churning butter with the cream Stephen had brought her earlier that morning. She heard the commotion in the school yard and peaked out the door. Oh, how she loved a beautiful snowfall. Grabbing her knitted wool shawl and its matching cap and mittens, she pulled them on and then stepped outside the kitchen.

Most of the adults had gathered at the schoolyard to enjoy a brief bit of fun with the children. George was challenging the boys to a snowball fight, for enough of the white stuff had fallen to allow for it.

Amanda decided not to join everyone else. Snow always held a magical quality for her and reminded her of rare childhood holidays with her dozen siblings in Ireland. She couldn't resist the urge to twirl in the snowfall and try to catch one of the fat flakes on her mittens. The frozen crystal made her think of her mother's fine tatted lace and it made her smile.

The wind pulled wisps of her auburn curls out from her knit cap and she made a pretty picture herself, causing Stephen to smile. He had come around the corner of the building to see the cook dancing with the snowflakes.

Stepping back so he didn't startle her, he watched her enjoy nature's beauty. It filled his heart with gratitude and he realized God had offered him something beautiful when he brought Miss Ingles into his life. He had thought that life was over when Lydia died, but his heart had reawakened with the kindness and concern the cook had shown him.

"You're beautiful, you know," he whispered, not wanting to break the lovely spell.

Amanda heard him and turned quickly to see him at the corner of the kitchen. Heat flamed her cheeks at being caught acting like a little girl. She covered her face with her mittens.

"Oh, you caught me bein' silly," she exclaimed.

"Not silly," Stephen said, coming toward her. "You're as pretty as this snow."

"Now you're teasin' me," Amanda said, for she never thought of herself as pretty. Self-consciously, she tried to brush the snow out of her hair.

"No, I'm serious," Stephen replied, coming closer still to stand in front of her. She felt her heart begin to pound, for he had a very serious expression on his face.

"Will you marry me, Miss Ingles?" he asked.

She caught her breath. She had loved this man since Lydia had told her about his selfless care for her. She had given her heart completely with his gift of the most costly of honey. She knew this man had a servant's heart.

"Yes," she whispered as her eyes filled with tears. "You do me a great honor to ask."

CHAPTER THIRTY-FIVE

Union Mission
Early Spring, 1822

Even six inches of snow could melt fast upon the prairie when a warm breeze blew up from the south a few days later. Stephen and Amanda shared the news of their engagement, but being two practical people, they decided to wait until after spring planting to wed.

The snow was followed by a very wet and stormy March making the fields difficult to plow and slowing traffic on the Trace. Stephen, Abraham and Robbie were out early each day to get as much field work done as possible. The prairie sod had to be plowed in both directions to break up the dirt before seed could ever be put into the ground.

One afternoon, Joseph Bogey came for a visit, bringing supplies and their annual pay from the Mission Society in New York. Clarissa was glad for the gold coin for she needed to purchase some material for clothes for Thea. It was getting warm enough that she could no longer simply be swaddled in a diaper and a blanket. She hoped she could get some soft flannel for gowns and hoped also that Mrs. Vaille and Martha would be willing to help her with the sewing.

"What is the news from Fort Smith?" Rev. Vaille asked Mr. Bogey as they gathered in the dining hall for supper.

"Colonel Arbuckle arrived last month with an additional 250 troops from the Seventh Infantry," Bogey responded. "I stopped in to meet him my last trip to Petite Roche."

"What sort of man is he?" Chapman wanted to know.

"Career military man," said Bogey. "No family to speak of. Seems sensible though and says he is quite determined to get Mad Buffalo to sign a peace treaty. He plans to make it one of his priorities this summer."

"Do you think Mad Buffalo will be inclined to sign a treaty?" John asked, expressing the skepticism Clarissa felt.

"Can't say," Bogey replied. "He's built his reputation among the Osages by taking a tough stand against the Cherokees. Don't see him backing down from that any time soon."

"And do you hear of any changes in the stand taken by the Cherokees?" asked Abraham.

"Their agent Mr. Brearley who came here last year seems to be working hard to get the Cherokees to the table to talk about peace and respect for hunting territories. And their last chief, Tahlonteeskee, was supportive of the mission down near Dardanelle. His brother is chief now. I think the Cherokees are closer to peace than Mad Buffalo."

"Has Dwight Mission seen many converts that you know of?" Rev. Chapman asked. Union, Harmony and Dwight Missions all had been authorized by the Mission Society at the same time, but Dwight had been operating longest having been established in a more settled area of Arkansas.

Bogey seemed a little sheepish at the question. "Well, not being much of a church man myself, I really don't know what the mission's been doing. But I hear that the Cherokees have developed their own written language and that the missionaries in Arkansas and Georgia are teaching it."

"That should greatly help with spreading the gospel," Will stated. Without a written form of Osage, Union had to rely solely on oral teaching. "All we can do is tell the Indians the gospel message; we can't really show it to them in writing."

"The Indians are comfortable with that," Bogey countered. "And you're showing them the gospel with how you live. I hear them talk. They are grateful for your hospitality and for your help, especially you, Doctor."

Marcus flushed a little at the praise and nodded his thanks. Clarissa felt a surge of pride for him. She knew that he worried that his failure to save Joseph Revoir and Whitestar might reflect poorly on the mission.

"You may just be closer than you think to seeing the Osages come around," Bogey concluded, as he finished sopping a bit of gravy with another piece of Amanda's light bread. He smacked his lips in satisfaction. "Miss Ingles," he said, rubbing his ample stomach, "I'd be a thin and sickly man were it not for your fine cooking."

Everyone chuckled at his exaggeration for Mr. Bogey was neither thin nor sickly and in no danger of becoming so. Amanda suspected that the trader knew every hospitable kitchen between Three Forks and Arkansas Post. He paid for his meals in news and gossip.

"I thank you kindly, sir." Amanda smiled at the incorrigible fellow.

"It's beginning to rain again, Mr. Bogey," Rachel said. "Won't you spend the night in the hay loft?"

"I don't mind if I do," Bogey said. That way he could enjoy Amanda's breakfast the next morning before heading back down the Trace.

Abraham was leading into the third verse of "O Worship the King," as a gentle drip of rain on the school building roof provided the only music for their Sabbath service. Despite the lack of musical instruments, Clarissa always enjoyed the Sunday morning songs and even little Thea seemed pleased with them as well. She rocked the baby gently in rhythm to the song.

"Thy bountiful care, what tongue can recite?
"It breathes in the air; it shines in the light,
"It streams from the hills; it descends to the plain,
"And sweetly distills in the dew and the rain."

The harmony of Mr. Woodruff's deep baritone and Miss Eliza's clear sweet tenor and all the other voices between carried out the open windows to their own bit of hill and plain.

As the last note of the song held and then quietly faded, the door to the schoolroom opened. Everyone turned to look for they had heard no one approach.

Buffalo Woman peeked inside as if afraid to enter. Teresa jumped up and went to draw her into the room.

"Welcome," Rev. Chapman greeted her in Osage.

Solemnly Buffalo Woman nodded and she let Teresa lead her to sit beside her on a chair George moved into place. Her tightly braided hair held raindrops and the blanket she wore like a shawl was damp.

Clarissa did not know what to think about the appearance of Mad Buffalo's wife at their worship service. Rev. Chapman stood to begin his sermon and seemed to exhibit an emotion that Clarissa had never seen before. Using his knowledge of the Osage language, he began to tell the story of Jesus' life and death and resurrection, weaving his words with Osage and English as he had observed Father Menard do.

The mission family all silently prayed that Buffalo Woman would understand what the minister was trying to convey as he sometimes stumbled over the Osage words. When Thea began to fuss to be fed, Clarissa handed her quickly to Mrs. Vaille, not wanting the child to be a distraction to the sermon. Everyone understood that this might be one of the most important Sunday services they would have in their little church.

Rev. Chapman reached the conclusion of the sermon and asked them all to stand for the benediction. After the prayer, Mrs. Chapman quickly turned to Buffalo Woman and invited her to stay and have dinner with them. She nodded after Teresa translated the invitation.

They all walked over to the dining hall where Amanda, Martha and Alice worked to finish the meal mostly prepared the evening before and set it on the tables.

Clarissa took a seat, now holding a sleeping Thea, and wondered why the Osage woman had come. Fear swirled in her mind for a brief moment. Perhaps Chief Claremont had sent her to get his daughter. The thought was like a knife to her heart. She could not imagine how hard it would be to give up the little girl.

Martha must have read her thoughts, for she gave the teacher an encouraging pat on the shoulder as she set a platter of cold fried chicken on the dining table. Clarissa would not be the only one of them who would sorely miss little Thea.

But Buffalo Woman showed no interest in the child, hardly even looking her way as Clarissa settled the baby on her lap.

The teacher felt her fears subside. It would seem the Osage woman's visit had nothing to do with Thea.

Everyone tried to include Buffalo Woman in the conversation during the meal, but she said little. She seemed pensive, but it was hard to read what her true thoughts might be. Curiosity showed on their faces, but everyone seemed hesitant to ask why Buffalo Woman had chosen to visit them today.

When the meal was completed, Clarissa settled Thea into her crib next to Joseph's near the fireplace. The missionaries usually lingered in the dining hall on Sundays since no work, except the necessities, was done. It was a chance to visit or read the last few issues of the *Arkansas Gazette* or study scripture. It was too damp for the children to play outside, so Phoebe and Abraham walked them over to the school building and would keep them entertained with quiet inside games for the afternoon.

Today was Clarissa's turn to help with clearing the dishes from the tables to be washed in the kitchen. Amanda insisted that dish washing was a necessity because she would have no bugs gathering in her work space. The cook was meticulously clean, a fact that all the missionaries appreciated.

Buffalo Woman lingered at the table and Teresa sat with her. The two women were not close friends, since they came from two different bands of their tribe, but Teresa tried to engage her in conversation, asking about her four children.

During the meal, Dr. Palmer noticed that Buffalo Woman had a recent burn on her hand and she seemed to move it carefully as if it gave her some pain. Asking permission of the two Osage women, he took a seat by Buffalo Woman and asked her about the wound.

"Inside fire," Buffalo Woman explained in her limited English. Normally the Indians spent the warm months living out of doors, but the rain would have necessitated cooking inside today.

Clarissa was wiping crumbs from the next table while Dr. Palmer carefully examined Buffalo Woman's hand.

"Miss Johnson," he said. She turned to come to the table where he sat. "Could you bring a cold, wet cloth for her hand?"

"Certainly, Doctor," Clarissa said, wondering again how she had become the designated nurse at the mission. She didn't mind it, really. Not unless it involved surgery. It was nice that Dr. Palmer looked to her for assistance.

She smiled a little as she walked to the kitchen to get the cloth he requested. They always kept strips of clean muslin there to use as bandages.

She quickly soaked a length of the cloth in the cold spring water and returned with it to Dr. Palmer. He carefully wrapped the cloth around the burn, explaining to Buffalo Woman that he wanted to cool the skin and keep it clean so it would heal more quickly. Teresa translated for him when Buffalo Woman looked puzzled.

After he had tucked the end of the bandage inside the wrap, the doctor started to stand, but Buffalo Woman stopped him.

"Why you help the *Wahzhazhe*?" she asked him.

Dr. Palmer considered the question carefully. He didn't want to give a glib answer for she seemed to be genuinely searching. "My God asks that his people care for others."

"The Jesus-God?" she asked.

"Yes. God's Son."

"He died?"

"Yes, but He lives now and directs our lives," he waved his hand to indicate all the missionaries. Quietly, as the others in the room became aware of the conversation, they began to silently pray.

"He tell you to be . . ." she searched for the English word and finally told Teresa in Osage what she was trying to say.

"To be kind, caring," Teresa explained.

"Yes. Jesus taught us to be caring . . . to help others." Dr. Palmer tried to keep his words simple but not demeaning. "He lives within us and directs our actions."

Teresa translated.

"Do you believe Jesus lives?" Dr. Palmer asked.

"Must live if he tell you what to do," Buffalo Woman said.

"Would you like Jesus to live within you?"

Buffalo Woman pondered the question, laying a hand over her heart as if trying to grasp the idea of God living within a person.

"Yes," she said. "I believe. I see this God shining out of you. I want him in me too."

Dr. Palmer felt the same thrill he received every time he brought a new baby into the world.

"Then because of your faith, he lives in you too."

Buffalo Woman smiled. It was the first time any of them had seen her smile.

She said something to Teresa and Teresa smiled too.

"She wants to know if you are going to water sprinkle her," she said.

Now everyone in the room was smiling.

"Yes, we can water sprinkle you," Rev. Chapman said, making no apology for entering the conversation.

They quickly arranged for the sacrament of baptism and with joy welcomed Buffalo Woman into the fellowship of believers.

Mrs. Chapman tried giving the Osage woman a hug, but she stiffened at the contact. She clearly was not used to this type of display of affection. All the other women simply smiled at her.

They couldn't seem to stop smiling. They had labored for well over a year to see this day. An ordinary, rainy Sunday had become one of the most important the mission had known and they knew the angels in heaven were rejoicing too.

When the rain stopped, Buffalo Woman mounted her patient mustang and rode toward her village. The missionaries watched her follow the Trace northward and Clarissa wondered what impact Buffalo Woman's conversion would have on her people. For the first time in a long while, she felt a hope that this field they had plowed would begin to bring a good harvest.

Several days later, Stephen paused behind the plow to enjoy the tin of cold water Amanda had brought him. They finally had a break in the rain and the fields were dry enough to set the furrows for the corn they would plant. They were late getting the seed into the ground and Stephen was impatient to finish the planting for more reasons than one.

"How many days?" Amanda asked and Stephen knew she was asking how long it would take to get the planting completed. She was also asking how long until they would be married.

The farmer waved away a mosquito and finished his water. Handing Amanda the tin cup, he took out his handkerchief to wipe his face. It had turned hot.

Exasperated at his delay in answering, Amanda pretended to pout. She turned to go, but Stephen caught her hand and drew her back to him.

"Three, maybe, four days at the most," he said.

"Promise?"

"Say your prayers that it doesn't rain," Stephen bargained. "That's the only way I can keep that promise."

"Then you know what I'll be speakin' to the Lord about this evening," Amanda smiled. Reluctantly she turned again to get to her kitchen chores, pulling her hand slowly from his. She threw him one last flirting smile over her shoulder.

Stephen watched her walk back toward the mission, then hupped the oxen into action. *It better not rain*, he thought, as he whistled a happy tune.

When Amanda arrived at the kitchen, she found Eliza bent over in the floor, a hard chill shaking her entire body. The young woman had suffered from a fever for several days. At first, the cook had suspected that the girl was faking the illness to get the doctor's attention, but she knew this suffering was real.

In fact, George, Robbie and Rev. Chapman had all been suffering as well. They had come to call this mysterious fever, "the intermittent," because it seemed to regularly assault one member of the family or another on warm, humid days.

"Oh, Miss Eliza," she said, hurrying over to her. "Let me help you." She worked to get Eliza up on her feet. "You need to be in bed."

"I'm so thirsty," Eliza said. "I was just going to get some water, but the chill hit me."

Her blue eyes were bright with fever and her skin felt hot to Amanda's touch. She took another tin cup and filled it with water from the pitcher on her work table, then handed it to Eliza.

The girl gulped the cool liquid as if she had been long in the desert. Her blonde curls were a tangled mess and that alone told Amanda that Miss Eliza did not feel well. She normally took great care in how she arranged her silky hair.

"Let me help you back to the cabin," Amanda offered. "You need to rest."

"Take me to Alice," Eliza said, sounding like a little girl.

Amanda felt pity for the young woman. She had been

brought to the mission without much say of her own in the matter. She had matured over the last year and tried harder to help with chores, but Amanda knew she missed the social life of New England. There was little to entertain on the prairie.

They walked to the Spaulding cabin and Alice quickly set down her sewing to help her sister to a chair. She brought a quilt from Billy's bed to wrap her in.

"Would you like me to bring some broth?" Amanda asked.

"That would be kind of you, Miss Ingles," Alice said. "Thank you."

Amanda nodded and then exited the cabin. She met Dr. Palmer in the yard and he walked with her to the kitchen. She told him about Eliza.

"George has been hit hard with the chills too," he said, looking concerned. "I've tried boneset and willow bark and Echinacea, but nothing seems to help."

"I'm goin' to prepare some broth for Miss Eliza," Amanda said. "I'll bring some for Mr. Requa too."

"Thank you, Miss Ingles."

A few days later, Rev. Chapman was recovered and Robbie seemed on the mend, but George and Eliza both remained bedfast with the fever.

"It's this awful heat," Alice said at supper one evening. There was worry in her voice. "I think we need to take Eliza north for a while . . . at least until the river is down and it isn't so damp here."

Would a change in climate help?" Rachel asked the doctor.

"It might," Marcus said, thoughtfully. "I don't think it would do any harm."

"Miss Ingles and I thought to travel to Missouri after we wed," Stephen spoke up. "Perhaps we could take Miss Cleaver to Harmony Mission for a respite."

Amanda smiled at her husband-to-be. He was so thoughtful.

"I would feel better about that if Dr. Palmer went with her," Alice stated. "I'd hate to think of her taking a turn for the worse out in the middle of nowhere."

"George needs some relief from this heat, too," Will added. "I'm getting concerned about him. He normally doesn't take this long to get over something."

After more discussion the group decided that Dr. Palmer would accompany George and Eliza with the newlywed Fullers to Missouri after their wedding on Sunday. They would begin the three-day journey early on Monday morning.

Amanda made a radiant bride and Stephen was a handsome and attentive groom. The mission sisters had insisted that Amanda not bake her own wedding cake. But as they ruefully surveyed the cake Rachel and Martha prepared and Phoebe and Clarissa frosted, they knew they were going to miss the cook while she was gone.

They all gathered near the corral yard at Monday sunrise as Stephen hitched their oxen team to the largest of their wagons. George was so sick Will practically had to lift him into the wagon. Eliza was some better, but still given to chills. She was eager for a change in scenery though and allowed Dr. Palmer to help her into the wagon. He climbed up to take a seat beside her.

Clarissa watched while she held Thea and felt a ripple of something like fear run through her middle. Poor George was pale and looked miserable. She prayed the journey wouldn't be too hard on him.

But as the wagon pulled onto the path leading to the Trace, Clarissa was surprised at another prayer that lifted from her heart. "Please bring him back to me," she whispered as she nuzzled Thea's downy hair. And this time she knew that she wasn't praying about George.

She watched the wagon grow smaller as it reached the Trace and thought of how much her life had changed since she had watched the keelboat leave the Pittsburgh port over two years ago. She had left home believing she would never know marriage or motherhood, yet God had blessed her already with a child to call her own.

Kissing Thea's forehead, she turned to go to breakfast. Looking around this place she now called home, she felt a sudden certainty that God had not forgotten her out here in this untamed land. She looked forward with hope now – hope that every dream of her heart would someday be fulfilled.

Watch for the **Missions of Indian Territory Book 2** coming soon. *Look unto the Fields* continues the story of the Union Mission as Arkansas Territory gives way to Indian Territory and missionary work spreads among the new tribes being moved into the land set aside for the native people.

Other books by Jonita Mullins can be purchased at Okieheritage.com.

CPSIA information can be obtained
at www.ICGtesting.com
Printed in the USA
LVHW04s1531230818
587903LV00009B/657/P